Motherless Brooklyn

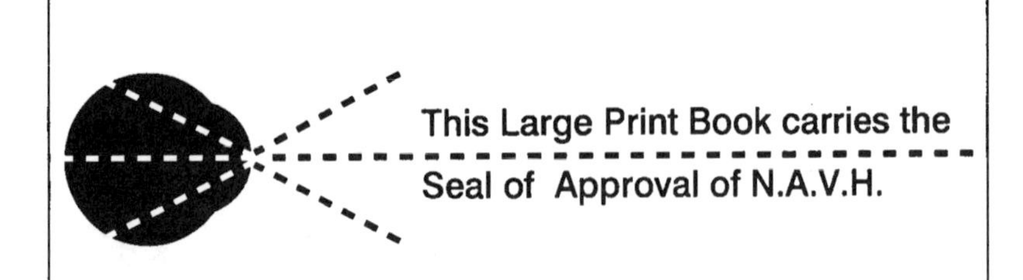
This Large Print Book carries the
Seal of Approval of N.A.V.H.

Motherless Brooklyn

Jonathan Lethem

Thorndike Press • Thorndike, Maine

Published in 2000 by arrangement with Doubleday,
a division of The Doubleday Broadway Publishing Group,
a division of Random House, Inc.

Thorndike Press Large Print Basic Series.

The tree indicium is a trademark of Thorndike Press.

The text of this Large Print edition is unabridged.
Other aspects of the book may vary from the original edition.

Set in 16 pt. Plantin by Al Chase.

Printed in the United States on permanent paper.

Library of Congress Cataloging-in-Publication Data

Lethem, Jonathan.
Motherless Brooklyn / Jonathan Lethem.
p. cm.
ISBN 0-7862-2695-1 (lg. print : hc : alk. Paper)
1. Private investigators — New York (State) — New York — Fiction. 2. Tourette syndrome — Patients — Fiction. 3. Brooklyn (New York, N.Y.) — Fiction. 4. Orphans — Fiction. 5. Large type books. I. Title.
PS3562.E8544 M68 2000
813′.54—dc21 00-033759

For my Father

Acknowledgments

I'm deeply indebted to the books of Lawrence Shainberg, Kosho Uchiyma, and Oliver Sacks, the words of Tuli Kupferberg, and to conversations with Blake Lethem, Cara O'Connor, David Bowman, Eliot Duhan, Matthew Burkhardt, Scott McCrossin, Janet Farrell, Diane Martel, Alice Ressner, and Maureen Linker and the Linker family.

Thanks also to Richard Parks, Bill Thomas, Walter Donohue, Zoe Rosenfeld, Tooley Cottage, the Zentrum für Kunst und Medientechnologie (ZKM) and the Corporation of Yaddo.

Walks Into

Context is everything. Dress me up and see. I'm a carnival barker, an auctioneer, a downtown performance artist, a speaker in tongues, a senator drunk on filibuster. *I've got Tourette's.* My mouth won't quit, though mostly I whisper or subvocalize like I'm reading aloud, my Adam's apple bobbing, jaw muscle beating like a miniature heart under my cheek, the noise suppressed, the words escaping silently, mere ghosts of themselves, husks empty of breath and tone. (If I were a Dick Tracy villain, I'd have to be Mumbles.) In this diminished form the words rush out of the cornucopia of my brain to course over the surface of the world, tickling reality like fingers on piano keys. Caressing, nudging. They're an invisible army on a peacekeeping mission, a peaceable horde. They mean no harm. They placate, interpret, massage. Everywhere they're smoothing down imperfections, putting hairs in place, putting ducks in a row, replacing divots. Counting and polishing the silver. Patting old ladies gently on the behind, eliciting a giggle. Only — here's the rub — when they find too much perfection, when the surface is already buffed smooth, the ducks already orderly, the old ladies complacent, then my little army rebels, breaks into the stores. Reality needs a prick here and there, the carpet needs a flaw. My words begin plucking at threads nervously, seeking purchase, a weak point, a vulnerable ear. That's when it comes, the urge to shout in the church, the nursery, the crowded movie house. It's an itch at first. Inconsequential. But that itch is soon a torrent behind a straining dam. Noah's flood. That itch is my whole life. Here it comes now. Cover your ears. Build an ark.

"Eat me!" I scream.

"Maufishful," said Gilbert Coney in response to my outburst, not even turning his head. I could barely make out the words — "My mouth is full" — both truthful and a joke, lame. Accustomed to my verbal ticcing, he didn't usually bother to comment. Now he nudged the bag of White Castles in my direction on the car seat, crinkling the paper. "Stuffinyahole."

Coney didn't rate any special consideration from me. "Eatmeeatmeeatme," I shrieked again, letting off more of the pressure in my head. Then I was able to concentrate. I helped myself to one of the tiny burgers. Unwrapping it, I lifted the top of the bun to examine the grid of holes in the patty, the slime of glistening cubed onions. This was another compulsion. I always had to look inside a White Castle, to appreciate the contrast of machine-tooled burger and nubbin of fried goo. Kaos and Control. Then I did more or less as Gilbert had suggested — pushed it into my mouth whole. The ancient slogan *Buy 'em by the sack* humming deep in my head, jaw working to grind the slider into swallowable chunks, I turned back to stare out the window at the house.

Food really mellows me out.

We were putting a stakeout on 109 East Eighty-fourth Street, a lone town house pinned between giant doorman apartment buildings, in and out of the foyers of which bicycle deliverymen with bags of hot Chinese flitted like tired moths in the fading November light. It was dinner hour in Yorktown. Gilbert Coney and I had done our part to join the feast, detouring up into Spanish Harlem for the burgers. There's only one White Castle left in Manhattan, on East 103rd. It's not as good as some of the suburban outlets. You can't watch them prepare your order anymore, and to tell the truth I've begun to wonder if they're microwaving the buns instead of steaming them. Alas. Taking our boodle of thusly compromised sliders and fries back downtown, we double-parked in front of the target address until a spot opened up. It only took a couple of minutes, though by that time the doormen on either side had made us — made us as out-of-place and nosy anyway. We were driving the Lincoln, which didn't have the "T"-series license plates or stickers or anything else to identify it as a Car Service vehicle. And we were large men, me and Gilbert. They probably thought we were cops. It didn't matter. We chowed and watched.

Not that we knew what we were doing there. Minna had sent us without saying why, which was usual enough, even if the address wasn't. Minna Agency errands mostly stuck us in Brooklyn, rarely far from Court Street, in fact. Carroll Gardens and Cobble Hill together made a crisscrossed game board of Frank Minna's alliances and enmities, and me and Gil Coney and the other Agency Men were the markers — like Monopoly pieces, I sometimes thought, tin automobiles or terriers (not top hats, surely) — to be moved around that game board. Here on the Upper East Side we were off our customary map, *Automobile* and *Terrier* in Candyland — or maybe in the study with Colonel Mustard.

"What's that sign?" said Coney. He pointed with his glistening chin at the town house doorway. I looked.

" 'Yorkville Zendo,' " I read off the bronze plaque on the door, and my fevered brain processed the words and settled with interest on the odd one. "Eat me Zendo!" I muttered through clenched teeth.

Gilbert took it, rightly, as my way of puzzling over the unfamiliarity. "Yeah, what's that *Zendo?* What's that?"

"Maybe like Zen," I said.

"I don't know from that."

"Zen like Buddhism," I said. "Zen master, you know."

"Zen master?"

"You know, like kung-fu master."

"Hrrph," said Coney.

And so after this brief turn at investigation we settled back into our complacent chewing. Of course after any talk my brain was busy with at least some low-level version of echolalia salad: *Don't know from Zendo, Ken-like Zung Fu, Feng Shui master, Fungo bastard, Zen masturbation, Eat me!* But it didn't require voicing, not now, not with White Castles to unscrew, inspect and devour. I was on my third. I fit it into my mouth, then glanced up at the doorway of One-oh-nine, jerking my head as if the building had been sneaking up on me. Coney and the other Minna Agency operatives loved doing stakeouts with me, since my compulsiveness forced me to eyeball the site or mark in question every thirty seconds or so, thereby saving them the trouble of swiveling their necks. A similar logic explained my popularity at wiretap parties — give me a key list of trigger words to listen for in a conversation and I'd think about nothing else, nearly jumping out of my clothes at hearing the slightest hint of one, while the same task invariably drew anyone else toward blissful sleep.

While I chewed on number three and monitored the uneventful Yorkville Zendo entrance my hands busily frisked the paper sack of Castles, counting to be sure I had three remaining. We'd purchased a bag of twelve, and not only did Coney know I had to have my six, he also knew he was pleasing me, tickling my Touretter's obsessive-compulsive instincts, by matching my number with his own. Gilbert Coney was a big lug with a heart of gold, I guess. Or maybe he was just trainable. My tics and obsessions kept the other Minna Men amused, but also wore them out, made them weirdly compliant and complicit.

A woman turned from the sidewalk onto the stoop of the town house and went up to the door. Short dark hair, squarish glasses, that was all I saw before her back was to us. She wore a pea coat. Sworls of black hair at her neck, under the boyish haircut. Twenty-five maybe, or maybe eighteen.

"She's going in," said Coney.

"Look, she's got a key," I said.

"What's Frank want us to do?"

"Just watch. Take a note. What time is it?"

Coney crumpled another Castle wrapper and pointed at the glove compartment. "You take a note. It's six forty-five."

I popped the compartment — the click-release of the plastic latch was a delicious hollow sound, which I knew I'd want to repeat, at least approximately — and found the small notebook inside. GIRL, I wrote, then crossed it out. WOMAN, HAIR, GLASSES, KEY. **6:45**. The notes were to myself, since I only had to be able to report verbally to Minna. If that. For all we knew, he might want us out here to scare someone, or to wait for some delivery. I left the notebook beside the Castles on the seat between us and slapped the compartment door shut again, then delivered six redundant slaps to the same spot to ventilate my brain's pressure by reproducing the hollow thump I'd liked. Six was a lucky number tonight, six burgers, six forty-five. So six slaps.

For me, counting and touching things and repeating words are all the same activity. Tourette's is just one big lifetime of tag, really. The world (or my brain — same thing) appoints me *it,* again and again. So I tag back.

Can *it* do otherwise? If you've ever been *it* you know the answer.

"Boys" came the voice from the street side of the car, startling me and Coney both.

"Frank," I said.

It was Minna. He had his trench-coat collar up against the breeze, not quite cloaking his unshaven Robert-Ryan-in-*Wild-Bunch* grimace. He ducked down to the level of my window, as if he didn't want to be seen from the Yorkville Zendo. Squeaky cabs rocking-horsed past over the pothole in the street behind him. I rolled down the window, then reached out compulsively and touched his left shoulder, a regular gesture he'd not bothered to acknowledge for — how long? Say, fifteen years now, since when I'd first begun manifesting the urge as a thirteen-year-old and reached out for his then twenty-five-year-old street punk's bomber-jacketed shoulder. Fifteen years of taps and touches — if Frank Minna were a statue instead of flesh and blood I've have buffed that spot to a high shine, the way leagues of tourists burnish the noses and toes of bronze martyrs in Italian churches.

"What you doing here?" said Coney. He knew it had to be important to not only get Minna up here, but on his own steam, when he could have had us swing by to pick him up somewhere. Something complicated was going on, and — surprise! — we stooges were out of the loop again.

I whispered inaudibly through narrowed lips, *Stakeout, snakeout, ambush Zendo.*

The Lords of Snakebush.

"Gimme a smoke," said Minna. Coney leaned over me with a pack of Malls, one tapped out an inch or so for the boss to pluck. Minna put it in his mouth and lit it himself, pursing his brow in concentration, sheltering the lighter in the frame of his collar. He drew in, then gusted smoke into our airspace. "Okay, listen," he said, as though we weren't already hanging on his words.

Minna Men to the bone.

"I'm going in," he said, narrowing his eyes at the Zendo. "They'll buzz me. I'll swing the door wide. I want you" — he nodded at Coney — "to grab the door, get inside, just inside, and wait there, at the bottom of the stairs."

"What if they come meet you?" said Coney.

"Worry about that if it happens," said Minna curtly.

"Okay, but what if —"

Minna waved him off before he could finish. Really Coney was groping for comprehension of his role, but it wasn't forthcoming.

"Lionel —" started Minna.

Lionel, my name. Frank and the Minna Men pronounced it to rhyme with *vinyl.* Lionel Essrog. *Line-all.*

Liable Guesscog.

Final Escrow.

Ironic Pissclam.

And so on.

My own name was the original verbal taffy, by now stretched to filament-thin threads that lay all over the floor of my echo-chamber skull. Slack, the flavor all chewed out of it.

★ ★ ★

"Here." Minna dropped a radio monitor and headphones in my lap, then patted his rib pocket. "I'm wired. I'll be coming over that thing live. Listen close. If I say, uh, 'Not if my life depended on it,' you get out of the car and knock on the door here, Gilbert lets you in, two of you rush upstairs and find me quick, okay?"

Eat me, dickweed was almost dislodged from my mouth in the excitement, but I breathed in sharply and swallowed the words, said nothing instead.

"We're not carrying," said Coney.

"What?" said Minna.

"A piece, I don't have a piece."

"What's with *piece?* Say *gun,* Gilbert."

"No gun, Frank."

"That's what I count on. That's how I sleep at night, you have to know. You with no gun. I wouldn't want you chuckleheads coming up a stairway behind me with a hairpin, with a harmonica, let alone a gun. I've got a gun. You just show up."

"Sorry, Frank."

"With an unlit cigar, with a fucking Buffalo chicken wing."

"Sorry, Frank."

"Just listen. If you hear me say, uh, 'First I gotta use the bathroom,' that means we're coming out. You get Gilbert, get back in the car, get ready to follow. You got it?"

Get, get, get, GOT! said my brain. *Duck, duck, duck, GOOSE!*

"Life depended, rush the Zendo," was what I said aloud. "Use the bathroom, start the car."

"Genius, Freakshow," said Minna. He pinched my cheek, then tossed his cigarette behind him into the street, where it tumbled, sparks scattering. His eyes were far away.

Coney got out of the car, and I scooted over to the driver's seat. Minna thumped the hood once, as if patting a dog on its head after saying *stay*, then slipped past the front bumper, put his finger up to slow Coney, crossed the pavement to the door of One-oh-nine, and hit the doorbell under the Zendo sign. Coney leaned against the car, waiting. I put on the headphones, got a clear sound of Minna's shoe scraping pavement over the wire so I knew it was working. When I looked up I saw the doorman from the big place to the right watching us, but he wasn't doing anything apart from watching.

I heard the buzzer sound, live and over the wire both. Minna went in, sweeping the door wide. Coney skipped over, grabbed the door, and disappeared inside, too.

Footsteps upstairs, no voices yet. Now suddenly I dwelled in two worlds, eyes and quivering body in the driver's seat of the Lincoln, watching from my parking spot the orderly street life of the Upper East Side, dog-walkers, deliverymen, girls and boys dressed as grown-ups in business suits shivering their way into gimmicky bars as the nightlife got under way, while my ears built a soundscape from the indoor echoes of Minna's movement up the stair, still nobody meeting him but he seemed to know where he was, shoe leather chafing on wood, stairs squeaking, then a hesitation, a rustle of clothing perhaps, then two wooden clunks, and the footsteps resumed more quietly. Minna had taken off his shoes.

Ringing the doorbell, then sneaking in? It didn't follow. But what in this sequence did follow? I palmed another Castle out of the paper sack — six burgers to restore order in a senseless world.

"Frank," came a voice over the wire.

"I came," said Minna wearily. *"But I shouldn't have to. You should clear up crap on your end."*

"I appreciate that," went the other voice. *"But things have gotten complicated."*

"They know about the contract for the building," said Minna.

"No, I don't think so." The voice was weirdly calm, placating. Did I recognize it? Perhaps not that so much as the rhythm of Minna's replies — this was someone he knew well, but who?

"Come inside, let's talk," said the voice.

"What about?" said Minna. *"What do we have to talk about?"*

"Listen to yourself, Frank."

"I came here to listen to myself? I can do that at home."

"But do you, in fact?" I could hear a smile in the voice. *"Not as often, or as deeply as you might, I suspect."*

"Where's Ullman?" said Minna. *"You got him here?"*

"Ullman's downtown. You'll go to him."

"Fuck."

"Patience."

"You say patience, I say fuck."

"Characteristic, I suppose."

"Yeah. So let's call the whole thing off."

More muffled footsteps, a door closing. A clunk, possibly a bottle and glass, a poured drink. Wine. I wouldn't have minded a beverage myself. I chewed on a Castle instead and gazed out the windshield, brain going *Characteristic autistic mystic my tic dipstick dickweed* and then I thought to take another note, flipped open the notebook and under

WOMAN, HAIR, GLASSES wrote ULLMAN DOWNTOWN, thought Dull Man Out of Town. When I swallowed the burger, my jaw and throat tightened, and I braced for an unavoidable copralalic tic — out loud, though no one was there to hear it. "Eat shit, Bailey!"

Bailey was a name embedded in my Tourette's brain, though I couldn't say why. I'd never known a Bailey. Maybe Bailey was everyman, like George Bailey in *It's a Wonderful Life.* My imaginary listener, he had to bear the brunt of a majority of my solitary swearing — some part of me required a target, apparently. If a Touretter curses in the woods and there's nobody to hear does he make a sound? Bailey seemed to be my solution to that conundrum.

"Your face betrays you, Frank. You'd like to murder someone."

"You'd do fine for a start."

"You shouldn't blame me, Frank, if you've lost control of her."

"It's your fault if she misses her Rama-lama-ding-dong. You're the one who filled her head with that crap."

"Here, try this." (Offering a drink?)

"Not on an empty stomach."

"Alas. I forget how you suffer, Frank."

"Aw, go fuck yourself."

"Eat shit, Bailey!" The tics were always worst when I was nervous, stress kindling my Tourette's. And something in this scenario was making me nervous. The conversation I overheard was too knowing, the references all polished and opaque, as though years of dealings lay underneath every word.

Also, where was the short-dark-haired girl? In the room with Minna and his supercilious conversational partner, silent? Or somewhere else entirely? My inability to visualize the interior space of One-oh-nine was agitating. Was the girl the "she" they were discussing? It seemed unlikely.

And what was *her Rama-lama-ding-dong?* I didn't have the luxury of worrying about it. I pushed away a host of tics and tried not to dwell on things I didn't understand.

I glanced at the door. Presumably Coney was still behind it. I wanted to hear *not if my life depended on it* so we could rush the stairs.

I was startled by a knock on the driver's window. It was the doorman who'd been watching. He gestured for me to roll down the window. I shook my head, he nodded his. Finally I complied, pulling the headphones off one ear so I could listen.

"What?" I said, triply distracted — the power window had seduced my magpie mind and now demanded purposeless raising and lowering. I tried to keep it subtle.

"Your friend, he wants you," said the doorman, gesturing back toward his building.

"What?" This was thoroughly confusing. I craned my neck to see past him, but there was nobody visible in the doorway of his building. Meanwhile, Minna was saying something over the wire. But not *bathroom* or *depended on it*.

"Your friend," the doorman repeated in his clumsy Eastern European accent, maybe Polish or Czech. "He asks for you." He grinned, enjoying my bewilderment. I felt myself knitting my brow exaggeratedly, a tic, and wanted to tell him to wipe the grin off his face: Everything he was seeing was not to his credit.

"What friend?" I said. Minna and Coney were both inside — I would have noticed if the Zendo door had budged.

"He said if you're waiting, he's ready," said the doorman, nodding, gesturing again. "Wants to talk."

Now Minna was saying something about "*. . . make a mess on the marble floor . . .*"

"I think you've got the wrong guy," I said to the doorman. *"Dickweed!"* I winced, waved him off, tried to focus on the voices coming over the headphones.

"Hey, hey," the doorman said. He held up his hands. "I'm just bringing you a message, friend."

I zipped down the power window again, finally pried my fingers away. "No problem," I said, and suppressed another *dickweed* into a high, chihuahuaesque barking sound, something like *yipke!* "But I can't leave the car. Tell my *friend* if he wants to talk to come out and talk to me here. Okay, *friend?*" It seemed to me I had too many friends all of a sudden, and I didn't know any of their names. I repeated my impulsive flapping motion with my hand, an expedient tic-and-gesture combo, trying to nudge this buffoon back to his doorway.

"No, no. He said come in."

"*. . . break an arm . . .*" I thought I heard Minna say.

"Get his name, then," I said, desperate. "Come back and tell me his name."

"He wants to talk to you."

"Okay, *eatmedoorman,* tell him I'll be right there." I powered up the window in his face. He tapped again, and I ignored him.

"*. . . first let me use your toilet . . .*"

I opened the car door and pushed the doorman out of the way, went to the Zendo door and knocked, six times, hard.

"Coney," I hissed. "Get out here."

Over the headset I heard Minna shut the bathroom door behind him, begin running water. *"Hope you heard that, Freakshow,"* he whispered into his microphone, addressing me directly. *"We're getting in a car. Don't lose us. Play it cool."*

Coney popped out of the door.

"He's coming out," I said, pulling the headphones down around my neck.

"Okay," said Coney, eyes wide. We were in the thick of the action, for once.

"You drive," I said, touching my fingertip to his nose. He flinched me away like a fly. We hustled into the car, and Coney revved the engine. I threw the bag of cooling Castles and paper wreckage into the backseat. The idiot doorman had vanished into his building. I put him out of my mind for the moment.

We sat facing forward, our car shrouded in its own steam, waiting, vibrating. My brain went *Follow that car! Hollywood star! When you wish upon a cigar!* My jaw worked, chewing the words back down, keeping silent. Gilbert's hands gripped the wheel, mine drummed quietly in my lap, tiny hummingbird motions.

This was what passed for playing it cool around here.

"I don't see him," said Coney.

"Just wait. He'll come out, with some other guys probably." *Probably, gobbledy.* I lifted one of the headphones to my right ear. No voices, nothing but clunking sounds, maybe the stairs.

"What if they get into a car behind us?" said Coney.

"It's a one-way street," I said, annoyed, but glancing backward at this cue to survey the parked cars behind us. "Just let them pass."

"Hey," said Coney.

They'd appeared, slipping out the door and rushing ahead of us on the sidewalk while I'd turned: Minna and another man, a giant in a black coat. The other man was seven feet tall if he was an inch, with shoulders that looked as though football pads or angel wings were hidden under his coat. Or perhaps the petite short-haired girl was curled under there, clutching the tall man's shoulders like a human backpack. Was this giant the man who'd spoken so insinuatingly? Minna hurried ahead of the giant, as if he were motivated to give us the slip instead of dragging his heels to keep us in the game. Why? A gun in his back? The giant's hands were hidden in his pockets. For some reason I envisioned them gripping loaves of bread or large chunks of salami, snacks hidden in the coat to feed a giant in winter, comfort food.

Or maybe this fantasy was merely my own self-comfort: a loaf of bread couldn't be a gun, which allotted Minna the only firearm in the scenario.

We watched stupidly as they crossed between two parked cars and slid into the backseat of a black K-car that had rolled up from behind us in the street, then immediately took off. Overanxious as we were, Coney and I had at some level timed our reactions to allow for their starting a parked car, and now they were getting away. "Go!" I said.

Coney swerved to pull the Lincoln out of our spot, batted bumpers, hard enough to dent. Of course we were locked in. He backed, more gently thumped the rear end, then found an arc sufficient to free us from the space, but not before a cab had rocketed past us to block the way. The K-car tucked around the corner up ahead, onto Second Avenue. "Go!"

"Look," said Coney, pointing at the cab. "I'm going. Keep your eyes up."

"Eyes up?" I said. "Eyes out. *Chin* up." Correcting him was an involuntary response to stress.

"Yeah, that too."

"Eyes open, eyes on the road, ears glued to the radio —" I suddenly had to list every workable possibility. That was how irritating *eyes up* had been.

"Yeah, and trap buttoned," said Coney. He got us right on the tail of the cab, better than nothing since it was moving fast. "What about gluing your ears to Frank while you're at it?"

I raised the headphones. Nothing but an overlay of traffic sounds to substitute for the ones I'd blotted out. Coney followed the cab onto Second Avenue, where the K-car obligingly waited in a thicket of cabs and other traffic for the light to change. We were back in the game, a notion exhilarating and yet pathetic by definition, since we'd lost them in the space of a block.

We merged left to pull around the first cab and into position behind another in the same lane as the car containing Minna and the giant. I watch the timed stoplights a half mile ahead turn red. Now there, I thought, was a job for someone with obsessive-compulsive symptoms — traffic management. Then our light turned green and we lurched all together, a floating quilt of black- and dun-colored private cars and the bright-orange cabs, through the intersection.

"Get closer," I said, pulling the phones from my ears again. Then an awesome tic wrenched its way out of my chest: *"Eat me Mister Dicky-weed!"*

This got even Gilbert's attention. "Mister Dicky-weed?" As the lights turned green in sequence for us the cabs threaded audaciously back and forth, seeking advantage, but the truth was the lights were timed for twenty-five-mile-an-hour traffic, and there wasn't any advantage to be gained. The still-unseen driver of the K-car was as impatient as a cabbie, and moved up to the front of the pack, but the timed lights kept us all honest, at least until they turned a corner. We remained stuck a car back. This was a chase Coney could handle, so far.

I was another story.

"Sinister mystery weed," I said, trying to find words that would ease the compulsion. It was as if my brain were inspired, trying to generate a really original new tic. Tourette's muse was with me. Rotten timing. Stress generally aggravated tics, but when I was engaged in a task the concentration kept me tic-free. I should have done the driving, I now realized. This chase was all stress and no place for it to go.

"Disturbed visitor week. Sisturbed."

"Yeah, I'm getting a little *sisturbed*

myself," said Coney absently as he jockeyed for an open spot in the lane to the right.

"Fister —" I sputtered.

"Spare me," groused Coney as he got us directly behind the K-car at last. I leaned forward to make out what I could of the interior. Three heads. Minna and the giant in the backseat, and a driver. Minna was facing straight ahead, and so was the giant. I picked up the headphones to check, but I'd guessed right: no talk. Somebody knew what they were doing and where they were going, and that somebody wasn't even remotely us.

At Fifty-ninth Street we hit the end of the cycle of green lights, as well as the usual unpleasantness around the entrance to the Queensborough bridge. The pack slowed, resigning itself to the wait through another red. Coney sagged back so we wouldn't be too obvious pulling in behind them for the wait, and another cab slipped in ahead of us. Then the K-car shot off through the fresh red, barely missing the surge of traffic coming across Fifty-eighth.

"Shit!"

"Shit!"

Coney and I both almost bounced out of our skins. We were wedged in, unable to follow and brave the stream of crosstown traffic if we'd wanted to try. It felt like a straitjacket. It felt like our fate overtaking us, Minna's losers, failing him again. Fuckups fucking up because that's what fuckups do. But the K-car hit another mass of vehicular stuff parked in front of the next red and stayed in sight a block ahead. The traffic was broken into chunks. We'd gotten lucky for a minute, but a minute only.

I watched, frantic. Their red, our red, my eyes flicked back and forth. I heard Coney's breath, and my own, like horses at the gate — our adrenalinated bodies imagined they could make up the difference of the block. If we weren't careful, at the sight of the light changing we'd pound our two foreheads through the windshield.

Our red did change, but so did theirs, and, infuriatingly, their vehicular mass surged forward while ours crawled. That mass was our hope — they were at the tail end of theirs, and if it stayed densely enough packed, they wouldn't get too far away. We were almost at the front of ours. I slapped the glove-compartment door six times. Coney accelerated impulsively and tapped the cab in front of us, but not hard. We veered to the side and I saw a silver scrape in the yellow paint of the cab's bumper. "Fuck it, keep going," I said. The cabbie seemed to have the same idea anyway. We all screeched across Fifty-ninth, a madcap rodeo of cabs and cars, racing to defy the immutable law of timed stoplights. Our bunch splayed and caught up with the rear end of their splaying bunch and the two blended, like video spaceships on some antic screen. The K-car aggressively threaded lanes. We threaded after them, making no attempt to disguise our pursuit now. Blocks flew past.

"Turning!" I shouted. "Get over!" I gripped the door handle as Coney, getting fully into the spirit of things, bent topological probability in moving us across three crowded lanes full of shrieking bald rubber and cringing chrome. Now my tics were quieted — stress was one thing, animal fear another. As when an airplane lands shakily, and all on board concentrate every gram of their will to stabilize the craft, the task of imagining I controlled things I didn't (in this case wheel, traffic, Coney, gravity, friction, etc.), imagining it with every fiber of my being — that was engagement enough for me at the moment. My Tourette's was overwhelmed.

"Thirty-sixth," said Coney as we rattled down the side street.

"What's that mean?"

"I dunno. Something."

"Midtown Tunnel. Queens."

There was something comforting about this. The giant and his driver were moving onto our turf, more or less. The boroughs. Not quite Brooklyn, but it would do. We bumped along with the thickening traffic into the two dense lanes of the tunnel, the K-car safely tied up two cars ahead of us, its windows now black and glossy with reflections from the strips of lighting that laced the stained tile artery. I relaxed a bit, quit holding my breath, and squeaked out a teeth-clenched, Joker-grimacing *eat me* just because I could.

"Toll," said Coney.

"What?"

"There's a toll. On the Queens side."

I started digging in my pockets. "How much?"

"Three-fifty, I think."

I'd just put it together, miraculously, three bills, a quarter, a dime and three nickels, when the tunnel finished and the two lanes branched out to meet the six or seven toll booths. I balled the fare and held it out to Coney in a fist. "Don't get stuck behind them," I said. "Get a fast lane. Cut someone off."

"Yeah." Coney squinted through the

windshield, trying to work an angle. As he edged to the right the K-car suddenly cut out of the flow, moving to the far left.

We both stared for a moment.

"Whuzzat?" said Coney.

"E-Z Pass," I said. "They've got an E-Z Pass."

The K-car slid into the empty E-Z Pass lane, and right through the booth. Meanwhile Coney had landed us third in line for EXACT CHANGE OR TOKEN.

"Follow them!" I said.

"I'm trying," said Coney, plainly dazed by this turn of events.

"Get over to the left!" I said. "Go through!"

"We don't got an E-Z Pass." Coney grinned painfully, displaying his special talent for rapid reversion to a childlike state.

"I don't care!"

"But we —"

I started to pry at the wheel in Coney's hands, to try and push us to the left, but it was too late by now. The spot before us opened, and Coney eased the car into place, then rolled down his window. I plopped the fare into his open palm, and he passed it over.

Pulling out of the tunnel to the right, we were suddenly in Queens, facing a tangle of indifferent streets: Vernon Boulevard, Jackson Avenue, Fifty-second Avenue. Et cetera.

The K-car was gone.

"Pull over," I said.

Chagrined, Coney parked us on Jackson. It was perfectly dark now, though it was only seven. The lights of the Empire State and the Chrysler loomed across the river. Cars whirred past us out of the tunnel, toward the entrance to the Long Island Expressway, mocking us in their easy purposefulness. With Minna lost, we were nobodies, nowhere.

"Eatmepass!" I said.

"They could of just been losing us," said Coney.

"I'd say they were, yes."

"No, listen," he said feebly. "Maybe they turned around and went back to Manhattan. Maybe we could catch them —"

"Shhh." I listened to the earphones. "If Frank sees we're off his tail, he might say something."

But there was nothing to hear. The sounds of driving. Minna and the giant were sitting in perfect silence. Now I couldn't believe that the man in the Zendo was the same as the giant — that garrulous, pretentious voice I'd heard couldn't have shut up this long, it seemed to me. It was surprising enough that Minna wasn't chattering, making fun of something, pointing out landmarks. Was he scared? Afraid to let on he was miked? Did he think we were still with him? Why did he want us with him anyway?

I didn't know anything.

I made six oinking sounds.

We sat waiting.

More.

"That's the way of a big Polish lug, I guess," said Minna. *"Always gotta stay within sniffing distance of a pierogi."*

Then: *"Urrhhf."* Like the giant had smashed him in the stomach.

"Where's Polish?" I asked Coney, lifting away one earphone.

"Wha?"

"Where around here's Polish? *Eat me pierogi lug!*"

"I dunno. It's all Polish to me."

"Sunnyside? Woodside? Come on, Gilbert. Work with me. He's somewhere Polish."

"Where'd the Pope visit?" mused Coney. It sounded like the start of a joke, but I knew Coney. He couldn't remember jokes. "That's Polish, right? What's it, uh, Greenpoint?"

"Greenpoint's Brooklyn, Gilbert," I said, before thinking. "We're in Queens." Then we both turned our heads like cartoon mice spotting a cat. The Pulaski Bridge. We were a few yards from the creek separating Queens and Brooklyn, specifically Greenpoint.

It was something to do anyway. "Go," I said.

"Keep listening," said Coney. "We can't just drive around Greenpoint."

We soared across the little bridge, into the mouth of Brooklyn.

"Which way, Lionel?" said Coney, as if he thought Minna were feeding me a constant stream of instructions. I shrugged, palms up toward the roof of the Lincoln. The gesture ticcified instantly, and I repeated it, shrug, palms flapped open, grimace. Coney ignored me, scanning the streets below for a sign of the K-car, driving as slow as he could down the Brooklyn side of the Pulaski's slope.

Then I heard something. Car doors opening, slamming, the scuff of footsteps. Minna and the giant had reached their destination. I froze in mid-tic, concentrating.

"Harry Brainum Jr.," said Minna in his mockingest tone. *"I guess we're gonna stop in for a quick installation, huh?"*

Nothing from the giant. More steps.

Who was Harry Brainum Jr.?

Meanwhile we came off the lit bridge, where the notion of a borough laid out for us, comprehensive, had been briefly indulgeable. Down instead onto McGuinness Boulevard, where at street level the dark industrial buildings were featureless and discouraging. Brooklyn is one big place, and this wasn't our end of it.

"You know — if you can't beat 'em, Brainum, right?" Minna went on in his needling voice. In the background I heard a car horn — they weren't indoors yet. Just standing on the street somewhere, tantalizingly close.

Then I heard a thud, another exhalation. Minna had taken a second blow.

Then Minna again: *"Hey, hey —"* Some kind of struggle I couldn't make out.

"Fucking —" said Minna, and then I heard him get hit again, lose his wind in a long, mournful sigh.

The scary thing about the giant was that he didn't talk, didn't even breathe heavy enough for me to hear.

"Harry Brainum Jr.," I said to Coney. Then, afraid it sounded like a tic to him, I added, "Name mean anything to you, Gilbert?"

"Sorry?" he said slowly.

"Harry Brainum Jr.," I repeated, furious with impatience. There were times when I felt like a bolt of static electricity communing with figures that moved through a sea of molasses.

"Sure," he said, jerking his thumb in the direction of his window. "We just passed it."

"What? Passed what?"

"It's like a tool company or something. Big sign."

My breath caught. Minna was talking to us, guiding us. "Turn around."

"What, back to Queens?"

"No, Brainum, wherever you saw that," I said, wanting to strangle him. Or at least find his fast-forward button and push it. "They're out of the car. Make a U-turn."

"It's just a block or two."

"Well, go, then. *Brain me, Junior!*"

Coney made the turn, and right away there it was. HARRY BRAINUM JR. INC. STEEL SHEETS., in giant circus-poster letters on the brick wall of a two-story plant that took up a whole block of McGuinness, just short of the bridge.

Seeing BRAINUM on the wall set off a whole clown parade of associations. I remembered mishearing *Ringling Bros. Barnum & Bailey*

Circus as a child. Barnamum Bailey. Like Osmium, Cardamom, Brainium, Barnamum, Where'smymom: the periodic table of elements, the heavy metals. Barnamum Bailey might also be George and Eat Me Bailey's older brother. Or were they all the same guy? Not now, I begged my Tourette's self. Think about it later.

"Drive around the block," I said to Coney. "He's here somewhere."

"Quit shouting," he said. "I can hear you."

"Shut up so I can hear," I said.

"That's all I said."

"What?" I lifted an earphone.

"That's all I said. Shut up."

"Okay! Shut up! Drive! Eat me!"

"Fucking freakball."

The block behind BRAINUM was dark and seemingly empty. The few parked cars didn't include the K-car. The windowless brick warehouse was laced with fire escapes, wrought-iron cages that ran the length of the second floor and ended in a crumpled, unsafe-looking ladder. On the side street a smallish, graffitied Dumpster was tucked halfway into the shadow of a double doorway. The doors behind were strapped with long exterior hinges, like a meat locker. One lid of the Dumpster was shut, the other open to allow some fluorescent bulbs sticking up. Street rubbish packed around the wheels made me think it hadn't moved in a while, so I didn't worry about the doors behind it. The other entrance was a roll-up gate on a truck-size loading dock, right out on the brightly lit boulevard. I figured I would have heard the gate sing if it had been raised.

The four stacks of the Newtown Creek Sewage Treatment Plant towered at the end of the street, underlit like ancient pylons in a gladiator movie. Fly an inflatable pig over and you'd have the sleeve of Pink Floyd's *Animals* album. Beneath its shadow we crept in the Lincoln around all four corners of the block, seeing nothing.

"Damn it," I said.

"You don't hear him?"

"Street noise. Hey, hit the horn."

"Why?"

"Do it."

I concentrated on the earphones. Coney honked the Lincoln's horn. Sure enough, it came through.

"Stop the car." I was in a panic now. I got out onto the sidewalk, slammed the door. "Circle slow," I said. "Keep an eye on me."

"What's the deal, Lionel?"

"He's here."

I paced the sidewalk, trying to feel the

pulse of the blackened building, to take the measure of the desolate block. It was a place made out of leftover chunks of disappointment, unemployment and regret. I didn't want to be here, didn't want Minna to be here. Coney paced me in the Lincoln, staring dumbly out the driver's window. I listened to the phones until I heard the approach of my own steps. My own heart beating made a polyrhythm, almost as loud. Then I found it. Minna's wire had been torn from his shirt and lay tangled in a little heap on the curb of the side street, at the other end of the block from the Dumpster. I picked it up and pushed it into my pants pocket, then ripped the headphones off my neck. Feeling the grimness of the street close around me I began to half-run down the sidewalk toward the Dumpster, though I had to stop once and mimic my own retrieval of the wire: hurriedly kneel at the edge of the sidewalk, grab, stuff, remove phantom headphones, feel a duplicate thrill of panic at the discovery, resume jogging. It was cold now. The wind punched me and my nose oozed in response. I wiped it on my sleeve as I came up to the Dumpster.

"You jerks," Minna moaned from inside.

I touched the rim of the Dumpster and my hand came away wet with blood. I pushed open the second lid, balanced it against the doorway. Minna was curled fetally in the garbage, his arms crossed around his stomach, sleeves covered in red.

"Jesus, Frank."

"Wanna get me out of here?" He coughed, burbled, rolled his eyes at me. "Wanna give me a hand? I mean, no sooner than the muse strikes. Or possibly you ought to get out your brushes and canvas. I've never been in an oil painting."

"Sorry, Frank." I reached in just as Coney came up behind me and looked inside.

"Oh, shit," he said.

"Help me," I said to Coney. Together we pulled Minna up from the bottom of the Dumpster. Minna stayed curled around his wounded middle. We drew him over the lip and held him, together, out on the dark empty sidewalk, cradling him absurdly, our knees buckled toward one another's, our shoulders pitched, like he was a giant baby Jesus in a bloody trench coat and we were each one of the Madonna's tender arms. Minna groaned and chuckled, eyes squeezed shut, as we moved him to the backseat of the Lincoln. His blood made my fingers tacky on the door handle.

"Nearest hospital," I breathed as we got into the front.

"I don't know around here," said Coney, whispering, too.

"Brooklyn Hospital," said Minna from the back, surprisingly loud. "Take the BQE, straight up McGuinness. Brooklyn Hospital's right off DeKalb. You boiled cabbageheads."

We held our breath and stared forward until Coney got us going the right way, then I turned and looked in the back. Minna's eyes were half open and his unshaven chin was wrinkled like he was thinking hard or sulking or trying not to cry. He saw me looking and winked. I barked twice — "yipke, yipke" — and winked back involuntarily.

"Fuck happened, Frank?" said Coney without taking his eyes off the road. We bumped and rattled over the Brooklyn-Queens Expressway, rottenest surface in the boroughs. Like the G train, the BQE suffered from low self-esteem, never going into citadel Manhattan, never tasting the glory. And it was choked with forty- or fifty-wheel trucks, day and night.

"I'm dropping my wallet and watch back here," said Minna, ignoring the question. "And my beeper. Don't want them stolen at the hospital. Remember they're back here."

"Yeah, but what the fuck happened, Frank?"

"Leave you my gun but it's gone," said Minna. I watched him shuck off the watch, silver smeared with red.

"They took your gun? Frank, what happened?"

"Knife," said Minna. "No biggie."

"You're gonna be all right?" Coney was asking and willing it at once.

"Oh, yeah. Great."

"Sorry, Frank."

"Who?" I said. "Who did this?"

Minna smiled. "You know what I want out of you, Freakshow? Tell me a joke. You got one you been saving, you must."

Minna and I had been in a joke-telling contest since I was thirteen years old, primarily because he liked to see me try to get through without ticcing. It was rare that I could.

"Let me think," I said.

"It'll hurt him if he laughs," said Coney to me. "Say one he knows already. Or one that ain't funny."

"Since when do I laugh?" said Minna. "Let him tell it. Couldn't hurt worse than your driving."

"Okay," I said. "Guy walks into a bar." I was watching blood pool on the backseat, at the same time trying to keep Minna from tracking my eyes.

"That's the ticket," rasped Minna. "Best jokes start the same fucking way, don't they, Gilbert? The guy, the bar."

"I guess," said Coney.

"Funny already," said Minna. "We're already in the black here."

"So guy walks into a bar," I said again. "With an octopus. Says to the bartender 'I'll bet a hundred dollars this octopus can play any instrument in the place.' "

"Guy's got an octopus. You like that, Gilbert?"

"Eh."

"So the bartender points at the piano in the corner says, 'Go ahead.' Guy puts the octopus on the piano stool — *Pianoctamus! Pianoctamum Bailey!* — octopus flips up the lid, plays a few scales, then lays out a little étude on the piano."

"Getting fancy," said Minna. "Showing off a little."

I didn't ask him to specify, since if I had he'd surely have said he meant me and the octopus both, for the *étude*.

"So guy says 'Pay up,' bartender says 'Wait a minute,' pulls out a guitar. Guy gives the octopus the guitar, octopus tightens up the E-string, closes its eyes, plays a sweet little fandango on the guitar." Pressure building up, I tagged Coney on the shoulder six times. He ignored me, driving hard, outracing trucks. "Guy says 'Pay up,' bartender says 'Hold on, I think I've got something else around here,' pulls a clarinet out of the back room. Octopus looks the thing over a couple of times, tightens the reed."

"He's milking it," said Minna, again meaning us both.

"Well, the octopus isn't good exactly, but he manages to squeak out a few bars on the clarinet. He isn't going to win any awards, but he plays the thing. *Clarinet Milk! Eat Me!* Guy says 'Pay up,' the bartender says 'Just wait one minute,' goes in the back rummages around finally comes out with a bagpipes. Plops the bagpipes up on the bar. Guy brings the octopus over, plops the octopus up next to the bagpipes. *Octapipes!*" I paused to measure my wits, not wanting to tic out the punch line. Then I started again, afraid of losing the thread, of losing Minna. His eyes kept closing and opening again and I wanted them open. "Octopus looks the bagpipes over, reaches out lifts one pipe lets it drop. Lifts another lets it drop. Backs up, squints at the bagpipes. Guy gets nervous, comes over to the bar says to the octopus — *Accupush! Reactapus!* — says to the octopush, *fuckit,* says *gonnafuckit* — says

'What's the matter? Can't you play it?' And the octopus says 'Play it? If I can figure out how to get its pajamas off, I'm gonna fuck it!' "

Minna's eyes had been closed through the windup and he didn't open them now. "You finished?" he said.

I didn't speak. We circled the ramp off the BQE, onto DeKalb Avenue.

"Where's the hospital?" said Minna, eyes still shut.

"We're almost there," said Coney.

"I need help," said Minna. "I'm dying back here."

"You're not dying," I said.

"Before we get in the emergency room, you want to tell us who did this to you, Frank?" said Coney.

Minna didn't say anything.

"They stab you in the gut and throw you in the fucking garbage, Frank. You wanna tell us who?"

"Go up the ambulance ramp," said Minna. "I need help back here. I don't wanna wait in some goddamn walk-in emergency room. I need immediate help."

"We can't drive up the ambulance ramp, Frank."

"What, you think you need an *E-Z Pass*, you stale meat loaf? Do what I said."

I gritted my teeth while my brain went, *Guy walks into the ambulance ramp stabs you in the goddamn emergency gut says I need an immediate stab in the garbage in the goddamn walk-in ambulance says just a minute looks in the back says I think I've got a stab in the goddamn walk-in immediate ambuloaf ambulamp octoloaf oafulope.*

"*Oafulope!*" I screamed, tears in my eyes.

"Yeah," said Minna, and now he laughed, then moaned. "A whole fucking herd of 'em."

"Someone ought to put you both out of your misery," muttered Coney as we hit the ambulance ramp behind Brooklyn Hospital, driving against the DO NOT ENTER signs, wheels squealing around a pitched curve to a spot alongside double swinging doors marked with yellow stencil EMS ONLY. Coney stopped. A Rastafarian in the costume of a private security guard was on us right away, tapping at Coney's window. He had bundled dreadlocks pushing sideways out of his hat, chiba eyes, a stick where a gun should be, and an embroidered patch on his chest indicating his first name, Albert. Like a janitor's uniform, or a mechanic's. The jacket was too big for his broomstick frame.

Coney opened the door instead of rolling down the glass.

"Get this car out of here!" said Albert.

"Take a look in the back," said Coney.

"Don't care, mon. This for ambulances only. Get back in the car."

"Tonight we're an ambulance, Albert," I said. "Get a stretcher for our friend."

Minna looked terrible. Drained, literally, and when we got him out of the car you could see what of. The blood smelled like a thunderstorm coming, like ozone. Two college students dressed as doctors in green outfits with rubber-band sleeves took him away from us just inside the doors and laid him onto a rolling steel cart. Minna's shirt was shreds, his middle a slush of itself, of himself. Coney went out and moved the car to quiet the security guard pulling on his arm while I followed Minna's stretcher inside, against the weak protests of the college students. I moved along keeping my eyes on his face and tapping his shoulder intermittently as though we were standing talking, in the Agency office perhaps, or just strolling down Court Street with two slices of pizza. Once they had Minna parked in a semiprivate zone in the emergency room, the students left me alone and concentrated on getting a line for blood into his arm.

His eyes opened. "Where's Coney?" he said. His voice was like a withered balloon.

If you didn't know its shape when it was full of air it wouldn't have sounded like anything at all.

"They might not let him back here," I said. "I'm not supposed to be here myself."

"Huhhr."

"Coney — *Eatme, yipke!* — Coney kind of had a point," I said. "You might want to tell us who, while we're, you know, waiting around here."

The students were working on his middle, peeling away cloth with long scissors. I turned my eyes away.

Minna smiled again. "I've got one for you," he said. I leaned in to hear him. "Thought of it in the car. Octopus and Reactopus are sitting on a bench, a fence. Octopus falls off, who's left?"

"Reactopus," I said softly. "Frank, who did this?"

"You know that Jewish joke you told me? The one about the Jewish lady goes to Tibet, wants to see the High Lama?"

"Sure."

"That's a good one. What's the name of that lama? You know, at the end, the punch line."

"You mean Irving?"

"Yeah, right. Irving." I could barely hear him now. "That's who." His eyes closed.

"You're saying it was someone named — *Dick! Weed!* — Irving who did this to you? Is that the name of the big guy in the car? Irving?"

Minna whispered something that sounded like "remember." The others in the room were making noise, barking out instructions to one another in their smug, technical dialect.

"Remember what?"

No answer.

"The name Irving? Or something else?"

Minna hadn't heard me. A nurse pulled open his mouth and he didn't protest, didn't move at all.

"Excuse me."

It was a doctor. He was short, olive-skinned, stubbled, Indian or Pakistani, I guessed. He looked into my eyes. "You have to go now."

"I can't do that," I said. I reached out and tagged his shoulder.

He didn't flinch. "What's your name?" he asked gently. Now I saw in his worn expression several thousand nights like this one.

"Lionel." I gulped away an impulse to scream my last name.

"Tourette's?"

"Yessrog."

"Lionel, we're going to do some emergency surgery here. You must go wait outside." He nodded his head quickly to point the way. "They'll be needing you to handle some papers for your friend."

I stood stupefied, looking at Minna, wanting to tell him another joke, or hear one of his. *Guy walks into —*

A nurse was fitting a hinged plastic tube, like a giant Pez dispenser, into Minna's mouth.

I walked out the way I'd come in and found the triage nurse. Thinking *arbitrage, sabotage,* I told her I was with Minna and she said she'd already spoken to Coney. She'd call out when she needed us, until then have a seat.

Coney sat crossed-legged and cross-armed with his chin clamped up angrily against the rest of his face, corduroy coat still buttoned, filling half of a kind of love seat with a narrow shelfload of splayed dingy magazines attached to it. I went and filled the other half. The waiting area was jammed with the sort of egalitarian cross-section only genuine misery can provide: Hispanics and blacks and Russians and various indeterminate, red-eyed teenage girls with children you prayed were siblings; junkie veterans petitioning for painkillers they wouldn't get; a tired housewife comforting her brother as he carped in an unceasing stream about his blocked digestion, the bowel movement he hadn't enjoyed for weeks; a terrified lover denied attendance, as I'd been, glaring viciously at the unimpressible triage nurse and the mute doors behind her; others guarded, defiant, daring you to puzzle at their distress, to guess on behalf of whom, themselves or another, they shared with you this miserable portion of their otherwise fine, pure and invulnerable lives.

I sat still for perhaps a minute and a half, tormented images of our chase and the Brainum Building and Minna's wounds strobing in my skull, tics roiling in my throat.

"*Walksinto,*" I shouted.

A few people looked up, confused by my bit of ventriloquism. Had the nurse spoken? Could it have been a last name? Their own, perhaps, mispronounced?

"Don't start now," said Coney under his breath.

"Guywalks, walksinto, guywalksinto," I said back to him helplessly.

"What, you telling a joke now?"

Very much in the grip, I modified the words into a growling sound, along the lines of "*whrywhroffsinko,*" — but the effort resulted in a side-tic: rapid eye blinks.

"Maybe you ought to stand outside, you know, like for a cigarette?" Poor dim Coney was just as much on edge as I was, obviously.

"Walks walks!"

Some stared, others looked away, bored. I'd been identified by the crowd as some sort of patient: spirit or animal possession, verbal epileptic seizure, whatever. I would presumably be given drugs and sent home. I wasn't damaged or ailing enough to be interesting here, only distracting, and slightly reprehensible in a way that made them feel better about their own disorders, so my oddness was quickly and blithely incorporated into the atmosphere.

With one exception: Albert, who'd been nursing a grudge since our jaunt up the ambulance ramp and now stood inside to get away from the cold, perhaps also to keep a bloodshot eye on us. I'd given him his angle, since, unlike the others in the waiting room, he knew I wasn't the patient in my party. He stepped over from where he'd been blowing on his hands and sulking in the doorway and pointed at me. "Yo, mon," he said. "You can't be like that in here."

"Be like what?" I said, twisting my neck and croaking *"Sothisguysays!"* as an urgent follow-up, voice rising shrilly, like a comedian who can't get his audience's attention.

"Can't be doing *that* shit," he said. "Gotta take it else*where*." He grinned at his own verbal flourish, openly pleased to provide this contrast to my lack of control.

"Mind your own business," said Coney.

"Piece! Of! String!" I said, recalling another joke I hadn't told Minna, also set in a bar. My heart sank. I wanted to barge in and begin reciting it to his doctors, to his white intubed face. *"String! Walks! In!"*

"What's the matter with you, mon?"

"WEDON'TSERVESTRING!"

I was in trouble now. My Tourette's brain had shackled itself to the string joke like an ecological terrorist to a tree-crushing bulldozer. If I didn't find a way out I might download the whole joke one grunted or shrieked syllable after another. Looking for the escape hatch I began counting ceiling tiles and beating a rhythm on my knees as I counted. I saw I'd reattracted the room's collective attention, too. *This guy might be interesting after all.*

Free Human Freakshow.

"He's gotta condition," said Coney to the guard. "So lay off."

"Well, tell the mon he best stand up and walk his condition out of here," said the guard. "Or I be calling in the armada, you understand?"

"You must be mistaken," I said, in a calm voice now. "I'm not a piece of string." The bargain had been struck, at a level beyond my control. The joke would be told. I was only a device for telling it.

"We stand up we're gonna lay a condition on *your* ass, Albert," said Coney. "You unnerstand that?"

Albert didn't speak. The whole room was watching, tuned to Channel Brooklyn.

"You gotta cigarette for us, Albert?" said Coney.

"Can't smoke in here, mon," said Albert softly.

"Now, that's a good, sensible rule," said Coney. " 'Cause you got all these people in here that's concerned about their *health*."

Coney was occasionally a master of the intimidating non sequitur. He certainly had Albert stymied now.

"I'm a *frayed knot,*" I whispered. I began to want to grab at the nightstick in Albert's holster — an old, familiar impulse to reach for things dangling from belts, like the bunches of keys worn by the teachers at St. Vincent's Home for Boys. It seemed like a particularly rotten idea right now.

"Afraid of what?" said Albert, confused,

though understanding the joke's pun, in a faint way.

"Afrayedknot!" I repeated obligingly, then added, "Eatmestringjoke!" Albert glared, unsure what he'd been called, or how badly to be insulted.

"Mr. Coney," called the triage nurse, breaking the stalemate. Coney and I both stood at once, still pathetically overcompensating for losing Minna in the chase. The short doctor had come out of the private room. He stood behind the triage nurse and nodded us over. As we brushed past Albert I indulged in a brief surreptitious fondling of his nightstick.

Half a fag, that's what Minna used to call me.

"Ah, are either of you a relative of Mr. Minna's?" The doctor's accent rendered this as *misdemeanors*.

"Yes and no," said Coney before I could answer. "We're his immediates, so to speak."

"Ah, I see," said the doctor, though of course he didn't. "Will you step this way with me —" He led us out of the waiting area, to another of the half-secluded rooms like the one where they'd wheeled Minna.

"I'mafrayed," I said under my breath.

"I'm sorry," said the doctor, standing

oddly close to us, examining our eyes. "There was little we could do."

"That's okay, then," said Coney, not hearing it right. "I'm sure whatever you can do is fine, since Frank didn't need so much in the first place —"

"I'mafrayedknot." I felt myself nearly choke, not on unspoken words for once but on rising gorge, White Castle-flavored bile. I swallowed it back so hard my ears popped. My whole face felt flushed with a mist of acids.

"Ahem. We were unable to revive misdemeanor."

"Wait a minute," said Coney. "You're saying unable to revive?"

"Yes, that's right. Loss of blood was the cause. I am sorry."

"Unable to revive!" shouted Coney. "He was *revived* when we brought him in here! What kind of a place is this? He didn't need to be revived, just patched up a little —"

I began to need to touch the doctor, to deliver small taps on either shoulder, in a pattern that was absolutely symmetrical. He stood for it, not pushing me away. I tugged his collar straight, matching the line to his salmon-colored T-shirt underneath, so that the same margin showed at either side of his neck.

Coney stood in deflated silence now, absorbing pain. We all stood waiting until I finally finished tucking and pinching the doctor's collar into place.

"Sometimes there is nothing we can do," said the doctor, eyes flicking to the floor now.

"Let me see him," said Coney.

"That isn't possible —"

"This place is full of crap," said Coney. "Let me see him."

"There is a question of evidence," said the doctor wearily. "I'm sure you understand. The examiners will also wish to speak with you."

I'd already seen police passing through from the hospital coffee shop, into some part of the emergency room. Whether those particular police were there to detain us or not, it was clear the law wouldn't be long in arriving.

"We ought to go, Gilbert," I told Coney. "Probably we ought to go right now."

Coney was inert.

"Problyreallyoughttogo," I said semi-compulsively, panic rising through my sorrow.

"You misunderstand," said the doctor. "We'll ask you to wait, please. This man will show you where to go —" He nodded at something behind us. I whipped around, my lizard instincts shocked at having allowed someone to sneak up on me.

It was Albert. The Thin Rastafarian Line between us and departure. His appearance seemed to trigger comprehension in Coney: The security guard was a cartoon reminder of the real existence of police.

"Outta the way," said Coney.

"We don't serve string!" I explained.

Albert didn't look any more convinced of his official status than we were. At moments like this I was reminded of the figure we Minna Men cut, oversize, undereducated, vibrant with hostility even with tear streaks all over our beefy faces. And me with my utterances, lunges, and taps, my symptoms, those extra factors Minna adored throwing into the mix.

Frank Minna, unrevived, empty of blood in the next room.

Albert held his palms open, his body more or less pleading as he said, "You better wait, mon."

"Nah," said Coney. "Maybe another time." Coney and I both leaned in Albert's direction, really only shifting our weight, and he jumped backward, spreading his hands over the spot he'd vacated as if to say *It was someone else standing there just now, not I.*

"But this is a thing upon which we must insist," said the doctor.

"You really don't wanna insist," said Coney, turning on him furiously. "You ain't got the insistence required, you know what I mean?"

"I'm not sure I do," said the doctor quietly.

"Well, just chew it over," said Coney. "There's no big hurry. C'mon, Lionel."

Motherless Brooklyn

I grew up in the library of St. Vincent's Home for Boys, in the part of downtown Brooklyn no developer yet wishes to claim for some up-scale, renovated neighborhood; not quite Brooklyn Heights, nor Cobble Hill, not even Boerum Hill. The Home is essentially set on the off-ramp to the Brooklyn Bridge, but out of sight of Manhattan or the bridge itself, on eight lanes of traffic lined with faceless, monolithic civil courts, which, gray and distant though they seemed, some of us Boys had seen the insides of, by Brooklyn's central sorting annex for the post office, a building that hummed and blinked all through the night, its gates groaning open to admit trucks bearing mountains of those mysterious items called letters, by the Burton Trade School for Automechanics, where hardened students attempting to set their lives dully straight spilled out twice a day for sandwich-and-beer breaks, overwhelming the cramped bodega next door, intimidating passersby and thrilling us Boys in their morose thuggish glory, by a desolate strip of park benches beneath a granite bust of Lafayette, indicating his point of entry into the Battle of Brooklyn, by a car lot surrounded by a high fence topped with wide curls of barbed wire and wind-whipped fluorescent flags, and by a redbrick Quaker Meetinghouse that had presumably been there when the rest was farmland. In short, this jumble of stuff at the clotted entrance to the ancient, battered borough was officially Nowhere, a place strenuously ignored in passing through to Somewhere Else. Until rescued by Frank Minna I lived, as I said, in the library.

I set out to read every book in that tomblike library, every miserable dead donation ever indexed and forgotten there — a mark of my profound fear and boredom at St. Vincent's and as well an early sign of my Tourettic compulsions for counting, processing, and inspection. Huddled there in the windowsill, turning dry pages and watching dust motes pinball through beams of sunlight, I sought signs of my odd dawning self in Theodore Dreiser, Kenneth Roberts, J. B. Priestley, and back issues of *Popular Mechanics* and failed, couldn't find the language of myself, as I failed to in watching television, those endless reruns of *Bewitched* and *I Dream of Jeannie* and *I Love Lucy* and *Gilligan* and *Brady Bunch* by which we nerdish unathletic Boys pounded our way through countless afternoons, leaning in close to the screen to study the antics of the women — women! exotic as letters, as phone calls, as forests, all things we orphans were denied — and the coping of their husbands, but I didn't find myself there, Desi Arnaz and Dick York and Larry Hagman, those harried earthbound astronauts, weren't showing me what I needed to see, weren't helping me find the language. I was closer on Saturday mornings, Daffy Duck especially gave me something, if I could bear to imagine growing up a dynamited, beak-shattered duck. Art Carney on *The Honeymooners* gave me something too, something in the way he jerked his neck, when we were allowed to stay up late enough to see him. But it was Minna who brought me the language, Minna and Court Street that let me speak.

We four were selected that day because we were four of the five white boys at St. Vincent's, and the fifth was Steven Grossman, fat as his name. If Steven had been thinner, Mr. Kassel would have left me in the stacks. As it was I was undersold goods, a twitcher and nose-picker retrieved from the library instead of the schoolyard, probably a retard of some type, certainly a regrettable, inferior offering. Mr. Kassel was a teacher at St. Vincent's who knew Frank Minna from the neighborhood, and his invitation to Minna to borrow us for the afternoon was a first glimpse of the glittering halo of favors and favoritism that extended around Minna — "knowing somebody" as a life condition. Minna was our exact reverse, we who knew no one and benefited nothing from it when we did.

Minna had asked for white boys to suit his clients' presumed prejudice — and his own certain ones. Perhaps Minna already had his fantasy of reclamation in mind, too. I can't know. He certainly didn't show it in the way he treated us that first day, a sweltering August weekday afternoon after classes, streets like black chewing gum, slow-creeping cars like badly projected science-class slides in the haze, as he opened the rear of his dented, graffitied van, about the size of those midnight mail trucks, and told us to get inside, then slammed and padlocked the doors without explanation, without asking our names. We four gaped at one another, giddy and astonished at this escape from our doldrums, not knowing what it meant, not really needing to know. The others, Tony, Gilbert and Danny, were willing to be grouped with me, to pretend I fit with them, if that was what it took to be plucked up by the outside world and seated in the dark on a dirty steel truck bed vibrating its way to somewhere that wasn't St. Vincent's. Of course I was vibrating too, vibrating before Minna rounded us up, vibrating inside always and straining to keep it from showing. I didn't kiss the other three boys, but I wanted to. Instead I made a kissing, chirping sound, like a bird's peep, over and over: "Chrip, chrip, chrip."

Tony told me to shut the fuck up, but his heart wasn't in it, not this day, in the midst of life's unfolding mystery. For Tony, especially, this was his destiny coming to find him. He saw more in Minna from the first because he'd prepared himself to see it. Tony Vermonte was famous at St. Vincent's for the confidence he exuded, confidence that a mistake had been made, that he didn't belong in the Home. He was Italian, better than the rest of us, who didn't know what we were (what's an Essrog?). His father was either a mobster or a cop — Tony saw no contradiction in this, so we didn't either. The Italians would return for him, in one guise or another, and that was what he'd taken Minna for.

Tony was famous for other things as well. He was older than the rest of us there in Minna's truck, fifteen to my and Gilbert's thirteen and Danny Fantl's fourteen (older St. Vincent's Boys attended high school elsewhere, and were rarely seen, but Tony had contrived to be left back), an age that made him infinitely dashing and worldly, even if he hadn't also lived outside the Home for a time and then come back. As it was, Tony was our God of Experience, all cigarettes and implication. Two years before, a Quaker family, attendees of the Meeting across the street, had taken Tony in, intending to give him a permanent home. He'd announced his contempt for them even as he packed his clothes. They weren't Italian. Still, he lived with them for a few months, perhaps happily, though he wouldn't have said so. They installed him at Brooklyn Friends, a private school only a few blocks away, and on his way home most afternoons he'd come and hang on the St. Vincent's fence and tell stories of the private-school girls he'd felt up and sometimes penetrated, the faggy private-school boys who swam and played soccer but were easily humiliated at basketball, not otherwise Tony's specialty. Then one day his foster parents found prodigious black-haired

Tony in bed with one girl too many: their own sixteen-year-old daughter. Or so the story went; there was only one source. Anyway, he was reinstalled at St. Vincent's the next day, where he fell easily into his old routine of beating up and befriending me and Steven Grossman each on alternating days, so that we were never in favor simultaneously and could trust one another as little as we trusted Tony.

Tony was our Sneering Star, and certainly the one of us who caught Minna's attention soonest, the one that fired our future boss's imagination, made him envision the future Minna Men inside us, aching to be cultivated. Perhaps Tony, with his will for his Italian rescue, even collaborated in the vision that became The Minna Agency, the strength of his yearning prompting Minna to certain aspirations, to the notion of having Men to command in the first place.

Minna was barely a man then himself, of course, though he seemed one to us. He was twenty-five that summer, gangly except for a tiny potbelly in his pocket-T, and still devoted to combing his hair into a smooth pompadour, a Carroll Gardens hairstyle that stood completely outside that year of

1979, projecting instead from some miasmic Frank Sinatra moment that extended like a bead of amber or a cinematographer's filter to enclose Frank Minna and everything that mattered to him.

Besides me and Tony in the back of Minna's van there was Gilbert Coney and Danny Fantl. Gilbert then was Tony's right hand, a stocky, sullen boy just passing for tough — he would have beamed at you for calling him a thug. Gilbert was awfully tough on Steven Grossman, whose fatness, I suspect, provided an uncomfortable mirror, but he was tolerant of me. We even had a couple of odd secrets. On a Home for Boys visit to the Museum of Natural History in Manhattan, two years before, Gilbert and I had split from the group and without discussion returned to a room dominated by a enormous plastic blue whale suspended from the ceiling, which had been the focus of the official visit. But underneath the whale was a double gallery of murky, mysterious dioramas of undersea life, lit and arranged so you had to press close to the glass to find the wonders tucked deep in the corners. In one a sperm whale fought a giant squid. In another a killer whale pierced a floor of ice. Gilbert and I wandered hypnotized from window to window. When a class of third- or fourth-graders were led away we found we had the giant hall to ourselves, and that even when we spoke our voices were smothered by the unearthly quiet of the museum. Gilbert showed me his discovery: A munchkin-size brass door beside the penguin diorama had been left unlocked. When he opened it we saw that it led both behind and into the penguin scene.

"Get in, Essrog," said Gilbert.

If I'd not wanted to it would have been bullying, but I wanted to desperately. Every minute the hall remained empty was precious. The lip of the doorway was knee-high. I clambered in and opened the flap in the ocean-blue-painted boards that made the side wall of the diorama, then slipped into the picture. The ocean floor was a long, smooth bowl of painted plaster, and I scooted down the grade on my bended knees, looking out at a flabbergasted Gilbert on the other side of the glass. Swimming penguins were mounted on rods extending straight from the far wall, and others were suspended in the plastic waves of ocean surface that now made up a low ceiling over my head. I caressed the nearest penguin, one mounted low, shown diving in pursuit of a delectable fish, patted its head, stroked its gullet as though helping it swallow a dry pill. Gilbert guffawed, thinking I was performing comedy for him, when in fact I'd been overwhelmed by a tender, touchy impulse toward the stiff, poignant penguin. Now it became imperative that I touch *all* the penguins, all I could, anyway — some were inaccessible to me, on the other side of the barrier of the ocean's surface, standing on ice floes. Shuffling on my knees I made the rounds, affectionately tagging each swimming bird before I made my escape back through the brass door. Gilbert was impressed, I could tell. I was now a kid who'd do anything, do crazy things. He was right and wrong, of course — once I'd touched the first penguin I had no choice.

Somehow this led to a series of confidences. I was crazy but also malleable, easily intimidated, which made me Gilbert's idea of a safe repository for what he regarded as his crazy feelings. Gilbert was a precocious masturbator, and looking for some triangulation between his own experiments and generic schoolyard lore. Did I do it? How often? One hand or two, held this way, or this? Close my eyes? Ever want to rub up against the mattress? I took his inquiries seriously, but I didn't really have the information he needed, not yet. My stupidity made Gilbert grouchy at first, and so he'd spend a week or two both pretending he hadn't spoken, didn't even know me, and glowering to let me know what galactic measures of pain awaited if I ratted him out. Then he'd suddenly come back, more urgent than ever. Try it, he'd say. It's not so hard. I'll watch and tell you if you do it wrong. I obeyed, as I had in the museum, but the results weren't as good. I couldn't yet treat myself with the tenderness I'd lavished on the penguins, at least not in front of Gilbert (though in fact he'd triggered my own private explorations, which were soon quite consuming). Gilbert became grouchy again, and prohibitively intimidating, and after two or three go-arounds the subject was permanently dropped. Still, the legacy of disclosure remained with us, a ghostly bond.

The last boy in Minna's van, Danny Fantl, was a ringer. He only looked white. Danny had assimilated to the majority population at St. Vincent's happily, effortlessly, down to his bones. In his way he commanded as much respect as Tony (and he certainly commanded Tony's respect, too) without bragging or posing, often without opening his mouth. His real language was basketball, and he was such a taut, fluid athlete that he couldn't help seeming a bit bottled up indoors, in the classroom. When he spoke it was to scoff at our enthusiasms, our displays of uncool, but distantly, as if his mind were really elsewhere plotting crossover moves, footwork. He listened to Funkadelic and Cameo and Zapp and was as quick to embrace rap as any boy at the Home, yet when music he admired actually *played,* instead of dancing he'd stand with arms crossed, scowling and pouting in time with the beat, his expressive hips frozen. Danny existed in suspension, neither black nor white, neither beating up nor beaten, beautiful but unfazed by the concept of girls, rotten at schoolwork but coasting through classes, and frequently unanchored by gravity, floating between pavement and the tangled chain-mesh of the St. Vincent's basketball hoops. Tony was tormented by his lost Italian family, adamant they would return; Danny might have coolly walked out on his parents one day when he was seven or eight and joined a pickup game that lasted until he was fourteen, to the day Minna drove up in his truck.

Tourette's teaches you what people will

ignore and forget, teaches you to see the reality-knitting mechanism people employ to tuck away the intolerable, the incongruous, the disruptive — it teaches you this because you're the one lobbing the intolerable, incongruous, and disruptive their way. Once I sat on an Atlantic Avenue bus a few rows ahead of a man with a belching tic — long, groaning, almost vomitous-sounding noises, the kind a fifth-grader learns to make, swallowing a bellyful of air, then forgets by high school, when charming girls becomes more vital than freaking them out. My colleague's compulsion was terribly specific: He sat at the back of the bus, and only when every head faced forward did he give out with his masterly digestive simulacra. We'd turn, shocked — there were fifteen or twenty others on the bus — and he'd look away. Then, every sixth or seventh time, he'd mix in a messy farting sound. He was a miserable-looking black man in his sixties, a drinker, an idler. Despite the peekaboo brilliance of his timing it was clear to everyone he was the source, and so the other riders hummed or coughed reprovingly, quit giving him the satisfaction of looking, and avoided one another's gaze. This was a loser's game, since not glancing back freed him to run together great uninterrupted phrases of his ripest noise. To all but me he was surely a childish jerk-off, a pathetic wino fishing for attention (maybe he understood himself this way, too — if he was undiagnosed, probably so). But it was unmistakably a compulsion, a tic — Tourette's. And it went on and on, until I'd reached my stop and, I'm sure, after.

The point is, I knew that those other passengers would barely recall it a few minutes after stepping off to their destinations. Despite how that maniacal froglike groaning filled the auditorium of the bus, the concertgoers were plainly engaged in the task of forgetting the music. Consensual reality is both fragile and elastic, and it heals like the skin of a bubble. The belching man ruptured it so quickly and completely that I could watch the wound instantly seal.

A Touretter can also be The Invisible Man.

Similarly, I doubt the other Boys, even the three who joined me in becoming Minna Men, directly recalled my bouts of kissing. I probably could have forced them to remember, but it would have been grudgingly. That tic was too much for us to encompass then, at St. Vincent's, as it would be now, anytime, anywhere. Besides, as my Tourette's bloomed I quickly layered the kissing behind hundreds of other behaviors, some of which, seen through the prism of Minna's rough endearments, became my trademarks, my Freakshow. So the kissing was gratefully forgotten.

By the time I was twelve, nine months or so after touching the penguins, I had begun to overflow with reaching, tapping, grabbing and kissing urges — those compulsions emerged first, while language for me was still trapped like a roiling ocean under a calm floe of ice, the way I'd been trapped in the underwater half of the penguin display, mute, beneath glass. I'd begun reaching for doorframes, kneeling to grab at skittering loosened sneaker laces (a recent fashion among the toughest boys at St. Vincent's, unfortunately for me), incessantly tapping the metal-pipe legs of the schoolroom desks and chairs in search of certain ringing tones, and worst, grabbing and kissing my fellow Boys. I grew terrified of myself then, and burrowed deeper into the library, but was forced out for classes or meals or bedtime. Then it would happen. I'd lunge at someone, surround him with my arms, and kiss his cheek or neck or forehead, whatever I hit. Then, compulsion expelled, I'd be left to explain, defend myself, or flee. I kissed

Greg Toon and Edwin Torres, whose eyes I'd never dared meet. I kissed Leshawn Montrose, who'd broken Mr. Voccaro's arm with a chair. I kissed Tony Vermonte and Gilbert Coney and tried to kiss Danny Fantl. I kissed Steven Grossman, pathetically thankful he'd come along just then. I kissed my own counterparts, other sad invisible Boys working the margins at St. Vincent's, just surviving, whose names I didn't know. "It's a game!" I'd say, pleadingly. "It's a game." That was my only defense, and since the most inexplicable things in our lives were games, with their ancient embedded rituals — British Bulldog, Ringolevio, Scully and Jinx — a mythos handed down to us orphans who-knew-how, it seemed possible I might persuade them this was another one, The Kissing Game. Just as important, I might persuade myself — wasn't it something in a book I'd read, a game for fevered teenagers, perhaps Sadie Hawkins Day? Forget the absence of girls, didn't we Boys deserve the same? That was it, then, I decided — I was single-handedly dragging the underprivileged into adolescence. I knew something they didn't. "It's a game," I'd say desperately, sometimes as tears of pain ran down my face. "It's a game." Leshawn Montrose cracked my head against a porcelain water fountain, Greg Toon and Edwin Torres generously only shucked me off onto the floor. Tony Vermonte twisted my arm behind my back and forced me against a wall. "It's a game," I breathed. He released me and shook his head, full of pity. The result, oddly enough, was I was spared a few months' worth of beatings at his hands — I was too pathetic and faggy to touch, might be better avoided. Danny Fantl saw my move coming and faked me out as though I were a lead-footed defender, then vanished down a stairwell. Gilbert stood and glared, deeply unnerved due to our private history. "A game," I reassured him. "It's a game," I told poor Steven Grossman and he believed me, just long enough to try kissing our mutual tormentor Tony, perhaps hoping it was a key to overturning the current order. He was not spared.

Meantime, beneath that frozen shell a sea of language was reaching full boil. It became harder and harder not to notice that when a television pitchman said to last the rest of a lifetime my brain went to rest the lust of a loaftomb, that when I heard "Alfred Hitchcock," I silently replied "Altered Houseclock" or "Ilford Hotchkiss," that when I sat reading Booth Tarkington in the library now my throat and jaw worked behind my clenched lips, desperately fitting the syllables of the prose to the rhythms of "Rapper's Delight" (which was then playing every fifteen or twenty minutes out on the yard), that an invisible companion named Billy or Bailey was begging for insults I found it harder and harder to withhold.

The kissing cycle was mercifully brief. I found other outlets, other obsessions. The pale thirteen-year-old that Mr. Kassel pulled out of the library and offered to Minna was prone to floor-tapping, whistling, tongue-clicking, winking, rapid head turns, and wall-stroking, anything but the direct utterances for which my particular Tourette's brain most yearned. Language bubbled inside me now, the frozen sea melting, but it felt too dangerous to let out. Speech was intention, and I couldn't let anyone else or myself know how intentional my craziness felt. Pratfalls, antics — those were accidental lunacy, and more or less forgivable. Practically speaking, it was one thing to stroke Leshawn Montrose's arm, or even to kiss him, another entirely to walk up and call him Shefawn Mongoose, or Lefthand Moonprose, or Fuckyou Roseprawn. So, though I collected words, treasured them like a drooling sadistic captor, bending them, melting them down, filing off their edges, stacking them into teetering piles, before release I translated them into physical performance, manic choreography.

And I was lying low, I thought. For every tic issued I squelched dozens, or so it felt — my body was an overwound watchspring, effortlessly driving one set of hands double-time while feeling it could as easily animate an entire mansion of stopped clocks, or a vast factory mechanism, a production line like the one in *Modern Times*, which we watched that year in the basement of the Brooklyn Public Library on Fourth Avenue, a version accompanied by a pedantic voice-over lecturing us on Chaplin's genius. I took Chaplin, and Buster Keaton, whose *The General* had been similarly mutilated, as models: Obviously blazing with aggression, disruptive energies barely contained, they'd managed to keep their traps shut, and so had endlessly skirted danger and been regarded as cute. I needn't exactly strain to find a motto: silence, golden, get it? Got it. Hone your timing instead, burnish those physical routines, your idiot wall-stroking, face-making, lace-chasing, until they're funny in a flickering black-and-white way, until your enemies don policeman's or Confederate caps and begin tripping over themselves, until doe-eyed women swoon. So I kept my tongue wound in my teeth, ignored the pulsing in my cheek, the throbbing in my gullet, persistently swallowed language back like vomit. It burned as hotly.

We rode a mile or two before Minna's van halted, engine guttering to a stop. Then a few minutes passed before he let us out of the back, and we found ourselves in a gated warehouse yard under the shadow of the Brooklyn-Queens Expressway, in a ruined industrial zone. Red Hook, I knew later. He led us to a large truck, a detached twelve-wheel trailer with no cab in evidence, then rolled up the back to reveal a load of identical sealed cardboard crates, a hundred, two hundred, maybe more. A thrill went through me: I'd secretly count them.

"Couple you boys get up inside," said Minna distractedly. Tony and Danny had the guile to leap immediately into the truck, where they could work shaded from the sun. "You're just gonna run this stuff inside, that's all. Hand shit off, move it up to the front of the truck, get it in. Straight shot, you got it?" He pointed to the warehouse. We all nodded, and I peeped. It went unnoticed.

Minna opened the big panel doors of the warehouse and showed us where to set the crates. We started quickly, then wilted in the heat. Tony and Danny massed the crates at the lip of the truck while Gilbert and I made the first dozen runs, then the older boys conceded their advantage and began to help us drag them across the blazing yard. Minna never touched a crate; he spent the whole time in the office of the warehouse, a cluttered room full of desks, file cabinets, tacked-up notes and pornographic calendars and a stacked tower of orange traffic cones, visible to us through an interior window, smoking cigarettes and jawing on the telephone, apparently not listening for replies — every time I glanced through the window his mouth was moving. The door was closed, and he was inaudible behind the glass. At some point another man appeared, from where I wasn't sure, and stood in the yard wiping his forehead as though he were the one laboring. Minna came out, the two stepped inside the office, the other man disappeared. We moved the last of the crates inside. Minna rolled down the gate of the truck and locked the warehouse, pointed us back to his van, but paused before shutting us into the back.

"Hot day, huh?" he said, looking at us directly for what might have been the first time.

Bathed in sweat, we nodded, afraid to speak.

"You monkeys thirsty? Because personally I'm dying out here."

Minna drove us to Smith Street, a few blocks from St. Vincent's, and pulled over in front of a bodega, then bought us beer, pop-top cans of Miller, and sat with us in the back of the van, drinking. It was my first beer.

"Names," said Minna, pointing at Tony, our obvious leader. We said our first names, starting with Tony. Minna didn't offer his own, only drained his beer and nodded. I began tapping the truck panel beside me.

Physical exertion over, astonishment at our deliverance from St. Vincent's receding, my symptoms found their opening again.

"You probably ought to know, Lionel's a freak," said Tony, his voice vibrant with self-regard.

"Yeah, well, you're all freaks, if you don't mind me pointing it out," said Minna. "No parents — or am I mixed up?"

Silence.

"Finish your beer," said Minna, tossing

his can past us, into the back of the van.

And that was the end of our first job for Frank Minna.

But Minna rounded us up again the next week, brought us to that same desolate yard, and this time he was friendlier. The task was identical, almost to the number of boxes (242 to 260), and we performed it in the same trepidatious silence. I felt a violent hatred burning off Tony in my and Gilbert's direction, as though he thought we were in the process of screwing up his Italian rescue. Danny was of course exempt and oblivious. Still, we'd begun to function as a team — demanding physical work contained its own truths, and we explored them despite ourselves.

Over beers Minna said, "You like this work?"

One of us said *sure*.

"You know what you're doing?" Minna grinned at us, waiting. The question was confusing. "You know what kind of work this is?"

"What, moving boxes?" said Tony.

"Right, moving. Moving work. That's what you call it when you work for me. Here, look." He stood to get into his pocket, pulled out a roll of twenties and a small stack of white cards. He stared at the roll for a minute, then peeled off four twenties and handed one to each of us. It was my first twenty dollars. Then he offered us each a card. It read: L&L MOVERS. NO JOB TOO SMALL. SOME JOBS TOO LARGE. GERARD & FRANK MINNA. And a phone number.

"You're Gerard or Frank?" said Tony.

"Minna, Frank." Like *Bond, James.* He ran his hand through his hair. "So you're a moving company, get it? Doing moving work." This seemed a very important point: that we call it *moving.* I couldn't imagine what else to call it.

"Who's Gerard?" said Tony. Gilbert and I, even Danny, watched Minna carefully. Tony was questioning him on behalf of us all.

"My brother."

"Older or younger?"

"Older."

Tony thought for a minute. "Who's L and L?"

"Just the name, L and L. Two L's. Name of the company."

"Yeah, but what's it mean?"

"What do you need it to mean, Fruitloop — Living Loud? Loving Ladies? Laughing at you Losers?"

"What, it doesn't mean anything?" said Tony.

"I didn't say that, did I?"

"Least Lonely," I suggested.

"There you go," said Minna, waving his can of beer at me. "L and L Movers, Least Lonely."

Tony, Danny and Gilbert all stared at me, uncertain how I'd gained this freshet of approval.

"Liking Lionel," I heard myself say.

"Minna, that's an Italian name?" said Tony. This was on his own behalf, obviously. It was time to get to the point. The rest of us could all go fuck ourselves.

"What are you, the census?" said Minna. "Cub reporter? What's your full name, Jimmy Olsen?"

"Lois Lane," I said. Like anyone, I'd read Superman comics.

"Tony Vermonte," said Tony, ignoring me.

"Vermont-ee," repeated Minna. "That's what, like a New England thing, right? You a Red Sox fan?"

"Yankees," said Tony, confused and defensive. The Yankees were champions now, the Red Sox their hapless, eternal victims, vanquished most recently by Bucky Dent's famous home run. We'd all watched it on television.

"Luckylent," I said, remembering. "Duckybent."

Minna erupted with laughter. "Yeah, Ducky fucking Bent! That's good. Don't look now, it's Ducky Bent."

"Lexluthor," I said, reaching out to touch Minna's shoulder. He only stared at my hand, didn't move away. "Lunchylooper, Laughyluck, Loopylip —"

"All right, Loopy," said Minna. "Enough already."

"Lockystuff —" I was desperate for a way to stop. My hand went on tapping Minna's shoulder.

"Let it go," said Minna, and now he returned my shoulder taps, once, hard. "Don't tug the boat."

To *tugboat* was to try Minna's patience. Any time you pushed your luck, said too much, overstayed a welcome, or overestimated the usefulness of a given method or approach, you were guilty of having tugged the boat. *Tugboating* was most of all a dysfunction of wits and storytellers, and a universal one: Anybody who thought himself funny would likely tug a boat here or there. Knowing when a joke or verbal gambit was right at its limit, quitting before the boat had been tugged, that was art (and it was a given that you wanted to push it as near as possible — missing an opportunity to score a laugh was deeply lame, an act undeserving of a special name).

Years before the word *Tourette's* was familiar to any of us, Minna had me diagnosed: Terminal Tugboater.

Distributing eighty dollars and those four business cards was all Minna had to do to instate the four of us forever — or anyway, for as long as he liked — as the junior staff of L&L Movers. Twenty dollars and a beer remained our usual pay. Minna would gather us sporadically, on a day's notice or no notice at all — and the latter possibility became incentive, once we'd begun high school, for us to return to St. Vincent's directly after classes and lounge expectantly in the schoolyard or recreation room, pretending not to listen for the distinctive grumble of his van's motor. The jobs varied enormously. We'd load merchandise, like the cartons in the trailer, in and out of storefront-basement grates all up and down Court Street, borderline shady activity that it seemed wholesalers ought to be handling themselves, transactions sealed with a shared cigar in the back of the shop. Or we'd bustle apartmentloads of furniture in and out of brownstone walk-ups, legitimate moving jobs, it seemed to me, where fretting couples worried we weren't old or expert enough to handle their belongings — Minna would hush them, remind them of the cost of distractions: "The meter's running." (This hourly rate wasn't reflected in our pay, of course. It was twenty dollars whether we hurried or not; we hurried.) We put sofas through third-story windows with a makeshift cinch and pulley, Tony and Minna on the roof, Gilbert and Danny in the window to receive, myself on the ground with the guide ropes. A massive factory building under the Brooklyn end of the Manhattan Bridge, owned by an important but unseen friend of Minna's, had been damaged in fire, and we moved most of the inhabitants for free, as some sort of settlement or concession — the terms were obscure, but Minna was terrifically urgent about it. When a couple of college-age artists objected to our rough handling of a pile of damaged canvases the firemen had heaped on the floor, he paced and seethed at the delay; the only meter running now was Minna's own time, and his credibility with his friend-client. We woke at five one August morning to collect and set up the temporary wooden stages for the bands performing in the Atlantic Antic, a massive annual street fair, then worked again at dusk to tear the stages down, the hot avenue now heaped with a day's torn wrappers and crumpled cups, a few fevered revelers still staggering home as we knocked the pine frames apart with hammers and the heels of our shoes. Once we emptied an entire electronics showroom into Minna's truck, pulling unboxed stereos off shelves and out of window displays, disconnecting the wires from lit, blinking amplifiers, eventually even taking the phone off the desk — it would have seemed a sort of brazen burglary had Minna not been standing on the sidewalk in front, drinking beer and telling jokes with the man who'd unpadlocked the shop gates for us as we filed past with the goods. Everywhere Minna connived and cajoled and dropped names, winking at us to make us complicit, and everywhere Minna's clients stared at us Boys, some wondering if we'd palm a valuable when they weren't looking, some trying to figure the angle, perhaps hoping to catch a hint of disloyalty, an edge over Minna they'd save for when they needed it. We palmed nothing, revealed no disloyalty. Instead we stared back, tried to make them flinch. And we listened, gathered information. Minna was teaching us when he meant to, and when he didn't.

It changed us as a group. We developed a certain collective ego, a presence apart at the Home. We grew less embattled from within, more from without: nonwhite Boys sensed in our privilege a hint of their future deprivations and punished us for it. Age had begun to heighten those distinctions anyway. So Tony, Gilbert, Danny and myself smoothed out our old antipathies and circled the wagons. We stuck up for one another, at the Home and at Sarah J. Hale, our local high school, a required stop except for those few who'd qualified for some special (i.e., Manhattan) destination, Stuyvesant or Music and Art.

There at Sarah J. we St. Vincent's Boys were disguised, blended with the larger population, a pretty rough crowd despite their presumably having parents and siblings and telephones and bedroom doors with locks and a thousand other unimaginable advantages. But we knew each other, kept an eye on each other, bad pennies circulating with the good. Black or white, we policed one another like siblings, reserved special degrees of scorn for one another's social or institutional humiliations. And there we mixed with girls for the first time, about as well as chunks of road salt in ice cream, though ice cream might be a generous comparison for the brutal, strapping black girls of Sarah J., gangs of whom laid after-school ambushes for any white boy daring enough to have flirted, even made eye contact, with one inside the building. They comprised the vast majority there, and the handful of white or Latin girls survived by a method of near-total invisibility. To pierce their cone of fear and silence was to be met with incredulous glares of resentment. Our lives are led elsewhere, those looks said, and yours ought to be too. The black girls were claimed by boyfriends too sophisticated to bother with school, who rode by for them at lunch hour in cars throbbing with amplified bass lines and sometimes boasting bullet-riddled doors, and their only use for us was as a dartboard for throwing lit cigarette butts, a frequent sport. Yes, relations between the sexes were strained at Sarah J., and I doubt any of us four, even Tony, so much as copped a feel from the girls we were schooled with there. For all of us that would wait for Court Street, for the world we would come to know through Minna.

* * *

Minna's Court Street was the old Brooklyn, a placid ageless surface alive underneath with talk, with deals and casual insults, a neighborhood political machine with pizzeria and butcher-shop bosses and unwritten rules everywhere. All was talk except for what mattered most, which were unspoken understandings. The barbershop, where he took us for identical haircuts that cost three dollars each, except even that fee was waived for Minna — no one had to wonder why the price of a haircut hadn't gone up since 1966, nor why six old barbers were working, mostly not working, out of the same ancient storefront, where the Barbicide hadn't been changed since the product's invention (in Brooklyn, the jar bragged), where other somewhat younger men passed through constantly to argue sports and wave away offers of haircuts; the barbershop was a retirement home, a social club, and front for a backroom poker game. The barbers were taken care of because this was Brooklyn, where people looked out. Why would the prices go up, when nobody walked in who wasn't part of this conspiracy, this trust? — though if you spoke of it you'd surely meet with confused denials, or laughter and a too-hard cuff on the cheek. Another exemplary mystery was the "arcade," a giant storefront paneled with linoleum, containing three pinball machines, which were in constant use, and six or seven video games — Asteroids, Frogger, Centipede — all pretty much ignored, and a cashier, who'd change dollars to quarters and accept hundred-dollar bills folded into lists of numbers, names of horses and football teams. The curb in front of the arcade was lined with Vespas, which had been in vogue a year or two before but now sat permanently parked, without anything more than a bicycle lock for protection, a taunt to vandals. A block away, on Smith, they would have been stripped, but here they were pristine, a curbside Vespa showroom. It didn't need explaining — this was Court Street. And Court Street, where it passed through Carroll Gardens and Cobble Hill, was the only Brooklyn, really — north was Brooklyn Heights, secretly a part of Manhattan, south was the harbor, and the rest, everything east of the Gowanus Canal (the only body of water in the world, Minna would crack each and every time we drove over it, that was 90 percent guns), apart from small outposts of civilization in Park Slope and Windsor Terrace, was an unspeakable barbarian tumult.

★ ★ ★

Sometimes he needed just one of us. He'd appear at the Home in his Impala instead of the van, request someone specific, then spirit him away, to the bruised consternation of those left behind. Tony was in and out of Minna's graces, his ambition and pride costing him as much as he won, but he was unmistakably our leader, and Minna's right hand. He wore his private errands with Minna like Purple Hearts, but refused to report on their content to the rest of us. Danny, athletic, silent and tall, became Minna's trusted greyhound, his Mercury, sent on private deliveries and rendezvous, and given early driving lessons in a vacant Red Hook lot, as though Minna were grooming him for work as an international spy, or Kato for a new Green Hornet. Gilbert, all bullish determination, was pegged for the grunt work, sitting in double-parked cars, repairing a load of ruptured cartons with strapping tape, unfastening the legs of an oversize dresser so as to fit it through a small doorway, and repainting the van, whose graffitied exterior some of Minna's neighbors had apparently found objectionable. And I was an extra set of eyes and ears and opinions. Minna would drag me along to back rooms and offices and barbershop negotiations, then debrief me afterward. What did I think of that guy? Shitting or not? A moron or retard? A shark or a mook? Minna encouraged me to have a take on everything, and to spit it out, as though he thought my verbal disgorgings were only commentary not yet anchored to subject matter. And he adored my echolalia. He thought I was doing impressions.

Needless to say, it wasn't commentary and impressions, but my verbal Tourette's flowering at last. Like Court Street, I seethed behind the scenes with language and conspiracies, inversions of logic, sudden jerks and jabs of insult. Now Court Street and Minna had begun to draw me out. With Minna's encouragement I freed myself to ape the rhythm of his overheard dialogues, his complaints and endearments, his for-the-sake-of arguments. And Minna loved my effect on his clients and associates, the way I'd unnerve them, disrupt some schmooze with an utterance, a head jerk, a husky *"Eatmebailey!"* I was his special effect, a running joke embodied. They'd look up startled and he'd wave his hand knowingly, counting money, not even bothering to look at me. "Don't mind him, he can't help it," he'd say. "Kid's shot out of a cannon." Or: "He likes to get a little nutty sometimes. Forget about it." Then he'd wink at me, acknowledge our conspiracy. I was evidence of life's unpredictability and rudeness and poignancy, a scale model of his own nutty heart. In this way Minna licensed my speech, and speech, it turned out, liberated me from the overflowing disaster of my Tourettic self, turned out to be the tic that satisfied where others didn't, the scratch that briefly stilled the itch.

"You ever listen to yourself, Lionel?" Minna would say later, shaking his head. "You really are shot out of a fucking cannon."

"*Scott Out of the Canyon!* I don't know why, I just—*fuckitup!*—I just can't stop."

"You're a freak show, that's why. Human freak show, and it's free. Free to the public."

"Freefreak!" I hit him on the shoulder.

"That's what I said: a free human freak show."

We were introduced to Matricardi and Rockaforte at their brownstone on Degraw Street one day in the fall, four or five months after meeting Minna. He'd gathered the four of us in the van in his usual way, without explaining our assignment, but there was a special degree of agitation about him, a jumpiness that induced a special ticcishness in me. He first drove us into Manhattan across the Brooklyn Bridge, then underneath the bridge, to the docks near Fulton Street, and I spent the whole time imitating the nervous jerks of his head as he negotiated traffic. We parked in the middle of a concrete yard in front of one of the piers. Minna disappeared inside a small, windowless shack made of corrugated steel sheets and had us stand outside the van, where we shivered in the wind coming off the East River. I danced around the van in a fit, counting suspension cables on the bridge that soared over us like a monstrous steel limb while Tony and Danny, chilliest in their thin plaid jackets, kicked and cursed at me. Gilbert was nicely insulated in a fake down coat which, stitched into bulging sections, made him look like the Michelin Man or the Red Queen from *Alice in Wonderland.* He stood a few feet from us and methodically tossed chunks of corroded concrete into the river, as though he could earn points by cleaning the pier of rubble.

Minna emerged just as the two small yellow trucks drove up. They were Ryder Rental vans, smaller than Minna's, and identically decorated, one pristine, the other dingy. The drivers sat smoking cigarettes in the cabs, with the motors running. Minna unlatched the backs of the trucks, which weren't padlocked, and directed us to move the contents into his van — quick.

The first thing I laid hands on was an electric guitar, one shaped into a flying V and decorated with enameled yellow and silver flames. A cable dangled from its socket. Other instruments, guitars and bass guitars, were in their hard black cases, but this one had been unplugged and shoved into the van in a hurry. The two trucks were full of concert gear — seven or eight guitars, keyboards, panels full of electronic switches, bundles of cable, microphones and stands, pedal effects for the floor, a drum kit that had been pushed into the truck whole instead of being disassembled, and a number of amplifiers and monitors, including six black stage amps, each half the size of a refrigerator, which alone filled the second Ryder truck and each took two of us to lift out and into Minna's van. The amplifiers and hard cases were stenciled with the band's name, which I recognized faintly. I learned later they were responsible for a minor AM hit or two, songs about roads, cars, women. I didn't grasp it then, but this was equipment enough for a small stadium show.

I wasn't sure we could fit the whole contents of the two trucks into the van but Minna only egged us to shut up and work faster. The men in the trucks never spoke or got out of the cabs, just smoked and waited. No one ever appeared from the corrugated shack. At the end there was barely room for Gilbert and me to crowd in behind the doors to ride with the band's calamitously piled equipment while Tony and Danny shared a spot up front with Minna.

We crossed the bridge back to Brooklyn like that, Gilbert and I fearing for our lives if the load shifted or toppled. After a few breathless turns and sudden stops Minna double-parked the van and freed us from the back. The destination was a brownstone in a row of brownstones on Degraw Street, red brick, stone detailing flaking to powder, genteel curtained windows. Some canny salesman had ten or twenty years before sold the entire block on defacing these hundred-year-old buildings with flimsy tin awnings over the elegant front doors; the only thing special about Matricardi and Rockaforte's house was that it lacked one of these.

"We're gonna have to take apart those drums," said Tony when he saw the doors.

"Just get it inside," said Minna. "It'll fit."

"Are there stairs?" said Gilbert.

"You'll see, you chocolate cheesepuffs," said Minna. "Just get it up the stoop already."

Inside, we saw. The brownstone which appeared so ordinary was an anomaly just through the doors. The insides — typical narrow halls and stairs, spoked banisters, high ornate ceilings — had all been stripped and gutted, replaced with a warehouse-style stairwell into the basement apartment and upstairs. The parlor floor where we stood was sealed off on the left by a clean white wall and single closed door. We ferried the equipment into the upper-floor apartment while Minna stood guarding the rear of the van. The drums went easily.

The band's equipment tucked neatly into one corner of the apartment, on wooden pallets apparently set out for that purpose. The upper floors of the building were empty apart from a few crates here and there and a single oak dining table heaped with silverware: forks, spoons in two sizes, and butter knives, hundreds of each, ornate and heavy, gleaming, bundled in disordered piles, no sense to them except that the handles all faced in one direction. I'd never seen so much silverware in one place, even in St. Vincent's institutional kitchen — anyway, those St. Vincent's forks were flat cutouts of dingy steel bent this way to make tines, that way to make a handle, barely better than the plastic "sporks" we were issued with our school lunches. These forks were little masterpieces of sculpture in comparison. I wandered away from the others and obsessed on the mountain of forks, knives and spoons, but especially those forks, as rich in their contours as tiny thumbless hands, or the paws of a silver animal.

The others shifted the last of the amplifiers up the stairs. Minna reparked the van. I stood at the table, trying to look casual. Jerking your head was good cover for jerking your head, I discovered. Nobody watched me. I pocketed one of the forks, trembling with lust and anticipation, joy in my fear, as I did it. I only just got away with it, too: Minna was back.

"The clients want to meet you," he said.

"Who's that?" said Tony.

"Just shut up when they talk, okay?" said Minna.

"Okay, but who are they?" said Tony.

"Practice shutting up now so you'll be good at it when you meet them," said Minna. "They're downstairs."

Behind that clean, seamless wall on the parlor floor lay hidden the brownstone's next surprise, a sort of double-reverse: The front room's old architecture was intact. Through the single door we stepped into a perfectly elegant, lavishly fitted brownstone parlor, with gold leaf on the ceiling's plaster scrollwork, antique chairs and desks and a marble-topped side table, a six-foot mirror-lined grandfather clock, and a vase with fresh flowers. Under our feet was an ancient carpet, layered with color, a dream map of the past. The walls were crowded with framed photographs, none more recent than the invention of color film. It was more like a museum diorama of Old Brooklyn than a contemporary room. Seated in two of the plush chairs were two old men, dressed in matching brown suits.

"So these are your boys," said the first of the two men.

"Say hello to Mr. Matricardi," said Minna.

"Yo," said Danny. Minna punched him on the arm.

"I said say hello to Mr. Matricardi."

"Hello," said Danny sulkily. Minna had never required politeness. Our jobs with him had never taken such a drab turn. We were used to sauntering with him through the neighborhood, riffing, honing our insults.

But we felt the change in Minna, the fear and tension. We would try to comply, though servility lay outside our range of skills.

The two old men sat with their legs crossed, fingers templed together, watching us closely. They were both trim in their suits, their skin white and soft wherever it showed, their faces soft, too, without being fat. The one called Mr. Matricardi had a nick in the top ridge of his large nose, a smooth indented scar like a slot in molded plastic.

"Say hello," Minna told me and Gilbert.

I thought *mister catch your body mixture bath retardy whistlecop's birthday* and didn't dare open my mouth. Instead I fondled the tines of my marvelous stolen fork, which barely fit the length of my corduroy's front pocket.

"It's okay," said Matricardi. His smile was pursed, all lips and no teeth. His thick glasses doubled the intensity of his stare. "You all work for Frank?"

What were we supposed to say?

"Sure," volunteered Tony. Matricardi was an Italian name.

"You do what he tells?"

"Sure."

The second man leaned forward.

"Listen," he said. "Frank Minna is a good man."

Again we were bewildered. Were we expected to disagree?

I counted the tines in my pocket, one-two-three-four, one-two-three-four.

"Tell us what you want to do," said the second man. "Be what? What kind of work? What kind of men?" He didn't hide his teeth, which were bright yellow, like the van we'd unloaded.

"Talk to Mr. Rockaforte," urged Minna.

"They do what you tell them, Frank?" said Rockaforte to Minna. It wasn't small talk, somehow, despite the repetitions. This was an intense speculative interest. Far too much rested on Minna's reply. Matricardi and Rockaforte were like that, the few times I glimpsed them: purveyors of banal remarks with terrifying weight behind them.

"Yeah, they're good kids," said Minna. I heard the hurry in his voice. We'd overstayed our welcome already.

"Orphans," said Matricardi to Rockaforte. He was repeating something he'd been told, rehearsing its value.

"You like this house?" said Rockaforte, gesturing upward at the ceiling. He'd caught me staring at the scrollwork.

"Yes," I said carefully.

"This is his mother's parlor," said Rockaforte, nodding at Matricardi.

"Exactly as she kept it," said Matricardi proudly. "We never changed a thing."

"When Mr. Matricardi and I were children like yourselves I would come to see his family and we would sit in this room." Rockaforte smiled at Matricardi. Matricardi smiled back. "His mother believe me would rip our ears if we spilled on this carpet, even a drop. Now we sit and remember."

"Everything exactly as she kept it," said Matricardi. "She would see it and know. If she were here, bless her sweet pathetic soul."

They fell silent. Minna was silent too, though I imagined I could feel his anxiety to be out of there. I thought I heard him gulp, actually.

My throat was calm. Instead I worked at my stolen fork. It now seemed so potent a charm, I imagined that if I had it in my pocket I might never need to tic aloud again.

"So tell us," said Rockaforte. "Tell us what you're going to be. What kind of men."

"Like Frank," said Tony, confident he was speaking for us all, and right to be.

This answer made Matricardi chuckle, still toothlessly. Rockaforte waited patiently until his friend was finished. Then he asked Tony, "You want to make music?"

"What?"

"You want to make music?" His tone was sincere.

Tony shrugged. We all held our breath, waiting to understand. Minna shifted his weight, nervous, watching this encounter ramble on beyond his control.

"The belongings you moved for us today," said Rockaforte. "You recognize what those things are?"

"Sure."

"No, no," said Minna suddenly. "You can't do that."

"Please don't refuse our gift," said Rockaforte.

"No, really, we can't. With respect." I could see this was imperative for Minna. The gift, worth thousands if not tens of thousands, must absolutely be denied. I shouldn't bother to form nutty fantasies about the electric guitars and keyboards and amplifiers. Too late, though: My brain had begun to bubble with names for our band, all stolen from Minna: *You Fucking Mooks*, *The Chocolate Cheeseballs*, *Tony and the Tugboats*.

"Why, Frank?" Matricardi. "Let us bring a little joy. For orphans to make music is a good thing."

"No, please."

Jerks From Nowhere. Free Human Freakshow. I pictured these in place of the band's logo on the skin of the bass drum, and stenciled onto the amplifiers.

"Nobody else will be permitted to take pleasure in that garbage," said Rockaforte, shrugging. "We can give it to your orphans, or a fire can be created with a can of gasoline — it would be no different."

Rockaforte's tone made me understand two things. First, that the offer truly meant nothing to him, nothing at all, and so it could be turned away. They wouldn't force Minna to allow us to take the instruments.

And second, that Rockaforte's strange comparison involving a can of gasoline wasn't strange at all to him. That was now exactly what would happen to the band's equipment.

Minna heard it too, and exhaled deeply. The danger was past. But at the same moment I turned a corner in the opposite direction. My magic fork failed. I began to want to pronounce a measure of the nonsense that danced in my head. *Bucky Dent and the Stale Doughnuts* —

"Here," said Matricardi. He raised his hand, a gentle referee. "We can see it displeases, so forget." He fished in the interior pocket of his suit jacket. "But we insist on a measure of gratitude for these orphan boys who have done us such a favor."

He came out with hundred-dollar bills, four of them. He passed them to Frank and nodded at us, smiling munificently, and why not? The gesture was unmistakably the source for Frank's trick of spreading twenties everywhere, and it instantly made Frank seem somehow childish and cheap that he would bother to grease palms with anything less than a hundred.

"All right," said Minna. "That's great, you'll spoil them. They don't know what to do with it." He was able to josh now, the end in sight. "Say thanks, you peanutheads."

The other three were dazzled, I was fighting my syndrome.

"Thanks."

"Thanks."

"Thanks, Mr. Matricardi."

"Arf!"

After that Minna got us out of there, hustled us through the brownstone's odd hallway too fast even to glance back. Matricardi and Rockaforte had never moved from their chairs, just smiled at us and one another until we were gone. Minna put us all in the back of the van, where we compared hundred-dollar bills — they were fresh, and the serial numbers ran in sequence — and Tony immediately tried to persuade us he should caretake ours, that they weren't safe in the Home. We didn't bite.

Minna parked us on Smith Street, near Pacific, in front of an all-night market called Zeod's, after the Arab who ran it. We sat and waited until Minna came around the back of the van with a beer.

"You jerks know about forgetting?" he said.

"Forgetting what?"

"The names of those guys you just met. They're not good for you to go around saying."

"What should we call them?"

"Call them nothing. That's a part of my work you need to learn about. Sometimes the clients are just the clients. No names."

"Who are they?"

"They're nobody," said Minna. "That's the point. Forget you ever saw them."

"They live there?" said Gilbert.

"Nope. They just keep that place. They moved to Jersey."

"Gardenstate," I said.

"Yeah, the Garden State."

"Garden State Brickface and Stucco!" I shouted. Garden State Brickface and Stucco was a renovation firm whose crummy homemade television ads came on channels 9 and 11 during Mets and Yankees games and during reruns of *The Twilight Zone.* The weird name of the firm was already an occasional tic. Now it seemed to me that Brickface and Stucco might actually be Matricardi and Rockaforte's secret names.

"What's that?"

"Garden State Bricco and Stuckface!"

I'd made Minna laugh again. Like a lover, I loved to make Minna laugh.

"Yeah," he said. "That's good. Call them Bricco and Stuckface, you goddamn beautiful freak." He took another slug of beer.

And if memory serves we never heard him speak their real names again.

"Makes you think you're Italian?" said Minna one day, as we all rode together in his Impala.

"What do I look like to you?" said Tony.

"I don't know, I was thinking maybe Greek," said Minna. "I used to know this Greek guy went around knocking up the

Italian girls down Union Street, until a couple their older brothers took him out under the bridge. You remind me of him, you know? Got that dusky tinge. I'd say half Greek. Or maybe Puerto Rican, or Syrian."

"Fuck you."

"Probably know all your parents, if you think about it. We're not talking the international jet set here — bunch of teen mothers, probably live in a five-mile radius, need to know the goddamn truth."

So it was, with this casual jaunt against Tony's boasts, that Minna appeared to announce what we already half suspected — that it was not only his life that was laced with structures of meaning but our own, that these master plots were transparent to him and that he held the power to reveal them, that he did know our parents and at any moment might present them to us.

Other times he taunted us, playing at knowledge or ignorance — we couldn't know which it was. He and I were alone when he said, "Essrog, Essrog. That name." He crunched up his mouth and squinted, as if trying to remember, or perhaps to read a name inscribed on the distant Manhattan skyline.

"You know an Essrog?" I said, my breath short, heart pounding. *"Edgehog!"*

"No. It's just — You ever look it up in the phone book? Can't be more than three or four Essrogs, for chrissakes. Such a weird name."

Later, at the Home, I looked. There were three.

Minna's weird views filtered down through the jokes he told and liked to hear, and those he cut short within a line or two of their telling. We learned to negotiate the labyrinth of his prejudices blind, and blindly. Hippies were dangerous and odd, also sort of sad in their utopian wrongness. ("Your parents must of been hippies," he'd tell me. "That's why you came out the superfreak you are.") Homosexual men were harmless reminders of the impulse Minna was sure lurked in all of us — and "half a fag" was more shameful than a whole one. Certain baseball players, Mets specifically (the Yankees were holy but boring, the Mets wonderfully pathetic and human), were half a fag — Lee Mazzilli, Rusty Staub, later Gary Carter. So were most rock stars and anyone who'd been in the armed services but not in a war. Lesbians were wise and mysterious and deserved respect (and how could we who relied on Minna for all our knowledge of women argue when he himself grew baffled and reverent?) but could still be comically stubborn or stuck up. The Arabic population of Atlantic Avenue was as distant and unfathomable as the Indian tribes that had held our land before Columbus. "Classic" minorities — Irish, Jews, Poles, Italians, Greeks and Puerto Ricans — were the clay of life itself, funny in their essence, while blacks and Asians of all types were soberly snubbed, unfunny (Puerto Ricans probably should have been in this second class but had been elevated to "classic" status single-handedly by *West Side Story* — and all Hispanics were "Ricans" even when they were Dominicans, as they frequently were). But bone stupidity, mental illness, and familial or sexual anxiety — these were the bolts of electricity that made the clay walk, the animating forces that rendered human life amusing and that flowed, once you learned to identify them, through every personality and interaction. It was a form of racism, not respect, that restricted blacks and Asians from ever being stupid like a Mick or Polack. If you weren't funny, you didn't quite exist. And it was usually better to be fully stupid, impotent, lazy, greedy or freakish than to seek to dodge your destiny, or layer it underneath pathetic guises of vanity or calm. So it was that I, Overt Freak Supreme, became mascot of a worldview.

I called the Brooklyn directory's Essrogs one day when I was left alone for twenty minutes in a warehouse office, waiting for Minna to return, slowly picking out the numbers on the heavy rotary dial, trying not to obsess on the finger holes. I'd perhaps dialed a phone twice at that point in my life.

I tried *F. Essrog and Lawrence Essrog and Murray and Annette Essrog*. F. wasn't home. Lawrence's phone was answered by a child. I listened for a while as he said "Hello? Hello?," my vocal cords frozen, then hung up.

Murray Essrog picked up the phone. His voice was wheezy and ancient.

"Essrog?" I said, and whispered *Chestbutt* away from the phone.

"Yes. This is the Essrog residence, Murray speaking. Who's this?"

"Baileyrog," I said.

"Who?"

"Bailey."

He waited for a moment, then said, "Well, what can I do for you, Bailey?"

I hung up the phone. Then I memorized the numbers, all three of them. In the years that followed I would never once step across the line I'd drawn with Murray or the other telephone Essrogs — never show up at their homes, never accuse them of being related to a *free human freak show*, never even properly introduce myself — but I made a ritual out of dialing their numbers and hanging up after a tic or two, or listening, just long enough to hear another Essrog breathe.

A true story, not a joke, though it was repeated as often, tugboated relentlessly, was of the beat cop from Court Street who routinely dislodged clumps of teenagers clustered at night on stoops or in front of bars and who, if met with excuses, would cut them off with "Yeah, yeah. Tell your story *walking*." More than anything, this somehow encapsulated my sense of Minna — his impatience, his pleasure in compression, in ordinary things made more expressive, more hilarious or vivid by their conflation. He loved talk but despised explanations. An endearment was flat unless folded into an insult. An insult was better if it was also self-deprecation, and ideally should also serve as a slice of street philosophy, or as resumption of some dormant debate. And all talk was finer on the fly, out on the pavement, between beats of action: We learned to tell our story walking.

* * *

Though Gerard Minna's name was printed on the L&L business card, we met him only twice, and never on a moving job. The first time was Christmas Day, 1982, at Minna's mother's apartment.

Carlotta Minna was an Old Stove. That was the Brooklyn term for it, according to Minna. She was a cook who worked in her own apartment, making plates of sautéed squid and stuffed peppers and jars of tripe soup that were purchased at her door by a constant parade of buyers, mostly neighborhood women with too much housework or single men, young and elderly, bocce players who'd take her plates to the park with them, racing bettors who'd eat her food standing up outside the OTB, barbers and butchers and contractors who'd sit on crates in the backs of their shops and wolf her cutlets, folding them with their fingers like waffles. How her prices and schedules were conveyed I never understood — perhaps telepathically. She truly worked an old stove, too, a tiny enamel four-burner crusted with ancient sauces and on which three or four pots invariably bubbled. The oven of this herculean appliance was never cool; the whole kitchen glowed with heat like a kiln. Mrs. Minna herself seemed to have been baked, her whole face dark and furrowed like the edges of an overdone calzone. We never arrived without nudging aside some buyers from her door, nor without packing off with plateloads of food, though how she could spare it was a mystery, since she never seemed to make more than she needed, never wasted a scrap. When we were in her presence Minna bubbled himself, with talk, all directed at his mother, banking cheery insults off anyone else in the apartment, delivery boys, customers, strangers (if there was such a thing to Minna then), tasting everything she had cooking and making suggestions on every dish, poking and pinching every raw ingredient or ball of unfinished dough and also his mother herself, her earlobes and chin, wiping flour off her dark arms with his open hand. She rarely — that I saw, anyway — acknowledged his attentions, or even directly acknowledged his presence. And she never once in my presence uttered so much as a single word.

That Christmas Minna had us all up to Carlotta's apartment, and for once we ate at her table, first nudging aside sauce-glazed stirring spoons and unlabeled baby-food jars of spices to clear spots for our plates. Minna stood at the stove, sampling her broth, and Carlotta hovered over us as we devoured her meatballs, running her floury fingers over the backs of our chairs, then gently touching our heads, the napes of our necks. We pretended not to notice, ashamed in front of one another and ourselves to show that we drank in her nurturance as eagerly as her meat sauce. But we drank it. It was Christmas, after all. We splashed, gobbled, kneed one another under the table. Privately, I polished the handle of my spoon, quietly aping the motions of her fingers on my nape, and fought not to twist in my seat and jump at her. I focused on my plate — eating was for me already by then a reliable balm. All the while she went on caressing, with hands that would have horrified us if we'd looked close.

Minna spotted her and said, "This is exciting for you, Ma? I got all of motherless Brooklyn up here for you. Merry Christmas."

Minna's mother only produced a sort of high, keening sigh. We stuck to the food.

"Motherless Brooklyn," repeated a voice we didn't know.

It was Minna's brother, Gerard. He'd come in without our noticing. A fleshier, taller Minna. His eyes and hair were as dark, his mouth as wry, lips deep-indented at the corners. He wore a brown-and-tan leather coat, which he left buttoned, his hands pushed into the fake-patch pockets.

"So this is your little moving company," he said.

"Hey, Gerard," said Minna.

"Christmas, Frank," said Gerard Minna absently, not looking at his brother. Instead he was making short work of the four of us with his eyes, his hard gaze snapping us each in two like bolt cutters on inferior padlocks. It didn't take long before he was done with us forever — that was how it felt.

"Yeah, Christmas to you," said Minna. "Where you been?"

"Upstate," said Gerard.

"What, with Ralph and them?" I detected something new in Minna's voice, a yearning, sycophantic strain.

"More or less."

"What, just for the holidays you're gonna go talkative on me? Between you and Ma it's like the Cloisters up here."

"I brought you a present." He handed Minna a white legal envelope, stuffed fat. Minna began to tear at the end and Gerard said, in a voice low and full of ancient sibling authority, "Put it away."

Now we understood we'd all been staring.

All except Carlotta, who was at her stove, piling together an improbable, cornucopic holiday plate for her older son.

"Make it to go, Mother."

Carlotta moaned again, closed her eyes.

"I'll be back," said Gerard. He stepped over and put his hands on her, much as Minna had. "I've got a few people to see today, that's all. I'll be back tonight. Enjoy your little orphan party."

He took the foil-wrapped plate and was gone.

Minna said, "What're you staring at? Eat your food!" He stuffed the white envelope into his jacket. The envelope made me think of Matricardi and Rockaforte, their pristine hundred-dollar bills. Brickface and Stucco, I corrected silently. Then Minna cuffed us, a bit too hard, the bulging gold ring on his middle finger clipping our crowns in more or less the same place his mother had fondled.

Minna's behavior with his mother oddly echoed what we knew of his style with women. I'd say girlfriends, but he never called them that, and we rarely saw him with the same one twice. They were Court Street girls, decorating poolrooms and movie-theater lounges, getting off work from the bakery still wearing disposable paper hats, applying lipstick without missing a chew of their gum, slanting their heavily elegant bodies through car windows and across pizza counters, staring over our heads as if we were four feet tall, and he'd apparently gone to junior high school with each and every one of them. "Sadie and me were in the sixth grade," he'd say, mussing her hair, disarranging her clothes. "This is Lisa — she used to beat up my best friend in gym." He'd angle jokes off them like a handball off a low wall, circle them with words like a banner flapping around a pole, tease their brassieres out of whack with pinching fingers, hold them by the two points of their hips and lean, as if he were trying to affect the course of a pinball in motion, risking *tilt.* They never laughed, just rolled their eyes and slapped him away, or didn't. We studied it all, soaked up their indifferent femaleness, that rare essence we yearned to take for granted. Minna had that gift, and we studied his moves, filed them away with silent, almost unconscious prayers.

"It's not that I only like women with large breasts," he told me once, years later, long after he'd traded the Court Street girls for his strange, chilly marriage. We were walking down Atlantic Avenue together, I think, and a woman passing had caused his head to turn. I'd jerked my head too, of course, my actions as exaggerated and secondhand as a marionette's. "That's a very common misunderstanding," he said, as if he were an idol and I his public, a mass audience devoted to puzzling him out. "Thing is, for me a woman has to have a certain amount of muffling, you know what I mean? Something between you, in the way of insulation. Otherwise, you're right up against her naked soul."

Wheels within wheels was another of Minna's phrases, used exclusively to sneer at our notions of coincidence or conspiracy. If we Boys ever dabbled in astonishment at, say, his running into three girls he knew from high school in a row on Court Street, two of whom he'd dated behind each other's backs, he'd bug his eyes and intone, *wheels within wheels.* No Met had ever pitched a no-hitter, but Tom Seaver and Nolan Ryan both pitched them after being traded away — *wheels within wheels.* The barber, the cheese man, and the bookie were all named Carmine — oh yeah, *wheels within wheels,* big time. You're onto something there, Sherlock.

By implication we orphans were idiots of connectivity, overly impressed by any trace of the familial in the world. We should doubt ourselves any time we imagined a network in operation. We should leave that stuff to Minna. Just as he knew the identity of our parents but would never reveal it to us, only Frank Minna was authorized to speculate on the secret systems that ran Court Street or the world. If we dared chime in, we'd surely only discovered more *wheels within wheels.* Business as usual. The regular fucking world — get used to it.

One day in April, five months after that Christmas meal, Minna drove up with all his windows thoroughly smashed, the van transformed into a blinding crystalline sculpture, a mirrorball on wheels, reflecting the sun. It was plainly the work of a man with a hammer or crowbar and no fear of interruption. Minna appeared not to have noticed; he ferried us out to a job without mentioning it. On our way back to the Home, as we rumbled over the cobblestones of Hoyt Street, Tony nodded at the windshield, which sagged in its frame like a beaded curtain, and said, "So what happened?"

"What happened to what?" It was a

Minna game, forcing us to be literal when we'd been trained by him to talk in glances, in three-corner shots.

"Somebody fucked up your van."

Minna shrugged, excessively casual. "I parked it on that block of Pacific Street."

We didn't know what he was talking about.

"These guys around that block had this thing about how I was uglifying the neighborhood." A few weeks after Gilbert's paint job the van had been covered again with graffiti, vast filled-in outlines of incoherent ballooning font and an overlay of stringy tags. Something made Minna's van a born target, the flat battered sides like a windowless subway car, a homely public surface crying for spray paint where both private cars and bigger, glossier commercial trucks were inviolate. "They told me not to park it around there anymore. Then after I did it a couple of times more, they told me a different way."

Minna lifted both hands from the wheel to gesture his indifference. We weren't totally convinced.

"Someone's sending a message," said Tony.

"What's that?" said Minna.

"I just said it's a message," said Tony. I

knew he wanted to ask about Matricardi and Rockaforte. Were they involved? Couldn't they protect Minna from having his windows smashed? We all wanted to ask about them and never would, unless Tony did it first.

"Yeah, but what are you trying to say?" said Minna.

"Fuckitmessage," I suggested impulsively.

"You know what I mean," said Tony defiantly, ignoring me.

"Yeah, maybe," said Minna. "But put it in your own words." I could feel his anger unfolding, smooth as a fresh deck of cards.

"Tellmetofuckitall!" I was like a toddler devising a tantrum to keep his parents from fighting.

But Minna wasn't distractable. "Quiet, Freakshow," he said, never taking his eyes from Tony. "Tell me what you said," he told Tony again.

"Nothing," said Tony. "Damn." He was backpedaling.

Minna pulled the van to the curb at a fire hydrant on the corner of Bergen and Hoyt. Outside, a couple of black men sat on a stoop, drinking from a bag. They squinted at us.

"Tell me what you said," Minna insisted.

He and Tony stared at one another, and

the rest of us melted back. I swallowed away a few variations.

"Just, you know, somebody's sending you a message." Tony smirked.

This clearly infuriated Minna. He and Tony suddenly spoke a private language in which *message* signified heavily. "You think you know a thing," he said.

"All I'm saying is I can see what they did to your truck, Frank." Tony scuffed his feet in the layer of tiny cubes of safety glass that had peeled away from the limp window and lay scattered on the floor of the van.

"That's not all you said, Dickweed."

That was the first I heard Minna use the term that would become lodged thereafter in my uppermost tic-echelon: *dickweed*. I didn't know whether he borrowed the nickname or invented it himself on the spot.

What it meant to me I still can't say. Perhaps it was inscribed in my vocabulary, though, by the trauma of that day: Our little organization was losing its innocence, although I couldn't have explained how or why.

"I can't help what I see," said Tony. "Somebody put a hit on your windows."

"Think you're a regular little wiseguy, don't you?"

Tony stared at him.

"You want to be Scarface?"

Tony didn't give his answer, but we knew what it was. *Scarface* had opened a month before, and Al Pacino was ascendant, a personal colossus astride Tony's world, blocking out the sky.

"See, the thing about Scarface," said Minna, "is before he got to be Scarface he was *Scabface.* Nobody ever considers that. You have to want to be Scabface first."

For a second I thought Minna was going to hit Tony, damage his face to make the point. Tony seemed to be waiting for it too. Then Minna's fury leaked away.

"Out," he said. He waved his hand, a Caesar gesturing to the heavens through the dented roof of his refitted postal van.

"What?" said Tony. "Right here?"

"Out," he said again, equably. "Walk home, you muffin asses."

We sat gaping, though his meaning was clear enough. We weren't more than five or six blocks from the Home anyway. But we hadn't been paid, hadn't gone for beers or slices or a bag of hot, clingy zeppole. I could taste the disappointment — the flavor of powdered sugar's absence. Tony slid open the door, dislodging more glass, and we obediently filed out of the van and onto the sidewalk, into the day's glare, the suddenly formless afternoon.

Minna drove off, leaving us there to bob together awkwardly before the drinkers on the stoop. They shook their heads at us, stupid-looking white boys a block from the projects. But we were in no danger there, nor were we dangerous ourselves. There was something so primally humiliating in our ejection that Hoyt Street itself seemed to ridicule us, humble row of brownstones, sleeping bodega. We were inexcusable to ourselves. Others clotted street corners, not us, not anymore. We rode with Minna. The effect was deliberate: Minna knew the value of the gift he'd withdrawn.

"Muffin ass," I said forcefully, measuring the shape of the words in my mouth, auditioning them for tic-richness. Then I sneezed, induced by the sunlight.

Gilbert and Danny looked at me with disgust, Tony with something worse.

"Shut up," he said. There was cold fury in his teeth-clenched smile.

"Tellmetodoit, muffinass," I croaked.

"Be quiet now," warned Tony. He plucked a piece of wood from the gutter and took a step toward me.

Gilbert and Danny drifted away from us warily. I would have followed them, but Tony had me cornered against a parked car.

The men on the stoop stretched back on their elbows, slurped their malt liquor thoughtfully.

"Dickweed," I said. I tried to mask it in another sneeze, which made something in my neck pop. I twitched and spoke again. *"Dickyweed! Dicketywood!"* I was trapped in a loop of self, one already too familiar, that of refining a verbal tic to free myself from its grip (not yet knowing how tenacious would be the grip of those particular syllables). Certainly I didn't mean to be replying to Tony. Yet *dickweed* was the name Minna had called him, and I was throwing it in his face.

Tony held the stick he'd found, a discarded scrap of lath with clumps of plaster stuck to it. I stared, anticipating my own pain as I'd anticipated Tony's, at Minna's hand, a minute before. Instead Tony moved close, stick at his side, and grabbed my collar.

"Open your mouth again," he said.

"Restrictaweed, detectorwood, vindictaphone," said I, prisoner of my syndrome. I grabbed Tony back, my hands exploring his collar, fingers running inside it like an anxious, fumbling lover.

Gilbert and Danny had started up Hoyt Street, in the direction of the Home. "C'mon, Tony," said Gilbert, tilting his head. Tony ignored them. He scraped his stick in the gutter, and came up with a smear of dog shit, mustard-yellow and pungent.

"Open," he said.

Now Gilbert and Danny were just slinking away, heads bowed. The street was brightly, absurdly empty. Nobody but the black men on the stoop, impassive witnesses. I jerked my head as Tony jabbed with his stick-tic as evasive maneuver — and he only managed to paint my cheek. I could smell it, though, powdered sugar's opposite made tangible, married to my face.

"Stickmebailey!" I shouted. Falling back against the car behind me, I turned my head again, and again, twitching away, enshrining the moment in ticceography. The stain followed me, adamant, on fire. Or maybe it was my cheek that was on fire.

Our witnesses crinkled their paper bag, offered ruminative sighs.

Tony dropped his stick and turned from me. He'd disgusted himself, couldn't meet my eye. About to speak, he thought better of it, instead jogged to catch Gilbert and Danny as they shrugged away up Hoyt Street, leaving the scene.

We didn't see Minna again until five weeks later, Sunday morning at the Home's yard, late May. He had his brother Gerard with him; it was the second time we'd ever laid eyes on him.

None of us had seen Frank in the intervening weeks, though I know that the others, like myself, had each wandered down Court Street, nosed at a few of his usual haunts, the barbershop, the beverage outlet, the arcade. He wasn't in them. It meant nothing, it meant everything. He might never reappear, but if he turned up and didn't speak of it we wouldn't think twice. *We* didn't speak of it to one another, but a pensiveness hung over us, tinged with orphan's melancholy, our resignation to permanent injury. A part of each of us still stood astonished on the corner of Hoyt and Bergen, where we'd been ejected from Minna's van, where we'd fallen when our inadequate wings melted in the sun.

A horn honked, the Impala's, not the van's. Then the brothers got out and came to the cyclone fence and waited for us to gather. Tony and Danny were playing basketball, Gilbert perhaps ardently picking his nose on the sidelines. That's how I picture it anyway. I wasn't in the yard when they drove up. Gilbert had to come inside and pull me out of the Home library, to which I'd mostly retreated since Tony's attack, though Tony had shown no signs of repeating it. I was wedged into a windowsill seat, in sunshine laced with shadows from the barred window, when Gilbert found me there, immersed in a novel by Allen Drury.

Frank and Gerard were dressed too warmly for that morning, Frank in his bomber jacket, Gerard in his patchwork leather coat. The backseat of the Impala was loaded with shopping bags packed with Frank's clothes and a pair of old leather suitcases that surely belonged to Gerard. I don't know that Frank Minna ever owned a suitcase in his life. They stood at the fence, Frank bouncing nervously on his toes, Gerard hanging on the mesh, fingers dangling through, doing nothing to conceal his impatience with his brother, an impatience shading into disgust.

Frank smirked, raised his eyebrows, shook his head. Danny held his basketball between forearm and hip; Minna nodded at it, mimed a set shot, dropped his hand at the wrist, and made a delicate O with his mouth to signify the *swish* that would result.

Then, idiotically, he bounced a pretend pass to Gerard. His brother didn't seem to notice. Minna shook his head, then wheeled back to us and aimed two trigger fingers through the fence, and gritted his teeth for *rat-a-tat,* a little imaginary schoolyard massacre. We could only gape at him dumbly. It was as though somebody had taken Minna's voice away. And Minna was his voice — didn't he know? His eyes said yes, he did. They looked panicked, as if they'd been caged in the body of a mime.

Gerard gazed off emptily into the yard, ignoring the show. Minna made a few more faces, wincing, chuckling silently, shaking off some invisible annoyance by twitching his cheek. I fought to keep from mirroring him.

Then he cleared his throat. "I'm, ah, going out of town for a while," he said at last.

We waited for more. Minna just nodded and squinted and grinned his closemouthed grin at us as though he were acknowledging applause.

"Upstate?" said Tony.

Minna coughed in his fist. "Oh yeah. Place my brother goes. He thinks we ought to just, you know. Get a little country air."

"When are you coming back?" said Tony.

"Ah, coming back," said Minna. "You got an unknown there, Scarface. Unknown factors."

We must have gaped at him, because he added, "I wouldn't wait underwater, if that's what you had in mind."

We were in our second year of high school. That measure loomed suddenly, a door of years swinging open into what had been a future counted in afternoons. Would we know Minna whenever it was he got back? Would we know each other?

Minna wouldn't be there to tell us what to think of Minna's not being there, to give it a name.

"All right, Frank," said Gerard, turning his back to the fence. "Motherless Brooklyn appreciates your support. I think we better get on the road."

"My brother's in a hurry," said Frank. "He's seeing ghosts everywhere."

"Yeah, I'm looking right at one," said Gerard, though in fact he wasn't looking at anyone, only the car.

Minna tilted his head at us, at his brother, to say *you know.* And *sorry.*

Then he pulled a book out of his pocket, a small paperback. I don't think I'd ever seen a book in his hands before. "Here," he said to me. He dropped it on the pavement and nudged it under the fence with the toe of his shoe. "Take a look," he said. "Turns out you're not the only freak in the show."

I picked it up. *Understanding Tourette's Syndrome* was the title, first time I'd seen the word.

"Meaning to get that to you," he said. "But I've been sort of busy."

"Great," said Gerard, taking Minna by the arm. "Let's get out of here."

Tony had been searching every day after school, I suspect. It was three days later that he found it and led us others there, to the edge of the Brooklyn-Queens Expressway, at the end of Kane Street. The van was diminished, sagged to its rims, tires melted. The explosion had cleared the windows of their crumbled panes of safety glass, which now lay in a spilled penumbra of grains on the sidewalk and street, together with flakes of traumatized paint and smudges of ash, a photographic map of force. The panels of the truck were layered, graffiti still evident in bone-white outline, all else — Gilbert's shoddy coat of enamel and the manufacturer's ancient green — now chalky black, and delicate like sunburned skin. It was like an X ray of the van that had been before.

We circled it, strangely reverent, afraid to touch, and I thought, *Ashes, ashes* — and then I ran away, up Kane, toward Court Street, before anything could come out of my mouth.

Over the next two years I grew larger —

neither fat nor particularly muscular, but large, bearlike, and so harder for the bantamweight Tony or anyone else to bully — and I grew stranger. With the help of Minna's book I contextualized my symptoms as Tourette's, then discovered how little context that was. My constellation of behaviors was "unique as a snowflake," oh, joy, and evolving, like some microscoped crystal in slow motion, to reveal new facets, and to spread from its place at my private core to cover my surface, my public front. The freak show was now the whole show, and my earlier, ticless self impossible anymore to recall clearly. I read in the book of the drugs that might help me, Haldol, Klonopin, and Orap, and laboriously insisted on the Home's once-weekly visiting nurse helping me achieving diagnosis and prescription, only to discover an absolute intolerance: The chemicals slowed my brain to a morose crawl, were a boot on my wheel of self. I might outsmart my symptoms, disguise or incorporate them, frame them as eccentricity or vaudeville, but I wouldn't narcotize them, not if it meant dimming the world (or my brain — same thing) to twilight.

We survived Sarah J. Hale in our different ways. Gilbert had grown, too, and grown a scowl, and he'd learned to sneer or lurch his way through difficulties. Danny coasted elegantly on his basketball skills and sophisticated musical taste, which had evolved through "Rapper's Delight" and Funkadelic to Harold Melvin and the Bluenotes and Teddy Pendergrass. If I saw him in certain company, I knew not to bother saying hello, as he was incapable of recognizing us others from deep within his cone of self-willed blackness. Tony more or less dropped out — it was hard to be officially expelled from Sarah J., so few teachers took attendance — and spent his high-school years on Court Street, hanging out at the arcade, milking acquaintanceships made through Minna for cigarettes and odd jobs and rides on the back of Vespas, and getting lucky with a series of Minna's ex-girlfriends, or so he said. For a six-month stint he was behind the counter at Queen Pizzeria, shoveling slices out of the oven and into white paper bags, taking smoking breaks under the marquee of the triple-X theater next door. I'd stop in and he'd batter me with cheap insults, un-Minna-worthy feints for the amusement of the older pizza men, then guiltily slip me a free slice, then shoo me away with more insults and maybe a slap on the head or a too-realistic fake jab to the spleen.

Me, I became a walking joke, preposterous, improbable, unseeable. My outbursts, utterances and tappings were white noise or static, irritating but tolerated, and finally boring unless they happened to provoke a response from some unsavvy adult, a new or substitute teacher. My peers, even the most unreachable and fearsome black girls, understood instinctively what the teachers and counselors at Sarah J., hardened into a sort of paramilitary force by dire circumstance, were slow to get: My behavior wasn't teenage rebellion in any sense. And so it wasn't really of *interest* to other teenagers. I wasn't tough, provocative, stylish, self-destructive, sexy, wasn't babbling some secret countercultural tongue, wasn't testing authority, wasn't showing colors of any kind. I wasn't even one of the two or three heedless, timid, green-mohawked and leather-clad punk rockers who required constant beatings for their audacity. I was merely crazy.

By the time Minna returned Gilbert and I were about to graduate — no great feat, mostly a matter of showing up, staying awake, and, in Gilbert's case, of systematically recopying my completed homework in his own hand. Tony had completely stopped showing his face at Sarah J. and Danny was somewhere in between — a presence in the yard and the gym, and in the culture of the school, he'd skipped most of his third-year classes and was being "held back," though the concept was a bit abstract to him, I think. You could have told him he was being returned to kindergarten and he would have shrugged, only asked how high the hoops were placed in the yard, whether the rims could hold his weight.

Minna had Tony in the car already when he drove up outside the school. Gilbert went to the yard to pull Danny out of a three-on-three while I stood on the curb, motionless in the rush of students out of the building, briefly struck dumb. Minna got out of the car, a new Cadillac, bruise-purple. I was taller than Minna now, but that didn't lessen his sway over me, the way his presence automatically begged the question of who I was, where'd I come from, and what kind of man or freak I was turning out to be. It had everything to do with the way, five years before, I'd begun discovering myself upon Minna's jerking me out of the library and into the world, and with the way his voice had primed the pump for mine. My symptoms loved him. I reached for him — though it was May, he was wearing a trench coat — and tapped his shoulder, once, twice, let my hand fall, then raised it again and let fly a staccato burst of Tourettic caresses. Minna still hadn't spoken.

"Eatme, Minnaweed," I said under my breath.

"You're a laugh and a half, Freakshow," said Minna, his face completely grim.

Soon enough I would understand that the Minna who'd returned was not the same as the one who'd left. He'd shed his old jocularity like baby fat. He no longer saw drolleries everywhere, had lost his taste for the spectrum of human comedy. The gate of his attention was narrowed, and what came through it now was pointed and bitter. His affections were more glancing, his laugh just a wince. He was quicker to show the spur of his impatience, too, demanded less *tell your story*, more *walking*.

But at that moment his austerity seemed utterly particular: He wanted us all in the car, had something to say. It was as though he'd been away a week or two instead of two years. He's got a job for us, I felt myself think, or hope, and the years between fell instantly away.

Gilbert brought Danny. We took the backseat; Tony sat in front with Minna.

Minna lit a cigarette while he steered with his elbows. We turned off Fourth Avenue, down Bergen. Toward Court Street, I thought. Minna put his lighter away and his hand came out of his trench-coat pockets with business cards.

L&L CAR SERVICE, they read. TWENTY-FOUR HOURS. And a phone number. No slogan this time, and no names.

"You mooks ever get learners' permits?" said Minna.

Nobody had.

"You know where the DMV is, up on Schermerhorn? Here." He dug out a roll, scrunched off four twenties onto the seat beside Tony, who handed them out. For Minna everything had the same price, was fixed and paid for by the quick application of twenty dollars. That hadn't changed. "I'll drop you up there. First I want you to see something."

It was a tiny storefront on Bergen, just short of Smith Street, boarded so tightly it looked like a condemned building. But I, for one, was already familiar with the inside of it. A few years earlier it had been a miniature candy store, with a single rack of comics and magazines, run by a withered Hispanic woman who'd pinioned my arm when I slipped a copy of *Heavy Metal* into my jacket and ducked for the door. Now Minna gestured at it grandly: the future home of L&L Car Service.

Minna had an arrangement with a certain Lucas, at Corvairs Driving School, on Livingston Street — we were all to receive lessons, free of charge, beginning tomorrow. The purple Caddy was the only vehicle in L&L's fleet, but others were on their way. (The car smelled poisonously new, vinyl squeaking like an Indian burn. My probing fingers investigated the backseat armrest ashtray — it contained ten neatly clipped fingernails.) In the meantime we'd be busy getting our licenses and rehabilitating the ruined storefront, fitting it with radios, office equipment, stationery, telephones, tape recorders, microphones (tape recorders? microphones?), a television and a small refrigerator. Minna had money to spend on these things, and he wanted us along to see him spend it. We might look for some suitable clothes while we're at it — did we know we looked like rejects from *Welcome Back, Kotter*? — the only thing to do was drop out of Sarah J. immediately. The suggestion didn't ruffle any feathers. In a blink we'd fallen into formation, Pavlov's orphans. We listened to Minna's new tonalities, distrusting and harsh, as they warmed into something like the old, more generous music, the tune we'd missed but not forgotten. He rolled on: We ought to have a CB-radio setup, this was the twentieth fucking century, had we heard? Who knew how to work a CB? Dead silence, punctured by *"Radiobailey!"* Fine, said Minna, the Freak volunteers. Hello? Hello? We almond-studded cheeseballs were staring like we didn't know English — what exactly *had* we been doing for two years anyway, apart from researching how many times a day we could clean out our fish tanks? Silence. Spank our monkeys, rough up our suspects, *jerk off,* Minna meant — did he have to spell it out? More silence. Hello? Hey, had we ever seen *The Conversation*? Best fucking movie in the world, Gene Hackman. We knew Gene Hackman? Silence again. We knew him only from *Superman* — Lex Luthor. It didn't seem likely Minna meant *that* Gene Hackman. (*Lexluthor, textlover, lostbrother,* went my brain, plumbing up trouble — where was Gerard, the other L in L&L? Minna hadn't said his name.) Well, we ought to see it, learn a thing or two about *surveillance.* Talking all the while, he drove us up to Schermerhorn, to the Department of Motor Vehicles. I saw Danny's eyes dart to the Sarah J. boys playing basketball in the park across the street — but now we were with Minna, a million miles away. We ought to get limousine-operator's licenses, he went on. They only cost ten dollars more, the test is the same. Don't smile for the picture, you'll look like the Prom Date Killers. Did we have girlfriends? Of course not, who'd want a bunch of jerks from nowhere. By the way, the Old Stove was dead. Carlotta Minna had passed two weeks ago; Minna was just settling her affairs now. We wondered what affairs, didn't ask. Oh, and Minna had gotten married, he thought to mention now. He and his new wife were moving into Carlotta's old apartment, after first scouring the thirty-year-old sauce off the walls. We jarheads could meet Minna's bride if we got ourselves haircuts first. Was she from Brooklyn? Tony wanted to know. Not exactly; she grew up on an *island.* No, you jerks, not Manhattan or Long Island — a real island. We'd meet her. Apparently first we had to be drivers who operated cameras, tape recorders and CB radios, with suits and haircuts, with unsmiling license photos. First we had to become *Minna Men,* though no one had said those words.

But here, here was *the beauty part.* By Minna's own admission, *he'd buried the lead:* L&L Car Service — it wasn't really a car service. That was just a front. L&L was a *detective agency.*

The joke Minna wanted to hear in the emergency room, the joke about Irving, went like this:

A Jewish mother — Mrs. Gushman, we'll call her — walks into a travel agency. "I vant to go to Tibet," she says. "Listen lady, take my word for it, you don't want to go to Tibet. I've got a nice package tour for the Florida Keys, or maybe Hawaii —" "No," says Mrs. Gushman, "I vant to go to *Tibet.*" "Lady, are you traveling alone? Tibet is no place —" "Sell me a ticket for Tibet!" shouts Mrs. Gushman. "Okay, okay." So she goes to Tibet. Gets off the plane, says to the first person she sees, "Who's the greatest holy man in Tibet?" "Why, that would be the High Lama," comes the reply. "That's who I vant to see," says Mrs. Gushman. "Take me to the High Lama." "Oh, no, you don't understand, American Lady, the High Lama lives on top of our highest mountain in total seclusion. No one can see the High Lama." "I'm Mrs. Gushman, I've come all the vay to Tibet, and I must see the High Lama!" "Oh, but you could never —" "Which mountain? How do I get there?" So Mrs. Gushman checks into a hotel at the base of the mountain and hires sherpas to take her to the monastery at the top. All the way up they're trying to explain to her, nobody sees the High Lama — his own monks have to fast and meditate for years before they're allowed to ask the High Lama a single question. She just keeps pointing her finger and saying "I'm Mrs. Gushman, take me up the mountain!" When they get to the monastery the sherpas explain to the monks — crazy American lady, wants to see the High Lama. She says, "Tell the High Lama Mrs. Gushman is here to see him." "You don't understand, we could never —" "Just tell him!" The monks go and come back and they're shaking their heads in confusion. "We don't understand, but the High Lama says he will grant you an audience. Do you understand what an honor —" "Yes, yes," she says. "Just take me!" So they lead her in to see the High Lama. The monks are whispering and they open the door and the High Lama nods — they can leave him alone with Mrs. Gushman. And the High Lama looks at Mrs. Gushman and Mrs. Gushman says, "Irving, when are you coming home? Your father's worried!"

Interrogation Eyes

Minna Men wear suits. Minna Men drive cars. Minna Men listen to tapped lines. Minna Men stand behind Minna, hands in their pockets, looking menacing. Minna Men carry money. Minna Men collect money. Minna Men don't ask questions. Minna Men answer phones. Minna Men pick up packages. Minna Men are clean-shaven. Minna Men follow instructions. Minna Men try to be like Minna, but Minna is dead.

Gilbert and I left the hospital so quickly, and drove back in such a perfect fog of numbness, that when we walked into L&L and Tony said, "Don't say it. We already heard," it was as though I were learning myself for the first time.

"Heard from who?" said Gilbert.

"Black cop, through here a few minutes ago, looking for you," said Tony. "You just missed him."

Tony and Danny stood furiously smoking cigarettes behind L&L's counter, their foreheads pasty with sweat, eyes fogged and distant, teeth grinding behind their drawn lips.

They looked like somebody had worked them over and they wanted to take it out on us.

The Bergen Street office was as we'd renovated it fifteen years before: divided in two by the Formica counter, thirty-inch color television playing constantly in the "waiting area" on this side of the counter, telephones, file cabinets and computer on the rear wall, underneath a massive laminated map of Brooklyn, Minna's heavy Magic Marker numerals scrawled across each neighborhood, showing the price of an L&L ride — five bucks to the Heights, seven to Park Slope or Fort Greene, twelve to Williamsburg or Borough Park, seventeen to Bushwick. Airports or Manhattan were twenty and up.

The ashtray on the counter was full of cigarette butts that had been in Minna's fingers, the telephone log full of his handwriting from earlier in the day. The sandwich on top of the fridge wore his bite marks. We were all four of us an arrangement around a missing centerpiece, as incoherent as a verbless sentence.

"How did they find us?" I said. "We've got Frank's wallet." I opened it up and took out the bundle of Frank's business cards and slipped them into my pocket. Then I dropped it on the counter and slapped the Formica five times to finish a six-count.

Nobody minded me except myself. This was my oldest, most jaded audience. Tony shrugged and said, "Him croaking out *L and L* as his dying words? A business card in his coat? Gilbert giving out names like a fucking idiot? You tell *me* how they found us."

"What did this cop want?" said Gilbert stoically. He would deal with one problem at a time, the plodder, even if they stacked up from here to the moon.

"He said you weren't supposed to leave the hospital, that's what he said. You gave some nurse your *name,* Gilbert."

"Fuck it," said Coney. "Fuck some fucking black cop."

"Yeah, well, you can express that sentiment in person, since he's coming back. And you might want to say, 'Fuck some fucking black homicide detective,' since that's actually what you're dealing with here. Smart cop, too. You could see it in his eyes."

"Fuckicide," I thought to add.

"Who's going to tell Julia?" said Danny quietly. His mouth, his whole face, was veiled in smoke. Nobody answered.

"Well, I won't be here when he comes

back," said Gilbert. "I'll be out doing his work for him, catching the motherfucker who did this. Gimme a coffin nail."

"Slow down, Sherlock," said Tony, handing him a cigarette. "I wanna know how'd it even happen in the first place? How'd the two of you even get involved? I thought you were supposed to be on a stakeout."

"Frank showed up," said Gilbert, trying to flick his depleted lighter again and again, failing to make it catch. "He went inside. Fuck. Fuck." His voice was clenched like a fist. I saw the whole stupid sequence playing behind his eyes: parked car, wire, traffic light, Brainum, the chain of banalities that somehow led to the bloody Dumpster and the hospital. The chain of banalities now immortalized by our guilt.

"Inside *where?*" said Tony, handing Gilbert a book of matches. The phone rang.

"Some kinda kung-fu place," said Gilbert. "Ask Lionel, he knows all about it —"

"Not kung fu," I started. "Meditation —"

"You're trying to say they killed him with *meditation?*" said Tony. The phone rang a second time.

"No, no, we saw who killed him — *Viable Guessfrog!* — a big Polish guy — *Barnamum Pierogi!* — I mean *really* big. We only saw him from behind."

"Which one of us is going to tell Julia?" said Danny again. The phone rang a third time.

I picked it up and said, "L and L."

"Need a car at One-eighty-eight Warren, corner of —" droned a female voice.

"No cars," I said by rote.

"You don't have any cars?"

"No cars." I gulped, ticking like a time bomb.

"How soon can you get a car?"

"Lionel Deathclam!" I shouted into the phone. That got the caller's attention, enough that she hung up. My fellow Minna Men glanced at me, jarred only slightly from their hard-boiled despair.

A real car service, even a small one, has a fleet of no fewer than thirty cars working in rotation, and at the very least ten on the street at any given time. Elite, our nearest rival, on Court Street, has sixty cars, three dispatchers, probably twenty-five drivers on a shift. Rusty's, on Atlantic Avenue, has eighty cars. New Relámpago, a Dominican-run service out of Williamsburg, has one hundred and sixty cars, a magisterial secret economy of private transportation hidden deep in the borough. Car services are completely dependent on phone dispatches — the drivers are forbidden by law to pick up customers on the street, lest they compete with medallioned taxicabs. So the drivers and dispatchers litter the world with business cards, slip them into apartment foyers like Chinese take-out menus, leave them stacked beside potted plants in hospital waiting rooms, palm them out with the change at the end of every ride. They sticker pay phones with their phone number, writ in phosphorescent font.

L&L had five cars, one for each of us, and we were barely ever available to drive them. We never handed out cards, were never friendly to callers, and had, five years before, removed our phone number from both the Yellow Pages and the sign over the Bergen Street storefront.

Nevertheless, our number circulated, so that one of our main activities was picking up the phone to say "no cars."

As I replaced the receiver Gilbert was explaining what he knew about the stakeout, doggedly. English might have been his fourth or fifth language from the sound of it, but you couldn't question his commitment. As *Bionic Dreadlog* was my likely contribution — my mourning brain had decided renaming itself was the evening's assignment — I was in no position to criticize. I stepped outside, away from the chain-smoking confusion, into the cold, light-washed night. Smith Street was alive, F train murmuring underneath, pizzeria, Korean grocer, and the Casino all streaming with customers. It could have been any night — nothing in the Smith Street scene required that Minna have died that day. I went to the car and retrieved the notebook from the glove compartment, doing my best not to glance at the bloodstained backseat. Then I thought of Minna's final ride. There was something I'd forgotten. When I steeled myself to look in the back I saw what it was: his watch and beeper. I fished them out from under the passenger seat where they'd slid and put them in my pocket.

I locked the car and rehearsed a few imaginary options. I could go back to the Yorkville Zendo by myself and have a look around. I could also seek out the homicide detective, earn his trust, pool my knowledge with him instead of the Men. I could walk down Atlantic Avenue, sit in an Arabic storefront where they knew me and wouldn't gape, and drink a tiny cup of mudlike black coffee and eat a baklava or Crow's Nest — acid, steam and sugar to poison my grief.

Or I could go back into the office. I went back into the office. Gilbert was still fumbling with the end of his account, our race up the ambulance ramp, the confusion at the hospital. He wanted Tony and Danny to know we'd done all we could do. I laid the notebook flat on the counter and with a red ballpoint circled WOMAN, GLASSES and ULLMAN, DOWNTOWN, those crucial new players on our stage. Paper-thin and unrevealing as they might be, they had more life than Minna now.

I had other questions: The building they'd spoken of. The doorman's interference. The unnamed woman Frank lost control of, the one who missed her *Rama-lama-ding-dong.* The wiretap itself: What did Minna hope I'd hear? Why couldn't he just tell me what to listen for?

"We asked him, in the back of the car," said Gilbert. "We asked him and he wouldn't tell us. I don't know why he wouldn't tell."

"Asked him what?" said Tony.

"Asked him who killed him," said Gilbert. "I mean, before he was dead."

I remembered the name Irving, but didn't say anything.

"Somebody's definitely going to have to tell Julia," said Danny.

Gilbert grasped the significance of the notebook. He stepped over and read what I'd circled. "Who's Ullman?" said Gilbert, looking at me. "You wrote this?"

"In the car," I said. "It's the note I took in the car. 'Ullman, downtown' was where Frank was supposed to go when he got into the car. The guy in the Zendo, who sent him out — that's where he was sending him."

"Sent him where?" said Tony.

"Doesn't matter," I said. "He didn't go. The giant took him and killed him instead. What matters is who sent him — *Failey! Bakum! Flakely!* — the guy inside the place."

"I'm not telling Julia," said Danny. "I don't care what anyone says."

"Well, it ain't gonna be me," said Gilbert, noticing Danny at last.

"We ought to go back to the East Side — *TrickyZendo!* — and have a look around." I was panting to get to the point, and Julia didn't seem to me to be it.

"All right, all right," said Tony. "We're gonna put our fucking heads together here."

At the word *heads* I was blessed with a sudden vision: Lacking Minna, ours, put together, were as empty and tenuous as balloons. Untethered by his death, the only question was how quickly they would drift apart, how far — and whether they'd burst or just wither.

"Okay," said Tony. "Gilbert, we gotta get you out of here. You're the name they've got. So we'll get you out doing some hoofwork. You look for this Ullman guy."

"How am I supposed to do that?" Gilbert wasn't exactly a specialist in digging up leads.

"Why don't you let me help him?" I said.

"I need you for something else," said Tony. "Gilbert can find Ullman."

"Yeah," said Gilbert. "But how?"

"Maybe his name's in the book," said Tony. "It's not so common, Ullman. Or maybe in Frank's book — you got that? Frank's address book?"

Gilbert looked at me.

"Must still be in his coat," I said. "Back at the hospital." But this triggered a compulsive self-frisking anyway. I patted each of my pockets six times. Under my breath I said, *"Franksbook, forkspook, finksblood —"*

"Great," said Tony. "That's just great. Well, show some initiative for once and find the guy. That's your *job*, Gilbert, for chrissakes. Call your pal, the garbage cop — he's got access to police records, right? Find Ullman and size him up. Maybe he's your giant. He might of been a little impatient for his date with Frank."

"The guy upstairs set Frank up," I said. I was frustrated that Gilbert and his jerk friend from the Sanitation Police were getting the assignment to track Ullman. "They were in it together, the guy upstairs and the giant. He knew the giant was waiting downstairs."

"Okay, but the giant could still be this guy Ullman," said Tony irritably. "And that's what Gilbert's going to find out, okay?"

I raised my hands in surrender, then snatched an imaginary fly out of the air.

"I'll go up to the East Side myself," said Tony. "Take a look around. See if I can get into this building. Danny, you mind the store."

"Check," said Danny, stubbing out his cigarette.

"That cop's gonna come back around," said Tony. "You talk to him. Cooperate, just don't give him anything. We don't want to look like we're panicking." Implicit in this assignment was the notion of Danny's superior rapport with the *fucking black cop.*

"You make it sound like we're the suspects," I said.

"That's how this cop made it sound," said Tony. "It isn't me."

"What about me?" I said. "You want me

— *Criminal Fishrug!* — to go with you? I know the place."

"No," said Tony. "You go explain to Julia."

Julia Minna had come back with Frank from wherever he'd gone between the dissolution of the moving company and the founding of the detective agency. She might have been the last and greatest of the Minna girls, for all we knew — she sure looked the part: tall, plush, blond by nurture, defiant around the jaw. It was easy to imagine Minna joshing with her, untucking her shirt, taking an elbow in the stomach. But by the time we got to meet her the two had initiated their long, dry stalemate. All that remained of their original passion was a faint crackle of electricity animating their insults, their drab swipes at one another. That was all that showed anyway. Julia terrified us at first, not for anything she did, but because of her cool grip on Minna, and also how tense he was around her, how ready to punish us with his words.

If Julia and Frank had still been animated, quickened with love, we might have remained in infantile awe of her, our fascination and lust still adolescent. But the chill between them was an opening. In our imaginations we became Frank and loved her, unchilled her, grew to manhood in her arms. If we were angry or disappointed with Frank Minna we felt connected to his beautiful, angry, disappointed wife, and were thrilled. She became an idol of disillusionment. Frank had shown us what girls were, and now he'd shown us a woman. And by failing to love her, he'd left a margin for our love to grow.

In our dreams we Minna Men were all Frank Minna — that wasn't news. But now we shot a little higher: If we had Julia we would do better than Frank, and make her happy.

Or so went dreams. I suppose over the years the other Minna Men conquered their fear and awe and desire of Julia, or anyway modulated it, by finding women of their own to make happy and unhappy, to enchant and disenchant and discard.

All except me, of course.

In the beginning Minna had Julia installed in the office of a Court Street lawyer, in a storefront as small as L&L's. We Men used to drop in on her there with little deliveries, messages or gifts from Frank, and watch her answering phones, reading *People*, making bad coffee. Minna seemed eager to show us off to her, more eager than he was to drop in himself. Similarly, he seemed pleased to have Julia on showcase there, under glass on Court Street. We all intuitively grasped Minna's instinct for human symbols, for moving us around to mark territory, so in this one sense Julia Minna had joined the Men, was on the team. Something went wrong, however, something soured between Julia and the lawyer, and Minna dragged her back to Carlotta Minna's old second-story apartment on Baltic Street, where she'd stayed for most of fifteen years, a sulking housewife. I could never visit without thinking of Carlotta's plates of food being carried down the stairwell by Court Street's assorted mugs. The old stove itself was gone, though. Julia and Frank mostly ate out.

I went to that apartment now, and knocked on the door, rolling my knuckles to get the right sound.

"Hello, Lionel," Julia said after peering at me through the peephole. She left the door unlatched and turned her back. I ducked inside. She wore a slip, her ripe arms bared, but below it she was already in stockings and heels. The apartment was dark, except for the bedroom. I shut the door behind me and followed her in, to where a dusty suitcase lay open on the bed, surrounded by heaps of clothing. It wasn't going to be my privilege to be first with the news anywhere, apparently. In a mass of lingerie already inside the suitcase I spotted something dark and shiny, half smothered there. A pistol.

Julia rummaged in her dresser, her back still turned. I propped myself in the closet doorframe, feeling awkward.

I could make out her labored breathing as she fumbled through the drawers.

"Who told you, Julia? *Eat, eat, eat* —" I ground my teeth, trying to check the impulse.

"Who do you think? I got a call from the hospital."

"Eat, ha ha, eat —" I revved like a motor.

"You want me to eat you, Lionel?" Her tone was grimly casual. "Just come out and say it."

"Okayeatme," I said gratefully. "You're packing? I mean, I don't mean the gun." I thought of Minna reprimanding Gilbert at the car, a few hours before. *You with no gun,* he'd said. *That's how I sleep at night.* "Packing your clothes —"

"Did they tell you to come over here and comfort me?" she said sharply. "Is that what you're doing?"

She turned. I saw the redness in her eyes

and the heaviness and softness of the flesh around her mouth. She groped for a pack of cigarettes that lay on the dresser, and when she put one between her grief-swollen lips I checked myself for a lighter I knew I wasn't carrying, just to make a show of it. She lit the cigarette herself, chopping at a match-book angrily, throwing off a little curl of spark.

The scene stirred me in about twelve different ways. Somehow Frank Minna was still alive in this room, alive in Julia in her slip with her half-packed suitcase, her cigarette, her gun. The two of them were closer at this moment than they had ever been. More truly married. But she was hurrying away. I sensed that if I let her go, that essence of him that I detected would go, too.

She looked at me and flared the end of the cigarette, then blew out smoke. "You jerks killed him," she said.

Her cigarette dangled in her fingers. I fought off a weird imagining: that she'd catch her slip on fire — it did seem flammable, practically looked aflame already — and that I'd have to put her out, drench her with a glass of water. This was an uncomfortable feature of Tourette's — my brain would throw up ugly fantasies, glimpses of pain, disasters narrowly averted. It liked to flirt with such images, the way my twitchy fingers were drawn near the blades of a spinning fan. Perhaps I also craved a crisis I could master, now, after failing Minna. I wanted to protect someone, and Julia would do.

"It wasn't us, Julia," I said. "We just didn't manage to keep him alive. He was killed by a giant, a guy the size of six guys."

"That's great," she said. "That sounds great. You've got it down, Lionel. You sound just like them. I hate the way you all talk, you know that?" She went back to stuffing clothes anarchically into the suitcase.

I mimed her striking of the match, one long motion away from my body, more or less keeping my cool. In fact, I wanted to run my hands through the clothes on the bed, snap the suitcase latches open and shut, lick the vinyl.

"Jerktalk!" I said.

She ignored me. A police siren sounded out on Smith Street and Baltic, and I shuddered. If the hospital had phoned her, the police couldn't be too far behind. But the sirens stopped half a block away. Just a traffic stop, a shakedown. Any given car on any given evening on Smith Street fit a profile, some profile. The cop's red light strobed through the margin of window under the shade, to throw a glow over the bed and Julia's glossy outline.

"You can't go, Julia."

"Watch."

"We need you."

She smirked at me. "You'll manage."

"No, really, Julia. Frank put L and L in your name. We work for you now."

"Really?" said Julia, interested now, or feigning interest — she made me too nervous to tell. "All I see before me is mine? Is that what you're telling me?"

I gulped, jerked my head to the side, as though she were looking behind me.

"You think I should come down and oversee the day-to-day business of a *car service,* Lionel? Have a look at the *books?* You think that might be a good occupation for the widow?"

"We're — *Detectapush! Octaphone!* — we're a detective agency. We're going to catch whoever did this." Even as I spoke, I tried to order my thoughts according to this principle: detectives, clues, investigation. I should be gathering information. I wondered for a moment if Julia were the *her* Frank had lost control of, according to the insinuating voice on the wire at the Zendo.

Of course, that would mean she missed

her *Rama-lama-ding-dong.* Whatever that was, I couldn't really picture Julia missing it.

"That's right," she said. "I forgot. I'm heir to a corrupt and inept detective agency. Get out of my way, Lionel." She set her cigarette on the edge of the dresser and pushed past me, into the closet.

Inupt and corrept, went the brain of Essrog the Idiotic. *You are corrept, sir!*

"God, look at these dresses," she said as she poked through the rack of hangers. Her voice was suddenly choked. "You see these?"

I nodded.

"They're worth more than the car service put together."

"Julia —"

"This isn't how I dress, really. This isn't how I look. I don't even like these dresses."

"How do you look?"

"You could never imagine. I can barely remember, myself. Before Frank dressed me up."

"Show me."

"Ha." She looked away. "I'm supposed to be the widow in black. You'd like that. I'd look really good. That's what Frank kept me around for, my big moment. No thanks. Tell Tony no thanks." She swept at the dresses, pushing them deeper into the closet. Then she abruptly pulled two out by the hangers and threw them onto the bed, where they spread over the suitcase like roosting butterflies. They weren't black.

"Tony?" I said. I was distracted, my eagle eye watching the ash burn longer, the glowing end of the abandoned cigarette inching toward the wood of the dresser.

"That's right, Tony. Fucking Frank Minna Junior. I'm sorry, Lionel, did you want to be Frank? Did I hurt your feelings? I'm afraid Tony has the inside track."

"That cigarette is going to burn the wood."

"Let it burn," she said.

"Is that a quote from a movie? 'Let it burn'? I feel like I remember that from some movie — *Burnamum Beatme!*"

She turned her back to me, moved again to the bed. Untangling the dresses from their hangers, she stuffed one into the suitcase, then held the other open and stepped into it, careful not to snag the heels of her shoes. I gripped the closet doorframe, stifling an impulse to bat like a kitten at the shimmery fabric as she slid the dress up around her hips and over her shoulders.

"Come here, Lionel," she said, without turning around. "Zip me up."

As I reached out, I was compelled to tap each of her shoulders twice, gently. She didn't seem to mind. Then I took hold of the zipper tab, eased it upward. As I did she took her hair in her hands, raised her arms above her head and turned, so that she rolled into my embrace. I kept hold of the tab, halfway up her back. Up close I saw how her eyes and lips looked like something barely rescued from drowning.

"Don't stop," she said.

She rested her elbows high on my shoulders and gazed up at my face while I tugged at the zipper. I held my breath.

"You know, when I met Frank I'd never shaved my armpits before. He made me shave." She spoke the words into my chest, her voice dopey now, absent-sounding. All the anger was gone.

I got the zipper to the nape of her neck and dropped my hands, then took a step back and exhaled. She still held her hair bunched above her head.

"Maybe I'll grow the hair back. What do you think, Lionel?"

I opened my mouth and what came out, soft but unmistakable, was "Double-breasts."

"All breasts are double, Lionel. Didn't you know that?"

"That was just a tic," I said awkwardly, lowering my eyes.

"Give me your hands, Lionel."

I lifted my hands again, and she took them.

"God, they're big. You have such big hands, Lionel." Her voice was dreamy and singsong, like a child, or a grownup pretending to be a child. "I mean — the way you move them around so quickly, when you do that thing you do, all that grabbing, touching stuff. What's that called again?"

"That's a tic, too, Julia."

"I always think of your hands as small because they move so fast. But they're big."

She moved them to her breasts.

Sexual excitement stills my Tourette's brain, not by numbing me, dimming the world like Orap or Klonopin, those muffling medications, but instead by setting up a deeper attentiveness in me, a finer vibration, which gathers and encompasses my urgent chaos, enlists it in a greater cause, like a chorus of voices somehow drawing a shriek into harmony. I'm still myself and still in myself, a rare and precious combination. Yes, I like sex very much. I don't get it very often. When I do, I find I want to slow it down to a crawl, live in that place, get to meet my stilled self, give him a little time to look around. Instead I'm hurried along by the conventional urgencies, by those awkward, alcohol-fueled juxtapositions of persons that have so far provided my few glimpses of arousal's haven. But oh, if I could have just spent a week or so with my hands on Julia's breasts, then I could think straight!

Alas, my very first straight thought guided my hands elsewhere. I went and plucked the smoldering cigarette off the dresser, rescuing the finish, and since Julia's lips were slightly parted I stuck it there, filter end first.

"Double, see?" she said as she drew on the cigarette. She combed her hair with her fingers, then straightened her slip under her dress where I'd held her.

"What's double?"

"You know, breasts."

"You shouldn't make fun of — *Lyrical Eggdog! Logical Assnog!* — you shouldn't make fun of me, Julia."

"I'm not."

"Did something — Is there something between you and Tony?"

"I don't know. Screw Tony. I like you better, Lionel. I just never told you." She was hurt, erratic, her voice straying wildly, searching for a place to rest.

"I like you, too, Julia. There's nothing — *Screwtony! Nertscrony! Screwtsony! Tootscrewny!* — sorry. There's nothing wrong with that."

"I want you to like me, Lionel."

"You're — you're not saying there could actually be something between us?" I turned and slapped the doorframe six times, feeling my face curdle with shame, regretting the question instantly — wishing, for once, that I'd ticced instead, something obnoxious to obliterate the conversation's meaning, to smother the words I'd let myself say.

"No," she said coldly. She set the cigarette, what was left of it, back on the dresser. "You're too strange, Lionel. Much too strange. I mean, take a look in the mirror." She resumed crushing her clothes into the suitcase, more than seemed possible, like a magician stuffing a prop for a trick.

I only hoped the gun wouldn't go off. "Where are you going, Julia?" I said tiredly.

"I'm going to a place of peace, if you must know, Lionel."

"A — what?" *Prays of peach? Plays of peas? Press-e-piece?*

"You heard me. A place of peace."

Then a horn sounded outside.

"That's my car," she said. "Would you go and tell them I'll be out in a minute?"

"Okay, but — *pressure pees* — that's a strange thing to say."

"Have you ever been out of Brooklyn, Lionel?"

Breasts, underarm hair, now Brooklyn — for Julia it was all just a measure of my inexperience. "Sure," I said. "I was in Manhattan just this afternoon." I tried not to think about what I'd been doing there, or failing to do.

"New York City, Lionel. Have you ever been out of New York City?"

While I considered this question I eyed the cigarette, which had at last begun to singe the dresser top. The blackening paint stood for my defeat here. I couldn't protect anything, maybe least of all myself.

"Because if you had, you'd know that anywhere else is a place of peace. So that's where I'm going. Would you please go hold my car for me?"

The car service double-parked in front of the building was Legacy Pool, the furthest upscale of the Brooklyn competitors, with all-black luxury models, tinted windows, cell phones for the customers, and built-in tissue-box holders under the rear window. Julia was running in style. I waved at the driver from the stoop of her building, and he nodded at me and leaned his head back on the rest. I was trying out his neck motions, *nod, lean,* when the gravelly voice appeared behind me.

"Who's the car for?"

It was the homicide detective. He'd been waiting, staking us out, slumped to one side of the doorway, huddled in his coat against the chilly November night. I made him right away — with his 10 P.M. Styrofoam cup of coffee, worn tie, ingrown beard, and interrogation eyes, he was unmistakable — but that didn't mean he had any idea who I was.

"Lady inside," I said, and tapped him once on the shoulder.

"Watch it," he said, ducking away from my touch.

"Sorry, friend. Can't help myself." I turned from him, back into the building.

The elegance of my exit was quickly thwarted, though — Julia was just then galumphing down the stairs with her overstuffed suitcase. I rushed to help her as the door eased slowly shut on its moaning hydraulic hinge. Too slowly: The cop stuck out his foot and held the door open for us.

"Excuse me," he said with a sly, exhausted authority. “You Julia Minna?”

“I was,” said Julia.

“You were?”

“Yes. Isn’t that funny? I was until just about an hour ago. Lionel, put my bag in the trunk.”

“In a hurry?” the detective asked Julia. I watched the two of them size one another up, as though I weren’t any more a factor than the waiting limo driver. *A few minutes ago,* I wanted to say, *my hands* — Instead I hoisted Julia’s luggage, and waited for her to move past me to the car.

“Sort of,” said Julia. “Plane to catch.”

“Plane to where?” He crushed his empty Styrofoam cup and tossed it over his shoulder, off the stoop, into the neighbor’s bushes. They were already decorated with trash.

“I haven’t decided yet.”

“She’s going to a *precipice, pleasure police, philanthropriest* —”

“Shut up, Lionel.”

The detective looked at me like I was crazy.

My life story to this point:

The teacher looked at me like I was crazy.

The social-services worker looked at me like I was crazy.

The boy looked at me like I was crazy and then hit me.

The girl looked at me like I was crazy.

The woman looked at me like I was crazy.

The black homicide detective looked at me like I was crazy.

"I'm afraid you can't go, Julia," said the detective, shaking off his confusion at my utterances with a sigh and a grimace. He'd seen plenty in his day, could cope with a little more before needing to bust my chops over it — that was the feeling I got. "We're going to want to talk to you about Frank."

"You'll have to arrest me," said Julia.

"Why would you want to say that?" said the detective, pained.

"Just to keep things simple," said Julia. "Arrest me or I'm getting in the car. Lionel, please."

I humped the huge, unwieldy suitcase down the stoop and waved at the driver to pop the trunk. Julia followed, the detective close behind. The limo's speakers were oozing Mariah Carey, the driver still mellow on the headrest. When Julia slid into the backseat, the detective caught the door in his two meaty hands and leaned in over the top.

"Don't you care who killed your husband,

Mrs. Minna?" He was plainly unnerved by Julia's blitheness.

"Let me know when you find out who killed him," she said. "Then I'll tell you if I care."

I pushed the suitcase in over the top of the spare tire. I briefly considered opening it up and confiscating Julia's pistol, then realized I probably didn't want to emerge with a gun in front of the homicide cop. He was liable to misunderstand. Instead I shut the trunk.

"That would involve us being in touch," the detective pointed out to Julia.

"I told you, I don't know where I'm going. Do you have a card?"

As he straightened to reach into his vest pocket she slammed the door, then rolled down her window to accept his card.

"We could have you stopped at the airport," he said severely, trying to remind her of his authority, or remind himself. But that we was weaker than he knew.

"Yes," said Julia. "But it sounds like you've decided to let me go. I appreciate it." She palmed his card into her purse.

"Where were you this afternoon when Frank was killed, Mrs. Minna?"

"Talk to Lionel," said Julia, looking back at me. "He's my alibi. We were together all day."

"Eat me alibailey," I breathed, as quietly as I could. The detective frowned at me. I held my hands open and made an Art Carney face, pleading for a common understanding between us — women, suspects, widows, whattayagonnado? Can't live with 'em, can't live without 'em, eh?

Julia powered her tinted window back up into place and the Legacy Pool limousine took off, idiot radio trickling away to silence, leaving me and the detective standing in the dark of Baltic Street by ourselves.

"Lionel."

Alibi hullabaloo gullible bellyflop smellafish, sang my brain, obliterating speech. I waved a farewell at the detective and started toward Smith Street. If Julia could leave him flat-footed, why couldn't I?

He followed. "We better talk, Lionel." He'd blown it, let her go, and now he was going to compensate with me, exercise his deductive and bullying powers.

"Can't it wait?" I managed, without turning — it took a considerable effort not to swivel my neck. But I felt him right on my heels, like a pacing man and his shadow.

"What's your full name, Lionel?"

"Lullaby Gueststar —"

"Come again?"

"Alibyebye Essmob —"

"Sounds Arabic," said the detective as he pulled even with me. "You don't look Arabic, though. Where were you and the lady this afternoon, Alibi?"

"Lionel," I forced myself to say clearly, and then blurted *"Lionel Arrestme!"*

"That's not gonna work twice in the same night," said the cop. "I don't have to arrest you. We're just taking a walk, Alibi. Only I don't know where we're going. You want to tell me?"

"Home," I said, before I recalled that he'd been to the place I called home once already this evening, and that it wasn't in my best interests to lead him there again. "Except actually I'd like to get a sandwich first. I'm starving. You want to get a sandwich with me? There's a place on Smith, called Zeod's, if that's okay, we'll get a sandwich and then maybe part ways there, since I'm kind of shy about bringing people back to my place —" As I turned to deliver my speech my shoulder-lust was activated, and I began reaching for him again.

He knocked my hand away. "Slow down, Alibi. What's the matter with you?"

"Tourette's syndrome," I said, with a grim sense of inevitability. Tourette's was my other name, and, like my name, my brain could never leave the words unmolested. Sure enough, I produced my own echo: "Tourette is the shitman!" Nodding, gulping, flinching, I tried to silence myself, walk quickly toward the sandwich shop, and keep my eyes down, so that the detective would be out of range of my shoulder-scope. No good, I was juggling too much, and when I reticced, it came out a bellow: *"Tourette Is the Shitman!"*

"He's the shitman, huh?" The detective apparently thought we were exchanging up-to-the-minute street jargon. "Can you take me to him?"

"No, no, there's no Tourette," I said, catching my breath. I felt mad for food, desperate to shake the detective, and choked with imminent tics.

"Don't worry," said the detective, talking down to me. "I won't tell him who gave out his name."

He thought he was grooming a stool pigeon. I could only try not to laugh or shout. Let Tourette be the suspect and maybe I'd get off the hook.

On Smith Street we veered into Zeod's Twenty-Four-Hour Market, where the odors of baloney and bad coffee mingled with those of pistachio, dates, and St. John's bread. If the cop wanted an Arab, I'd give him an Arab. Zeod himself stood on the elevated ramp behind the Plexiglas-and-plywood counter. He saw me and said, "Crazyman! How are you my friend?"

"Not so good," I admitted. The detective hovered behind me, tempting me to turn my head again. I resisted.

"Where's Frank?" said Zeod. "How I never see Frank anymore?"

Here was my chance to deliver the news at last, and my heart wasn't up to it. "He's in the hospital," I said, unable now to keep from glancing nervously at the homicide detective. *"Doctorbyebye!"* recalled my Tourette's.

"Some crazyman you are," said Zeod, smiling and arching his hedge of eyebrows knowingly at my official shadow. "You tell Frank Zeod asks, okay, partner?"

"Okay," I said. "I'll do that. How about a sandwich for now? Turkey on a kaiser, plenty of mustard."

Zeod nodded at his second, an indolent Dominican kid, who moved to the slicer. Zeod never made sandwiches himself. But he'd taught his countermen well, to slice extraordinarily thin and drape the meat as it slid off the blade so it fell in bunches, rather than stacking airlessly, to make a sandwich with that fluffy compressibility I craved. I let myself be hypnotized by the whine of the slicer, the rhythm of the kid's arm as he received the slices and dripped them onto the kaiser roll. Zeod watched me. He knew I obsessed on his sandwiches, and it pleased him. "You and your friend?" he said magnanimously.

The detective shook his head. "Pack of Marlboro Lights," he said.

"Okay. You want a soda, Crazyman? Get yourself." I went and got a Coke out of the cooler while Zeod put my sandwich and the cop's cigarettes into a brown paper bag with a plastic fork and a sheaf of napkins.

"Charge it to Frank, yes, my friend?"

I couldn't speak. I took the bag and we stepped back out onto Smith Street.

"Sleeping with the dead man's wife," said the detective. "Now you're eating on his tab. That takes some gall."

"You misunderstand," I said.

"Then maybe you better set me straight," he said. "Gimme those cigarettes."

"I work for Frank —"

"Worked. He's dead. Why didn't you tell your friend the A-rab?"

"*Arab-eye!* — I don't know. No reason." I handed the cop his Marlboros. "*Eatmebailey, repeatmebailey, repeatmobile* — could we continue this maybe another time? Because — *retreatmobile!* — because now I really urgently have to go home and — *eatbail! beatmail!* — eat this sandwich."

"You work for him where? At the car service?"

Detective agency, I silently corrected. "Uh, yeah."

"So you and his wife were, what? Driving around? Where's the car?"

"She wanted to go shopping." This lie came out so blessedly smooth and un-tic-laden it felt like the truth. For that reason or some other, the detective didn't challenge it.

"So you'd describe yourself as, what? A friend of the deceased?"

"*Trend the decreased! Mend the retreats!* — sure, that's right."

He was learning to ignore my outbursts. "So where are we going now? Your house?" He lit a cigarette without breaking stride. "Looks like you're headed back to work."

I didn't want to tell him how little difference there was between the two.

"Let's go in here," I said, jerking my neck sideways as we crossed Bergen Street, letting my physical tic lead me — navigation by Tourette's — into the Casino.

The Casino was Minna's name for Smith Street's hole-in-the-wall newspaper shop, which had a single wall of magazines and a case of Pepsi and Snapple crammed into a space the size of a large closet. The Casino was named for the lines that stretched each morning to buy Lotto and Scratchers and Jumble 6 and Pickball, for the fortune being made on games of chance by the newsstand's immigrant Korean owners, for the hearts being quietly broken there round the clock. There was something tragic in the way they stood obediently waiting, many of them elderly, others new immigrants, illiterate except in the small language of their chosen game, deferring to anyone with real business, like the purchase of a magazine, a pack of double-A batteries, or a tube of lip gloss. That docility was heartbreaking. The games were over almost before they started, the foil scraped off tickets with a key or a dime, the contrived near-misses underneath bared. (New York is a Tourettic city, and this great communal scratching and counting and tearing is a definite symptom.) The sidewalk just outside the Casino was strewn with discarded tickets, the chaff of wasted hope.

But I was hardly in a position to criticize lost causes. I had no reason for visiting the Casino except that I associated it with Minna, with Minna alive. If I visited enough of his haunts before news of his death spread along Court and Smith Street, I might persuade myself against the evidence of my own eyes — and against the fact of the homicide cop on my heels — that nothing had happened.

"What're we doing?" said the detective.

"I, uh, need something to read with my sandwich."

The desultory magazines were shelved two deep in the rack — there weren't more than one or two customers for *GQ* or *Wired* or *Brooklyn Bridge* per month around here. Me, I was bluffing, didn't read magazines at all. Then I spotted a familiar face, on a magazine called *Vibe*: The Artist Formerly Known as Prince. Before a blurred cream background he posed resting his head against the neck of a pink guitar, his eyes demure. The unpronounceable typographical glyph with which he had replaced his name was shaved into the hair at his temple.

"Skrubble," I said.

"What?"

"Plavshk," I said. My brain had decided to try to pronounce that unpronounceable glyph, a linguistic foray into the lands *On Beyond Zebra*. I lifted up the magazine.

"You're telling me you're gonna read *Vibe*?"

"Sure."

"You trying to make fun of me here, Alibi?"

"No, no, I'm a big fan of *Skursvshe*."

"Who?"

"The Artist Formerly Known As *Plinvstk*." I couldn't quit tackling the glyph. I plopped the magazine on the counter and Jimmy, the Korean proprietor, said, "For Frank?"

"Yeah," I gulped.

He waved my money away. "Take it, Lionel."

Back outside, the cop waited until we'd turned the corner, into the relative gloom of Bergen Street, just past the F-train entrance and a few doors from L&L's storefront, then collared me, literally, two hands bunching my jacket at my neck, and pushed me up against the tile-mosaic wall. I gripped my magazine, which was curled into a baton, and the bag from Zeod's with sandwich and soda, held them protectively in front of me like an old lady with her purse. I knew better than to push back at the cop. Anyway, I was bigger, and he didn't really frighten me, not physically.

"Enough with the double-talk," he said. "Where's this going? Why are you pretending your man Minna's still with us, Alibi? What's the game?"

"Wow," I said. "This was unexpected. You're like good cop and bad cop rolled into one."

"Yeah, used to be they could afford two different guys. Now with all the budget cuts and shit they've got us doing double shifts."

"Can we go back to — *fuckmeblackcop* — back to talking nice now?"

"What you say?"

"Nothing. Let go of my collar." I'd kept the outburst down to a mumble — and I knew to be grateful my Tourette's brain hadn't dialed up *nigger*. Despite the detective's roughhousing, or because of it, our frenzy had peaked and abated, and we'd earned a quiet moment together. He was close enough to invite intimacy. If my hands hadn't been full I would have begun stroking his pebbly jaw or clapping him on the shoulders.

"Talk to me, Alibi. Tell me things."

"Don't treat me like a suspect."

"Tell me why not."

"I worked for Frank. I miss him. I want to catch his killer as much as you."

"So let's compare notes. The names Alphonso Matricardi and Leonardo Rockaforte mean anything to you?"

I was silenced.

Matricardi and Rockaforte: The homicide cop didn't know you weren't supposed to say those names aloud. Not anywhere, but especially not out on Smith Street.

I'd never even heard their first names, Alphonso and Leonardo. They seemed wrong, but what first names wouldn't? Wrongness surrounded those names and their once-in-a-blue-moon uttering. Don't say Matricardi and Rockaforte.

Say "The Clients" if you must.

Or say "Garden State Brickface and Stucco." But not those names.

"Never heard of them," I breathed.

"Why don't I believe you?"

"Believemeblackman."

"You're fucking sick."

"I am," I said. "I'm sorry."

"You should be sorry. Your man got killed and you're not giving me anything."

"I'll catch the killer," I said. "That's what I'll give you."

He eased off me. I barked twice. He made another face, but it was clear it all would get chalked up to harmless insanity now. I was smarter than I knew leading the cop into Zeod's and letting him hear the Arab call me Crazyman.

"You might want to leave that to me,

Alibi. Just make sure you're telling me all you know."

"Absolutely." I made an honorable Boy Scout face. I didn't want to point out to *good cop* that *bad cop* hadn't learned anything from me, just got tired of asking.

"You're making me sad with your sandwich and your goddamn magazine. Get out of here."

I straightened my jacket. A strange peace had come over me. The cop had caused me to think about The Clients for a minute, but I pushed them out of view. I was good at doing that. My Tourette's brain chanted *Want to catch him as much as miss him as much as a sad-wich* but I didn't need to tic now, could let it live inside me, a bubbling brook, a deep well of song. I went to the L&L storefront and let myself in with my key. Danny wasn't anywhere to be seen. The phone was ringing. I let it ring. The cop stood watching me and I waved at him once, then shut the door and went into the back.

Sometimes I had trouble admitting I lived upstairs in the apartment above the L&L storefront, but I did, and had since the day so long ago when I left St. Vincent's. The stairs ran down into the back of the storefront. Apart from that inconvenient fact, I tried to keep the two places separated in my mind, decorating the apartment conventionally with forties-style furniture from the decrepit discount showrooms far down Smith Street and never inviting the other Minna Men up if I could help it, and adhering to certain arbitrary rules: drinking beer downstairs and whiskey upstairs, playing cards downstairs but setting out a board with a chess problem upstairs, Touch-Tone phones downstairs, a Bakelite dial phone upstairs, et cetera. For a while I even had a cat, but that didn't work out.

The door at the top of the stair was acned with a thousand tiny dents, from my ritual rapping of my keys before opening the door. I added six more quick key-impressions — my counting nerve was stuck on six today, ever since the fatal bag of White Castles — and then let myself in. The phone downstairs went on ringing. I left my lights off, not wanting to signal to the detective, if he was still outside watching, the connection between upstairs and down. Then I crept to my front window and peered out. The corner was empty of cop. Still, why take a chance? Enough light leaked in from the streetlamps for me to make my way around. So I left the lamps dimmed, though I had to run my hands under the shades and fondle the switches, ritual contact just to make myself feel at home.

Understand: The possibility that I might at any time have to make the rounds and touch every visible item in my apartment dictated a sort of faux-Japanese simplicity in my surroundings. Beneath my reading lamp were five unread paperbacks, which I would return to the Salvation Army on Smith Street as soon as I'd finished them. The covers of the books were already scored with dozens of minute creases, made by sliding my fingernails sideways over their surfaces. I owned a black plastic boom box with detachable speakers, and a short row of Prince/Artist Formerly Known As CDs — I wasn't lying to the homicide cop about being a fan. Beside the CDs lay a single fork, the one I'd stolen from Matricardi and Rockaforte's table full of silverware fourteen years before. I placed the *Vibe* magazine and the bag with the sandwich on my table, which was otherwise clean. I wasn't so terribly hungry anymore. A drink was more urgent. Not that I really liked alcohol, but the ritual was essential.

The phone downstairs went on ringing. L&L didn't have a machine to pick it up — callers usually gave up after nine or ten rings and tried another car service. I tuned it out.

I emptied my jacket pockets and rediscovered Minna's watch and beeper. I put them on the table, then poured myself a tumblerful of Walker Red and dropped in a couple of ice cubes and sat down there in the dark to try to let the day settle over me, to try to make some sense of it. The way my ice shimmered made me need to bat at it like a cat fishing in a goldfish bowl, but otherwise the scene was pretty calm. If only the phone downstairs would stop ringing. Where was Danny? For that matter, shouldn't Tony be back from the East Side by now? I didn't want to think he'd go into the Zendo without some backup, without letting us other Minna Men in on the score. I pushed the thought away, tried to forget about Tony and Danny and Gilbert for the moment, to pretend it was my case alone and weight the variables and put them into some kind of shape that made sense, that produced answers or at least a clear question. I thought of the giant Polish killer we'd watched drive our boss away to a Dumpster — he already seemed like something I'd imagined, an impossible figure, a silhouette from a dream. The phone downstairs went on ringing. I thought about Julia, how she'd toyed with the homicide detective and then flown, how she'd almost seemed too ready for the news from the hospital, and I considered the bitterness laced into her sorrow. I tried not to think of how she'd toyed with me, and how little I knew it meant. I thought about Minna himself, the mystery of his connection in the Zendo, his caustic familiarity with his betrayer, his disastrous preference for keeping his Men in the dark and how he'd paid for it. As I gazed past the streetlight to the flickering blue-lit curtains of the bedrooms in the apartments across Bergen Street, I lingered over my paltry clues: Ullman downtown, the girl with glasses and short hair, "the building" that the sardonic voice in the Yorkville Zendo had mentioned, and Irving — if Irving really was a clue.

While I thought about these things, another track in my brain intoned brainyoctomy brainyalimony bunnymonopoly baileyoctopus brainyanimal broccopotamus. And the phone downstairs kept on ringing. Sighing, I resigned myself to my fate, went back downstairs and picked up the phone.

"No cars!" I said forcefully.

"That you, Lionel?" said Gilbert's friend Loomis, the sanitation inspector — the garbage cop.

"What is it, Loomis?" I disliked the garbage cop intensely.

"Gotta problem over here."

"Where's here?"

"Sixth Precinct house, in Manhattan."

"*Dickweed!* What are you doing at the precinct house, Loomis?"

"Well, they're saying it's too late, no way they're gonna arraign him tonight, he's gonna have to spend the night in the bullpen."

"Who?"

"Who'd you think? Gilbert! They got him up on killing some guy name Ullman."

Have you ever felt, in the course of reading a detective novel, a guilty thrill of relief at having a character murdered before he can step onto the page and burden you with his actual existence? Detective stories always have too many characters anyway. And characters mentioned early on but never sighted, just lingering offstage, take on an awful portentous quality. Better to have them gone.

I felt some version of this thrill at the news that the garbage cop delivered, of Ullman's demise. But too, I felt its opposite: a panic that the world of the case was shrinking. Ullman had been an open door, a direction, a whiff of something. I couldn't spare any grief for the death of Ullman the human being — especially not on The Day Frank Minna Died — but I mourned nonetheless: My clue had been murdered.

A few other things I felt:

Annoyed — I would have to deal with Loomis tonight. My reverie was snapped. The ice would melt in my glass of Walker Red upstairs. My sandwich from Zeod's would go uneaten.

Confused — let Gilbert glower and lurch all he wanted, but he'd never kill a man. And I'd watched him blink dumbly at the name Ullman. It had meant nothing to him. So no motive, unless it was self-defense. Or else he'd been set up. Therefore:

Frightened. Someone was hunting Minna Men.

I took an agency car into Manhattan and tried to see Gilbert at the precinct house, but didn't have any luck. He'd already been shifted out of the front cage, to the back, where he'd been grouped with a bunch of other fresh arrests for a night of what the cops euphemistically called "bullpen therapy" — eating baloney sandwiches, using the toilet in the open if he had to go, shrugging off petty advances on his watch and wallet, and trading cigarettes, if he had any, for a razor blade to protect himself. Industrious Loomis had already exhausted the cops' patience for Gilbert's rights and privileges: He'd had his phone call, his moment's visitation at the cell bars, and nothing more would be allowed to happen to him until the next morning at the soonest. Then he could hope to be arraigned and sent out to the Tombs to wait for someone to bail him out. So my effort was rewarded by learning nothing yet being saddled with driving Loomis back to Brooklyn. I took the opportunity to try to find out what the garbage cop had heard from Gilbert.

"He didn't want to say much without a lawyer, and I don't blame him. The walls have ears, you know? Just that Ullman was dead when he got there. The homicides picked him up coming out the place like they'd been tipped. Time I saw him, he'd mouthed a little and been roughed around, asked for a lawyer, they told him he had to wait for tomorrow. I guess he tried to call L&L but you weren't picking up, fortunately I was around — Hey, sorry about Frank, by the way. It's a shame a thing happens. Gilbert didn't look too good about it either I can tell you. I don't know what he said or didn't but the guys weren't too happy with him by the time I showed. I tried reasoning with the guys, let them see my badge, but they treat me like I was lower than a fucking prison guard, you know? Like I couldn't make the fucking cut."

Gilbert had befriended Loomis somewhere near the end of high school, when they both were hanging around the Carroll Street park watching the old men play bocce. Loomis called to Gilbert's lazy, sloppy side, the nose-picker and cigarette-grubber, the part of him that didn't want to always have to keep up with Minna and us other Men. Loomis wasn't sharpened up the way even the most passive and recalcitrant of us orphans had to be — he was a sort of shapeless inadvertent extension of his parents' couch and television set and refrigerator, and he assumed independent life only grudgingly. At Gilbert's side he'd come slouching around L&L in the formative days and never show a glimmer of interest in either our cover-story car service or the detective agency lurking just underneath — we might have an open packet of Sno-Balls or Chocodiles sitting on the counter, though.

Loomis was nudged by his parents toward police work. He struck out twice at the civil-service qualification test to become a regular beat cop, and some kindhearted career counselor nudged him again, gently downward, to the easier test for the sanitation police, which he squeaked past. Before he was the Garbage Cop, though, Minna used to call him *Butt Trust,* a term he would apply with a measure of real tenderness.

Me and the other Boys let it go the first five or six times, thinking an explanation would be offered, before finally asking Minna what he meant.

"You got your brain trust, your most-valued," said Minna. "Then you got the rest of them. The ones you let hang around anyway. That would be the butt trust, right?"

I was never overfond of the butt trust. In fact, I hated Loomis — let me count the ways. His imprecision and laziness maddened my compulsive instincts — his patchiness, the way even his speech was riddled with drop-outs and glitches like a worn cassette, the way his leaden senses refused the world, his attention like a pinball rolling past unlit blinkers and frozen flippers into the hole again and again: *game over.* He was permanently impressed by the most irrelevant banalities and impossible to impress with real novelty, meaning, or conflict. And he was too moronic to be properly self-loathing — so it was my duty to loathe him instead.

Tonight, as we roared across the metal grating of the Brooklyn Bridge's roadway, he settled into his usual dull riff: The sanitation force gets no respect. "You think they'd know what it's like for a cop in this city, me and those guys are on the same team, but this one cop keeps saying, 'Hey, why don't you come around my block, somebody keeps stealing my garbage.' If it weren't for Gilbert I would of told him to stick it —"

"What time did Gilbert call you?" I interrupted.

"I don't know, around seven or eight, maybe nine almost," he said, succinctly demonstrating his unfitness for the force.

"It's — *Tourette is the stickman!* — only ten now, Loomis."

"Okay, it was just after eight."

"Did you find out where Ullman lived?"

"Downtown somewhere. I gave Gilbert the address."

"You don't remember where it was?"

"Nah."

Loomis wasn't going to be any help. He seemed to know this as well as I, and immediately launched into another digression, as if to say, *I'm useless, but no hard feelings, okay?* "So you heard the one about how many Catholics does it take to screw in a lightbulb?"

"I've heard that one, Loomis. No jokes, please."

"Ah, come on. What about why did the blonde stare at the carton of orange juice?"

I was silent. We came off the bridge, at Cadman Plaza. I'd be rid of him soon.

" 'Cause it said 'concentrate,' get it?"

This was another thing I hated about Loomis. Years ago he'd latched on to Minna's joke-telling contests, decided he could compete. But he favored idiot riddles, not jokes at all, no room for character or nuance. He didn't seem to know the difference.

"Got it," I admitted.

"What about how do you titillate an ocelot?"

"What?"

"Titillate an ocelot. You know, like a big cat. I think."

"It's a big cat. How do you titillate it, Loomis?"

"*You oscillate its tit a lot,* get it?"

"Eat me Ocelot!" I screamed as we turned onto Court Street. Loomis's crappy punning had slid right under the skin of my symptoms. "Lancelot ancillary oscillope! Octapot! Tittapocamus!"

The garbage cop laughed. "Jesus, Lionel, you crack me up. You never quit with that routine."

"It's not a — *root* — *ocelot,*" I shrieked through my teeth. Here, finally, was what I hated most in Loomis: He'd always insisted, from the time we met as teenagers to this day, that I was elaborately feigning and could keep from ticcing if I wanted to. Nothing would dissuade him, no example or demonstration, no program of education. I'd once shown him the book Minna gave me; he glanced at it and laughed. I was making it up. As far as he was concerned, my Tourette's was just an odd joke, one going mostly over his head, stretched out over the course of fifteen years.

"Tossed salad!" he said. "Gotcha!" He liked to think he was playing along.

"Go touchalot!" I slapped him on the thickly padded shoulder of his coat, so suddenly the car swerved with my movement.

"Christ, look out!"

I tapped him five more times, my driving steady now.

"I can't get over you," he said. "Even at a time like this. I guess it's sentimental, like a way of saying, *if Frank were still here.* Since that routine always did keep him busted up."

We pulled up outside L&L. The lights in the storefront were on. Somebody had returned since my jaunt to the Sixth Precinct.

"I thought you were driving me home." Loomis lived on Nevins Street, near the projects.

"You can walk from here, *gofuckacop*."

"C'mon, Lionel."

I parked in the open spot across from the storefront. The sooner Loomis and I were out of each other's presence, the better.

"Walk," I said.

"At least lemme use the can," he whined. "Those jerks at the station wouldn't let me. I been holding it."

"If you'll do one thing for me."

"Whuzzat?"

"Ullman's address," I said. "You found it once. I need it, Loomis."

"I can get it tomorrow morning when I'm back at my desk. You want me to call you here?"

I took one of Minna's cards out of my pocket and handed it to him. "Call the beeper number. I'll be carrying it."

"Okay, all right, now will you lemme take a leak?"

I didn't speak, just clicked the car locks up and down automatically six times, then got out. Loomis followed me to the storefront, and inside.

Danny came out of the back, stubbing a cigarette in the countertop ashtray as he passed. He always dressed the prettiest of us Minna Men, but his lean black suit suddenly looked like it had been worn too many days in a row. He reminded me of an out-of-work mortician. He glanced at me and Loomis and pursed his lips but didn't speak, and I couldn't really get anything out of his eyes. I felt I didn't know him with Minna gone. Danny and I functioned as expressions of two opposed ends of Frank Minna's impulses: him a tall, silent body that attracted women and intimidated men, me a flapping inane mouth that covered the world in names and descriptions. Average us and you might have Frank Minna back, sort of. Now, without Minna for a conduit between us, Danny and I had to begin again grasping one another as entities, as though we were suddenly fourteen years old again and occupying our opposite niches at St. Vincent's Home for Boys.

In fact, I had a sudden yearning that Danny should be holding a basketball, so that I could say "Good shot!" or exhort him to dunk it. Instead we stared at one another.

" 'Scuse me," said Loomis, scooting past

me and waving his hand at Danny. "Gotta use your toilet." He disappeared into the back.

"Where's Tony?" I said.

"I was hoping you could tell me."

"Well, I don't know. I hope he's doing better than Gilbert. I just left him in the lockup at the Sixth." I realized it sounded as if I'd actually seen him, but I let the implication stand. Loomis wouldn't call me on it, even if he heard from the bathroom.

Danny didn't look all that surprised. The shock of Minna's death made this new turn unimpressive by comparison, I supposed. "What's he in for?"

"*Ullmanslaughter!* — the guy Tony sent Gilbert to find, he turned up dead. They pinned it on Gilbert."

Danny only scratched at the end of his nose thoughtfully.

"So where were you?" I said. "I thought you were minding the store."

"Went for a bite."

"I was here for forty-five minutes." A lie — I doubted it was more than fifteen, but I felt like pushing him.

"Guess we missed each other."

"Any calls? See that *homosapien, homogenize, genocide, can'tdecide, candyeyes,* homicide cop?"

He shook his head. He was holding something back — but then it occurred to me that I was too.

Danny and I stood pensively regarding each other, waiting for the next question to form. I felt a vibration deep inside, profounder tics lurking in me, gathering strength. Or perhaps I was only feeling my hunger at last.

Loomis popped out of the back. "Jesus, you guys look bad. What a day, huh?"

We stared at him.

"Well, I think we owe Frank a moment of silence, don't you guys?"

I wanted to point out that what Loomis had interrupted *was* a moment of silence, but I let it go.

"Little something in the way of remembrance? Bow your heads, you turkeys. The guy was like your father. Don't end the day arguing with each other, for crying out loud."

Loomis had a point, or enough of one anyway, to shame me and Danny into letting him have his way. So we stood in silence, and when I saw that Danny and Loomis had each closed their eyes I closed mine too. Together we made up some lopped-off, inadequate version of the Agency — Danny standing for himself and Tony, I for myself, and Loomis, I suppose, for Gilbert. But I was moved anyway, for a second.

Then Loomis ruined it with a clearly audible fart, which he coughed to cover, unsuccessfully. "Okay," he said suddenly. "How's about that ride home, Lionel?"

"Walk," I said.

Humbled by his own body, the garbage cop didn't argue, but headed for the door.

Danny volunteered to sit by the L&L phone. He already had a pot of coffee brewing, he pointed out, and I could see he was in a pacing mood, that he wanted the space of the office to himself. It suited me well enough to leave him there. I went upstairs, without our exchanging more than a few sentences.

Upstairs I lit a candle and stuck it in the center of my table, beside Minna's beeper and watch. Loomis's clumsy pass at ritual haunted me. I needed one of my own. But I was also hungry. I poured out the diluted drink and made myself a fresh one, set it out on the table too. Then I unwrapped the sandwich from Zeod's. I considered for a moment, fighting the urge just to sink my teeth into it, then went to the cabinet and brought back a serrated knife and small plate. I cut the sandwich into six equal pieces, taking unexpectedly deep pleasure in the texture of the kaiser roll's resistance to the knife's dull teeth, and arranged the pieces so they were equidistant on the plate. I returned the knife to my counter, then centered plate, candle and drink on the table in a way that soothed my grieving Tourette's. If I didn't stem my syndrome's needs I would never clear a space in which my own sorrow could dwell.

Then I went to my boom box and put on the saddest song in my CD collection, Prince's "How Come U Don't Call Me Anymore."

I don't know whether The Artist Formerly Known as Prince is Tourettic or obsessive-compulsive in his human life, but I know for certain he is deeply so in the life of his work. Music had never made much of an impression on me until the day in 1986 when, sitting in the passenger seat of Minna's Cadillac, I first heard the single "Kiss" squirting its manic way out of the car radio. To that point in my life I might have once or twice heard music that toyed with feelings of claustrophobic discomfort and expulsive release, and which in so doing passingly charmed my Tourette's, gulled it with a sense of recognition, like Art Carney or Daffy Duck — but here was a song that lived entirely in that territory, guitar and voice twitching and throbbing within obsessively delineated bounds, alternately silent and plosive. It so pulsed with Tourettic energies that I could surrender to its tormented, squeaky beat and let my syndrome live outside my brain for once, live in the air instead.

"Turn that shit down," said Minna.

"I like it," I said.

"That's that crap Danny listens to," said Minna. *Danny* was code for *too black.*

I knew I had to own that song, and so the next day I sought it out at J&R Music World — I needed the word "funk" explained to me by the salesman. He sold me a cassette, and a Walkman to play it on. What I ended up with was a seven-minute "extended single" version — the song I'd heard on the radio, with a four-minute catastrophe of chopping, grunting, hissing and slapping sounds appended — a coda apparently designed as a private message of confirmation to my delighted Tourette's brain.

Prince's music calmed me as much as masturbation or a cheeseburger. When I listened to him I was exempt from my symptoms. So I began collecting his records, especially those elaborate and frenetic remixes tucked away on the CD singles. The way he worried forty-five minutes of variations out of a lone musical or verbal phrase is, as far as I know, the nearest thing in art to my condition.

"How Come U Don't Call Me Anymore" is a ballad, piano strolling beneath an aching falsetto vocal. Slow and melancholy, it still featured the Tourettic abruptness and compulsive precision, the sudden shrieks and silences, that made Prince's music my brain's balm.

I put the song on repeat and sat in the light of my candle and waited for the tears. Only after they came did I allow myself to eat the six turkey-sandwich portions, in a ritual for Minna, alternating them with sips of Walker Red. *The body and the blood,* I couldn't keep from thinking, though I was as distant from any religious feeling as a mourning man could be. *The turkey and the booze,* I substituted. A last meal for Minna, who didn't get one. Prince moaned, finished his song, began it again. The candle guttered. I counted *three* as I finished a portion of sandwich, then *four.* That was the extent of my symptoms. I counted sandwiches and wept. At *six* I killed the music, blew out the candle and went to bed.

(Tourette Dreams)

(in Tourette dreams you shed your tics)

(or your tics shed you)

(and you go with them, astonished to leave yourself behind)

Bad Cookies

There are days when I get up in the morning and stagger into the bathroom and begin running water and then I look up and I don't even recognize my own toothbrush in the mirror. I mean, the object looks strange, oddly particular in its design, strange tapered handle and slotted, miter-cut bristles, and I wonder if I've ever looked at it closely before or whether someone snuck in overnight and substituted this new toothbrush for my old one. I have this relationship to objects in general — they will sometimes become uncontrollably new and vivid to me, and I don't know whether this is a symptom of Tourette's or not. I've never seen it described in the literature. Here's the strangeness of having a Tourette's brain, then: no control in my personal experiment of self. What might be only strangeness must always be auditioned for relegation to the domain of symptom, just as symptoms always push into other domains, demanding the chance to audition for their moment of acuity or relevance, their brief shot — coulda been a contender! — at centrality. Personalityness. There's a lot of traffic in my head, and it's two-way.

This morning's strangeness was refreshing, though. More than refreshing — revelatory. I woke early, having failed to draw my curtains, the wall above my bed and the table with melted candle, tumbler quarter full of melted ice, and sandwich crumbs from my ritual snack now caught in a blaze of white sunlight, like the glare of a projector's bulb before the film is threaded. It seemed possible I was the first awake in the world, possible the world was new. I dressed in my best suit, donned Minna's watch instead of my own, and clipped his beeper to my hip. Then I made myself coffee and toast, scooped the long-shadowed crumbs off the table, sat and savored breakfast, marveling at the richness of existence with each step. The radiator whined and sneezed and I imitated its sounds out of sheer joy, rather than helplessness. Perhaps I'd been expecting that Minna's absence would snuff the world, or at least Brooklyn, out of existence. That a sympathetic dimming would occur. Instead I'd woken into the realization that I was Minna's successor and avenger, that the city shone with clues.

It seemed possible I was a detective on a case.

I crept downstairs past Danny, who was

sleeping on his arms on the countertop, black suit jacket shrugged up around his shoulders, small patch of drool on his sleeve. I switched off the coffee machine, which was roasting a quarter inch of coffee into sour perfume, and went outside. It was a quarter to seven. The Korean keeper of the Casino was just rolling up his gate, tossing his bundles of the *News* and the *Post* inside. The morning was clarifyingly cold.

I started the L&L Pontiac. Let Danny sleep, let Gilbert wait in his cell, let Tony be missing. I'd go to the Zendo. Let it be too early for the monks or mobsters hidden there — I'd have the advantage of surprise.

By the time I'd parked and made my way to the Zendo, the Upper East Side was warming into life, shopkeepers rolling fruit stands out of their shops, sidewalk vendors of stripped paperbacks unloading their boxes, women already dressed for business glancing at their watches as they hustled their dogs' waste into Baggies. The doorman at the entranceway next door was someone new, a kid with a mustache and uniform, not my harasser from yesterday. He was probably green, without tenure, stuck working the end of the overnight shift. I figured it was worth a shot anyway. I crooked a finger at him through the glass and he came out into the cold.

"What's your name?" I said.

"Walter, sir."

"Walter sir — what?" I broadcast a cop-or-employer vibe.

"Walter is, uh, my last name. Can I help you with something?" He looked concerned, for himself and his building.

"*Helpmewalter* — I need the name of the doorman working last night, about six-thirty, seven. Older gentleman than yourself, maybe thirty-five, with an accent."

"Dirk?"

"Maybe. You tell me."

"Dirk's the regular man." He wasn't sure he should be telling me this.

I averted my gaze from his shoulder. "Good. Now tell me what you know about the Yorkville Zendo." I indicated the bronze plaque next door with a jerk of my thumb. "Dirkweed! Dirkman!"

"What?" He goggled his eyes at me.

"You see them come and go?"

"I guess."

"Walter Guessworth!" I cleared my throat deliberately. "Work with me here, Walter. You must see stuff. I want your impressions."

I could see him sorting through layers of

exhaustion, boredom, and stupidity. "Are you a cop?"

"Why'd you think that?"

"You, uh, talk funny."

"I'm a guy who needs to know things, Walter, and I'm in a hurry. Anyone come and go from the Zendo lately? Anything catch your eye?"

He scanned the street to see if anyone saw us talking. I took the opportunity to cover my mouth with my hand and make a brief panting sound, like an excited dog.

"Uh, not much happens late at night," said Walter. "It's pretty quiet around here."

"A place like the Zendo must attract some weird traffic."

"You keep saying Zendo," he said.

"It's right there, etched in brass." *Itched in Ass.*

He stepped toward the street, craned his neck, and read the plaque. "Hmmm. It's like a religious school, right?"

"Right. You ever see anyone suspicious hanging around? Big Polish guy in particular?"

"How would I know he was Polish?"

"Just think about big. We're talking really, really big."

He shrugged again. "I don't think so." His numb gaze wouldn't have taken in a crane and wrecking ball going through next door, let alone an outsize human figure.

"Listen, would you keep an eye out? I'll give you a number to call." I had a stash of L&L cards in my wallet, and I fished one out for him.

"Thanks," he said absently, glancing at the card. He wasn't afraid of me anymore. But he didn't know what to think of me if I wasn't a threat. I was interesting, but he didn't know how to be interested.

"I'd appreciate hearing from you — *Doorjerk! Doorjam! Jerkdom!* — if you see anything odd."

"You're pretty odd," he said seriously.

"Something besides me."

"Okay, but I get off in half an hour."

"Well, just keep it in mind." I was running out of patience with Walter. I freed myself to tap his shoulder farewell. The dull young man looked down at my hand, then went back inside.

I paced the block to the corner and back, flirting with the Zendo, seeking my nerve. The site aroused reverence and a kind of magical fear in me already, as though I were approaching a shrine — *the martyrdom of Saint Minna.* I wanted to rewrite their plaque to tell the story. Instead I rang the doorbell once. No answer. Then four more times, for a total of *five,* and I stopped, startled by a sense of completeness.

I'd shrugged off my tired old friend *six.*

I wondered if it was in some way commemorative — my counting tic moving down a list, subtracting a digit for Frank.

Somebody is hunting Minna Men, I thought again. But I couldn't be afraid. I wasn't game but hunter this morning. Anyway, the count was off — four Minna Men plus Frank made five. So if I was counting heads, I should be at four. I had an extra aboard, but who? Maybe it was Bailey. Or Irving.

A long minute passed before the girl with the short black hair and glasses opened the door and squinted at me against the morning sun. She wore a T-shirt, jeans, had bare feet, and held a broom. Her smile was slight, involuntary, and crooked. And sweet.

"Yes?"

"Could I ask you a few questions?"

"Questions?" She didn't seem to recognize the word.

"If it's not too early," I said gently.

"No, no. I've been up. I've been sweeping." She showed me the broom.

"They make you clean?"

"It's a privilege. Cleaning is treasured in

Zen practice. It's like the highest possible act. Usually Roshi wants to do the sweeping himself."

"No vacuum cleaner?" I said.

"Too noisy," she said, and frowned as if it should be obvious. A city bus roared past in the distance, damaging her point. I let it go.

Her eyes adjusted to the brightness, and she looked past me, to the street, examining it as though astonished to discover that the door opened onto a cityscape. I wondered if she'd been out of the building since I saw her enter the evening before. I wondered if she ate and slept there, whether she was the only one who did or whether there were dozens, foot soldiers of Zen.

"I'm sorry," she said. "What were you saying?"

"Questions."

"Oh, yes."

"About the Zendo, what you do here."

She looked me over now. "Do you want to come inside? It's cold."

"I'd like that very much."

It was the truth. I didn't feel unsafe following her into the dark temple, the Deathstar. I would gather information from within the Trojan Horse of her Zen grace. And I was conscious of my ticlessness, didn't want to break the rhythm of the conversation.

The foyer and stairwell were plain, with unadorned white walls and a wooden banister, looking as if it had been clean before she began sweeping, clean forever. We bypassed a door on the ground floor and went up the stairs, she carrying the broom ahead of her, turning her back to me trustingly. Her walk had a gentle jerkiness to it, a quickness like her replies.

"Here," she said, pointing to a rack with rows of shoes on it.

"I'm fine," I said, thinking I was supposed to select from among the motley footgear.

"No, take yours off," she whispered.

I did as she told me, removed my shoes and pushed them into an orderly place at the end of one of the racks. A chill went through me when I recalled that Minna had removed his shoes the evening before, presumably at this same landing.

Now in my socks, I followed her as the banister wrapped around through a corridor, past two sealed doors and one that opened onto a bare, dark room with rows of short cloth mats laid out across a parquet floor and a smell of candles or incense, not a morning smell at all. I wanted to peer inside but she hurried us along, up another flight.

On the third landing she led me to a small

kitchen where a wooden table and three chairs were arranged around a thwarted back window, through which an emaciated shaft of sunlight negotiated a maze of brick. If the massive buildings on either side had existed when this room was built they might not have bothered with a window. The table, chairs and cabinets of the kitchen were as undistinguished and homely as a museum diorama of Cree or Shaker life, but the teapot she set out was Japanese, and its hand-painted calligraphic designs were the only stretch, the only note of ostentation.

I seated myself with my back to the wall, facing the door, thinking of Minna and the conversation I'd heard through the wire. She took water off a low flame and filled the pot, then put a tiny mug without a handle in front of me and filled it with an unstrained swirling confetti of tea. I warmed my chapped hands around it gratefully.

"I'm Kimmery."

"Lionel." I felt *Kissdog* rising in me and fought it back.

"You're interested in Buddhism?"

"You could say that."

"I'm not really who you should talk to but I can tell you what they'll say. It's not about getting centered, or, you know, *stress reduction.* A lot of people — Americans, I mean

— have that idea. But it's really a religious discipline, and not easy at all. Do you know about zazen?"

"Tell me."

"It'll make your back hurt a *lot.* That's one thing." She rolled her eyes at me, already commiserating.

"You mean meditation."

"*Zazen,* it's called. Or *sitting.* It sounds like nothing, but it's the heart of Zen practice. I'm not very good at it."

I recalled the Quakers who'd adopted Tony, and their brick meetinghouse across eight lanes of traffic from St. Vincent's. Sunday mornings we could look through their tall windows and see them gathered in silence on hard benches.

"What's to be good at?" I said.

"You have no idea. Breathing, for starters. And thinking, except it's not supposed to *be* thinking."

"Thinking about not thinking?"

"*Not* thinking about it. One Mind, they call it. Like realizing that everything has Buddha nature, the flag and the wind are the same thing, that sort of stuff."

I wasn't exactly following her, but *One Mind* seemed an honorable goal, albeit positively chimerical. "Could we — could I sit with you sometime? Or is it done alone?"

"Both. But here at the Zendo there's regular sessions." She lifted her cup of tea with both hands, steaming her glasses instantly. "Anyone can come. And you're really lucky if you stick around today. Some important monks from Japan are in town to see the Zendo, and one of them is going to talk this evening, after zazen."

Important monks, imported rugs, unimportant ducks — jabber was building up in the ocean of my brain like flotsam, and soon a wave would toss it ashore. "So it's run out of Japan," I said. "And now they're checking up on you — like the Pope coming in from Rome."

"Not exactly. Roshi set the Zendo up on his own. Zen isn't centralized. There are different teachers, and sometimes they move around."

"But Roshi did come here from Japan." From the name I pictured a wizened old man, a little bigger than Yoda in *Return of the Jedi.*

"No, Roshi's American. He used to have an American name."

"Which was?"

"I don't know. *Roshi* just basically means teacher, but that's the only name he has anymore."

I sipped my scalding tea. "Does anyone

else use this building for anything?"

"Anything like what?"

"*Killing me!* — sorry. Just anything besides sitting."

"You can't shout like that in here," she said.

"Well, if — *kissing me!* — something strange was going on, say if Roshi were in some kind of trouble, would you know about it?" I twisted my neck — if I could I would have tied it in a knot, like the top of a plastic garbage bag. *"Eating me!"*

"I guess I don't know what you're talking about." She was oddly blasé, sipping her tea and watching me over the top of the cup. I recalled the legends of Zen masters slapping and kicking students to induce sudden realizations. Perhaps that practice was common here in the Zendo, and so she'd inured herself to outbursts, abrupt outlandish gestures.

"Forget it," I said. "Listen: Have you had any visitors lately?" I was thinking of Tony, who'd ostensibly called on the Zendo after our conference at L&L. "Anyone come sniffing around here last night?"

She only looked puzzled, and faintly annoyed. "No."

I considered pushing it, describing Tony to her, then decided he must have visited unseen, at least by Kimmery. Instead I asked, "Is there anybody in the building right now?"

"Well, Roshi lives on the top floor."

"He's up there now?" I said, startled.

"Sure. He's in *sesshin* — it's like an extended retreat — because of these monks. He took a vow of silence, so it's been a little quiet around here."

"Do you live here?"

"No. I'm cleaning up for morning zazen. The other students will show up in an hour. They're out doing work service now. That's how the Zendo can afford to pay the rent here. Wallace is downstairs already, but that's basically it."

"Wallace?" I was distracted by the tea leaves in my cup settling gradually into a mound at the bottom, like astronauts on a planet with barely any gravity.

"He's like this old hippie who hardly ever does anything but sit. I think his legs must be made of plastic or something. We went past him on the way up."

"Where? In the room with the mats?"

"Uh-huh. He's like a piece of furniture, easy to miss."

"Biggish, you mean?"

"Not so big. I meant still, he sits still." She whispered, "I always wonder if he's dead."

"But he's not a really *big* person."

"You wouldn't say that."

I plunged two fingers into my cup, needing to unsettle the floating leaves again, force them to resume their dance. If the girl saw me do it she didn't say anything.

"You haven't seen any really big people lately, have you?" Though I'd not encountered them yet, Roshi and Wallace seemed both unpromising suspects to be the Polish giant. I wondered if instead one might be the sardonic conversationalist I'd heard taunting Minna over the wire.

"Mmmmm, no," she said.

"Pierogi monster," I said, then coughed five times for cover. Thoughts of Minna's killers had overwhelmed the girl's calming influence — my brain sizzled with language, my body with gestures.

In reply she only refilled my cup, then moved the pot to the countertop. While her back was turned I stroked her chair, ran my palm over the warmth where she'd been sitting, played the spokes of the chair's back like a noiseless harp.

"Lionel? Is that your name?"

"Yes."

"You don't seem very calm, Lionel." She'd pivoted, almost catching my chair-molestation, and now she leaned back against the counter instead of retaking her seat.

I didn't ordinarily hesitate to reveal my syndrome, but something in me fought it now. "Do you have something to eat?" I said. Perhaps calories would restore my equilibrium.

"Um, I don't know," she said. "You want some bread or something? There might be some yogurt left."

"Because this tea is corked with caffeine. It only looks harmless. Do you drink this stuff all the time?"

"Well, it's sort of traditional."

"Is that part of the Zen thing, getting punchy so you can see God? Isn't that cheating?"

"It's more just to stay awake. Because we don't really have God in Zen Buddhism." She turned away from me and began rifling through the cabinets, but didn't quit her musings. "We just sit and try not to fall asleep, so I guess in a way staying awake *is* seeing God, sort of. So you're right."

The little triumph didn't thrill me. I was feeling trapped, with the wizened teacher a floor above me and the plastic-legged hippie a floor below. I wanted to get out of the Zendo now, but I hadn't figured a next move.

And when I left I wanted to take Kimmery with me. I wanted to protect her — the impulse surged in me, looking to affix to a suitable target. Now that I'd failed Minna, who deserved my protection? Was it Tony? Was it Julia? I wished that Frank would whisper a clue in my ear from the beyond. In the meantime, Kimmery would do.

"Here, do you want some Oreos?"

"Sure," I said distractedly. "Buddhists eat Oreos?"

"We eat anything we want, Lionel. This isn't Japan." She took a blue carton of cookies and put it on the table.

I helped myself, craving the snack, glad we weren't in Japan.

"I used to know this guy who once worked for Nabisco," she said, musing as she bit into a cookie. "You know, the company that makes Oreos? He said they had two main plants for making Oreos, in different parts of the country. Two head bakers, you know, different quality control."

"Uh —" I took a cookie and dunked it in my tea.

"And he used to swear he could tell the difference just by tasting them. This guy, when we ate Oreos, he would just go through the pack sniffing them and tasting the chocolate part and then he'd put the bad ones in a pile. And like, a really good package was one where less than a third had to go in the bad pile, because they were from the wrong bakery, you know? But sometimes there wouldn't be more than five or six good ones in a whole package."

"Wait a minute. You're saying every package of Oreos has cookies from *both* bakeries?"

"Uh-huh."

I tried to keep from thinking about it, tried to keep it in the blind spot of my obsessiveness, the way I would flinch my eyes from a tempting shoulder. But it was impossible. "What motive could they possibly have for mixing batches in the same package?"

"Well, easy. If word got out that one bakery was better than the other, they wouldn't want people, you know, *shunning* whole cartons, or maybe even whole truckloads, whole deliveries of Oreos. They'd have to keep them mixed up, so you'd buy any package knowing you'd probably get some good ones."

"So you're saying they ship batches from the two bakeries to one central boxing location just to mix them together."

"I guess that's what it would entail, isn't it?" she said brightly.

"That's stupid," I said, but it was only the sound of my crumbling resistance.

She shrugged. "All I know is we'd eat them and he'd be frantically building this pile of rejected cookies. And he'd be pushing them at me saying, 'See, see?' I could never tell the difference."

No, no, no, no.

Eatmeoreo, I mouthed inaudibly. I crinkled in the cellophane sleeve for another cookie, then nibbled off the overhang of chocolate top. I let the pulverized crumbs saturate my tongue, then reached for another, performed the same operation. They were identical. I put both nibbled cookies in the same pile. I needed to find a good one, or a bad one, before I could tell the difference.

Maybe I'd only ever eaten bad ones.

"I thought you didn't believe me," said Kimmery.

"Mushytest," I mumbled, my lips pasty with cookie mud, my eyes wild as I considered the task my brain had set for my sorry tongue. There were three sleeves in the box of Oreos. We were into just the first of them.

She nodded at my pile of discards. "What are those, good ones or bad ones?"

"I don't know." I tried sniffing the next. "Was this guy your boyfriend or something?"

"For a little while."

"Was he a Zen Buddhist too?"

She snorted lightly. I nibbled another cookie and began to despair. I would have been happy now for an ordinary interruptive tic, something to throw my bloodhoundlike obsessions off the scent. The Minna Men were in shambles, yes, but I'd get to the bottom of the Oreo conundrum.

I jumped to my feet, rattling both our teacups. I had to get out of there, quell my panic, restart my investigation, put some distance between myself and the cookies.

"Barnamum Bakery!" I yelped, reassuring myself.

"What?"

"Nothing." I jerked my head sideways, then turned it slowly, as if to work out a kink. "We'd better go, Kimmery."

"Go where?" She leaned forward, her pupils big and trusting. I felt a thrill at being taken so seriously. This making the rounds without Gilbert could get to be a habit. For once I was playing lead detective instead of comic — or Tourettic — relief.

"Downstairs," I said, at a loss for a better answer.

"Okay," she said, whispering conspiratorially. "But be quiet."

We crept past the half-open door on the

second landing, and I retrieved my shoes from the rack. This time I got a look at Wallace. He sat with his back to us, limp blond hair tucked behind his ears and giving way to a bald spot. He wore a sweater and sweatpants and sat still as advertised, inert, asleep, or, I suppose, dead — though death was not a still thing to me at the moment, more a matter of skid marks in blood and the Brooklyn-Queens Expressway. Wallace looked harmless anyway. Kimmery's idea of a hippie, apparently, was a white man over forty-five not in a business suit. In Brooklyn we would have just said *loser.*

She opened the front door of the Zendo. "I've got to finish cleaning," she said. "You know, for the monks."

"*Im*portantmonks," I said, ticcing gently.

"Yes."

"I don't think you should be alone here." I looked up and down the block to see if anyone was watching us. My neck prickled, alert to wind and fear. The Upper East Siders had retaken their streets, and walked obliviously crinkling doggie-doo bags and the *New York Times* and the wax paper around bagels. My feeling of advantage, of beginning my investigation while the world was still asleep, was gone.

"I'm *con — worried,*" I said, Tourette's

mangling my speech again. I wanted to get away from her before I shouted, barked, or ran my fingers around the neck of her T-shirt.

She smiled. "What's that — like confused and worried?"

I nodded. It was close enough.

"I'll be okay. Don't be conworried." She spoke calmly, and it calmed me. "You'll come back later, right? To sit?"

"Absolutely."

"Okay." She craned up on her toes and kissed my cheek. Startled, I couldn't move, stood instead feeling her kiss-print burning on my flesh in the cold morning air. Was it personal, or some sort of fuzzy Zen coercion? Were they that desperate to fill mats at the Zendo?

"Don't do that," I said. "You just met me. This is New York."

"Yes, but you're my friend now."

"I have to go."

"Okay," she said. "Zazen is at four o'clock."

"I'll be there."

She shut the door. I was alone on the street again, my investigation already at a standstill. Had I learned anything inside the Zendo? Now I felt dazed with loss — I'd penetrated the citadel and spent my whole time contemplating Kimmery and Oreos. My mouth was full of cocoa, my nostrils full of her scent from the unexpected kiss.

Two men took me by the elbows and hustled me into a car waiting at the curb.

The four of them wore identical blue suits with black piping on the legs, and identical black sunglasses. They looked like a band that plays at weddings. Four white guys, assortedly chunky, pinched in the face, with pimples, and indistinct. Their car was a rental. Chunky sat in the backseat waiting and when the two who'd picked me up crushed me into the back beside him, he immediately put his arm around my neck in a sort of brotherly choke hold. The two who'd picked me off the street — Pimples and Indistinct — jammed in beside me, to make four of us on the backseat. It was a bit crowded.

"Get in the front," said Chunky, the one holding my neck.

"Me?" I said.

"Shut up. Larry, get out. There's too many. Go in the front."

"Okay, okay," said the one on the end, Indistinct or Larry. He got out of the back and into the empty front passenger seat and the one driving — Pinched — took off. Chunky loosened his hold when we got into the downtown traffic on Second Avenue, but left his arm draped over my shoulders.

"Take the Drive," he said.

"What?"

"Tell him take the East Side Drive."

"Where are we going?"

"I want to be on the highway."

"Why not just drive in circles?"

"My car is parked up here," I said. "You could drop me off."

"Shut up. Why can't we just drive in circles?"

"You shut up. It should look like we're going somewhere, stupid. We're really scaring him going in circles."

"I'm listening to what you say no matter how you drive," I said, wanting to make them feel better. "There's four of you and one of me."

"We want more than listening," said Chunky. "We want you scared."

But I wasn't scared. It was eight-thirty in the morning, and we were fighting traffic on Second Avenue. There weren't even any circles to go in, just honking delivery trucks tied up by pedestrians. And the closer I looked at these guys the less I was impressed. For one thing, Chunky's hand on my neck was soft, his skin was soft, and his hold on me rather tender. And he was the toughest of the bunch. They weren't calm, they weren't good at what they were doing, and they weren't tough. None of them, as far as I could tell, was wearing a gun.

For another thing, all four of their sunglasses still bore price tags, dangling fluorescent orange ovals reading $6.99!

I reached out and batted at Pimples's price tag. He turned away, and my finger hooked the earpiece and jerked the shades off his face, into his lap. "Shit," said Pimples, and hurried the glasses back onto his face as if I might recognize him without them.

"Hey, none of that," said Chunky, and hugged me again. He reminded me of my long-ago kissing tic, the way he was crowding me close to him in the car.

"Okay," I said, though I knew it would be hard not to bat at the price tags if they came within reach. "But what's the game here, guys?"

"We're supposed to throw a scare into you," said Chunky, distracted, watching Pinched drive. "Stay away from the Zendo, that sort of thing. Hey, take the fucking Drive. Seventy-ninth Street there's an on-ramp."

"I can't get over," complained Pinched,

eyeing lanes of traffic.

"What so great about the FDR?" said Indistinct. "Why can't we stay on the streets?"

"What, you want to pull over and rough him up on Park Avenue?" said Chunky.

"Maybe just a scare without the roughing-up will do," I suggested. "Get this over with, get on with the day."

"Stop him talking so much."

"Yeah, but he's got a point."

"Eatmepointman!"

Chunky clamped his hand over my mouth. At that moment I heard a high-pitched two-note signal. The four of them, and me, began looking around the car for the source of the noise. It was as if we were in a video game and had crossed up to the next level, were about to be destroyed by aliens we couldn't see coming. Then I realized that the beeping issued from my coat pocket: Minna's beeper going off.

"What's that?"

I twisted my head free. Chunky didn't fight me. "Barnamum Beeper," I said.

"What's that, some special kind? Get it out of his pocket. Didn't you chumps frisk him?"

"Screw you."

"Jesus."

They put their hands on me and quickly found the beeper. The digital readout showed a Brooklyn-Queens-Bronx prefix on the number. "Who's that?" said Pimples.

I frowned and shrugged: didn't know. Truly, I didn't recognize the number. Someone who thought Minna was still alive, I guessed, and shuddered a little. That scared me more than my abductors did.

"Make him call it," said Pinched from the front.

"You want to pull over to let him call?"

"Larry, you got the phone?"

Indistinct turned in his seat and offered me a cell phone.

"Call the number."

I dialed, they waited. We inched down Second Avenue. The airspace of the car hummed with tension. The cell phone rang, *dit-dit-dit,* a miniature, a toy that effortlessly commanded our focus, our complete attention. I might have popped it in my mouth and gulped it down instead of holding it to my ear. *Dit-dit-dit,* it rang again, then somebody picked up.

Garbage Cop.

"Lionel?" said Loomis.

"Mmmmhuh," I replied, squelching an outburst.

"Get this. What's the difference between

three hundred sixty-five blow jobs and a radial tire?"

"Don'tcare!" I shouted. The four in the car all jumped.

"One's a Goodyear, the other's a *great year,*" said Loomis proudly. He knew he'd nailed the riddle, no faltering this time, not a word out of place.

"Where are you calling from?" I asked.

"You called me."

"You beeped me, Loomis. Where are you?"

"I don't know" — his voice dimmed — "hey, what's the name of this place? Oh, yeah? Thanks. Bee-Bee-Que? Really, just like that, three letters? Go figure. Lionel, you there?"

"Here."

"It's a diner called B-B-Q, just like barbecue, only three letters. I eat here all the time, and I never even knew that!"

"Why'd you beep me, Loomis?" *Beep and Rebeep are sitting on a fence —*

"You told me to. You wanted that address, right? Ullman, the dead guy."

"Uh, that's right," I said, shrugging at Chunky, who still held my neck, but lightly, leaving me room to place the phone. He scowled at me, but it wasn't my fault if he was confused. I was confused, too. Confused and conworried.

"Well, I got it right here," said the Garbage Cop pridefully.

"What's the good of driving him around watching him make a phone call?" complained Pimples.

"Take it away from him," said Pinched from the driver's seat.

"Just punch him in the stomach," said Indistinct. "Make him scared."

"You got someone there with you?" said Loomis.

The four in the car had begun to chafe at seeing their faint authority slip away, devolve to the modern technology, the bit of plastic and wire in my palm. I had to find a way to calm them down. I nodded and widened my eyes to show my cooperation, and mouthed a just-wait signal to them, hoping they'd recall the protocol from crime movies: pretend they weren't there listening, and thus gather information on the sly.

I couldn't help it that they *weren't* actually listening.

"Tell me the address," I said.

"Okay, here goes," said Loomis. "Got a pen?"

"Whose address?" whispered Chunky in my other ear. He'd caught my hint. He was schooled enough in the clichés to be manipulable; his compatriots I wasn't so sure of.

"Tell me *Ullman's* address," I said for their sake. *Man-Salad-Dress* went my brain. I swallowed hard to keep it from crossing the threshold.

"Yeah, I got it," said the Garbage Cop sarcastically. "Whose else would you want?"

"Ullman?" said Chunky, not to me but to Pimples. "He's talking about *Ullman?*"

"Whose! A! Dress!" I shrieked.

"Aw, quit," said Loomis, jaded by now. My other audience wasn't so blasé. Pimples ripped the cell phone out of my hand, and Chunky wrestled my arm behind my back so I was wrenched forward nearly against the back of the driver's seat, and down. It was like he wanted me draped in his lap for a spanking. Meanwhile, up front, Pinched and Indistinct began arguing fiercely about parking, about whether they'd fit in some spot.

Pimples put the phone to his own ear and listened, but Loomis hung up, or maybe just got quiet and listened back, so they were silent together. Pinched managed to park, or double-park — I couldn't tell which from my strained vantage. The two up front were still muttering at one another, but Chunky was quiet, just turning my arm another degree or two, experimenting with actually hurting me, trying it on for size.

"You don't like hearing the name *Ullman,*" I said, wincing.

"Ullman was a friend," said Chunky.

"Don't let him talk about Ullman," said Pinched.

"This is stupid," said Indistinct, with consummate disgust.

"You're stupid," said Chunky. "We're supposed to scare a guy, let's do it."

"I'm not so scared," I said. "You guys seem more scared to me. Scared of talking about Ullman."

"Yeah, well, if we're scared you don't know why," said Chunky. "And don't guess either. Don't open your trap."

"You're scared of a big Polish guy," I said.

"This is stupid," said Indistinct again. He sounded like he might cry. He got out of the car and slammed the door behind him.

Pimples finally quit listening to the silence Loomis had left behind on the cell phone, shut it down, and put it on the seat between us.

"What if we are scared of him?" said Chunky. "We ought to be, take it from us. We wouldn't be working for him if we weren't." He loosened his grip on my arm, so I was able to straighten up and look around. We were parked outside a popular coffee shop on Second. The window was full of sullen kids flirting by working on tiny computers and reading magazines. They didn't notice us, carful of lugs, and why should they?

Indistinct was nowhere to be seen.

"I sympathize," I said, to keep them talking. "I'm scared of the big guy, too. It's just you can't throw a scare so good when you're scared."

I thought of Tony. If he'd come to the Zendo last night shouldn't he have triggered the same alarm I had? Shouldn't he have drawn these would-be toughs, this clown car loaded with fresh graduates from Clown College?

"What's so not scary about us?" said Pinched. He said to Chunky, "Hurt him already."

"You can hurt me but you still won't scare me," I said distractedly. One part of my brain was thinking, *Handle with scare, scandal with hair,* and so on. Another part was puzzling over the Tony question.

"Who was that on the phone?" said Pimples, still working on the problem he'd selected as his own.

"You wouldn't believe me," I said.

"Try us," said Chunky, twisting my arm.

"Just a guy doing research for me, that's all. I wanted Ullman's address. My partner got arrested for the murder."

"See, you shouldn't *have* a guy doing research," said Chunky. "That's the whole problem. Getting involved, visiting Ullman's apartment, that's the kind of thing we're supposed to scare you about."

Scare me, skullman, sang my disease. *Skullamum Bailey. Skinnyman Brainy.*

"Hurt him and scare him and let's get out of here," said Pinched. "I don't like this. Larry was right, it is stupid. I don't care about who's doing research."

"I still want to know who was on the phone," said Pimples.

"Listen," said Chunky, now trying to reason with me, as his gang's morale and focus — and actual numbers — were dwindling. "We're here on behalf of the big guy you're talking about, see? That's who sent us." He offered the morphic resonance theory: "So if he scares you you ought to be scared by us, without us having to hurt you."

"Guys like you could *kill* me and you still wouldn't scare me," I said.

"This was a bad idea," concluded

Pinched, and he, too, got out of the car. The front seats were empty now, the steering wheel unmanned. "This isn't us," he said, leaning back in, addressing Pimples and Chunky. "We're no good at this." He raised his eyebrows at me. "You'll have to forgive us. This isn't what we do. We're men of peace." He shut the door. I turned my head enough to see him scooting down the block, his walk like a hectic bird's.

"Scaredycop!" I shouted.

"Where?" said Chunky, immediately releasing my arm. They both swiveled their heads in a panic, eyes wild behind the dark glasses, orange price tags dancing like fishing lures. Freed at last, I turned my head too, not searching for anything, of course, instead for the pleasure of aping their movements.

"Screw this," muttered Pimples.

He and Chunky both fled the rental car, hot on Pinched's heels, leaving me alone there.

Pinched had taken the car keys, but Indistinct's cell phone sat abandoned on the seat beside me. I put it in my pocket. Then I leaned over the seat, popped the glove compartment, and found the rental agency's registration card and receipt. The car was on a six-month lease to the Fujisaki Corporation, 1030 Park Avenue. The zip code, I was pretty sure, put it in the same zone as the Zendo. Which is where I was, as it happened. I rapped on the rental car's glove compartment door five times, but it wasn't particularly resonant or satisfying.

On my walk over to 1030 Park I flipped open the cell phone and rang L&L. I'd never made a street call before, and felt quite Captain Kirk-ish.

"L&L," said a voice, the one I'd hoped to hear.

"Tony, it's me," I said. "Essrog." That was how Minna always started a phone call: *Lionel, it's Minna.* You're the first name, I'm the last. In other words: You're the jerk and I'm the jerk's boss.

"Where are you?" said Tony.

Crossing Lexington at Seventy-sixth Street was the answer. But I didn't want to tell him.

Why? I wasn't sure. Anyway, I let a tic do my talking: "Kiss me, scareyman!"

"I got worried about you, Lionel. Danny said you went off with the Garbage Cop on some kind of a mission."

"Well, sort of."

"He with you now?"

"Garbage cookie," I said seriously.

"Why don't you head back here, Lionel? We ought to talk."

"I'm investigating a case," I said. *A guess tic eating a vest.*

"Oh, yeah? Where's it taking you?"

A well-coiffed man in a blue suit turned off Lexington ahead of me. He had a cell phone pressed to his right ear. I aligned myself behind him and imitated his walk.

"Various places," I said.

"Name one."

The harder Tony asked, the less I wanted to say. "I was hoping we could, you know, triangulate a little. Compare data."

"Give me an example, Lionel."

"Like did you — *Vesticulate! Guessticalot!* — did you get anything out of that, uh, Zendo place last night?"

"I'll tell you about it when I see you. Right now there's something important, you ought to get back here. What are you, at a pay phone?"

"Vestphone!" I said. "By any chance did a carful of guys try to warn you off?"

"Fuck you talking about?"

"What about the girl I saw go in before Minna? Did you find out about her?" Even as I asked I got the answer to the question I was asking, the real question.

I didn't trust Tony.

I felt the truth of it in the pause before he replied.

"I learned a few things," he said. "But at the moment we need to pool our resources, Lionel. You need to get back here. Because we got some problems coming up."

Now I could hear the bluff in his voice. It was casual, easy. He wasn't straining particularly. It was only Essrog on the line, after all.

"I know about problems," I said. "Gilbert's in jail on a murder charge."

"Well, that's just one."

"You weren't at the Zendo last night," I said. The man in the blue suit turned onto Park Avenue, still gabbing. I let him go, and stood in a crowd at the corner, waiting for the light to change.

"Maybe you ought to worry about your own fucking self and not me, Lionel," said Tony. "Where were *you* last night?"

"I did what I was supposed to do," I said, wanting to provoke him now. "I told Julia. Actually, she already knew." I left out the part about the homicide cop.

"That's interesting. I've been sort of wondering where Julia goes off to. I hope you found out."

Alarms went off. Tony was trying to make his voice casual, but it wasn't working.

"Wondering when? You mean she goes out of town a lot?"

"Maybe."

"Anyway, how'd you know she went anywhere?"

"Fuck you think we do around here, Lionel? We learn things."

"Yeah, we're a leading outfit. Gilbert's in jail, Tony." My eyes were suddenly full of tears. I knew I should be trying to focus on the Julia problem, but our betrayal of Gilbert felt more immediate.

"I know. He's safer there. Come in and talk, Lionel."

I crossed with the crowd but stopped halfway, at the traffic island in the middle of Park Avenue. The thumbnail of garden was marked with a sign that read VALIANT DAFFODIL (N. AMERICA), but the ground was chewed and pocked and vacant, as if someone had just dug up a plot of dead bulbs. I sat on the wooden embankment there and let the crowd pass by, until the light turned red again and the traffic began to whiz past me. A strip of sunshine laced the avenue and warmed me on the bench. Park Avenue's giant apartment buildings were ornate with shadow in the midmorning light. I was like a castaway on my island there, in a river of orange cabs.

"Where are you, Freakshow?"

"Don't call me Freakshow," I said.

"What should I call you — Buttercup?"

"Valiant Daffodil," I blurted. "Alibi Diffident."

"Where are you, Daffodil?" said Tony rather sweetly. "Should we come get you?"

"Goodcop, buttercup," I said, ticcing on through my tears. By calling me Freakshow — Minna's nickname — Tony had cued my Tourette's, had cut right through the layers of coping strategies and called out my giddy teenage voice. It should have been a relief to tic freely with one who knew me so well. But I didn't trust him. Minna was dead and I didn't trust Tony and I didn't know what it meant.

"Tell me where your little investigation led you," said Tony.

I looked up at Park Avenue, the monolithic walls of old money stretched out, a furrow of stone.

"I'm in Brooklyn," I lied. *"Eatmegreenpoint."*

"Oh, yeah? What's in Greenpoint?"

"I'm looking for the — *Greenpope!* — the guy who killed Minna, the Polish guy. What do you think?"

"Just wandering around looking for him, huh?"

"Eatmephone!"

"Hanging out in Polish bars, that sort of thing?"

I barked and clicked my tongue. My agitated jaw jerked against the redial button and a sequence of tones played on the line. The light changed and the cabs crossing Park blared their horns, working through gridlock. Another raft of pedestrians passed over my island and back into the river.

"Doesn't sound like Greenpoint," said Tony.

"They're filming a movie out here. You should see this. They've got Greenpoint — *Greenphone! Creepycone! Phonyman!* — Greenpoint Avenue set up to look like Manhattan. All these fake buildings and cabs and extras dressed up like they're on Park Avenue or something. So that's what you're hearing."

"Who's in it?"

"What?"

"Who's in the movie?"

"Somebody said Mel — *Gisspod, Gasspoint, Pissphone* —"

"Mel Gibson."

"Yeah. But I haven't seen him, just a lot of extras."

"And they really got fake buildings out there?"

"Did you sleep with Julia, Tony?"

"Why'd you want to go and say that?"

"Did you?"

"Who you trying to protect, Daffodil? Minna's dead."

"I want to know."

"I'll tell you in person when you get in here already."

"Dickety Daffodil! Dissident Crocophile! Laughable Chocodopolus!"

"Ah, I heard it all before."

"Likable lunchphone, veritable spongefist, teenage mutant Zendo lungfish, penis Milhaus Nixon tuning fork."

"You fucking Tugboat."

"Good-bye, Tonybailey."

Ten-thirty Park Avenue was another stone edifice, unremarkable among its neighbors. The oak doors split the difference between magnificence and military sturdiness, tiny windows barred with iron: French Colonial Bomb Shelter. The awning showed just the numerals, no gaudy, pretentious building name like you'd see on Central Park West or in Brooklyn Heights — here nothing remained to be proved, and anonymity was a value greater than charisma. The building had a private loading zone and a subtle curb cut, though, which sang of money, payoffs to city officials, and of women's-shoe heels too fragile to tangle with the usual four-inch step, too expensive to risk miring in dog shit. A special curb man stood patrolling the front, ready to open car doors or kick dogs or turn away unwanted visitors before they even tarnished the lobby. I came down the block at a good clip and swiveled to the door at the last minute, faking him out.

The lobby was wide and dark, designed to blind an unfamiliar visitor coming in from the sunlight. A crowd of doormen in white gloves and familiar blue suits with black piping on the legs surrounded me the minute I stumbled through the doors. It was the same uniform worn by the lugs in the rental car.

So they hadn't been lugs by training — that much was obvious. They were doormen, no shame in that. But *men of peace?*

"Help you with something?"

"Help you sir?"

"Name?"

"All visitors must be announced."

"Delivery?"

"Have you got a name?"

They encircled me, five or six them, not on special assignment but instead doing exactly what they were trained to do. Loom in the gloom. In their white gloves and their right context they were much scarier than they had been loaded into a rental car and fumbling as hoods. Their propriety was terrifying. I didn't see Pinched, Pimples, Chunky or Indistinct among them, but it was a big building. Instead I'd drawn Shadowface, Shadowface, Shadowface, Tallshadowface, and Shadowface.

"I'm here to see Fujisaki," I said. "Man, woman or corporation."

"There must be a mistake."

"Wrong building, surely."

"There is no Fujisaki."

"Name?"

"Fujisaki Management Corporation," I said.

"No."

"No. Not here. That isn't right."

"No."

"Name? Who's calling, sir?"

I took out one of Minna's cards. "Frank Minna," I said. The name came easily, and I didn't feel any need to distort it the way I would my own.

The band of doormen around me loosened at the sight of a business card. I'd shown a first glimmer of legitimacy. They were a top grade of doorman, finely tuned, factoring vigilance against hair-trigger sycophantic instincts.

"Expected?"

"Sorry?"

"Expected by the party in question? Appointment? Name? Contact?"

"Dropping in."

"Hmmm."

"No."

"No."

Another minute correction ensued. They bunched closer. Minna's card disappeared.

"There may be some confusion."

"Yes."

"Probably there is."

"Wrong building completely."

"Should there be a destination for a message, what would a message be?"

"On the chance that the destination in question is this one. You understand, sir."

"Yes."

"Yes."

"No message," I said. I tapped the nearest doorman's suit breast. He darted back, scowling. But they were penguins now. I had to touch them all. I reached for the next, the tallest, tried to high-five his shoulder and just grazed it. The circle loosened around me again as I spun. They might have thought I was staining them with invisible swatches of blacklight paint for future identification or planting electronic bugs or just plain old spreading cooties, from the way they jumped.

"No."

"Look out."

"Can't have this."

"Can't have this here."

"Out."

Then two of them had me by the elbows, and I was steered out onto the sidewalk.

I took a stroll around the block, just to glean what I could from the north face of the building. I was shadowed by the curb man, of course, but I didn't mind. The staff entrance smelled of a private dry-cleaning service, and the disposal bins showed signs of bulk food orders, perhaps an in-house grocery. I wondered if the building housed a private chef, too. I thought about poking my head in to see but the curb man was muttering tensely into a walkie-talkie, and I figured I'd probably better distance myself. I waved good-bye and he waved back involuntarily — everyone's a little ticcish that way sometimes.

Between bites of hot dog and gulps of papaya juice I dialed the Garbage Cop's office. The Papaya Czar on Eighty-sixth Street and Third Avenue is my kind of place

— bright orange and yellow signs pasted on every available surface screaming, PAPAYA IS GOD'S GREATEST GIFT TO MAN'S HEALTH! OUR FRANKFURTERS ARE THE WORKING MAN'S FILET MIGNON! WE'RE POLITE NEW YORKERS, WE SUPPORT MAYOR GIULIANI! And so on. Papaya Czar's walls are so layered with language that I find myself immediately calmed inside their doors, as though I've stepped into a model interior of my own skull.

I washed down the tangy nubbin of the first dog while the phone rang. Papaya Czar's product did emulate an expensive steak's melting-in-your-mouthiness, frankfurters apparently skinless and neither bun nor dog crisped in the cooking, so they slid together into hot-dog cream on the tongue. These virtues could be taken in excess and leave one craving the greater surface tension of a Nathan's dog, but I was in the mood for the Czar's today. I had four more laid out in a neat row on the counter where I sat, each with a trim line of yellow mustard for an exclamation — *five* was still my angel.

As for papaya itself, I might as well be drinking truffula seed nectar or gryphon milk, for all I knew — I'd never encountered the fruit in any form except the Czar's chalky beverage.

"Sanitation Inspector Loomis," answered the Garbage Cop.

"Listen, Loomis. I'm working on this Gilbert thing." I knew I needed to tie it in to his friend's plight to keep him focused. In fact, Gilbert was now the furthest thing from my mind. "I need you to pull up some information for me."

"That you, Lionel?"

"Yeah. Listen. Ten-three-oh Park Avenue. Write that down. I need some records on the building, management company, head of the board, whatever you can find out. See if any names you recognize pop up."

"Recognize from where?"

"From, uh, around the neighborhood." I was thinking *Frank Minna,* but I didn't want to say it. "Oh, one in particular. Fujisaki. It's Japanese."

"I don't know any Fujisaki from around the neighborhood."

"Just look up the records, Loomis. Call me back when you get something."

"Call you back where?"

I'd gotten the beeper and the cell phone mixed up. I was collecting other people's electronics. In fact, I didn't know the number of the phone I'd borrowed from the doorman in sunglasses. I wondered for the first time who I'd find myself talking to if I answered the incoming calls.

"Forget it," I said. "You've still got Minna's beeper number?"

"Sure."

"Use that. I'll call you."

"When do we bail out Gilbert?"

"I'm working on it. Listen, Loomis, I'd better go. Get back to me, all right?"

"Sure thing, Lionel. And, buddy?"

"What?"

"Good stature, man," said Loomis. "You're holding up great."

"Uh, thanks Loomis." I ended the call, put the cell phone back into my jacket pocket.

"Kee-rist," said a man sitting on my right. He was a guy in his forties. He wore a suit. As Minna said more than once, in New York any chucklehead can wear a suit. Satisfied he wasn't a doorman, I ignored him, worked on dog number three.

"I was in this restaurant in L.A.," he started. "Great place, million-dollar place. All the food is tall, you know what I mean? Tall food? There's this couple at a table, both of them talking on fucking cell phones, just like you got there. Two different conversations through the whole meal, yakking all over each other, what *Cindy* said, get away for the *weekend,* gotta work on my *game,* the whole nine yards. You couldn't hear yourself think over the racket."

I finished dog three in five evenly spaced bites, licked the mustard off my thumb tip, and picked up number four.

"I thought L.A., fair enough. Chalk it up. You can't expect any different. So couple months ago I'm trying to impress a client, take him to Balthazar, you know, downtown? Million-dollar place, take it from me. Tall food, *gangly* food. So what do I see but a couple of bozos at the bar talking on cell phones. My water's getting hot, but I figure, bar, fair enough, that's showing decent respect. Adjust my standards, whatever. So we get a table after waiting fifteen fucking minutes, sit down and my client's phone rings, he takes it out at the table! Guy I was with! Sits there yakking! Ten, fifteen minutes!"

I enjoyed dog four in Zen-like calm and silence, practicing for my coming *zazen.*

"Never thought I'd see it in here, though. Fucking California, Balthazar, whatever, all these guys with crap in their hair and million-dollar wristwatches like Dick Tracy I guess I gotta adjust my standards to the modern universe but I thought at the very least I could sit here eat a fucking hot dog without listening to yak yak yak."

I'd apportioned a fifth of my papaya juice for rinsing down the last dog. Suddenly impatient to leave, I stuffed a wad of napkins in my jacket pocket and took the dog and the drink in hand and headed back out into the bright cold day.

"Fucking people talking to themselves in a public place like they got some kind of illness!"

The beeper went off just as I got to the car. I drew it out for a look: another unfamiliar number in 718. I got into the car and called from the cell phone, ready to be irritated with Loomis.

"DickTracyphone," I said into the mouthpiece.

"This is Matricardi and Rockaforte," went a gravelly voice. Rockaforte. Though I'd heard them speak just two or three times in fifteen years, I would have known his voice anywhere.

Through the windshield I viewed Eighty-third Street, midday, November. A couple of women in expensive coats mimed a Manhattan conversation for my benefit, trying to persuade me of their reality. On the line, though, I heard an old man's breathing, and what I saw through the windshield wasn't real at all.

I considered that I was answering Minna's beeper. Did they know he was dead? Would I have to deliver the news to The Clients? I felt my throat constrict, instantly throbbing with fear and language.

"Speak to me," rasped Rockaforte.

"Larval Pushbug," I said softly, trying to offer my name. Did The Clients even know it? "Papaya Pissbag." I was tic-gripped, helpless. "*Not*Minna," I said at last. "*Not*Frank. Frank's*dead.*"

"We know, Lionel," said Rockaforte.

"Who told you?" I whispered, controlling a bark.

"Things don't escape," he said. He paused, breathed, went on. "We're very sorry for you in this time."

"You found out from Tony?"

"We found out. We find out what we need. We learn."

But do you kill? I wanted to ask. *Do you command a Polish giant?*

"We're concerned for you," he said. "The information is that you are running, going here and there, unable to sit still. We hear this, and it concerns."

"What information?"

"And that Julia has left her home in this time of mourning. That nobody knows where she has gone unless it is you."

"Nojulia, nobody, nobodyknows."

"You still suffer. We see this and we suffer as well."

This was somewhat obscure to me, but I wasn't going to ask.

"We wish to speak with you, Lionel. Will you come and talk to us?"

"We're talking now," I breathed.

"We wish to see you standing before us. It's important in this time of pain. Come see us, Lionel."

"Where? New Jersey?" Heart racing, I allowed soothing permutations to course through my brain: *Garden state bricko and stuckface garbage face grippo and suckfast garter snake ticc-o and circus.* My lips rustled at the phone, nearly giving the words breath.

"We're in the Brooklyn house," he said. "Come."

"Scarface! Cigarfish!"

"What's got you running, Lionel?"

"Tony. You've been talking to Tony. He said I'm running. I'm not running."

"You sound running."

"I'm looking for the killer. Tony's trying to stop me, I think."

"You have a problem with Tony?"

"I don't trust him. He's acting — *Stuccotash!* — he's acting strangely."

"Let me speak," came a voice in the background of the call. Rockaforte's voice was replaced with Matricardi's: higher, more mellifluous, a single-malt whiskey instead of Dewar's.

"What's wrong with Tony?" said Matricardi. "You don't trust him in this matter?"

"I don't trust him," I repeated dumbly. I thought about ending the call. Again I consulted my other senses: I was in the sunshine in Manhattan in an L&L vehicle talking on a doorman's cell phone. I could discard Minna's beeper, forget about the call, go anywhere. The Clients were like players in a dream. They shouldn't have been able to touch me with their ancient, ethereal voices. But I couldn't bring myself to hang up on them.

"Come to us," said Matricardi. "We'll talk. Tony doesn't have to be there."

"Forgettaphone."

"You remember our place? Degraw Street. You know where?"

"Of course."

"Come. Honor us in this time of disappointment and regret. We'll talk without Tony. What's wrong we'll straighten."

While I considered what to do I used the

doormen's phone again, called information and got the number of the *Daily News*' obituary page and bought a notice for Minna. I put in on a credit card of Minna's to which he'd added my name. He had to pay for his own notice, but I knew he'd have wanted it, considered it fifty bucks well spent. He was always an avid reader of the obituaries, studying them each morning in the L&L office like a tip sheet, a chance for him to pick up or work an angle. The woman on the line did it all by rote, and so did I: billing information, name of deceased, dates, survivors, until we got to the part where I gave out a line or two about who Minna was supposed to have been.

"Beloved something," said the woman, not unkindly. "It's usually Beloved something."

Beloved Father Figure?

"Or something about his contributions to the community," she suggested.

"Just say detective," I told her.

One Mind

There were only and always two things Frank Minna would not discuss in the years following his return from exile and founding of the Minna Agency. The first was the nature of that exile, the circumstances surrounding his disappearance that day in May when his brother Gerard hustled him out of town. We didn't know why he left, where he went or what he did while he was gone, or why he came back when he did. We didn't know how he met and married Julia. We didn't know what happened to Gerard. There was never again any sign or mention of Gerard. The sojourn "upstate" was covered in a haze so complete it was sometimes hard to believe it had lasted three years.

The other was The Clients, though they lurked like a pulse felt here or there in the body of the Agency.

L&L wasn't a moving company anymore, and we never again saw the inside of that hollowed-out brownstone on Degraw. But we were as much errand boys as detectives, and it wasn't hard, in the early days, to sense Matricardi and Rockaforte's shadow in some percentage of our errands. Their assignments were discernible for the deep unease they provoked in Minna. Without explanation he'd alter his patterns, stop dropping in at the barbershop or the arcade for a week or so, close the L&L storefront and tell us to get lost for a few days. Even his walk changed, his whole manner of being. He'd refuse to be seated anywhere but in the corners of restaurants, his back to the wall. He'd turn his head on the street for no reason, which I of course cobbled into a lifelong tic. For cover he'd joke harder but also more discontinuously, his stream of commentary and insult turned balky and riddled with grim silences, his punch lines become non sequiturs. And the jobs we did for The Clients were discontinuous too. They were fractured stories, middles lacking a clear beginning or end. When we Minna Men tracked a wife for a husband or watched an employee suspected of pilferage or cooking the books we mastered their pathetic dramas, encompassed their small lives with our worldliness. What we gathered with our bugs and cameras and etched into our reports was true and complete. Under Minna we were secret masters, writing a sort of social history of Cobble Hill and Carroll Gardens into our duplicate files. But when the hand of Matricardi and

Rockaforte moved the Minna Men we were only tools, glancing off the sides of stories bigger than we understood, discarded and left wondering at the end.

Once in the early days of the Agency we were dispatched to stand guard in broad daylight around a car, a Volvo, and we picked up a scent of The Clients in Minna's stilted, fragmentary instructions. The car was empty as far as we could tell. It was parked on Remsen Street near the Promenade, at a placid dead-end traffic circle overlooking Manhattan. Gilbert and I sat on a park bench, trying to look casual with our backs to the skyline, while Tony and Danny idled at the mouth of Remsen and Hicks, glaring at anyone who turned onto the block. We knew only that we were supposed to give way at five o'clock, when a tow truck would come for the car.

Five o'clock stretched into six, then seven, with no truck. We took pee breaks in the children's park at Montague Street, ran through cigarettes, and paced. Evening strollers appeared on the Promenade, couples, teenagers with paper-bagged bottles of beer, gays mistaking us for cruisers. We shrugged them away from our end of the walk, muttered, glanced at our watches. The Volvo couldn't have been less conspicuous if it were invisible, but for us it glowed, screamed, ticked like a bomb. Every kid on a bike or stumbling wino seemed an assassin, a disguised ninja with aims on the car.

When the sun began to set Tony and Danny started arguing.

"This is stupid," said Danny. "Let's get out of here."

"We can't," said Tony.

"You know there's a body in the trunk," said Danny.

"How am I supposed to know that?" said Tony.

"Because what else would it be?" said Danny. "Those old guys had someone killed."

"That's stupid," said Tony.

"A body?" said Gilbert, plainly unnerved. "I thought the car was full of money."

Danny shrugged. "I don't care, but it's a body. I'll tell you what else: We're being set up for it."

"That's stupid," said Tony.

"What does Frank know? He just does what they tell him." Even in rebellion Danny obeyed Minna's stricture against speaking The Clients' names.

"You really think it's a body?" said Gilbert to Danny.

"Sure."

"I don't want to stay if it's a body, Tony."

"Gilbert, you fat fuck. What if it is? What do you think we're doing here? You think you're never gonna see a body working for Minna? Go join the garbage cops, for chrissakes."

"I'm cutting out," said Danny. "I'm hungry anyway. This is stupid."

"What should I tell Minna?" said Tony, daring Danny to go.

"Tell him what you want."

It was a startling defection. Tony and Gilbert and I were all problems in our various ways, while Danny in his silence and grace was Minna's pillar, his paragon.

Tony couldn't face this mutiny directly. He was accustomed to bullying Gilbert and me, not Danny. So he reverted to form. "What about you, Freakshow?"

I shrugged, then kissed my own hand. It was an impossible question. Devotion to Minna had boiled down to this trial of hours watching over the Volvo. Now we had to envision disaster, betrayal, rotting flesh.

But what would it mean to turn from Minna?

I hated The Clients then.

The tow truck came grinding down Remsen before I could speak. It was manned by a couple of fat lugs who laughed at our jumpiness and told us nothing about the car's importance, just shooed us off and began chaining the Volvo's bumper to their rig. Less Men than Boys in suits, we felt as though this had been designed as a test of our fresh-grown nerves. And we'd failed, even if Minna and The Clients didn't know about it.

We grew tougher, though, and Minna became unflappable, and we came to take the role of The Clients in the life of the Agency more in stride. Who had to make sense of everything? It wasn't always certain when we were acting for them anyway. Seize a given piece of equipment from a given office: Was that on The Clients' behalf or not? Collect this amount from such and such a person: When we passed the take to Minna did he pass it along to The Clients? Unseal this envelope, tap this phone: Clients? Minna kept us in the dark and turned us into professionals. Matricardi and Rockaforte's presence became mostly subliminal.

The last job I felt certain was for The Clients was more than a year before Minna's murder. It bore their trademark of total inexplicability. A supermarket on Smith Street had burned and been razed earlier that summer, and the empty lot was filled with crushed brick and turned into an informal peddlers' market, where sellers of one fruit — oranges, say, or mangoes — would set up a few crates and do a summer afternoon's business, alongside the hot-dog and shaved-ice carts that began to gather there. After a month or so a Hispanic carnival took over the site, setting up a Tilt-a-Whirl and a miniature Ferris wheel, each a dollar a ride, along with a grilled-sausage stand and a couple of lame arcades: a water-gun balloon game and a grappling hook over a glass case full of pink and purple stuffed animals. The litter and smells of grease were a blight if you got too close, but the Ferris wheel was lined with white tubes of neon, and it was a glorious thing to see at night down Smith Street, a bright unexpected pinwheel almost three stories high.

We'd been so bored that summer that we'd fallen into working regularly as a car service, taking calls when they came, ferrying dates home from nightclubs, old ladies to and from hospitals, vacationers to La Guardia for the weekend flight to Miami Beach. Between rides we'd play poker in the air-conditioned storefront. It was after one-thirty on a Friday night when Minna came in. Loomis was sitting in on the game, losing hands and eating all the chips, and Minna told him to get lost, go home already.

"What's the matter, Frank?" said Tony.

"Nothing's the matter. Got something for us to do, that's all."

"Something what? For who?"

"Just a job. What do we have in here that's like a crowbar or something?" Minna smoked furiously to mask his unease.

"A crowbar?"

"Just something you can swing. Like a crowbar. I've got a bat and a lug wrench in my trunk. Stuff like that."

"Sounds like you want a gun," said Tony, raising his eyebrows.

"If I wanted a gun I'd get a gun, you diphthong. This doesn't take a gun."

"You want chains?" said Gilbert, meaning to be helpful. "There's a whole bunch of chains in the Pontiac."

"Crowbar, crowbar, crowbar. Why do I even bother with you mystic seers anymore? If I wanted my mind read I'd call Gladys Knight for chrissakes."

"Dionne Warwick," said Gilbert.

"What?"

"Psychic Hotline's Dionne Warwick, not Gladys Knight."

"Psychicwarlock!"

"Got some pipe downstairs," mused

Danny, only now laying down the hand he'd been holding since Minna barged into the office. It was a full house, jacks and eights.

"It's gotta be swingable," said Minna. "Let's see."

The phone rang and I grabbed for it and said, "L&L."

"Tell them we don't have any cars," said Minna.

"This needs all four of us?" I said. I was courting fond notions of missing the crowbar-and-lug-wrench project, whatever it was, and driving someone out to Sheepshead Bay instead.

"Yes, Freakboy. We're all going."

I got rid of the call. Twenty minutes later we were loaded up with pipes, lug wrench, car jack and a souvenir Yankee bat from Bat Day in Minna's old Impala, the least distinguished of L&L's many cars, and another bad sign if I was trying to read signs. Minna drove us down Wyckoff, past the projects, then circled around, south on Fourth Avenue down to President Street, and back toward Court. He was stalling, checking his watch.

We turned on Smith, and Minna parked us a block below the empty supermarket lot. The carnival had shut down for the night, plywood boards up over the concessions, rides stilled, the evening's discarded beer cups and sausage wrappers glowing against the moonlit rubblescape. We crept onto the lot with our implements, following Minna wordlessly now, no longer chafing at his leadership, instead lulled into our deep obedient rhythm as his Men. He pointed at the Ferris wheel.

"Take it out."

"Eh?"

"Destroy the wheel, you candied yams."

Gilbert understood soonest, perhaps because the task suited his skills and temperament so well. He took a swing at the nearest line of neon with his chunk of pipe, smashing it easily, bringing a rain of silver dust. Tony and Danny and I followed his lead. We attacked the body of the wheel, our first swings tentative, measuring our strength, then lashing out, unloading. It was easy to damage the neon, not easy at all to impress the frame of the wheel, but we set at it, attacked any joint or vulnerable weld, prying up the electrical cable and chopping at it with the sharpest edge of the wrench until insulation and wire were bare and mangled, then frayed. Minna himself wielded the Yankee bat, splintering its wood against the gates that held riders into their seats, not breaking them but changing their shape. Gilbert and I got inside the frame of the wheel and with all our weight dragged at one of the chairs until we ruptured the hinge. Then we found the brake and released the wheel to turn so that we could apply our malicious affection to the whole of it. A couple of Dominican teenagers stood watching us from across the street. We ignored them, bore down on the Ferris wheel, hurrying but not frantic, absolutely Minna's to direct but not even needing direction. We acted as one body to destroy the amusement. This was the Agency at its mature peak: unquestioning and thorough in carrying out an action even when it bordered on sheer Dada.

"Frank loved you, Lionel," said Rockaforte.

"I, uh, I know."

"For that reason we care for you, for that reason we are concerned."

"Though we have not seen you since you were a boy," said Matricardi.

"A boy who barked," said Rockaforte. "We remember. Frank brought and you stood before us in this very room and you barked."

"And Frank spoke of your sickness many times."

"He loved you though he considered you a freak."

"He used that very word."

"You helped him build, you were one of his boys, and now you are a man and you stand before us in this hour of pain and misunderstanding."

Matricardi and Rockaforte had looked sepulchral to me as a teenager and they looked no worse now, their skin mummified, their thin hair in a kind of spider-web sheen over their reflective pates, Matricardi's ears and scarred nose dwarfing his other features, Rockaforte's face puffier and more potatolike. They were dressed as twins in black suits, whether consciously in mourning or not I couldn't know. They sat together on the tightly upholstered couch and when I stepped through the door I thought I saw their hands first joined on the cushions in the space between them, then jerking to their laps. I stood far enough back that I wasn't tempted to reach out and play pattycake, to slap at their folded hands or the place their hands had been resting.

The Degraw Street brownstone was unchanged, outside and in, apart from a dense, even layer of dust on the furniture and carpet and picture frames in the parlor. The air in the room swam with stirred dust, as though Matricardi and Rockaforte had arrived just a few moments before. They visited their Brooklyn shrine less often than in the past, I supposed. I wondered who drove them in from Jersey and whether they took any pains not to be seen coming here or whether they cared. Perhaps no one alive in Carroll Gardens knew them by sight anymore.

A neighborhood's secret lords could also be Invisible Men.

"What is between you and Tony?" said Matricardi.

"I want to find Frank's killer." I'd already heard myself say this too many times, and meaning was leaking out of the phrase. It threatened to become a sort of moral tic: *findfrank'skiller.*

"Why don't you follow Tony in this? Shouldn't you act as one, as brothers?"

"I was there. When they took Frank. Tony — *Hospitabailey!* — Tony wasn't there."

"You're saying then that he should follow you."

"He shouldn't get in my way. *Essway! Wrongway!*" I winced, hating to tic now, in front of them.

"You're upset, Lionel."

"Sure I'm upset." Why should I confess

my distrust to those I distrusted? The more Matricardi and Rockaforte spoke Tony's name, the more certain I was they were tangled together in this somehow, and that Tony was far more familiar with The Clients than I'd been in the years since our first visit to this crypt, this mausoleum. I'd come away with a fork, he with something more. Why should I accuse one half of a conspiracy to the other? Instead I squinted and turned my head and pursed my lips, trying to avoid the obvious, finally acceded to The Clients' power of suggestion and barked once, loudly.

"You are afflicted and we feel for you. A man shouldn't run, and he shouldn't woof like a dog. He should find peace."

"Why doesn't Tony want me looking into Frank's murder?"

"Tony wishes this thing to be done correctly and with care. Work with him, Lionel."

"Why do you speak for Tony?" I gritted my teeth as I spoke the words. It wasn't exactly ticcing, but I'd begun to echo The Clients' verbal rhythms, the cloistered Ping-Pong of their diction.

Matricardi sighed and looked at Rockaforte. Rockaforte raised his eyebrows.

"Do you like this house?" said Matricardi.

I considered the dust-covered parlor, the load of ancient furnishing between the carpet and the ceiling's scrollwork, how it all hung suspended inside the shell of the warehouse-brownstone. I felt the presence of the past, of mothers and sons, deals and understandings, one dead hand gripping another — dead hands were nested here on Degraw Street like a series of Chinese boxes. Including Frank Minna's. There were so many ways I didn't like it I didn't know where to begin, except that I knew I shouldn't allow myself to begin at all.

"It's not a house," I said, offering the very least of my objections. "It's a room."

"He says it's a room," said Matricardi. "Lionel, this is my mother's house where we sit. Where you stand so full of fury it makes you like a cornered dog."

"Somebody killed Frank."

"Are you accusing Tony?"

"Accusatony! Excusebaloney! Funny-monopoly!" I squeezed my eyes shut to interrupt the seizure of language.

"We wish you to understand, Lionel. We regret Frank's passing. We miss him sorely. It is a soreness in our hearts. Nothing could please us more than to see his killer torn by birds or picked apart by insects with claws. Tony should have your help in bringing that day closer. You should stand behind him."

"What if my search brings me to Tony?" I'd let The Clients lead me to this pass in the conversation, and now there wasn't any reason to pretend.

"The dead live in our hearts, Lionel. From there Frank will never be dislodged. But now Tony has replaced Frank in the world of the living."

"What does that mean? You've replaced Frank with Tony?"

"It means you shouldn't act against Tony. Because our wishes go with him."

I understood now. It was Tony's Italian apotheosis at last. I was thrilled for him.

Unless it had been this way for years without my knowing. Maybe Tony Vermonte and The Clients ran deeper than Frank Minna and The Clients ever had.

I considered the word *replaced.* I decided it was time to go.

"I need your permission —" I began, then stopped. Who were The Clients, and what did their permission consist of? What was I thinking?

"Speak, Lionel."

"I'm going to keep looking," I said. "With or without Tony's help."

"Yes. We can see. And so we have an assignment for you. A suggestion."

"A place for you to apply your passion for justice."

"And your talent for detection. The training instilled."

"What?" Just a measure of the day's angled brightness penetrated the heavy curtains of the parlor. I glared back at a row of thuggish midcentury faces staring out from picture frames, wondering which was Matricardi's mom. The hot dogs I'd eaten were rumbling in my stomach. I longed to be outside, on the Brooklyn streets, anywhere but here.

"You spoke with Julia," said Matricardi. "You should find her. Bring her in as we brought you. Let us speak with her."

"She's afraid," I said. *A frayed knot.*

"Afraid of what?"

"She's like me. She doesn't trust Tony."

"Something is wrong between them."

This was exhausting. "Of course something's wrong. They slept together."

"Making love brings people closer, Lionel."

"Maybe they feel guilty about Frank."

"Guilty, yes. Julia knows something. We called her to see us. Instead she runs. Tony says he doesn't know where."

"You think Julia has something to do with Frank's murder?" I let my hand trace a vague line in the dust on the marble mantelpiece. A mistake. I tried to forget I'd done it.

"There's something on her mind, something weighing. You want to help us, Lionel, find her."

"Learn her secrets and share them with us. Do this without telling Tony."

Losing control somewhat, I inserted my finger into the grooved edge of the mantel and pushed, gathering a shaggy clot of dust.

"I don't get it," I said. "Now you want me to go behind Tony's back?"

"We listen, Lionel. We hear. We consider. Questions occur. If your suspicions are grounded the answers may lie with Julia. Tony has been less than clear in this one area. However strange and damaged, you'll be our hands and feet, our eyes and ears, you'll learn and return to us and share."

"Founded," I said. I reached the end of the mantel and thrust the accumulated dustball past the edge, following through like a one-fingered shot-putter.

"*If* they are," said Matricardi. "You don't know. That's what you'll find out."

"No, I mean founded, not grounded. Suspicions *founded.*"

"He's correcting," said Rockaforte to Matricardi, gritting his teeth.

"Find her, Essrog! Founder! Grounder!

Confessrub!" I tried to wipe my finger clean on my jacket and made a gray stripe of clingy dust.

Then I belched, really, and tasted hot dogs.

"There's a little part of Frank in you," said Matricardi. "We speak to that part and it understands. The rest of you may be inhuman, a beast, a freak. Frank was right to use that word. You're a freak of nature. But the part of you that Frank Minna cared for and that cares so much for his memory is the part that will help us find Julia and bring her home."

"Go now, because you sicken us to see you playing with the dust that gathers in the home of his beloved mother, bless her sweet dishonored and tormented soul."

Conspiracies are a version of Tourette's syndrome, the making and tracing of unexpected connections a kind of touchiness, an expression of the yearning to touch the world, kiss it all over with theories, pull it close. Like Tourette's, all conspiracies are ultimately solipsistic, sufferer or conspirator or theorist overrating his centrality and forever rehearsing a traumatic delight in reaction, attachment and causality, in roads out from the Rome of self.

The second gunman on the grassy knoll wasn't part of a conspiracy — we Touretters know this to be true. He was ticcing, imitating the action that had startled and allured him, the shots fired. It was just his way of saying, Me too! I'm alive! Look here! Replay the film!

The second gunman was tugging the boat.

I'd parked in the shade of an elderly, crippled elm, trunk knotted and gnarled from surviving disease, with roots that had slowly nudged the slate sidewalk upward and apart. I didn't see Tony waiting in the Pontiac until I nearly had my key in the door. He was sitting in the driver's seat.

"Get in." He leaned over and opened the passenger door. The sidewalk was empty in both directions. I considered strolling away, ran into the usual problem of where to go.

"Get in, Freakshow."

I went to the passenger side and slid into the seat beside him, then reached out disconsolately and caressed his shoulder, leaving a smudge of dust. He raised his hand and slapped me on the side of the head.

"They lied to me," I said, flinching away.

"I'm shocked. Of course they lied. What

are you, a newborn baby?"

"*Barnamum* baby," I mumbled.

"Which particular lie are you worrying about, Marlowe?"

"They warned you I was coming here, didn't they? They set me up. It was a trap."

"Fuck did you *think* was going to happen?"

"Never mind."

"You think you're smart," said Tony, his voice twangy with contempt. "You think you're Mike fucking Hammer. You're like the Hardy Boys' retarded kid brother, Lionel." He slapped my head again. "You're Hardly Boy."

My home borough had never felt so like a nightmare to me as it did on this bright sunlit day on Matricardi and Rockaforte's block of Degraw: a nightmare of repetition and enclosure. Ordinarily I savored Brooklyn's unchangeability, the bullying, Minna-like embrace of its long memory. At the moment I yearned to see this neighborhood razed, replaced by skyscrapers or multiplexes. I longed to disappear into Manhattan's amnesiac dance of renewal. Let Frank be dead, let the Men disperse. I only wanted Tony to leave me alone.

"You knew I had Frank's beeper," I said sheepishly, putting it together.

"No, the old guys have X-ray vision, like Superman. They don't know shit if I don't tell them, Lionel. You need to find a new line of work, McGruff. Shitlock Holmes."

I was familiar enough with Tony's belligerence to know it had to run awhile, play itself out. Me, I slid my hands along the top of the dashboard at the base of the windshield, smoothing away the crumbs and dust accumulated there, riffling my fingers over the plastic vents. Then I began buffing the corner of the windshield with my thumb tip. Visiting Matricardi's mother's parlor had triggered a dusting compulsion.

"You idiot freak."

"Beepmetwice."

"I'll beep you twice, all right."

He lifted his hand, and I flinched again, ducking underneath like a boxer. While I was near I licked the shoulder of his suit, trying to clean off the smudge of dust I'd left. He pushed me away disgustedly, an ancient echo of St. Vincent's hallway.

"Okay, Lionel. You're still half a fag. You got me convinced."

I didn't speak, no small achievement. Tony sighed and put both hands on the wheel. He appeared to be through buffeting me for the moment. I watched my saliva-stripe evaporate into the weave of his jacket.

"So what did they tell you?"

"The Clients?"

"Sure, The Clients," said Tony. "Matricardi and Rockaforte. Frank's dead, Lionel. I don't think he's gonna, like, spin in his grave if you say their names."

"Fork-it-hardly," I whispered, then glanced over my shoulder at their stoop. "Rocket-fuck-me."

"Good enough. So what did they tell you?"

"The same thing the — *Duckman! Dogboy! Confessdog!* — same thing the doormen told me: Stay off the case." I was mad with verbal tics now, making up for lost time, feeling at home. Tony was still a comfort to me in that way.

"What doorman?"

"Door*men*. A whole bunch of them."

"Where?"

But Tony's eyes said he knew perfectly well where, only needed to measure what I knew. He looked a little panicked, too.

"Ten-thirty Park Avenue," I said. *Energy pocket angle. Rectangle sauce!*

His hands tightened on the wheel. Instead of looking at me, he squinted into the distance. "You were there?"

"I was following a lead."

"Answer my question. *You were there?*"

"Sure."

"Who'd you see?"

"Just a lot of doormen."

"You discuss this with Matricardi and Rockaforte? Tell me you didn't, you goddamn motormouth."

"They talked, I listened."

"Oh yeah, that's likely. Fuck."

Oddly, I found myself wanting to reassure Tony. He and The Clients had drawn me back to Brooklyn and ambushed me in my car, but some old orphans' solidarity worked against my claustrophobia. Tony scared me, but The Clients scared me more. And now I knew they still scared Tony, too. Whatever deal he'd struck was incomplete.

It was cold in the car, but Tony was sweating.

"Be serious with me now, Lionel. Do they know about the building?"

"I'm always serious. That's the tragedy of my life."

"Talk to me, Freakshow."

"*Anybuilding! Nobuilding!* Nobody said anything about a building." I reached for his collar, wanting to straighten it, but he batted my hands away.

"You were in there awhile," he said. "Don't fuck with me, Lionel. What was said?"

"They want me to find Julia," I said, wondering if it was a good idea to mention her name. "They think she knows something."

Tony took a gun out from under his arm and pointed it at me.

I'd returned to Brooklyn suspecting Tony of colluding with The Clients, and now — sweet irony! — Tony suspected me of the same thing. It wasn't that much of a leap. Matricardi and Rockaforte didn't have any motive for humoring me. If they trusted Tony, they wouldn't have required him to wait and bag me outside in the car afterward. He would have been hidden inside, behind the proverbial curtain, soaking up the whole conversation.

I had to give The Clients credit. They'd played us like a Farfisa organ.

On the other hand, Tony had a secret from The Clients: the building on Park Avenue. And despite his fears his secret seemed intact. No point of this particular quadrangle had a monopoly on information. Tony knew something they didn't. I knew something Tony didn't, didn't I? I hoped so. And Julia knew something neither Tony nor The Clients knew, or else she knew something Tony didn't want The Clients to know. Julia, Julia, Julia, I needed to figure out the Julia angle, even if Matricardi and Rockaforte wanted me to.

Or was I outsmarting myself? I knew what Minna would have said.

Wheels within wheels.

I'd never faced Tony at gunpoint before, but at some level I'd been preparing for this moment all my life. It didn't feel at all unnatural. Rather it was a sort of culmination, the rarefied end point of our long association. Now, if I'd had a gun on him, *that* would've freaked me out.

The gun also served splendidly to concentrate my attention. I felt my ticcishness ease, and a flood of excess language instantly evaporate, like cartoon blemishes in a television commercial. Gunplay: another perfectly useless cure.

Tony didn't seem all that impressed by the situation. His eyes and mouth were tired. It was only four in the afternoon and we'd been sitting in the parked car too long already. He had questions, urgent, particular, and the gun would help move things along.

"You talk to anyone else about the building?" he asked.

"Who would I talk to?"

"Danny, say. Or Gilbert."

"I was just up there. I haven't seen

Danny. And Gilbert's in jail." I left out the part about the Garbage Cop, and prayed Minna's beeper didn't go off anytime soon.

Meanwhile, with his questions Tony was telling me more than I was telling him: Danny and Gilbert weren't with him in the Park Avenue caper. Yes, this Hardly Boy was still on the case.

"So it's just you," Tony said. "You're the jerk I've gotta deal with. You're Sam Spade."

"When someone kills your partner you're supposed to do something about it," I said.

"Minna wasn't your partner. He was your sponsor, Freakshow. He was Jerry Lewis, and you were the thing in the wheelchair."

"Then why'd he call for me instead of you when he was in trouble yesterday?"

"He was an idiot bringing you up there."

A shadow strolled past the car, indifferent to our curbside melodrama. This was my second time imperiled in a parked vehicle in the space of three hours. I wondered what goonish spectacles I'd overlooked in my own career as a pavement walker.

"Tell me about Julia, Tony — *Tulip Attorney!*" The magic curative of being at gunpoint was beginning to fade.

"Shut up a little. I'm thinking."

"What about Ullman?" I said. As long as

he was allowing my questions I might as well ask. "Who was Ullman? — *Doofus Allplan!*" I wanted to ask about the Fujisaki Corporation, but I figured the extent of what I knew was one of the only things I knew and he didn't. I needed to preserve that advantage, however minuscule. Besides, I didn't want to hear what hay my syndrome would make of the word *Fujisaki*.

Tony made a particularly sour face. "Ullman's a guy who didn't figure numbers right. He's one of a little group of somebodies who tried to make themselves rich. Frank was another one."

"So you and the Polish killer took him out, huh?"

"That's so wrong it's funny."

"Tell me, Tony."

"Where would I start?" he said. I heard a note of bitterness, and wondered if I could play on it. Tony likely missed Minna in his way, and missed the Agency, no matter how he'd been corrupted or what poisonous information he knew that I didn't.

"Be sentimental for a change," I said. "Make me know you didn't kill him."

"Go fuck yourself."

"That was persuasive," I said. Then I made a sour face like an uptight British butler: *"Per-shwoosh-atively!"*

"The problem with you, Lionel, is you don't know anything about how the world really works. Everything you know comes from Frank Minna or a book. I don't know which is worse."

"Gangster movies." I fought to keep the butler-face from reappearing.

"What?"

"I watched a lot of gangster movies, like you. Everything we both know comes from Frank Minna or gangster movies."

"Frank Minna was two guys," said Tony. "The one I learned from and the chucklehead who thought you were funny and got himself killed. You only knew the chucklehead."

Tony held the gun floppily between us, using it to gesture, to signal punctuation. I only hoped he understood how literally it could punctuate. None of us had ever carried guns so far as I knew, apart from Minna. He'd rarely allowed us even to see his. Now I wondered what private teaching had gone on when I wasn't around, wondered how seriously I should take Tony's notion of the two Minnas.

"I suppose it was the smart Frank Minna who taught you to wave guns around," I said. It came out a bit more sarcastic than I'd intended, then I yelled, *"Frankensmart!"*

which pretty much undercut my delivery. Tony really was waving the gun, though. The only thing it never pointed at was himself.

"I'm carrying this for protection. Like I'm protecting you with it right now, by convincing you to shut up and quit asking questions. And stay in Brooklyn."

"I hope you don't have to protect me — *Protectmebailey! Detectorbaby!* — by pulling the trigger."

"Let's both hope. Too bad you weren't clever like Gilbert, to get himself put under police protection for a week or so."

"Is that the current sentence for murder? A week?"

"Don't make me laugh. Gilbert didn't kill anybody."

"You sound disappointed."

"I'm long over my disappointment that Frank liked to surround himself with a cavalcade of clowns. It was a way of life. I won't be making the same mistake."

"No, you'll think up a whole bunch of new ones."

"Enough of this. Does every conversation with you have to be the director's cut? Get out of the car."

At that moment there came a tap on the window, driver's side. It was a gun muzzle that tapped. The arm holding the gun extended from behind the trunk of the elm tree. A head poked out too: the homicide detective.

"Gentlemen," he said. "Do step out of the car — slowly."

Ambushes within ambushes.

He still had that threadbare, jaded, coffee-isn't-working-anymore air about him, even in daylight. It didn't look like he'd gotten out of his suit since the night before. I believed him with a gun better than I did Tony, though. He waved us over to the front of the car and had us spread our legs, to the wonderment of a couple of old ladies, then took away Tony's gun. He had Tony open his jacket and show the open holster and lift his pant legs to prove there was nothing strapped to his ankles. Then he tried to pat me down and I began to pat him back.

"Goddamn it, Alibi, cut that out." He was still fond of that nickname he'd invented for me. It made me fond of him.

"I can't help it," I said.

"What's that? A phone? Take it out."

"It's a phone." I showed him.

Tony looked at me strangely, and I just shrugged.

"Get back in the car. Give me the keys first." Tony handed over the keys and we got back into the front seat. The homicide detective opened the back doors and eased into the seat behind us, training his gun on the backs of our heads.

"Hands on the wheel and the dash, that's good. Face forward, gentlemen. Don't look at me. Smile like they're taking your picture. They will be soon enough."

"What did we do?" said Tony. "A guy can't show another guy a gun anymore?"

"Shut up and listen. This is a murder investigation. I'm the investigating officer. I don't care about your goddamn gun."

"So give it back."

"I don't think so, Mr. Vermonte. You people make me nervous. I found out a few things about this neighborhood in the last twenty-four hours."

"Mister Gobbledy Gun."

"Shut up, Alibi."

Shut up shut up shut up! I kneaded the petrified foam of the Pontiac's dashboard like a nursing kitten, just trying to keep still and shut up. Someday I'd change my name to Shut Up and save everybody a lot of time.

"I got this case because you jokers brought Frank Minna into Brooklyn Hospital. That's where he died and that's in my jurisdiction. I don't get to work this side of Flatbush Avenue that often, you get me? I don't know all that much about your neighborhood, but I'm learning, I'm learning."

"Not so many murders over here, eh, Chief?" said Tony.

"Not so many *niggers* on this side of Flatbush, that what you're trying to say?"

"Whoa, slow down," said Tony. "You're leading the witness. Isn't that against the rules?" Tony kept his hands on the steering wheel and grinned into the windshield. I don't think the homicide cop had really meant to inspire such a smile.

"Okay, Tony," said the cop, his voice a little husky. I heard him breathing heavily through his nose. I suppose unsheathing his gun had gotten him a bit worked up. I imagined I could feel its muzzle centering first on my ear, then on Tony's. "Tell me what you meant," he said. "Set me straight."

"All I meant was not so many murders — am I right?"

"Yeah, you got the lid clamped down pretty tight around here. No murders and no niggers. Nice clean streets, nothing but old guys carrying around racing forms and tiny pencils. Makes me nervous."

It was honest of him to admit it. I wondered what Mafia horror stories he'd gathered in his day-old investigation.

"Around here people watch out for each other," said Tony.

"Yeah, right up until you off each other. What's the connection between Minna and Ullman, Tony?"

"Who's Ullman?" said Tony. "I never met the guy."

That was a Minna-ism: *never met the guy.*

"Ullman kept the books for a property-management firm in Manhattan," said the homicide detective. "Until your friend Coney shot him through the skull. Looks like tit for tat to me. I'm impressed with how quick you guys get to work."

"What's your name, Officer?" said Tony. "I get to ask that, don't I?"

"I'm not an officer, Tony. I'm a detective. My name is Lucius Seminole."

"Luscious? You gotta be kidding me."

"*Lu*cius. Call me Detective Seminole."

"What is that, like an Indian name?"

"It's a Southern name," said Seminole. "Slave name. Keep laughing, Tony."

"Detectahole!"

"Alibi, you are not making me happy."

"Inspectaholic!"

"Don't kill him, Superfly," said Tony, grinning broadly. "I know it's pitiful, but he can't help himself. Think of it as a free human freak show."

"Licorice Smellahole!" Not turning my head was driving me crazy: I had to rename what I couldn't see.

"You a car service or a comedy team?" said Seminole.

"Lionel's just jealous because you're asking me all the questions," said Tony. "He likes to talk."

"I already heard from Alibi last night. He near about drove me crazy with his talk. Now I'm looking for answers from you, straight man."

"We're not a car service," I said. "We're a detective agency." The assertion fought its way out of me, a tic disguised as a common statement.

"Turn around, Alibi. Let's talk about the lady who ran to Boston — Mrs. Deadguy."

"Boston?" said Tony.

"We'readetectiveagency," I ticced again.

"She booked the flight under her own name," said Seminole. "It's not the first time either. What's in Boston?"

"Beats me. She goes up there a lot?"

"Don't play stupid."

"It's news to me," said Tony. He scowled at me, and I made a dopey face back, stumped. Julia in Boston? I wondered if Seminole had his information straight.

"She was ready to fly," said Seminole. "Somebody tipped her."

"She got a call from the hospital," I said.

"Nope," said Seminole. "I checked that. Try another one. Maybe your boy Gilbert gave her a call. Maybe Gilbert took out Frank Minna before he took out Ullman. Maybe he and the lady are in this together."

"That's crazy," I said. "Gilbert didn't kill anybody. We're *detectives*."

I finally got Seminole's attention. "I looked into that rumor," he said. "None of you carry investigators' credentials, according to the computer. Just limousine operators' licenses."

"We work for Frank Minna," I said, and heard my own unconcealed nostalgia, my pining. "We assist a detective. We're, uh, operatives."

"You do stooge work for a penny-ante hood, according to what I can see. A *dead* penny-ante hood. You were in the pocket of a guy in the pocket of Alphonso Matricardi and Leonardo Rockaforte, two relatively deep old dudes. Only it appears the pocket got turned inside out."

Tony winced: These clichés hurt. "We work for the clients that come in," he said, oddly sincere. For a moment Minna again came alive in Tony's voice. "We don't ask questions we shouldn't, or we wouldn't have any clients at all. The cops do the same, don't try to tell me any different."

"Cops don't have *clients*," said the homicide detective stiffly. I would have liked to see the real Frank Minna handle Seminole.

"What are you, Abraham Jefferson Jackson?" said Tony. "You running for office with that speech? Give me a break."

I snorted. Despite everything, Tony was cracking me up. I threw in a flourish of my own:

"Abracadabra Jackson!"

The gun, and Seminole's status as a law-enforcement officer, didn't matter — he was losing control of this interview. What happened was this: Tony and I, so deeply estranged, had been drawn together by the point of the detective's gun. In this post-Minna era we Men were a little panicked and raw at facing one another head on. But triangulated by Seminole we'd rediscovered the kinship that lurked in our old routines. If we couldn't trust each other, Tony and I were at least reminded we were two of a kind, especially in the eyes of a cop. And Tony, seeing chinks in the detective's confidence, was turning on him with his old orphan's savagery. A bully knows the parameters and half-life of a brandished threat — the only thing weaker than a gun so long ignored was no gun at all. The cop had had to arrest us or hurt us or turn us against each other by now, and he hadn't. Tony would cut him apart with his tongue for the mistake.

In the meantime I considered what Seminole had been saying, and tried to sift the information from his dingbat theories. If Julia didn't get a call from the hospital how did she know about Minna's death?

Again I wondered: Was it Julia who missed her *Rama-lama-ding-dong?* Did she keep it in Boston?

"Listen, you scumbags," said Seminole. He was compensating desperately for his plummeting authority. "I'd rather tangle with *homies* doing *drive-bys* all day than wade into this Italianate mobster shit. Don't get big-headed, now — I can see you're just a couple of fools. It's the wiseguys pulling your strings I'm worried about."

"Great," said Tony. "A paranoid cop. *Wiseguys pulling strings* — you read too many comic books, Cleopatra Jones."

"Clapperdapper Bailey Johnson!"

"You think I'm stupid," continued Seminole, on a real tear now. "You think a dumb black cop is going to stumble into your little nest and take it on face value. Car service, detective agency, give me a break. I'm going to push this murder bag just far enough to turn it over to the Federal Bureau of Investigation, and then I'm going to get my ass out of here for good. Might even take a vacation, sit on the beach and read about you losers in the Metro section."

Stumble, wade: Seminole's choice of words betrayed him. He really and truly feared he'd already gotten in further than was good for him. I wanted to find a way to allay his fears, I really did. I sort of liked the homicide detective. But everything out of my mouth sounded vaguely like a racial slur.

"Federal Bureau of what?" said Tony. "I never met those guys."

"Let's go upstairs and see if Uncle Alphonso and Uncle Leonardo can explain it to you," said Seminole. "Something tells me they've got a working familiarity with the FBI."

"I don't think the old guys are home anymore," said Tony.

"Oh yeah? Where'd they go?"

"They went through a tunnel in the basement," said Tony. "They had to get back to their hideout, since they've got James Bond — or Batman, I can't remember which — roasting over a slow fire."

"What are you talking about?"

"Don't worry, though. Batman always gets away. These supervillains never learn."

"Uncle Batman!" I shouted. They couldn't know how much work it was for me to keep my hands on that dashboard, my neck straight. "Unclebailey Blackman! *Barnamum Bat-a-potamus!*"

"That's enough, Alibi," said Seminole. "Get out of the car."

"What?"

"Get lost, go home. You annoy me, man. Tony and me are going to have a little talk."

"C'mon, Blacula," complained Tony. "We've been talking for hours. I've got nothing to say to you."

"Every name you call me I think up a couple more questions," said Seminole. He waved at me with his gun. "Get lost."

I gaped at Seminole, incredulous.

"I mean it. Get."

I opened the door. Then I thought to find the Pontiac's keys and hand them to Tony.

Tony glared at me. "Go back to the office and wait for me."

"Oh, sure," I said, and stepped out onto the curb.

"Close the door," said Seminole, training gun and gaze on Tony.

"Thanks, *Count Chocula,*" I said, and skipped away, literally.

Have you noticed yet that I relate everything to my Tourette's? Yup, you guessed it, it's a tic. Counting is a symptom, but counting symptoms is also a symptom, a tic *plus ultra.* I've got meta-Tourette's. Thinking about ticcing, my mind racing, thoughts reaching to touch every possible symptom. Touching touching. Counting counting. Thinking thinking. Mentioning mentioning Tourette's. It's sort of like talking about telephones over the telephone, or mailing letters describing the location of various mailboxes. Or like a tugboater whose favorite anecdote concerns actual tugboats.

There is nothing Tourettic about the New York City subways.

Though at each step I felt the gaze of an army of invisible doormen on my neck, I was nevertheless exultant to be back on the Upper East Side. I hurried down Lexington from the Eighty-sixth Street station, with only ten minutes to spare before five o'clock: zazen. I didn't want to be late for my first. While I was still on the street, though, I took out the cell phone and called Loomis.

"Yeah, I was just about to call you." I could hear him chewing a sandwich or a chicken leg, and pictured his open mouth, smacking lips. Hadn't he been at lunch two hours before? "I got the goods on that building."

"Let's have it — quick."

"This guy in Records, he was going on and on about it. That's a sweet little building, Lionel. Way outta my class."

"It's Park Avenue, Loomis."

"Well, there's Park Avenue and then there's this. You gotta have a hundred million to get on the waiting list for this place, Lionel. This kind of people, their other house is an *island*."

I heard Loomis quoting someone smarter than himself. "Right, but what about Fujisaki?"

"Hold your horses, I'm getting there. This sort of place, there's a whole staff — it's like a bunch of mansions stacked together. They got secret passages, wine cellars, a laundry service, swimming pool, servants' quarters, private chef. Whole secret economy. There's only five or six buildings like this in the city — the place where Bob Dylan got killed, what's it, the *Nova Scotia*? That's a doghouse in comparison. This place is for the old-money people, they'll turn down Seinfeld, *Nixon*, doesn't matter. They don't even give a shit."

"Include me in that category," I said, unable to discern any useful information in the Garbage Cop's jabber. "I'm looking for names, Loomis."

"Your Fujisaki's the management corporation. Whole bunch of other Jap names in there — guess they own half of New York if you started digging. This is a serious money operation, Lionel. Ullman, far as I can tell, he was just Fujisaki's accountant. So clue me in: Why would Gilbert go after an accountant?"

"Ullman was the last guy Frank was supposed to see," I said. "He never got to him."

"Minna was supposed to kill Ullman?"

"I don't know."

"Or vice versa?"

"I don't know."

"Or did the same guy kill them both?"

"I don't know, Loomis."

"So you aren't learning much besides what I'm digging up for you, huh?"

"Eat me, Loomis."

★ ★ ★

"I'm so glad you're here," said Kimmery when she opened the door to me. "You're just in time. Mostly everybody's sitting already." She kissed me on the cheek again. "There's a lot of excitement about the monks."

"I'm feeling a lot of excitement myself." In fact, I felt an instant euphoria at Kimmery's alleviating presence. If this was the prospect of Zen I was ready to begin my training.

"You'll have to take a cushion right away. Just sit anywhere but up at the front of the line. We'll work on your posture some other time — for now you can sit and concentrate on your breathing."

"I'll do that." I followed her up the stairs.

"That's really everything anyway, breathing. You could work on just that for the rest of your life."

"I'll probably have to."

"Take off your shoes."

Kimmery pointed, and I added my shoes to a neat row in the hallway. It was a bit disconcerting to surrender them and with them my street-readiness, but in fact my aching dogs were grateful for the chance to breathe and stretch.

The second-floor sitting room was

gloomy now, overhead track lighting still dark, the fading November daylight insufficient. I spotted the source of the heavy smell this time, a pot of smoldering incense on a high shelf beside a jade Buddha. The walls of the room were covered with undecorated paper screens, the glossy parquet floor with thin cushions. Kimmery led me to a spot near the back of the room and sat beside me, folded her legs and straightened her back, then nodded wide-eyed to suggest I imitate her moves. If only she knew. I sat and worked my big legs into position, grabbing my shins with both hands, only once jostling the sitter ahead of me, who turned and quickly glared, then resumed his posture of grace. The rows of cushions around us were mostly full with Zen practitioners, twenty-two when I counted, some in black robes, others in beatniky street clothes, corduroy or sweatpants and turtlenecks, not one in a suit like me. In the dimness I couldn't make out any faces.

So I sat and waited and wondered exactly what I was there for, though it was tough to keep my back straight as those I saw around me. I glanced at Kimmery. Her eyes were already peacefully shut. In twenty-four hours — it was only slightly more than that since Gilbert and I had parked at the curb outside the day before — my confusion at the Zendo's significance had doubled and re-doubled, become veiled in successive layers. The conversation I'd heard on the wire, those sneering insinuations, now seemed impossible to fix to this place. Kimmery's voice, ingenuous, unconspiring, was all I heard now. That, of course, against a back-ground of my own interior babble. As I sat beside Kimmery, sheltered inside her tic-canceling field, I felt all the more keenly the uneasy, half-stoppered force of my own language-generator, my Multi-Mind, that tangle of responses and mimickings, of interruptions of interruptions.

I gazed at her again. She was *sitting* sincerely, not wondering about me. So I shut my eyes and, taking my own little crack at enlightenment, tried to unify my mind and get a fix on my Buddha nature.

The first thing I heard was Minna's voice: *I dare you to shut up for a whole twenty minutes sometime, you free human freakshow.*

I pushed it away, thought *One Mind* instead.

One Mind.

Tell me one, Freakshow. One I don't already know.

I vant to go to Tibet.

One Mind. I focused on my breathing.

Come home, Irving.

One Mind. Sick Mind. Dirty Mind. Bailey Mind.

One Mind.

Oreo Man.

When I opened my eyes again, I'd adjusted to the gloom. At the front of the room was a large bronze gong, and the cushions nearest the gong were empty as if readied for celebrity sitters, perhaps the *important monks.* The rows of heads had developed features, though mostly I was looking at ears and napes, the neckline of haircuts. The crowd was a mix of sexes, the women mostly skinny, with earrings and hairstyles that cost something, the men on average more lardish and scruffy, their haircuts overdue. I spotted Wallace's ponytail and bald spot and furniture-stiff posture up near the front. And a row ahead of me, closer to the entrance, sat Pinched and Indistinct, my would-be abductors. At last I understood: They *were* men of peace. Was there a severe shortage of human beings on the Upper East Side, so the same small cast of doormen was required to pose in costume, here as goons, there as seekers after serenity? At least they'd shed their blue suits, made a greater commitment to this new identity. Garbed in black robes, their postures were admirably erect, presumably earned by extensive training, years of sacrifice. They hadn't been working all that time on their strong-arm patter, that was for sure.

So much for my breathing. I managed to check my voice, though. Pinched and Indistinct both had their eyes shut, and I'd arrived last, so I had the drop on them. They weren't exactly my idea of big trouble anyway. But I was reminded that the stolen cell phone and borrowed beeper in my jacket might shatter this ancient Eastern silence at any moment. Moving quietly as possible, I drew them out and turned off the cell phone's ringer, set Minna's beeper to "vibrate." As I slipped them back into my jacket's inner pocket an open hand slapped the back of my head and neck, hard.

Stung, I whipped around. But my attacker was already past me, marching solemnly between the mats to the front of the room, the first in a file of six bald Japanese men, all draped in robes revealing glimpses of sagging brown skin and threads of white underarm hair. Important monks. The lead monk had swerved out of his way to deliver the blow. I'd been reprimanded or perhaps offered a jolt of enlightenment — did I now know the sound of one hand clapping? Either way, I felt the heat of blood rushing to my ears and scalp.

Kimmery hadn't noticed, just placidly Zenned right through the whole sequence. Maybe she was further along on her spiritual path than she realized.

The six moved to the front and took the unoccupied mats near the gong. And a seventh entered the room, a little behind the others, also robed, also with a polished bald skull. But he wasn't small and Japanese and his body hair wasn't white and it wasn't limited to his underarms. He had silky black plumes of back and shoulder hair, rising from all sides to circle his neck with a fringe. It wasn't a look the designer of the robe had likely had in mind. He moved to the front of the room and took the last of the VIP spots before I could see his face, but I thought of Kimmery's description and decided this must be the American teacher, founder of the Zendo, the Roshi.

Irving. When are you coming home, Irving? *Your family misses you.*

The joke nagged at me, but I couldn't put it to work. Was that Roshi's original name, his American name: Irving? Was Roshi-Irving the voice on the wire?

If so, why? What linked Minna to this place?

They settled into quietude up front. I stared at the row of bald heads, the six monks and Roshi, but discerned nothing. Even Pinched and Indistinct were meditating serenely. Minutes crept past and I was the only set of open eyes. Someone coughed and I faked a cough in imitation. If I kept one eye on Kimmery I was mostly calm, though. It was like having a bag of White Castles beside me on the car seat. I wondered how deep her influence over my syndrome could run if given the chance, how much of that influence I could hope to import. How close I could get. I shut my eyes, trusting Pinched and Indistinct to stay planted obliviously on their cushions, and drifted into some pleasant thoughts about bodies, about Kimmery's body, her nervous elegant limbs. Perhaps this was the key to Zen, then. *We don't exactly have God,* she'd said. *We just sit and try to stay awake.* Well, I wasn't having any trouble staying awake. And as my penis stiffened it occurred to me I'd found my One Mind.

I was jostled from my reverie by a sound at the door. I opened my eyes and turned to see the Polish giant standing in the entrance to the sitting room, filling the doorway with his square shoulders, holding in his fist a plastic produce bag full of kumquats and gazing at the roomful of Zen practitioners with an expression of absolute and utter serenity. He wasn't in a robe, but he might have been Buddha himself for the benignity of his gaze.

Before I could figure a plan or response there came a commotion at the front of the room. A commotion by the local standards anyway: One of the Japanese monks stood and bowed to Roshi, then to the other monks in his party, then to the room at large. You still would have heard a pin drop, but the rustling of his robe was signal enough, and eyes opened everywhere. The giant stepped into the room, still clutching his kumquats like a bag of live goldfish, and took a mat — a couple actually — on the other side of Kimmery, between us and the door. I reminded myself that the giant hadn't seen me, at least not yesterday. He certainly wasn't giving me any special notice — or anyone else for that matter. Instead he settled into his spot, looking ready for the monk's lecture. Quite a gathering we made now, the various mugs and lugs attending to the wise little men from the East. Pinched and Indistinct might be real Zen students playing at thuggishness, but Pierogi Monster was undoubtedly the opposite. The kumquats, I was pretty sure, were a giveaway — weren't they a Chinese fruit, not Japanese at all? I wanted to hug Kimmery toward me, away from the killer's reach, but then I wanted to do a lot of things — I always do.

The monk bowed to us again, searched our faces briefly, then began speaking, so abruptly and casually it was as if he were resuming a talk he'd been having with himself.

"Daily life, I fly on an airplane, I take a taxicab to visit Yorkville Zendo" — this came out *Yolkville-ah* — "I feel excitement, thoughts, anticipations, what will my friend Jerry-Roshi show me? Will I go to a very good Manhattan restaurant, sleep on a very good bed in New York City hotel?" He stomped his sandaled foot as though testing out a mattress.

I vant to go to Tibet! The joke insisted itself upon me again. My calm was under pressure from all sides, the goons everywhere, my echolalia provoked by the monk's speech. But I couldn't turn and gaze and refresh my dose of Kimmery without also taking in Minna's titanic killer — he was so big that his outline framed her on all sides despite his being farther away, an optical trick I couldn't afford to find fascinating.

"All these moods, impulses, this daily life, nothing wrong with them. But daily life, island, dinner, airplane, cocktail, daily life is not Zen. In zazen practice all that matters is the sitting, the practice. American, Japan, doesn't matter. Only sitting."

I vant to speak to the Lama! The American monk, Roshi, had half turned in his spot to better contemplate the master from across the ocean. The profile below Roshi's gleaming dome stirred me unexpectedly. I recognized some terrible force of authority and charisma in his features.

Jerry-Roshi?

Meanwhile the giant sat disrespectfully pinching the skin of a kumquat, pressing it to his monstrous lips, sucking its juice.

"It is easy practice zazen in its external form, sit on the cushion and waste time on the cushion. So many forms of nothing — Zen, meaningless Zen, only one form of true Zen: actual making contact with own Buddha-self."

The High Lama will grant you an audience.

"There is *chikusho* Zen, Zen of domesticated animals who curl up on pillows like cats in homes, waiting to be fed. They sit to kill time between meals. Domesticated animal Zen useless! Those who practice chikusho should be beaten and thrown out of the zendo."

I obsessed on Jerry-Roshi's face while the monk sputtered on.

"There is *ningen* Zen, Zen practiced for self-improvement. Ego-Zen. Make skin better, make bowel movement better, think positive thoughts and influence people. Shit! Ningen Zen is shit Zen!"

Irving, come home, went my brain. *No soap, Zendo. Tibettapocamus. Chickenshack Zen. High Oscillama Talkalot.* The monk's wonky syllables, the recursions of the Tibet joke, my own fear of the giant — all were conspiring to bring me to a boil. I wanted to trace Roshi's enthralling profile with my fingertip — perhaps I'd recognize its significance by touch. Instead I practiced Essrog Zen, and stifled myself.

"Consider also *gaki* Zen: the Zen of insatiable ghosts. Those who study gaki Zen chase after enlightenment like spirits who crave food or vengeance with a hunger can never be satisfied. These ghosts never even enter the house of Zen they are so busy howling at the windows!"

Roshi looked like Minna.

Your brother misses you, Irving.

Irving equals Lama, Roshi equals Gerard.

Roshi was Gerard Minna.

Gerard Minna was the voice on the wire.

I couldn't say which got me there first, his profile in front of me or the joke's subliminal nagging. It felt like a dead heat. Of course, the joke had been designed to get me there sooner, spare me figuring it out while in the belly of the whale. Too bad.

I tried to quit staring, failed. Up front, the monk continued to enumerate false Zens, the various ways we could go wrong. I personally could think of a few he probably hadn't come across yet.

But why had Minna buried the information in a joke to begin with? I thought of a couple of reasons. One: He didn't want us to know about Gerard *unless* he died. If he survived the attack he wanted his secret to survive as well. Two: He didn't know who among his Men to trust, even down to Gilbert Coney. He could be certain I'd puzzle over the Irving clue while Gilbert would write it off as our mutual inanity.

And he felt, rightly, that no conspiracy around him could possibly include his pet Freakshow. The other Boys would never let me play. I could be flattered at the implied trust, or insulted by the dis. It didn't really matter now.

I stared at Gerard. Now I understood the

charismatic force of his profile, but it inspired only bitterness. It was as though the world imagined it could take Minna away and offer this clumsy genetic substitution. A resemblance.

"California Roll Zen. This is the Zen of sushi so full of avocado and cream cheese might as well be a marshmallow for all you know. The pungent fish of zazen smothered in easy pleasures, picnics, get-togethers, Zendo becomes a dating service!"

"Zengeance!" I shouted.

Not every head turned. Gerard Minna's did, though. So did Pinched's, and Indistinct's. And so did the giant's. Kimmery was among those who practiced their calm by ignoring me.

"Ziggedy zendoodah," I said aloud. My erection dimmed, energy venting elsewhere. *"Pierogi Monster Zen master zealous neighbor.* Zazen zaftig Zsa Zsa go-bare." I rapped the scalp of the sitter in front of me. "Zippity go figure."

The roomful of gurus and acolytes came to agitated life but not one of them spoke a word, so my burst of verbiage sang in the silence. The lecturing monk glared at me and shook his head. Another of his posse rose from his cushion and lifted a wooden paddle I hadn't previously noticed from a hook on the wall, then started through the rows of students in my direction. Only Wallace sat immobile, eyes shut, still meditating. I began to appreciate his reputation for imperturbability.

"Pierogi kumquat sushiphone! Domestic marshmallow ghost! Insatiable Mallomar! *Smothered pierogiphone!*" The flood came with such force, I twisted my neck and nearly barked the words.

"Silence!" commanded the lecturing monk. "Very bad to make disturbance in the Zendo! Time and place for everything!" Anger wasn't good for his English. "Shouting is for outside, New York City full of shouting! Not in Zendo."

"Knock knock Zendo!" I shouted. "Monk monk goose!"

The monk with the paddle approached. He gripped it cross-handed, like Hank Aaron. The giant stood, shoved his baggie of kumquats into the pocket of his Members Only jacket and rubbed his sticky hands together, readying them for use. Gerard turned and stared at me, but if he recognized in me the twitchy teenager he'd left behind at the St. Vincent's schoolyard fence nineteen years before, he didn't show any sign. His eyebrows were delicately knit, his mouth pursed, his expression bemused.

Kimmery put her hand on my knee and I put my hand on hers, reciprocity-ticcing. Even in a shitstorm such as I was in at this moment, my syndrome knew that God was in the details.

"Keisaku is more than ceremonial implement," said the monk with the paddle. He applied it to my shoulder blades so gently it was like a caress. "Unruly student can do with a blow." Now he clouted my back with the same muscular Buddhist glee his colleague had applied to my scalp.

"Ouch!" I fished behind me for the paddle, snagged it, tugged. It came out of the monk's grasp and he staggered backward. By now the giant was headed in our direction. Those between us rolled or scuttled out of his path, according to their ability to unlock their elaborately folded legs. Kimmery darted away just as he loomed over us, not wanting to be crushed. Pierogi Man hadn't checked his shoes at the door.

That was when I saw the nod.

Gerard Minna nodded ever so slightly at the giant, and the giant nodded back. That was all it took. The same team that had doomed Frank Minna was back in the saddle. I would be the sequel.

The giant wrapped me in his arms and lifted, and the paddle clattered to the floor.

★ ★ ★

I weigh nearly two hundred pounds, but the giant didn't strain at all moving me down the stairs and out onto the street, and when he plumped me onto the sidewalk I was more shaken and winded than he by far. I straightened my suit and confirmed the alignment of my neck with a string of jerks while he unloaded his bag of kumquats and got back to sucking out their juice and pulp, reducing their bodies to husks that looked like orange raisins in his massive hands.

The narrow street was nearly dark now, and the dog-walkers were far enough away to give us privacy.

"Want one?" he said, holding out the bag. His voice was a dull thing where it began in his throat but it resonated to grandeur in the tremendous instrument of his torso, like a mediocre singer on the stage of a superb concert hall.

"No, thanks," I said. Here was where I should grow large with anger, facing Minna's killer right at the spot of the abduction. But I was diminished, ribs aching from his squeezing, confused and worried — conworried — by my discovery of Gerard Minna inside the Zendo, and unhappy to have left Kimmery and my shoes upstairs. The pavement was cold through my socks, and my feet tingled oddly as they flushed with the blood denied them by Zen posture.

"So what's the matter with you?" he said, discarding another of the withered kumquats.

"I've got Tourette's," I said.

"Yeah, well, threats don't work with me."

"Tourette's," I said.

"Eh? My hearing's not so good. Sorry." He put the bag of fruit away again, and when his hand reemerged it was holding a gun. "Go in there," he said. He pointed with his chin at the three steps leading to the narrow channel between the Zendo and the apartment building on the right, a lane filled with garbage cans and darkness. I frowned, and he reached out and with the hand not holding the gun shoved me backward toward the steps. "Go," he said again.

I considered the giant and myself as a tableau. Here was the man I'd been hunting and wishing to go up against, howling for a chance at vengeance like an insatiable ghost or marshmallow — yet had I planned a way to take advantage of him, a method or apparatus to give me any real edge, let alone narrow the immense gap in force his size presented? No. I'd come up pathetically empty. And now he had a gun to ice the cake. He shoved me again, straight-armed my shoulder, and when I tried, ticcishly, to shove his shoulder in return I found I was held at too great a distance, couldn't brush his shoulder even with long-stretched fingertips, and it conjured some old memory of Sylvester the Cat in a boxing ring with a kangaroo. My brain whispered, *He's just a big mouse, Daddy, a vigorous louse, big as a house, a couch, a man, a plan, a canal, apocalypse.*

"Apocamouse," I mumbled, language spilling out of me unrestrained. "Unplan-a-canal. Unpluggaphone."

"I said get in there, Squeaky." Had he caught my mouse reference, even with his impaired hearing? But then, who wouldn't be squeaky to him? He was so big he only had to shrug to loom. I took a step backward. I had Tourette's, he had threats. "Go," he said again.

It was the last thing I wanted to do and I did it.

The minute I stepped down into the darkness he swung the gun at my head.

So many detectives have been knocked out and fallen into such strange swirling darknesses, such manifold surrealist voids ("something red wriggled like a germ under a microscope" — Philip Marlowe, *The Big*

Sleep), and yet I have nothing to contribute to this painful tradition. Instead my falling and rising through obscurity was distinguished only by nothingness, by blankness, by lack and my resentment of it. Except for grains. It was a grainy nothing. A desert of grains. How fond can you be of flavorless grains in a desert? How much better than nothing at all? I'm from Brooklyn and I don't like wide-open spaces, I guess. And I don't want to die. So sue me.

Then I remembered a joke, a riddle like one the Garbage Cop would tell, and it was my lifeline, it sang like a chorus of ethereal voices beckoning me from the brink of darkness:

Why don't you starve in the desert?

Because of the *sand which is* there.

Why didn't I want to die or leave New York?

The sandwiches. I concentrated on the sandwiches. For a while that's all there was, and I was happy. The sandwiches were so much better than the desert of grains.

"Lionel?"

It was Kimmery's voice.

"Mhrrggh."

"I brought your shoes."

"Oooh."

"I think we should go. Can you stand?"

"Rrrrssp."

"Lean against the wall. Careful. I'll get a cab."

"Cabbabbab."

I flickered awake again and we were slicing through the park, East Side to West, in that taxicab channel of tree-topped stone, my head on Kimmery's bony shoulder. She was putting my shoes back on, lifting my leaden feet one after the other, then tying the laces. Her small hands and my large shoes made this an operation rather like saddling a comatose horse. I could see the cabbie's license — his name was Omar Dahl, which invited tics I couldn't muster in my state — and a view upward through the side window. For a moment I thought it was snowing and everything seemed precious and distant — Central Park in a snow globe. Then I realized it was snowing inside the cab, too. The grains again. I closed my eyes.

Kimmery's apartment was on Seventy-eighth Street, in an old-lady apartment building, gloriously shabby and real after the gloss of the East Side, the chilling dystopian lobby of 1030 Park Avenue especially. I got upright and into the elevator on my own steam, with only Kimmery to hold the doors for me, which was how I liked it — no doormen. We rode to the twenty-eighth floor in an empty car, and Kimmery leaned against me as if we were still in the cab. I didn't need the support to stand anymore, but I didn't stop it from happening. My head throbbed — where Pierogi Man had clubbed me, it felt as though I were trying to grow a single horn, and failing — and the contact with Kimmery was a kind of compensation. At her floor she parted from my side with that nervous quick walk I already considered her trademark, her confession of some kernel of jerkiness I could cultivate and adore, and unlocked the door to her place so frantically I wondered if she thought we'd been followed.

"Did the giant see you?" I said when we were inside.

"What?"

"The giant. Are you afraid of the giant?" I felt a body-memory, and shuddered. I was still a little *unsteady on my pins,* as Minna would have said.

She looked at me strangely. "No, I just — I'm an illegal sublet here. There are people in this building who can't mind their own business. You should sit down. Do you want some water?"

"Sure." I looked around. "Sit where?"

Her apartment consisted of a brief foyer, a minuscule kitchen — really more an astronaut's cockpit full of cooking equipment — and a large central room whose polyurethaned floor mirrored the vast moonlit city nightscape featured in its long, uncurtained window. The reflected image was uninterrupted by carpet or furniture, just a few modest boxes tucked into the corners, a tiny boom box and a stack of tapes, and a large cat that stood in the center of the floor, regarding our entrance skeptically. The walls were bare. Kimmery's bedding was a flattened mattress on the floor of the foyer where we stood now, just inside the apartment's door. We were almost on top of it.

"Go ahead and sit on the bed," she said, with a nervous half smile.

Beside the bed was a candle, a box of tissues, and a small stack of paperbacks. It was a private space, a headquarters. I wondered if she hosted much — I felt I might be the first to see past her door.

"Why don't you sleep in there?" I said, pointing at the big empty room. My words came out thickened and stupid, like those of a defeated boxer in his dressing room, or a Method actor's, while playing a defeated boxer. My Tourette's brain preferred precision, sharper edges. I felt it waking.

"People look in," said Kimmery. "I'm not comfortable."

"You could have curtains." I gestured at the big window.

"It's too big. I don't really like that room. I don't know why." Now she looked like she regretted bringing me here. "Sit. I'll bring you some water."

The room she didn't like was the whole of the apartment. She lived instead in the foyer. But I decided not to say anything more about it. There was something anyway that suited me in her use of the space, as though she'd planned to bring me here to hide, knew I'd have something to fear from the skyline, the big world of conspiracies and doormen that was Manhattan.

I took a seat on her bed, back against the wall, legs straightened to cross the mattress, so my shoes reached the floor. I felt my tailbone meet the floor through the pancake-thin mattress. Now I saw that Kimmery had double-knotted my laces. I lingered awkwardly over this detail, used it to measure my returning consciousness, allowing my obsessiveness to play over the intricacy of the knots and my stroboscopic memories of Kimmery tugging at my feet in the cab. I imagined I could feel the dented place in my skull and the damaged language flowing in a new direction through this altered inner topography and the words went *sandwiches sandwiches I scream for ice cream dust to dust* and so on.

I decided to distract myself with the books stacked near the bed. The first was called *The Wisdom of Insecurity*, by Alan Watts. Tucked into it as an oversize bookmark was a pamphlet, a glossy sheet folded in thirds. I pulled out the pamphlet. It was for Yoshii's, a Zen Buddhist retreat center and roadside Thai and Japanese restaurant on the southern coast of Maine. The phone number beneath the schematic road map on the back was circled with blue ballpoint. The heading on the front of the pamphlet said A PLACE OF PEACE.

Pleasure police.

Pressure peas.

The cat walked in from the main room and stood on my outstretched thighs and began kneading them with its front paws, half-retracted claws engaging the material to make a *pocka-pocka-pocka* sound. The cat was black and white with a Hitler mustache, and when it finally noticed I had a face it squeezed its eyes at me. I folded the pamphlet into my jacket pocket, then took off my jacket and put it on the corner of Kimmery's bed. The cat went back to working my thighs.

"You probably don't like cats," said Kimmery, returning with two glasses of water.

"Chickencat," I said, ticcing stupidly. *"Cream of soup salad sandwich."*

"Are you hungry?"

"No, no," I said, though maybe I was. "And I like cats fine." But I kept my hands away, not wanting to begin obsessing on its body — kneading back or mimicking its uneven, cackling purr.

I can't own a cat, because my behaviors drive them insane. I know because I tried. I had a cat, gray and slim, half the size of Kimmery's, named Hen for the chirping and cooing sounds she made, for the barnyard pecking motions her initial sniffing inspections of my apartment reminded me of. She enjoyed my attentions at first, my somewhat excessive fondling. She'd purr and push against my hand as I tapped her, taking her pleasure. I'd refine my impulses toward her as well as I could, stroking her neck smoothly, rubbing her cheeks sideways to stimulate her kittenish memories of being licked, or whatever it is that makes cats crave that sensation. But from the very first Hen was disconcerted by my head-jerks and utterances and especially by my barking. She'd turn her head to see what I'd jumped at, to see what I was fishing for in the air with my hand. Hen recognized those behaviors — they were supposed to be *hers*. She never felt free to relax. She'd cautiously advance to my lap, a long game of half measures and imaginary distractions before she'd settle. Then I'd issue a string of bitten-off shrieks and bat at the curtain.

Worse, her bouts of joy at my petting hands became a focal point for Tourettic games of disruption. Hen would purr and nudge at my hand, and I'd begin stroking her smooth, sharklike face. She'd lean into the pressure, and I'd push back, until she was arched into my hand and ready to topple. Then the tic — I'd withdraw my hand. Other times I'd be compelled to follow her around the apartment, reaching for her when she'd meant to be sly or invisible; I'd stalk her, though it was obvious that like any cat her preference was to come to me. Or I'd fixate on the limits of her pleasure at being touched — would she keep purring if I rubbed her fur backward? If I tickled her cheeks would I be allowed to simultaneously grasp her sacrosanct tail? Would she permit me to clean the sleep from her eyes? The answer was often yes, but there was a cost. As with a voodoo doll, I'd begun investing my own ticcishness in my smaller counterpart: Tourette's Cat. She'd been reduced to a distrustful, skittish bundle of reactions, anticipatory flinchings and lashings-out. After six months I had to find her a new home with a Dominican family in the next building. They were able to straighten her out, after some cooling-off time spent hidden behind their stove.

The big Nazi cat went on raking up thread-loops from my trousers, seemingly intent on single-handedly reinventing Velcro. Meanwhile Kimmery returned with water, in two glasses she placed on the floor near my feet. Though the room was dim — we were lit as much by the reflected skyline in the big room behind us as by the faint bulb there in the foyer — she'd removed her eyeglasses for the first time, and her eyes looked tender and small and searching. She slid down to seat herself against the wall, so we were arranged like clock hands on the face of the floor, our shoes at the center. According to the clock of us it was four o'clock. I tried not to root for midnight.

"Have you been living here long?" I asked.

"I know, it looks like I'm camping out,"

she said. "It's been about a month. I just broke up with this guy. It's pretty obvious, isn't it?"

"The Oreo Man?" I pictured a weather-beaten cowboy in front of a sunset, holding a cookie to his lips like a cigarette. Then, in frantic compensation, I conjured a tormented nerd in goggle-glasses, peering at cookie crumbs through a microscope, trying to discern their serial numbers.

"Uh-huh," said Kimmery. "A friend was moving out and she gave me this place. I don't even like it. I'm hardly ever here."

"Where instead — the Zendo?"

She nodded. "Or the movies."

I wasn't ticcing much, for a couple of reasons. The first was Kimmery herself, still an unprecedented balm to me this late in the day. The second was the day itself, the serial tumult of unsorted clues, the catastrophe of my visit to the Zendo; that extra track in my brain had plenty of work to do threading beads together, smoothing the sequence into order: Kimmery, doormen, Matricardi and Rockaforte, Tony and Seminole, Important Monks, Gerard Minna and the killer. Minna's killer.

"Did you lock your door?" I said.

"You're really afraid," said Kimmery,

widening her eyes. "Of the, uh, giant."

"You didn't see him?" I said. "The big guy who took me outside?" I didn't mention what happened next. It was shameful enough that Kimmery had had to mop it up.

"He's a *giant?*"

"Well, what do you call it?"

"Isn't gigantism a genetic condition?"

"I'd say it is. He didn't *earn* that height." I touched the delicate spot on my head with one hand, kept the other calm at my side, ignoring every impulse to return the cat's pulsing and pawing at my legs. Instead I fingered the homely, hand-stitched coverlet on Kimmery's mattress, traced its inelegant, lumpy seams.

"I guess I didn't notice," she said. "I was, you know — sitting."

"You've never seen him before?"

She shook her head. "But I never met you before today either. I guess I should have told you not to bring anyone like that to the Zendo. And not to make noise. Now I missed practically the whole lecture."

"You're not saying the lecture went on?"

"Sure, why not? After you and your friend *the giant* were gone."

"Why didn't you stay?"

"Because my concentration isn't that good," she said, bitterly philosophical now.

"If you're really Zen you sit right through distractions, like Roshi did. And *Wallace.*" She rolled her eyes.

I was tempted to remind her that she'd moved to avoid being trampled, but it was just one objection among thousands.

"You don't understand," I said. "I didn't bring him to the Zendo. Nobody knew I was coming there."

"Well, I guess he followed you." She shrugged, not wanting to argue. To her it was self-evident that the giant and I were dual phenomena. I'd caused his presence at the Zendo, was likely responsible for his very existence.

"Listen," I said. "I know Roshi's American name. He's not who you think he is."

"I don't think he's anyone."

"What do you mean?"

"I didn't say, like, *Roshi's really Johnny Carson* or something. I just said I didn't know."

"Okay, but he's not a Zen teacher. He's involved in a murder."

"That's silly." She made it sound like a virtue, as though I'd meant to entertain her. "Besides, anyone who teaches Zen is a Zen teacher, I think. Probably even if they were a murderer. Just like anyone who sits is a student. Even you."

"What's wrong with me?"

"Nothing's wrong with you, at least according to a Zen outlook. That's my whole point."

"Taken."

"Don't be so sour, Lionel. I'm only joking. You sure you're happy with that cat?"

"Doesn't it have a name?" Feline Hitler had settled ponderously between my thighs, was purring in broken measures, and had begun to feature tiny bubbles of drool at the corners of its mouth.

"Shelf, but I never call him that."

"Shelf?"

"I know, it's completely stupid. I didn't name him. I'm just cat-sitting."

"So this isn't your apartment and this isn't your cat."

"It's sort of a period of crisis for me." She reached for her glass of water, and I immediately reached for mine, grateful: The mirroring scratched a tiny mental itch. Anyway, I was thirsty. Shelf didn't budge. "That's why I got involved with Zen," Kimmery went on. "For more *detachment.*"

"You mean like no apartment and no cat? How detached can you get?" My voice was irrationally bitter. Disappointment had crept over me, impossible to justify or perfectly define. I suppose I'd imagined us sheltered in Kimmery's childlike foyer, her West Side tree house, three cats hiding. But now I understood that she was rootless, alienated in this space. The Oreo Man's house was her home, or possibly the Zendo, just as L&L was mine, just as Shelf's was elsewhere, too. None of us could go to those places, so we huddled here together, avoiding the big room and the forest of skyscrapers.

Now, before Kimmery could reply, I ticced loudly, *"Detach-me-not!"* I tried to block myself, interrupt my own ticcing with the glass of water, which I moved to my lips just in time to shout into the glass, fevering the surface of the water with my breath, *"Go-shelf-a-lot!"*

"Wow," said Kimmery.

I didn't speak. I gulped down water and fondled the stitching of her coverlet again, seeking to lose my Tourette's self in texture.

"You say really weird stuff when you get angry," she said.

"I'm not —" I turned my neck, put the glass of water down on the floor. This time I jostled Shelf, who looked up at me with jaded eyes. "I'm not angry."

"What's wrong with you, then?" The question was delivered evenly, without sarcasm or fear, as though she really wanted an answer. Her eyes no longer looked small to me without the black frames around them. They felt as round and inquisitive as the cat's.

"Nothing — at least from a Zen outlook. I just shout sometimes. And touch things. And count things. And think about them too much."

"I've heard of that, I think."

"You're the exception to the rule if you have."

She reached into my lap and patted Shelf's head, distracting the cat from its interrogative gaze. Instead it squeezed its eyes together and craned its neck to press back against her palm. I'd have craned as far.

"Don't you want to know Roshi's real name?" I said.

"Why should I?"

"What?"

"Unless you're really going to shock me and say he's, like, J. D. Salinger, what's the difference? I mean, it's just going to be Bob or Ed or something, right?"

"Gerard Minna," I said. I wanted it to mean as much to her as Salinger, wanted her to understand everything. "He's Frank Minna's brother."

"Okay, but who's Frank Minna?"

"He's the guy who got killed." Strangely, I had a name for him now, a name flat and terrible and true: *the guy who got killed.* When before I could never have answered that question, or if I started answering it I'd never have finished. Frank Minna is the secret king of Court Street. Frank Minna is a mover and a talker, a word and a gesture, a detective and a fool. *Frank Minna c'est moi.*

"Oh, that's terrible."

"Yes." I wondered if I could ever share with her how terrible it was.

"I mean, that's got to be one of the worst things I've ever heard, practically."

Kimmery leaned closer, comforting the cat, not me. But I felt comforted. She and I were drawn close within her dawning understanding. Perhaps this foyer had only waited for this moment, for me and my story, to become a real space instead of a provisional one. Here Minna would be properly mourned. Here I'd find surcease for my pain and the answer to the puzzle of Tony and The Clients and why Minna and Ullman had to die and where Julia was and who Bailey was, and here Kimmery's hand would move from Shelf's head to my thigh and I would never tic again.

"He sent his brother out to die," I said. "He set him up. I heard it happen. I just don't know why yet."

"I don't understand. How did you hear?"

"Frank Minna was wearing a bug when he went into the Zendo. I heard him and Gerard talking. You were there too, in the building."

I recalled revising my surveillance note, trying to decide whether to declare Kimmery *girl* or *woman,* and my writing hand twitched, reenacting my crossing-out across the soft threads of her coverlet.

"When?"

"Yesterday," I said, though it seemed a long time ago now.

"Well, that's impossible. It must have been someone else."

"Tell me why."

"Roshi is under a vow of silence." She whispered, as if she were breaking such a vow at this moment. "He hasn't said a word for the last five days. So you couldn't have heard him talk."

I was tongue-tied for once. It was the logic of the Oreo Man, invading my moral puzzle. Or another Zen conundrum: What's the sound of a silent monk condemning his brother to death?

The quieter the monk, the gaudier the patter I thought, remembering the conversation on the wiretap.

"I can't believe you go around *bugging*

people," she said, still whispering. Perhaps she imagined there was a bug in the room now. "Were you trying to frame this Frank person?"

"No, no, no. Frank wanted me to listen."

"He wanted to be caught?"

"He didn't *do* anything," I said. "Except get bumped off by his brother, the silent monk."

Though she regarded me skeptically, Kimmery went on rubbing the cat's neck and head while it nestled in my lap. I had more than the usual panicky reasons to ignore the captivating sensations, the fricative purring and chafing down there. I was suppressing two different kinds of response, two possible ways of poking back. I kept my eyes level on Kimmery's face.

"I think you've got a few things mixed up," she said gently. "Roshi's a very gentle man."

"Well, Gerard Minna's a punk from Brooklyn," I said. "And they're positively the same guy."

"Hmmm. I don't know, Lionel. Roshi once told me he'd never been to Brooklyn. He's from Vermont or Canada or something."

"Maine?" I asked, thinking of the pamphlet I'd secreted in my jacket, the retreat center by the water.

She shrugged. "I don't know. You should take my word for it, though, he isn't from *Brooklyn.* He's a very important man." She made it sound as if the two were mutually exclusive.

"Eat me Brooklyn Roshi!"

I was ticcing out of sheer frustration. In squaring her perceptions to mine I not only had a world of knowledge to build up but a preexisting one to tear down. Anyone faintly Zen was to her beyond reproach. And Gerard Minna, for the cheap act of shaving his likely-already-balding head, was secure in a pantheon of the holy.

And Gerard had a lot of damn gall to renounce the borough.

"Lionel?"

I grabbed for my glass, took another sip of water, averted my eyes from Kimmery's.

"How does it feel when you do that?" she said. "I mean, what are you thinking?"

She was close enough now, and I succumbed completely and reached for her shoulder, tapped it five times quickly with paired fingertips. Then I moved my water glass to the floor and leaned forward, forcing Shelf to make another bleary, pleasure-addled adjustment to his position in my lap, and straightened Kimmery's collar with both hands. The material was floppy, and I tried to prop it up as if it were starched, put the collar-tips on point like a ballerina's toes. And my brain went, *How are you feeling and how are you thinking and think how you're feeling*, and that became the chorus, the soundtrack to my adamant necessary collar-play.

"Lionel?" She didn't push my hands away.

"Liable," I said softly, my gaze lowered. "Think-a-mum Feely."

"What do the words mean?"

"They're just words. They don't mean anything." The question depressed me a little, took the wind out of my sails, and this was a good thing: I was able to release her collar, still my wriggling fingers.

Kimmery touched one hand, just briefly, as I withdrew it. I was numb to her now, though. She no longer soothed my tics, and the attention she'd begun to give them was humiliating. I needed to get this interview back on an official basis. Sitting here purring and being purred at wasn't going to accomplish anything. In the city on the other side of the door a giant killer lurched around unafraid, and it was my job to find him.

"What do you know about ten-thirty Park Avenue?" I said, resuming my investigation, the legitimate inquiry.

"Is that that big apartment building?" Her hand was back riffling Shelf's fur, her body ever closer to mine.

"Big building," I said. "Yes."

"A lot of Roshi's students do their work service there," she said lightly. "Working in the kitchen, cleaning up, that kind of thing. I was telling you about it, remember?"

"Doormen? Any — doormen?" My syndrome wanted to call them dogshirts, doorsnips, diphthongs. I gritted my teeth.

She shrugged. "I think so. I never went there myself. Lionel?"

"Yes?"

"You didn't really come to the Zendo because you were interested in Buddhism, did you?"

"I guess I thought that was obvious by now."

"It is obvious."

I wasn't sure what to say. I was narrowed to a fine point, thinking only of Frank and Gerard and the places I might have to go to finish my investigation. I'd shuttered myself against Kimmery's tenderness toward me, even shuttered away my own tenderness toward her. She was an incompetent witness, beyond that a distraction. And I was an investigator who supplied plenty of my own distractions, too many.

"You came to make trouble," she said.

"I came *because* of trouble, yes."

Kimmery rubbed the fur of Shelf's flank in the wrong direction, aggravating my senses. I put my hand on the cat for the first time, nudged Kimmery's fingers away from the chaos of up-sticking fur she'd caused, and smoothed the fur back into place.

"Well, I'm glad I met you anyway," she said.

I made a sound, half dog, half cat, something like *"Chaarff."*

Our hands collided in Shelf's fur, Kimmery's moving to rough up the area I'd just smoothed into sense, mine preemptively slipping underneath to preserve my work. It took a big indifferent loaf of a cat like Shelf to withstand it; Hen would have been across the room reordering herself with her own tongue by now.

"You're strange to me," said Kimmery.

"Don't feel bad about it," I said.

"No, but I mean strange in a good way, too."

"Uh." She was tugging on my fingers, and I tugged systematically back, so our hands were tangling, squirming, the cat a benign mattress underneath, one vibrating like a cheap hotel's.

"You can say whatever you want," Kimmery whispered.

"What do you mean?"

"The words."

"I don't really need to when you're touching my hand like that."

"I like to."

"Touch?" Touch shoulders, touch penguins, touch Kimmery — who didn't like to touch? Why shouldn't she? But this vaguest of questions was all I could manage. I wasn't only strange to her, I was strange to myself at that moment: tugging, lulled, resistant. Conworried.

"Yes," she said. "You. Here —"

She groped at the wall behind her head and switched off the light. We were still outlined in white, Manhattan's radiation leaking in from the big room. Then she moved closer: It was a minute after twelve. Somewhere as she fit herself in beside me the cat was jostled loose and wandered ungrudgingly away.

"That's better," I said lamely, like I was reading from a script. The distance between us had narrowed, but the distance between me and me was enormous. I blinked in the half-light, looking straight ahead. Now her hand was on my thigh where the cat had been. Mirroring, I let my fingers play lightly at the parallel spot on her leg.

"Yes," she said.

"I can't seem to interest you fully in my case," I said.

"Oh, I'm interested," she said. "It's just — It's hard to talk about things that are important to you. With a new person. Everyone is so strange, don't you think?"

"I think you're right."

"So you have to trust them at first. Because everything makes sense after a while."

"So that's what you're doing with me?"

She nodded, then leaned her head against my shoulder. "But you're not asking me anything about myself."

"I'm sorry," I said, surprised. "I guess — I guess I don't know where to start."

"Well, so you see what I mean, then."

"Yes."

I didn't have to turn her face to mine to kiss her. It was already there when I turned. Her lips were small and soft and a little chapped. I'd never before kissed a woman without having had a few drinks. And I'd never kissed a woman who hadn't had a few herself. While I tasted her Kimmery drew circles on my leg with her finger, and I did the same back.

"You do everything I do," she whispered into my mouth.

"I don't really need to," I said again. "Not if we're this close." It was the truth. I was never less ticcish than this: aroused, pressing toward another's body, moving out of my own. But just as Kimmery had somehow spared me ticcing aloud in conversation, now I felt free to incorporate an element of Tourette's into our groping, as though she were negotiating a new understanding between my two disgruntled brains.

"It's okay," she said. "You need a shave, though."

We kissed then, so I couldn't reply, didn't want to. I felt her press her thumb very gently against the point of my Adam's apple, a touch I couldn't exactly return. I stroked her ear and jaw instead, urging her nearer. Then her hand fell lower, and mine too, and at that moment I felt my hand and mind lose their particularity, their pointiness, their countingness, instead become clouds of general awareness, dreamy and yielding with curiosity. My hand felt less a hand than a catcher's mitt, or Mickey Mouse's hand, something vast and blunt and soft. I didn't count her where I touched her. I conducted a general survey, took a tender sampling.

"You're excited," she breathed.

"Yes."

"It's okay."

"I know."

"I just wanted to mention it."

"Okay, yes."

She unbuttoned my pants. I fumbled with hers, with a thin sash knotted at her front for a belt. I couldn't undo it with one hand. We were breathing into one another's mouths, lips slipping together and apart, noses mashed. I found a way in around the knotted sash, untucked her shirt. I put my finger in her belly button, then found the crisp margin of her pubic hair, threaded it with a finger. She tremored and slid her knee between mine.

"You can touch me there," she said.

"I am," I said, wishing for accuracy.

"You're so excited," she said. "It's okay."

"Yes."

"It's okay. Oh, Lionel, that's okay. Don't stop, it's okay."

"Yes," I said. "It's okay." *Okay, okay:* Here was Kimmery's tic, in evidence at last. I couldn't begrudge it. I turned my whole hand, gathering her up, surrounding her. She spilled as I held her. Meanwhile she'd found the vent in my boxer shorts. I felt two fingertips contact a part of me through that window, the blind men and the elephant. I wanted and didn't want her to go on, terribly.

"You're so excited," she said again, incantatory.

"Uh." She jostled me, untangled me from my shorts and my self.

"Wow, God, Lionel you're sort of huge."

"And bent," I said, so she wouldn't have to say it.

"Is that normal?"

"I guess it's a little unusual-looking." I panted, hoping to be past this moment.

"More than a little, Lionel."

"Someone — a woman once told me it was like a beer can."

"I've heard of that," said Kimmery. "But yours is, I don't know, like a beer can that's been crushed, like for recycling."

So it was for me. In my paltry history I'd never been unveiled without hearing something about it — freak shows within freak shows. Whatever Kimmery thought, it didn't keep her from freeing me from my boxer shorts and palming me, so that I felt myself aching heavily in her cool grasp. We made a circuit: mouths, knees, hands and what they held. The sensation was okay. I tried to match the rhythm of her hand with mine, failed. Kimmery's tongue lapped my chin, found my mouth again. I made a whining sound, not a part of any word. Language was destroyed. Bailey, he left town.

"It's okay to talk," she whispered.

"Uh."

"I like, um, I like it when you talk. When you make sounds."

"Okay."

"Tell me something, Lionel."

"What?"

"I mean, say something. The way you do."

I looked at her open-mouthed. Her hand urged me toward an utterance that was anything but verbal. I tried to distract her the same way.

"Speak, Lionel."

"Ah." It really was all I could think to say.

She kissed me gaspingly and drew back, her look expectant.

"One Mind!" I said.

"Yes!" said Kimmery.

"Fonebone!" I shouted.

Another key contributor to my Tourette's lexicon was a cartoonist named Don Martin, first encountered in a pile of tattered *Mad* magazines in a box in the Ping-Pong room in the basement of St. Vincent's when I was eleven or twelve. I used to pore over his drawings, trying to find what it was about his characters, drawn with riotously bulging eyes, noses, chins, Adam's apples and knees, elongated tongues and fingers and feet that flapped like banners, named Professor Bleent, P. Carter Franit, Mrs. Freenbeen and Mr. Fonebone, that stirred such a deep chord in me. His image of life was garish and explosive, heads being stretched and shrunk, surgeons lopping off noses and dropping brains and sewing hands on backward, falling safes and metal presses squashing men flat or into boxlike packages, children swallowing coat hangers and pogo sticks and taking on their shapes. His agonized characters moved through their panels with a geeky physicality, seeming to strain toward their catastrophic contact with fire hoses, whirring blades, and drawbridges, and his sophomoric punch lines mostly hinged on reversals or literalizations — "The kids are upstairs with their ears glued to the radio" — or else on outright destruction. *Mad* often held the concluding panel of a Don Martin cartoon to the following page, and part of the pleasure of his work was never knowing whether the payoff would be a visual pun or verbal riff or merely the sight of a man in a full-body cast falling out a window into the path of a steamroller. Mostly, though, I recall the distortion, the torque in the bodies he drew: These characters had met disaster in being born onto the page, and their more extreme fates were only realizations of their essential nature. This made sense to me. And Fonebone made sense, too. He had a name I could get behind. For a while he almost supplanted Bailey, and he was lastingly traceable in my tendency to append *phone* or *bone* to the end of a phrase.

When I had sex with another person and my body began to convulse and move faster, my toes to curl, my eyes to roll, I felt like a Don Martin character, a Fonebone, all elbows and bowlegs and boomerang penis and gurgling throat in a halo of flung-off sweat drops and sound effects: *Fip, Thwat, Zwip, Sproing, Flabadab.* More than Daffy Duck, more than Art Carney, more than any other icon of my discomfort. Don Martin's drawings throbbed with the suggestion that disruptive feeling was all sexual. Though his venue denied him any overt reference his characters overflowed with lewd energies, which had to be manifested instead in tics and seizures, eruptions and deformations. His poor doomed Fonebones seemed to chart my path from twitch to orgasm, the way sex first smoothed away tics, then supplanted them with a violent double: little death, big tic. So perhaps it was Don Martin's fault that I always expected a punishment after sex, cringed in anticipation of the steamroller or plummeting anvil to follow.

Possibly Kimmery sensed it in me, this dread of a page about to be turned, revealing some ludicrous doom on the last panel of my cartoon. Another fact about Don Martin: He never used the same character twice — each was an innocent pawn with no carry-over from one episode to the next, no understanding of his role or fate. A Fonebone was a placeholder, a disposable clone or stooge. A member of the Butt Trust.

"Is something the matter?" she said, stopping what she was doing, what I was doing.

"Everything's fine. I mean, better than fine."

"You don't look fine."

"Just one thing, Kimmery. Promise me you won't go back to the Zendo. At least for a few days."

"Why?"

"Just trust me, okay?"

"Okay."

With that, her magic word, we were done talking.

* * *

Once Kimmery was asleep I dressed and tiptoed to her phone, which was on the floor in the big room. Shelf followed me in. I tapped his head five times, instantly reigniting his ragged purring, then pushed him away. The phone showed a number under its plastic window. I fed the number into the speed dial of the doormen's cell phone, wincing at the beeping tones, which echoed in the silent empty room like musical gunshots. Kimmery didn't stir on her mattress, though. She lay splayed like a child making a snow angel. I wanted to go and kneel and trace her shape with my fingertips or my breath. Instead I found her key ring and separated the five keys. The key to the apartment was easy to identify, and that was the only one I left behind — she'd have to deal with her suspicious neighbors to get into the lobby downstairs. I took the other four, figuring one would get me into the Zendo. The last two probably unlocked Oreo Man's place. Those I'd lose.

Auto Body

See me now, at one in the morning, stepping out of another cab in front of the Zendo, checking the street for cars that might have followed, for giveaway cigarette-tip glows through the windows of the cars parked on the deadened street, moving with my hands in my jacket pockets clutching might-be-guns-for-all-they-know, collar up against the cold like Minna, unshaven like Minna now, too, shoes clacking on sidewalk: think of a coloring-book image of the Green Hornet, say. That's who I was supposed to be, that black outline of a man in a coat, ready suspicious eyes above his collar, shoulders hunched, moving toward conflict.

Here's who I was instead: that same coloring-book outline of a man, but crayoned by the hand of a mad or carefree or retarded child, wild slashes of idiot color, a blizzard of marks violating the boundaries that made *man* distinct from *street*, from *world.* Some of those colors were my fresh images of Kimmery, flashing me back to the West Side an hour before, crayon stripes and arrows like flares over Central Park in the night sky. Others weren't so pretty, roaring scrawls of mania, *find-a-man-kill-a-phone-fuck-a-plan* in sloppy ten-foot-high letters drawn like lightning bolts or Hot Wheels race-car flames through the space of my head. And the blackened steel-wool scribble of my guilt-deranged investigation: I pictured the voices of the two Minna brothers and Tony Vermonte and The Clients as gnarled above and around me, in a web of betrayal I had to penetrate and dissolve, an ostensible world I'd just discovered was really only a private cloud I carried everywhere, had never seen the outside of. So, crossing the street to the door of the Zendo, I might have appeared less a single Green Hornet than a whole inflamed nest of them.

My first act was to drop in next door. I found the original doorman, Dirk, asleep on his stool.

I lifted his head up with my hand and he jerked awake and away from my grasp. "Hello!" he shouted.

"You remember me, Dirk?" I said. "I was sitting in a car. You told me I had a message from my 'friend.' "

"Oh? Sure, I remember. Sorry, I was just doing what I was told."

"Sure you were. And I suppose you never

saw the guy before, did you — *dirtyworker, dirketyname?*"

"I never saw the guy before." He breathed out, wide-eyed.

"He was a very big man, yes?"

"Yes!" He rolled his eyes upward to show it. Then he held his hands out, begging my patience. I backed off a little and he stood and neatened his coat. I helped him with it, especially around the collar. He was too sleepy or confused by my questions to object.

"He pay you or just scare you into giving me the bum steer?" I asked more gently. My anger was wasted on Dirk. Anyway, I felt vaguely grateful to him for confirming the giant's existence. My only other sure witness was Gilbert, in jail. Kimmery had begun to make me doubt my eyes.

"A man that big doesn't have to pay," said Dirk honestly.

One of the stolen keys got me inside. This time I held on to my shoes as I passed the sitting room and headed upstairs, past the floor where Kimmery and I had sat at tea, up to the Roshi's private quarters — a.k.a. Gerard Minna's hideout. The halls were darker the higher I climbed, until at the top I could only grope my way toward a thin margin of light squeezed out underneath a sealed door. I turned the handle and pushed the door open, impatient with my own fear.

His bedroom had the integrity of his self-reinvention. It was bare of furnishings except for a long low shelf against the wall, a board, really, propped on bricks and bearing a few candles and books, a glass of water and a small bowl of ashes, decorated with Japanese script, presumably some kind of tiny shrine. The spareness reminded me of Kimmery's empty studio apartment but I resented the echo, not wishing to see Kimmery as influenced by Gerard's Zen pretensions, not wishing to imagine her visiting his private floor, his lair, at all. Gerard sat propped on pillows on a flat mattress on the floor, his legs crossed, the book at his knees shut, his posture calm, as though he'd been waiting for me. I faced him head on for what might have been the first time — I don't know that I'd ever addressed him directly, stolen more than a glance as a teenager. In the candlelight I first made out his silhouette: He'd thickened around the jaw and neck, so that his bald head seemed to rise from his round shoulders like the line of a cobra's hood. I might have been overly influenced by that bald head but as my eyes adjusted I couldn't keep from understanding the difference between his features and Frank Minna's as the same as that between Brando's in *Apocalypse Now!* and *On the Waterfront.*

"Thehorrorthehorror," I ticced. *"Icouldabeenacontender!"* It was like a couplet.

"You're Lionel Essrog, aren't you?"

"Unreliable Chessgrub," I corrected. My throat pulsed with ticcishness. I was overly conscious of the open door behind me, so my neck twitched, too, with the urge to look over my shoulder. Doormen could come through open doors, anyone knew that. "Is there anyone else in the building?" I said.

"We're alone."

"Mind if I close this?"

"Go ahead." He didn't budge from his position on the mattress, just gazed at me evenly. I closed the door and moved just far enough into the room not to be tempted to grope behind me for the door's surface. We faced each other across the candlelit gloom, each a figure out of the other's past, each signifying to the other the lost man, the man killed the day before.

"You broke your vow of silence just now," I said.

"I'm finished with my sesshin," he said. "Anyway, you brought silence to a rather conclusive finish during today's sitting."

"I think your hired killer had something to do with that."

"You're speaking without thinking," he said. "I recall your difficulties in that area."

I took a deep breath. Gerard's serenity called out of me a storm of compensatory voices, a myriad possible shrieks and insults to stanch. A part of me wanted to cajole him out from behind his Zen front, expose the Lord of Court Street lurking, make him Frank's older brother again. What came out of my mouth was the beginning of a joke, one from the deepest part of the made-Frank-Minna-laugh-once archive:

"So there's this order of nuns, right?"

"An order of nuns," Gerard repeated.

"*Ordinary nunphone!* — an order of nuns. Like the Cloisters. You know, a monastery."

"A monastery is for monks."

"Okay, a nunastery. *A plannery, a nunnetarium!* — a nunnery. And they've all, these nuns, they've all taken a vow of silence, a lifetime vow of silence, right?" I was driven, tears at the edges of my eyes, wishing for Frank to be alive to rescue me, tell me he'd heard this one already. Instead I had to go on. "Except one day a year one of the nuns gets to say something. They take turns, one nun a year. Understand?"

"I think I understand."

"So the big day comes — *Barnamum-big-nun! Domesticated ghost-phone!* — the big day is here and the nuns are all sitting at the dinner table and the one who gets to talk this year opens her mouth and says 'The soup is terrible.' And the other nuns all look at each other but nobody says anything because of the vow of silence, and that's it, back to normal. Another year of silence."

"A very disciplined group," said Gerard, not without admiration.

"Right. So a year later the day comes and it's this other nun's turn. So they're sitting and the second nun turns to the first and says 'I don't know, maybe it's just me, but I don't think the soup's that bad' — and that's it, silence. Another year."

"Hmmm. Imagine the states of contemplation one could achieve in such a year."

"I never thought about it myself. Anyway, so the calendar pages flip, and the special day — *Flip-a-thon! Fuck-a-door! Flipweed! Fujisaki! Flitcraft!* — the special day comes around again. This third nun, it's her turn — *Nun-fuck-a-phone!* — so this third nun, she looks at the first nun and the second nun and she says 'Bicker, bicker, bicker.' "

There was silence, then Gerard nodded and said, "That would be the punch line."

"I know about the building," I said, working to catch my breath. "And the Fujisaki Corporation." *Unfuckafish* whispered under my palate.

"Ah. Then you know much."

"Yeah, I know a thing. And I've met your killing machine. But you saw that, when he dragged me out, downstairs. The kumquat-eater."

I was desperate to see him flinch, to impress him with the edge I had, the things I'd learned, but Gerard wasn't ruffled. He raised his eyebrows, which got a lot of play across the empty canvas of his forehead. "You and your friends, what are their names?"

"Who? The Minna Men?"

"Yes — Minna Men. That's a very good description. My brother was very important to the four of you, wasn't he?"

I nodded, or not, but anyway he went on.

"He really taught you everything, I suppose. You sound just like him when you speak. What an odd life, really. You realize that, don't you? That Frank was a very odd man, living in a strange and anachronistic way?"

"What's *cartoonistic* about it?"

"Anachronistic," said Gerard patiently. "From another time."

"I know what it means," I said. "I mean what's so *akakonistic* about it?" I was too wound up to go back and repair the tic-pocked surface of my speech. "Anyway, *enactoplasmic* as opposed to what? A million-year-old mystical Japanese cult?"

"You wear your ignorance as aggressively as Frank," said Gerard. "I suppose you're making my point for me."

"Point being what?"

"My brother taught you only what he knew, and not even all of that. He kept you charmed and flattered but also in the dark, so your sense of even his small world was diminished, two-dimensional. Cartoonistic, if you like. What's astonishing to me is that you didn't know about the Park Avenue building until just now. It really must come as a shock."

"Enlighten me."

"Surely you've got my brother's money in your pocket even as we speak, Lionel. Do you really believe that it came from detective work, from those scuffling little assignments he contrived to keep you children busy? Or perhaps you imagine he *crapped* money. That's just as likely."

Was *crapped* a chink in Gerard's Zen façade, a bit of Brooklyn showing through? I recalled the elder monk proclaiming the worthlessness of "Bowel Movement Zen."

"Frank consorted with dangerous people," Gerard went on. "And he stole from them. The remuneration and the risk were high. The odds that he would flourish in such a life forever, low."

"Talk to me about *fool-me-softly — Fujisaki.*"

"They own the building. Minna had a hand in managing it. The money involved would dazzle your senses, Lionel." He gave me an expectant look, as though this assertion ought to dazzle me in the money's stead, ought to astonish me right out of my investigation, and his bedroom.

"These people, their other home is an island," I said, quoting the Garbage Cop — not that the phrase was likely to have originated with him.

Gerard smiled at me oddly. "For every Buddhist, Japan is his other home. And yes, it is an island."

"Who's a Buddhist?" I said. "I was talking about the money."

He sighed, without losing the smile. "You are so like Frank."

"What's your role, Gerard?" I wanted to sicken him the way I was sickened. "I mean, besides sending your brother out into the Polack's arms to die."

Now he beamed munificently. The worse I attacked him, the deeper his forgiveness and grace would be — that's what the smile said. "Frank was very careful never to expose me to any danger if he could help it. I was never introduced to anyone from Fujisaki. I believe I have yet to make their acquaintance, apart from the large hit man you led here yesterday."

"Who's Ullman?"

"A bookkeeper, another New Yorker. He was Frank's partner in fleecing the Japanese."

"But you *never met the guy.*"

I meant him to hear the sarcasm, or rather Frank Minna's sarcasm in quotation. But he went on obliviously. "No. I only supplied the labor, in return for consideration equal to my mortgage here on the Zendo. Buddhism is spread by what means it finds."

"Labor for what?" My brain tangled on *spread by means it finds, fed in springs by mimes, bled by mingy spies,* but I shook it off.

"My students performed the maintenance and service work for the building, as part of their training. Cleaning, cooking, the very sort of labor they'd perform in a monastery, only in a slightly different setting. The contract for those services in such a building is worth millions. My brother and

Ullman tithed the difference mostly into their own pockets."

"Doormen," I said.

"Yes. Doormen, too."

"So Fujisaki sicced the giant on Frank and the bookkeeper."

"I suppose that's right."

"And he just happened to use the Zendo as his trap yesterday?" I aired out another Minna-ism: "Don't try to hand me no two-ton feather." I was dredging up Minna's usages on any excuse now, as though I could build a golem of his language, then bring it to life, a figure of vengeance to search out the killer or killers.

I was aware of myself standing in Gerard's room, planted on his floor, arms at my sides, never moving nearer to him where he sat beaming Zen pleasantness in my direction, ignoring my accusations and my tics. I was big but I was no golem or giant. I hadn't startled Gerard in deep sleep nor upended his calm with my griefy hostility. I wasn't holding a gun on him. He didn't have to answer my questions.

"I don't really believe in sophisticated killers," said Gerard. "Do you?"

"Go-fisticate-a-killphone," I ticced.

"The Fujisaki Corporation is ruthless and remorseless — in the manner of corporations. And yet in the manner of corporations their violence is also performed at a remove, by a force just nominally under their control. In the giant you speak of they seem to have located a sort of primal entity — one whose true nature is killing. And sicced him, as you say, on the men who they feel betrayed them. I'm not sure the killer's behavior is explicable in any real sense, Lionel. Any human sense."

Gerard's persuasiveness was a variant of the Minna style, I saw now. I felt the force of it, moving me authentically. Yet his foray against the notion of a sophisticated killer also made me think of Tony mocking Detective Seminole with jokes about Batman and James Bond supervillains. Was it a giveaway, a clue that Gerard and Tony were in league? And what about Julia? I wanted to quote Frank's conversation with Gerard the night he died: *She misses her Rama-lama-ding-dong,* find out what he meant. I wanted to ask about Boston, and I wanted to ask about Frank and Julia's marriage — had Gerard been at the ceremony? I wanted to ask him about whether he missed Brooklyn, and how he got his head so shiny. I searched for a single question that could stand for my thousands and what popped out was this:

"What's human sense?"

"In Buddhism, Lionel, we come to understand that everything on this earth is a vessel for Buddha-nature. Frank had Buddha-nature. You have Buddha-nature. I feel it."

Gerard allowed a long minute to pass while we contemplated his words. *Buddha nostril,* I nearly blurted. When he spoke again, it was with a confidence that sympathy flowed between us untrammeled by doubt or fear.

"There's another of your Minna Men, Lionel. He's pushing his way into this, and I fear he may have aroused the killer's ire. Tony, is that his name?"

"Tony Vermonte," I said, marveling — it was as if Gerard had read my mind.

"Yes. He'd like to walk in my brother's footsteps. But Fujisaki will be keeping a keener eye on their money from this point, I'd think. There's nothing to be gained and everything to be lost. Perhaps you'll have a word with him."

"Tony and I aren't exactly . . . communicating well, since yesterday."

"Ah."

I felt a surge of care in me, for Tony. He was only a heedless adventurer, with a poignant urge to imitate Frank Minna in all things. He was a member of my family — L&L, the Men. Now he was in above his head, threatened on all sides by the giant, by Detective Seminole, by The Clients. Only Gerard and I understood his danger.

I must have been silent for a minute or so — a veritable sesshin by my standards.

"You and Tony are together in your pain at the loss of my brother," said Gerard softly. "But you haven't come together in actuality. Be patient."

"There's another factor," I said, tentative now, lulled by his compassionate tones. "Someone else may be involved in this somehow. Two of them, actually — *Monstercookie and Antifriendly!* — uh, Matricardi and Rockaforte."

"You don't say."

"I do."

"You can't know how sorry I am to hear those names." *Never say those names!* warned Minna in the echo chamber of my memory. Gerard went on, "Those two are the prototype, aren't they, for my brother's tendency to dangerous associations — and his tendency to exploit those associations in dangerous ways."

"He stole from them?"

"Do you recall that he once had to leave New York for a while?"

Did I recall! Suddenly Gerard threatened to solve the deepest puzzles of my existence.

I practically wanted to ask him, *So who's Bailey?*

"I'd hoped they were no longer in the picture," said Gerard reflectively. It was the nearest to thrown I'd seen him, the closest I'd come to pushing his buttons. Only now I wasn't sure I wanted to. "Avoid them, Lionel, if you can," he continued. "They're dangerous men."

He returned his gaze to my face, batted his lashes, moved his expressive eyebrows. If I'd been in striking distance I'd have tried to span his head with my hands and stroke his eyebrows with my thumb tips, just to soothe this one small worry I'd raised.

"Can I ask one more thing?" I nearly called him Roshi, so complete was my conversion. "Then I'll leave you alone."

Gerard nodded. *The High Lama will grant you an audience, Mrs. Gushman.*

"Is there anyone else — *Zonebone!* — anyone else at the Zendo who's involved in this thing? Anyone — *Kissmefaster! Killmesooner! Cookiemonster!* — anyone the killer might target? That old hippie, Wallace? Or the girl — *Kissingme!* — Kimmery?" I tried not to divulge the special freight of tenderness and hope behind this query. Whether the string of shrieks I issued in the course of its delivery made me appear more or less blasé, I couldn't say.

"No." Gerard spoke benevolently. "I compromised myself personally, but not my students or my practice as a teacher. Wallace and Kimmery should be safe. It's kind of you to be concerned."

I'm concerned about Pinched and Indistinct, too, I wanted to say. I doubted students could get any more compromised than that.

And then there was that nod of complicity I saw pass between Gerard and the giant.

The three of them — Pinched, Indistinct, and the nod — were three sour notes in a very pretty song. But I kept my tongue, feeling I'd learned what I could here, that it was time to go. I wanted to find Tony before the giant did. And I needed to step outside the candle glow of Gerard's persuasiveness to sort out the false and the real, the Zen and the chaff in our long discussion.

"I'm going now," I said awkwardly.

"Good night, Lionel." He was still watching me as I closed the door.

On second thought, there *is* a vaguely Tourettic aspect to the New York City subway, especially late at night — that dance of attention, of stray gazes, in which every rider must engage. And there's a lot of stuff you shouldn't touch in the subway, particularly in a certain order: this pole and then your lips, for instance. And the tunnel walls are layered, like those of my brain, with expulsive and incoherent language —

But I was in a terrible hurry, or rather two terrible hurries: to get back to Brooklyn, and to sort out my thinking about Gerard before I got there. I couldn't spare a minute to dwell in myself as a body riding the Lexington train to Nevins Street — I might as well have been teleported, or floated to Brooklyn on a magic carpet, for all that I was allured or distracted by the 4 train's sticky, graffitied immediacy.

The lights were burning in the L&L storefront. I approached from the opposite sidewalk, confident I was invisible on the darkened street to those in the office — I'd been on the other side of that plate of glass only two or three thousand nights in preparation for the act of spying on my fellow Men from the street. I didn't want to go waltzing into a trap. Detective Seminole might be there or, who knew, maybe Tony and a passel of doormen. If there was something to learn at a distance, I'd learn it.

It was almost two-thirty now, and Bergen Street was shut up tight, the night cold enough to chase the stoop-sitting drinkers indoors. Smith Street showed a bit more life, Zeod's Market lit up like a beacon, catering to the all-night cigarette cravings, to the squad-car cops in need of a bagel or LifeSaver or some other torus. Four L&L cars were scattered in parking spots near the storefront: the Minna death car, which hadn't moved since Gilbert and I returned from the hospital and parked it, the Pontiac in which Tony had shanghaied me in front of The Clients' brownstone, a Caddy that Minna had liked to drive himself, and a Tracer, an ugly modernistic bubble of a car that usually fell to me or Gilbert to pilot. I slowed my walk as I drew up even with the storefront, then turned my neck. It was pleasing to have a good solid reason behind turning my neck for once, retroactive validation for a billion tics. As I passed, I made out the shapes of two Men inside: Tony and Danny, both in a cloud of cigarette smoke, Danny seated behind the counter with a folded newspaper, radiating cool, Tony pacing, radiating cool's opposite. The television was on.

I walked past, to the corner of Smith, then swiveled and went back. This time I set up shop on the brief stoop of the big apartment building directly across from L&L. It was a safe outpost. I could duck my head and watch them through a parked car's windows if I thought they were in any danger of spotting me. Otherwise I'd sit back in the wings and study them in the limelight of the storefront until something happened or I'd decided what to do.

Danny — I gave Danny Fantl a moment of my time. He was sliding through this crisis as he'd slid through life to this point, so poised he was practically an ambient presence. Gilbert was in jail and I was hunted high and low and Danny sat in the storefront all day, refusing car calls and smoking cigarettes and reading sports. He wasn't exactly my candidate for any plot's criminal mastermind, but if Tony conspired with or even confided in anyone inside L&L's circle, it would be Danny. In the present atmosphere, I decided, there was no way I could take Danny for granted, trust him with my back.

Which meant I wasn't going inside to talk with either one of them until they were apart. If then — the image of Tony pulling his wobbly gun on me was fresh enough to give pause.

Anyway, something happened before I'd decided what to do — why was I not surprised? But it was a relatively banal something, reassuring, even. A tick of the clock of everyday life on Bergen Street, an everyday life that already felt nostalgic.

A block east, on the corner of Bergen and Hoyt, was an elegantly renovated tavern called the Boerum Hill Inn, with a gleaming antique inlaid-mirror bar, a CD jukebox weighted toward Blue Note and Stax, and a Manhattanized clientele of professional singles too good for bars with televisions, for subway rides home, or for the likes of the Men. Only Minna ever visited the Boerum Hill Inn, and he cracked that anyone who drank there was someone else's assistant: a district attorney's, an editor's, or a video artist's. The dressed-up crowd at the inn gabbled and flirted every night of the week until two in the morning, oblivious to the neighborhood's past or present reality, then slept it off in their overpriced apartments or on their desks the next day in Midtown. Typically a few parties would stagger down the block after last call and try to engage an L&L car for a ride home — sometimes it was a woman alone or a newly formed couple too drunk to throw to the fates, and we'd take the job. Mostly we claimed not to have any cars.

But the inn's bartenders were a couple of young women we adored, Siobhain and Welcome. Siobhain was properly named, while Welcome bore the stigma of her parents' hippie ideals, but both were from Brooklyn and Irish to their ancient souls — or so had declared Minna. They were roommates in Park Slope, possibly lovers (again according to Minna), and bartending their way through graduate school. Each night one or the other was stuck with closing — the owner of the inn was stingy and didn't let them double up after midnight. If we weren't actually busy on some surveillance job we'd always drive the closer home.

It was Welcome, at the door of L&L, now going inside. I saw Tony nod at Danny, then Danny stood and stubbed out a butt, checked in his pocket for the keys and nodded too. He and Welcome moved to the door and out. I lowered my head. Danny led her to the Caddy, which sat at the front of the row of parked cars, on the corner of Smith. She went around to the front passenger seat, not like the usual ride who'd sit in the back. Danny slammed his door and the interior light shut off, then he started the engine. I glanced back to see that Tony was now going through the drawers behind the L&L counter, searching for something, his desperado's energy suddenly lashed to a purpose. He used both hands, his cigarette stuck in his mouth, and unpacked papers onto the countertop hurriedly. I'd gathered a piece of vague information, I supposed: Tony didn't trust Danny with everything.

Then I saw a hulking shadow stir, in a parked car on L&L's side of the street, just a few yards from the storefront.

Unmistakable.

The Kumquat Sasquatch.

The car was an economy model, bright red, and he filled it like it had been cast around his body. I saw him lean sideways to watch the Cadillac with Danny and Welcome inside round the corner of Smith and disappear with a pulse of brakelights. Then he turned his attention back to the storefront; I read the movement in the disappearance of a nose from the silhouette, its replacement by an elephantine ear. The giant was doing what I was doing, staking out L&L.

He watched Tony, and I watched them both. Tony was a lot more interesting at the moment. I hadn't often seen him reading, and never this intently. He was searching for something in the sheaf of papers he'd pulled from Minna's drawers, his brow furrowed, cigarette in his lips, looking like Edward R. Murrow's punk brother. Now, unsatisfied, he dug in another drawer, and worked over a notebook I recognized even from across the street as the one containing my own stakeout jottings from the day before. I tried not to take it personally when he thrust this aside even more hastily and went back to tearing up the drawers.

The large shadow took it all in, complacent. His hand moved from somewhere below the line of the car window and briefly covered his mouth; he chewed, then leaned forward to dribble out some discarded seeds or pits. A bag of cherries or olives this time, something a giant would gobble in a handful. Or Cracker Jack, and he didn't like peanuts. He watched Tony like an operagoer who knew the libretto, was curious only to gather details of how the familiar plot would play out this time.

Tony exhausted the drawers, started in on the file cabinets.

The giant chewed. I blinked in time with his chewing, and counted chews and blinks, occupying my Tourette's brain with this nearly invisible agitation, tried to stay otherwise still as a lizard on the stoop. He had only to turn this way to spot me. My whole edge consisted of seeing without being seen; I had nothing more on the giant, had never had. If I wanted to preserve that wafer-thin edge I needed to find a better hiding place

— and it wouldn't hurt to get in out of the stiff, cold wind.

The three remaining L&L cars were my best option. But the Pontiac, which I would have preferred, was up ahead of the giant's car, easily in his line of sight. I was sure I didn't want to face whatever ghosts or more tangibly olfactory traces of Minna might be trapped inside the sealed windows of the Death Car. Which left the Tracer. I felt in my pocket for my bunch of keys, found the three longest, one of which was the Tracer's door and ignition. I was preparing to duckwalk down the pavement and slip into the Tracer when the Cadillac reappeared, hurtling down Bergen, with Danny at the wheel.

He parked in the same spot at the front of the block and walked back toward L&L. I slumped on the stoop, played drunk. Danny didn't see me. He went inside, surprising Tony in his filework. They exchanged a word or two, then Tony slid the drawer closed and bummed another cigarette from Danny. The shadow in the little car went on watching, sublimely confident and peaceful. Neither Tony nor Danny had ever seen the giant, I suppose, so he had less to worry about in attracting attention than I did. But reason alone couldn't account for the giant's composure. If he wasn't a student of Gerard's, he should have been: He possessed true Buddha-nature, and would have surpassed his teacher. Three hundred and fifty-odd pounds instill a cosmic measure of gravity, I suppose. *What did the Buddhist say to the hot-dog vendor?* was the joke I remembered now, one of Loomis's measly riddles. *Make me one with everything.* I would have been happy to be one with everything at that moment.

Heck, make me one with anything.

I was pretty hungry, too, if I thought about it. A stakeout was customarily a gastronomic occasion, and I was beginning to get that itch for something between two slices of bread. Why shouldn't I be hungry? I'd missed dinner, had Kimmery instead.

With thoughts of food and sex my attention slipped, so that I was startled now to see Tony pop out of the storefront, his expression still as fierce as it had been when he was poring over the paperwork. For a moment I thought I'd been spotted. But he turned toward Smith Street, crossed Bergen, and disappeared around the corner.

The giant watched, unimpressed, unworried.

We waited.

Tony returned with a large plastic shopping bag, probably from Zeod's. The only thing I could discern was a carton of Marlboros sticking out of the top, but the bag was heavy with something. Tony opened the passenger door of the Pontiac and put the bag on the seat, glanced quickly up the street without spotting either me or the giant, then relocked the car and went back to L&L.

Figuring it was status quo for the time being, I made my way back down Bergen, up Hoyt Street, and around the block the long way, and checked into Zeod's myself.

Zeod liked to work the late hours, do the overnight, check in the newspaper deliveries at six and then sleep through the bright hours of the morning and early afternoon. He was like the Sheriff of Smith Street, eyes open while we all slept, seeing the drunks stagger home, keeping his eye on the crucial supplies, the Ding Dongs and Entenmann's cookies, the forty-ounce malt liquor and the cups of coffee "regular" with a picture of the Parthenon on the cup. Except now he had company down the street at L&L, Tony and Danny and the giant and myself enacting our strange vigil, our roundelay of surveillance. I wondered if Zeod knew about Minna yet. As I slipped up to the counter the groggy counter boy was punishing the slicer with a steaming white towel, replenishing the towel in a basin of hot suds, while Zeod stood exhorting him, telling him how he could be doing it better, squeezing some value out of him before he quit like all the others.

"Crazyman!"

"Shhh." I imagined that Tony or the giant could hear Zeod bellow through the shop window and around the corner of the block.

"You're working so late for Frank tonight? Something important, eh? Tony just came."

"Important Freaks! Important Franks!"

"Ho ho ho."

"Listen, Zeod. Can you tell me what Tony bought?"

Zeod screwed up his face, finding this question sensational. "You can't ask him yourself?"

"No, I can't."

He shrugged. "Six-pack of beer, four sandwiches, carton of cigarettes, Coca-Cola — whole picnic."

"Funny picnic."

"Wasn't funny to him," said Zeod. "Couldn't make him smile. Like you, Crazyman. On a very serious case, eh?"

"What — *becausewhich, besideswhich* —

what sandwiches did he buy?" It was my suddenly ravenous appetite that steered this inquiry.

"Ah!" Zeod rubbed his hands together. He was always ready to savor his own product on someone else's behalf. "Turkey with Thousand, very nice on a kaiser roll, pepperoni-and-provolone hero with peppers inside, two roast beef with horseradish on rye bread."

I had to clutch the counter to keep from falling over, this storm of enticements was so heady.

"You like what you hear, I can see that," said Zeod.

I nodded, turned my head sideways, took in the fresh-gleaming slicer, the elegant curve of the fender that sheathed the blade.

Zeod said, "You want something, Crazyman, don't you?"

I saw the counter boy's eyes roll in weary anticipation. The slicer rarely saw this much action at two or three in the morning. They'd have to sluice it down with suds again before the night was done.

"Please — *ghostradish, pepperpony, kaiserphone* — please, uh, the same as Tony."

"You want the same? All four the same?"

"Yes," I gasped. I couldn't think past

Tony's list of sandwiches. My hunger for them was absolute. I had to match Tony sandwich for sandwich, a gastronomic mirroring-tic — I'd understand him by the time I was through the fourth, I figured. We would achieve a Zeod's mind-meld, with Thousand Island dressing.

While Zeod rode his counter boy to complete the large order I hid in the back near the beverage cases, picked out a liter of Coke and a bag of chips, and reorganized and counted a disorderly shelf of cat-food cans.

"Okay, Lionel." Zeod was always most gentle with me when handing over his precious cargo — we shared that reverence for his product. "Put it on Frank's tab, right?" He gathered my soda and chips in a large bag with the paper-wrapped sandwiches.

"No, no —" I rustled in my pockets for a tight-folded twenty.

"What's the matter? Why not the boss man pick it up?"

"I want to pay you." I pushed the bill across the counter. Zeod took it and arched his eyebrows.

"Very funny business," he said, and made a *chuck-chuck-chuck* sound with his tongue in his cheek.

"What?"

"Same thing as Tony, before you," he said. "He says he wants to pay. Same thing."

"Listen, Zeod. If Tony comes back in here tonight" — I fought off a howling sound that wanted to come out of me, the cry of a sandwich predator over fresh kill he has yet to devour — "don't tell him you saw me, okay?"

Zeod winked. Somehow this made sense to him. I felt a thing that was either a nauseous wave of paranoia — perhaps Zeod was an agent of Tony's, absolutely in his pocket, and would be on the phone to him the minute I was out of the shop — or else my stomach spasming in anticipation of food. "Okay, Chief," said Zeod as I went out the door.

I came around the block the long way again, quickly confirmed that the giant and Tony were still in their places, then swerved across the street and slipped up beside the Tracer, key in hand. The giant's compact was six cars ahead, but I couldn't see his clifflike silhouette from where I stood as I unlocked the car. I only hoped that meant he couldn't see me. I plopped Zeod's bag on the passenger seat, jumped inside, and slammed the door shut as quickly as I could, praying that the brief flash of the interior light hadn't registered in the giant's rearview. Then I slumped down in my place so I'd be invisible, on the slight chance he did turn and could make anything out through a thickness of twelve darkened windshields. Meanwhile I got my hands busy unfurling the paper around one of Zeod's roast beef and horseradish specials. Once I had it free, I gobbled the sandwich like a nature-film otter cracking an oyster on its stomach: knees up in the wiring under the dashboard, my elbows jammed against the steering wheel, my chest serving as a table, my shirt as a tablecloth.

Now it was a proper stakeout — if only I could figure what it was I was waiting to see happen. Not that I could see much from inside the Tracer. The giant's car was still in its place but I couldn't confirm his existence inside it. And at this extreme angle all I could see was a thin slice of bright L&L window. Twice Tony paced to the front of the store, just long enough for me to identify his form in shadow and a flash of an elbow, a left-behind plume of cigarette exhalation across the edge of Minna's destination map, the Queens airports at the left margin showing Minna's Magic Marker scrawl: $18. Bergen Street was a void in my rearview, Smith Street only marginally brighter ahead of me. It was a quarter to four. I felt the F train's rumble underneath Bergen, first as it slowed into the station and paused there, then a second tremor as it departed. A minute later the 67 bus rolled like a great battered appliance down Bergen, empty apart from the driver. Public transportation was the night's pulse, the beep on the monitor at the patient's bedside. In a few hours those same trains and buses would be jammed with jawing, caffeinated faces, littered with newspapers and fresh gum. Now they kept the faith. Me, I had the cold to keep me awake, that and the liter of Coca-Cola and my assignment, my will to influence the outcome of the night's strange stalemate. Those would have to slug it out with the soporific powers of the roast-beef sandwich, the dreamy pull of my fresh memories of Kimmery, the throb of my skull where the giant had clubbed me with his gun.

What was the giant waiting for?

What did Tony want to find in Minna's files?

Why were his sandwiches in the car?

Why had Julia flown to Boston?

Who was Bailey anyway?

I opened my bag of chips, took a slug of

my cola, and put myself to work on those new and old questions and on staying awake.

Insomnia is a variant of Tourette's — the waking brain races, sampling the world after the world has turned away, touching it everywhere, refusing to settle, to join the collective nod. The insomniac brain is a sort of conspiracy theorist as well, believing too much in its own paranoiac importance — as though if it were to blink, then doze, the world might be overrun by some encroaching calamity, which its obsessive musings are somehow fending off.

I've spent long nights in that place. This night, though, consisted of summoning up that state I'd so often worked to banish. I was alone now, no Minna, no Men, my own boss on this stakeout with who-knew-what riding on its outcome. If I fell asleep the little world of my investigation would crumble. I needed to find my insomniac self, to agitate my problem-solving brain, if not to solve actual problems, then to worry at them for the purpose of keeping my dumb eyeballs propped open.

Avoiding becoming one with everything: that was my big challenge at the moment.

It was four-thirty. My consciousness was

distended, the tics like islands in an ocean of fog.

Who needed sleep? I asked myself. *I'll sleep when I'm dead,* Minna had liked to say.

I guess he had his chance now.

I'll die when I'm dead, my brain recited in Minna's voice. Not a minute sooner, you kosher macaroons!

A diet of bread. A guy on a bed.

No, no bed. No car. No phone.

Phone.

The cell phone. I pulled it out, rang the L&L number. It rang three times before a hand picked it up.

"No cars," said Danny lazily. If I knew him, he'd been sleeping with his head on the counter, weary of pretending to listen to whatever Tony was ranting about.

I'd have given a lot, of course, to know what Tony was ranting about.

"It's me, Danny. Put Tony on."

"Yo," he said, unsurprisable. "Here you go."

"What?" said Tony.

"It's me," I said. *"Deskjob."*

"You fucking little freak," said Tony. "I'll kill you."

I outweighed Tony only by about fifty pounds. "You had your chance," I heard myself say. Tony still brought out the romantic in me. We'd be two Bogarts to the end. "Except if you'd pulled that trigger, you might have blown a hole in your foot, or in some far-off toddler on his bike."

"Oh, I'd of straightened it out," Tony said. "I wish I had put a coupla holes in you. Leaving me with that fucking cop."

"Remember it any way you like. I'm trying to help you at the moment."

"That's a good one."

"Eat me St. Vincent!" I held the phone away from my face until I was sure the tic was complete. "You're in danger, Tony. Right now."

"What do you know about it?"

I wanted to say, *Going out of town? What's in the files? Since when do you like horseradish?* But I couldn't let him know I was outside and have him rush into the giant's arms. "Trust me," I said. "I really wish you would."

"Oh, I trust you — to be Bozo the Clown," he said. "The point is, what can you tell me that's worth the time to listen?"

"That hurts, Tony."

"For chrissake!" Now he held his receiver away from his mouth and swore. "I got problems, Freakshow, and you're A-number one."

"If I were you, I'd worry more about Fujisaki."

"What do you know about Fujisaki?" He was hissing. "Where are you?"

"I know — *undress-a-phone, impress-a-clown* — I know a few things."

"You better hide," he said. "You better hope I don't catch you."

"Aw, Tony. We're in the same situation."

"That's a laugh, only I'm not laughing. I'm gonna kill you."

"We're a family, Tony. Minna brought us together —" I caught myself wanting to quote the Garbage Cop, suggest another *moment of silence.*

"There's too long a tail on that kite, Freakshow. I don't have the time."

Before I could speak he hung up the phone.

It was after five, and bakery trucks had begun to roll. Soon a van would come and deliver Zeod's newspapers, with Minna's obituary notice in them.

I was in a comalike state when Tony came out of L&L and got into the Pontiac. A sentinel part of my brain had kept a watch on the storefront while the rest of me slept, and so I was startled to find that the sun was up, that traffic now filled Bergen Street. I glanced at Minna's watch: It was twenty minutes to seven. I was chilled through, my head throbbed, and my tongue felt as if it had been bound in horseradish-and-cola-soaked plaster and left out on the moon overnight. I shook my head and my neck crackled. I tried to keep my eyes on the scene even as I worked my jaw sideways to revive the mechanism of my face. Tony steered the Pontiac into Smith Street's morning flow. The giant poked his compact into the traffic a moment later, first allowing two cars to creep in behind Tony. I turned the Tracer's ignition key and the engine scuffed into life, and I followed, keeping my own safe distance behind.

Tony led us up Smith, onto Atlantic heading toward the waterfront, into a stream of commuters and delivery trucks. In that stream I lost sight of Tony pretty quickly, but held on to the giant's pretty red compact.

Tony took the Brooklyn-Queens Expressway at the foot of Atlantic. The giant and I slid onto the ramp behind him in turn. Greenpoint, that was my first guess. I shuddered at recalling the Dumpster behind Harry Brainum's, off McGuinness Boulevard, where Minna had met his finish. How had the giant contrived to lure Tony out to that spot?

But I was wrong. We passed the

Greenpoint exit, heading north. I saw the black Pontiac in the distance ahead as we rounded the expressway's curve toward the airports and Long Island, but I kept dropped back, at least two cars behind the red compact. I had to trust the giant to track Tony, another exercise in Zen calm. We threaded the various exits and cloverleafs out of Brooklyn, through Queens toward the airport exits. When we turned momentarily toward JFK I generated a new theory: Someone from Fujisaki was disembarking at the Japan Air Lines terminal, some chief of executions, or a courier with a ticking package to deliver. Minna's death might be the first blow in an international wave of executions. And a flight to meet explained Tony's long, nervous overnight wait. Even as I settled on this explanation, I watched the red car peel away from the airport option, to the northbound ramp, marked for the Whitestone Bridge. I barely made it across three lanes to stay on their vehicular heels.

Four sandwiches, of course. If I weren't prone to multiple sandwiches myself I might have made more of this clue. Four sandwiches and a six-pack. We were headed out of town. Fortunately I *had* rounded up my clone version of Tony's picnic, so I was outfitted too. I wondered if the giant had anything to eat besides the bag of cherries or olives I'd seen him gobbling. Our little highway formation reminded me of a sandwich, actually, a Minna Man on either side of the giant — we were a goon-on-orphan, with wheels. As we soared over the Whitestone I took another double shot of cola. It would have to stand in for morning coffee. I only had to solve the problem of needing to pee rather badly. Hence I hurried to finish the Coke, figuring I'd go in the bottle.

Half an hour later we'd passed options for the Pelhams, White Plains, Mount Kisco, a few other names I associated with the outer margins of New York City, on into Connecticut, first on the Hutchinson River Parkway, then on something called the Merritt Parkway. I kept the little red car in my sights. The cars were thick enough to keep me easily camouflaged. Every now and again the giant would creep near enough to Tony's Pontiac that I could see we were still three, bound like secret lovers through the indifferent miles of traffic.

Highway driving was maximally soothing. The steady flow of attention and effort, the nudging of gas pedal and checking of mirrors and blind spots with a twist of the neck subsumed my ticcishness completely. I was still bleary, needing sleep, but the novelty of this odd chase and of being farther out of New York City than I'd ever been worked to keep me awake. I'd seen trees before — so far Connecticut offered nothing I didn't know from suburban Long Island, or even Staten Island. But the *idea* of Connecticut was sort of interesting.

The traffic tightened as we skirted a small city called Hartford, and for a moment we were bricked into a five-lane traffic jam. It was just before nine, and we'd caught Hartford's endearing little version of a rush hour. Tony and the giant were both in view ahead of me, the giant in the lane to my right, and as I cinched forward a wheel-turn at a time, I nearly drew even with him. The red car was a Contour, I saw now. I was a Tracer following a Contour. As though I'd taken a pencil and followed the giant's route on a road map. My lane crept forward while his stood still, and soon I'd nearly pulled up even with him. He was chewing something, his jaw and neck pulsing, his hand now moving again to his mouth. I suppose to maintain that size he had to keep it coming. The car was probably brimful with snacks

— perhaps Fujisaki paid him for his hits directly in food, so he wouldn't have to bother converting cash. They should have gotten him a bigger car, though.

I braked to keep him in front of me. Tony's lane began to slide ahead of the others and the giant merged into it without signaling, as though the Contour conveyed the authority of his brutish body. I was content to let some distance open between us, and before long Hartford's miniature jam eased. *Heartfood handfoot hoofdog horseradish* went the tinny song in my brain. I took a cue from the giant's chewing and rustled in the bag of sandwiches on the passenger seat. I groped for the hero, wanting to taste the wet crush of the Zeod's marinated peppers mixed with the spicy, leathery pepperoni.

I had the hero half devoured when I spotted Tony's black Pontiac slowing into a rest area, while the giant's Contour soared blithely past.

It could mean only one thing. Having reached this point behind Tony, the giant didn't need to trail him anymore. He knew where Tony was going and in fact preferred to arrive sooner, to be waiting when Tony arrived.

It wasn't Boston. Boston might be on the

way, but it wasn't the destination. I'd finally put *men of peace* and *place of peace* together. I'm not so slow.

And appropriate to the manner of the evening's stakeout and the morning's chase, I still stood in relation to the giant as the giant stood to Tony. I knew where the giant was going — *a freakshow chasing a context* — I knew where they were both going. And I had reasons to want to get there soonest. I was still seeking my edge over the giant. Maybe I could poison his sushi.

I pulled into the next rest stop and gassed up the car, peed, and bought some ginger ale, a cup of coffee and a map of New England. Sure enough, the diagonal across Connecticut pointed through Massachusetts and a nubbin of coastal New Hampshire to the entrance of the Maine Turnpike. I fished the "Place of Peace" brochure out of my jacket and found the place where the Turnpike left off and the brochure's rudimentary map took over, a coastal village called Musconguspoint Station. The name had a chewy, unfamiliar flavor that tantalized my syndrome. I spotted others like it on the map. Whether or not Maine's wilderness impressed me more than suburban Connecticut, the road signs would provide some nourishment.

Now I had only to take the lead in this secret interstate race. I was relying on the giant's overconfidence — he was so certain he was the pursuer he'd never stopped to wonder whether he might be pursued. Of course, I hadn't spent a lot of time looking over *my* shoulder either. I twitched the notion off with a few neck-jerks and got back in my car.

She answered on the second ring, her voice a little groggy.

"Kimmery."

"Lionel?"

"Yessrog."

"Where did you go?"

"I'm in — I'm almost in Massachusetts."

"What do you mean, almost? Is that like a state of mind or something, Massachusetts?"

"No, I mean almost there, literally. I'm on the highway, Kimmery. I've never been this far from New York."

She was quiet for a minute. "When you run you really run," she said.

"No, no, don't misunderstand. I had to go. This is my investigation. I'm — *invest-in-a-gun, connect-a-cop, inventachusetts* —" I mashed my tongue against the cage of my gritted teeth, trying to bottle up the flow.

Ticcing with Kimmery was especially abhorrent to me, now that I'd declared her my cure.

"You're what?"

"I'm on the giant's tail," I said, squeezing out the words. "Well, not *actually* on his tail, but I know where he's going."

"You're still looking for your giant," she said thoughtfully. "Because you feel bad about that guy Frank who got killed, is that right?"

"No. Yes."

"You make me sad, Lionel."

"Why?"

"You seem so, I don't know, guilty."

"Listen, Kimmery. I called because — *Missmebailey!* — because I missed you. I mean, I miss you."

"That's a funny thing to say. Um, Lionel?"

"Yes?"

"Did you take my keys?"

"It was part of my investigation. Forgive me."

"Okay, whatever, but I thought it was pretty creepy."

"I didn't mean anything creepy by it."

"You can't do that kind of thing. It freaks people out, you know?"

"I'm really sorry. I'll bring them back."

She was quiet again. I coursed in the fast lane with a band of other speeders, every so often slipping to the right to let an especially frantic one go by. The highway driving had begun to inspire a Tourettic fantasy, that the hoods and fenders of the cars were shoulders and collars I couldn't touch. I had to keep adequate distance so I wouldn't be tempted to try to brush up against those gleaming proxy bodies.

I hadn't seen any sign of either Tony or the giant, but I had reason to hope that Tony at least was already behind me. The giant would have to stop for gas if he hadn't, and that was when I would pass him.

"I'm going to a place you might know about," I said. "Yoshii's. A retreat."

"That's a good idea," she said grudgingly, curiosity winning over her anger. "I always wanted to go there. Roshi said it was really great."

"Maybe —"

"What?"

"Maybe sometime we'll go together."

"I should get off the phone, Lionel."

The call had made me anxious. I ate the second of the roast-beef sandwiches. Massachusetts looked the same as Connecticut.

I called her back.

"What did you mean by *guilty?*" I said. "I don't understand."

She sighed. "I don't know, Lionel. It's just, I'm not really sure about this *investigation.* It seems like you're just running around a lot trying to keep from feeling sad or guilty or whatever about this guy Frank."

"I want to catch the killer."

"Can't you hear yourself? That's like something O. J. Simpson would say. Regular people, when someone they know gets killed or something they don't go around trying to *catch the killer.* They go to a *funeral.*"

"I'm a detective, Kimmery." I almost said, *I'm a telephone.*

"You keep saying that, but I don't know. I just can't really accept it."

"Why not?"

"I guess I thought detectives were more, uh, subtle."

"Maybe you're thinking of detectives in movies or on television." I was a fine one to be explaining this distinction. "On TV they're all the same. Real detectives are as unalike as fingerprints, or snowflakes."

"Very funny."

"I'm trying to make you laugh," I said. "I'm glad you noticed. Do you like jokes?"

"You know what *koans* are? They're like Zen jokes, except they don't really have punch lines."

"What are you waiting for? I've got all day here." In truth the highway had grown fat with extra lanes, and complicated by options and merges. But I wasn't going to interrupt Kimmery while things were going so well, ticless on my end, bubbly with digressions on hers.

"Oh, I can never remember them, they're too vague. Lots of monks hitting each other on the head and stuff."

"That sounds hilarious. The best jokes usually have animals in them, I think."

"There's plenty of animals. Here —" I heard a rustle as she braced the phone between her shoulder and chin and paged through a book. I'd had her in the middle of the big empty room — now I adjusted the picture, envisioned her with the phone stretched to reach the bed, perhaps with Shelf on her lap. "So these two monks are arguing over a cat and this other monk cuts the cat in half — Oh, that's not very nice."

"You're killing me. I'm busting a gut over here."

"Shut up. Oh, here, this is one I like. It's about death. So this young monk comes to visit this old monk to ask about this other, older monk who's just died. Tendo, that's the dead monk. So the young monk is asking about Tendo and the old monk says stuff like 'Look at that dog over there' and 'Do you want a bath?' — all this irrelevant stuff. It goes on like that until finally the young monk is enlightened."

"Enlightened by what?"

"I guess the point is you can't really say anything about death."

"Okay, I get it. It's just like in *Only Angels Have Wings*, when Cary Grant's best friend Joe crashes his plane and dies and then Rosalind Russell asks him 'What about Joe?' and "Aren't you going to do anything about Joe?' and Cary Grant just says, 'Who's Joe?' "

"Speaking of watching too much movies and television."

"Exactly." I liked the way the miles were flying past for me now, ticless, aloft on Kimmery's voice, the freeway traffic thinning.

The moment I observed the way our talk and my journey were racing along, though, we lapsed into silence.

"Roshi says this thing about guilt," she said after a minute. "That it's selfish, just a way to avoid taking care of yourself. Or thinking about yourself. I guess that's sort of two different things. I can't remember."

"Please don't quote Gerard Minna to me on the subject of guilt," I said. "That's a little hard to swallow under the present circumstances."

"You really think Roshi's guilty of something?"

"There's more I need to find out," I admitted. "That's what I'm doing. That's why I had to take your keys."

"And why you're going to Yoshii's?"

"Yes."

In the pause that followed I detected the sound of Kimmery believing me, believing in my case, for the first time.

"Be careful, Lionel."

"Sure. I'm always careful. Just keep your promise to me, okay?"

"What promise?"

"Don't go to the Zendo."

"Okay. I think I'm getting off the phone now, Lionel."

"You promise?"

"Sure, yeah, okay."

Suddenly I was surrounded by office buildings, carports, stacked overhead freeways clogged with cars. I realized too late I probably should have navigated around Boston instead of through it. I suffered through the slowdown, munched on chips and tried not to hold my breath, and before too long the city's grip loosened, gave way to suburban sprawl, to the undecorated endless interstate. I only hoped I hadn't let Tony and the giant get ahead of me, lost my lead, my edge. *Gotta have an edge*. I was beginning to obsess on *edge* too much: edge of car, edge of road, edge of vision and what hovered there, nagging and insubstantial. How strange it began to seem that cars have bodies that never are supposed to touch, a disaster if they do.

Don't hover in my blind spot, Fonebone!

I felt as though I would begin ticcing with the body of the car, would need to flirt with the textured shoulder of the highway or the darting, soaring bodies all around me unless I heard her voice again.

"Kimmery."

"Lionel."

"I called you again."

"Aren't these car-phone calls kind of expensive?"

"I'm not the one paying," I burbled. I was exhilarated by the recurrent technomagic, the cell phone reaching out across space and time to connect us again.

"Who is?"

"Some Zen doormat I met yesterday in a car."

"Doormat?"

"Doorman."

"Mmmm." She was eating something. "You call too much."

"I like talking to you. Driving is . . . boring." I undersold my angst, let the one word stand in for so many others.

"Yeah, mmmm — but I don't want anything, you know, crazy in my life right now."

"What do you mean by crazy?" Her tonal swerves had caught me by surprise again. I suppose it was this strange lurching dance, though, that kept my double brain enchanted.

"It's just — A lot of guys, you know, they tell you they understand about giving you space and stuff, they know how to talk about it and that you need to hear it. But they don't really have any idea what it means. I've been through a lot recently, Lionel."

"When did I say anything about giving you space?"

"I just mean this is a lot of calls in a pretty short period is all."

"Kimmery, listen. I'm not like other, ah, people you meet. My life is organized around certain compulsions. But it's different with you, I feel different."

"That's good, that's nice —"

"You have no idea."

"— but I'm just coming out of something pretty intense. I mean, you swept me off my feet, Lionel. You're kind of overwhelming, actually, if you don't already know. I mean, I like talking to you, too, but it isn't a good idea to call three times right after, you know, *spending the night.*"

I was silent, unsure how to decode this remarkable speech.

"What I mean is, this is exactly the kind of craziness I just got through with, Lionel."

"Which kind?"

"Like this," she said in a meek voice. "Like with you."

"Are you saying Oreo Man had *Tourette's syndrome?*" I felt a weird thrill of jealousy. She collected us freaks, I understood now. No wonder she took us in stride, no wonder she damped our symptoms. I was nothing special after all. Or rather my fistlike penis was my only claim.

"Who's Oreo Man?"

"Your old boyfriend."

"Oh. But what's the other thing you said?"

"Never mind."

We were silent for a while. My brain went, *Tourette's slipdrip stinkjet's blessdroop mutual-*

of-overwhelm's wild kissdoom —

"All I mean is I'm not ready for anything too intense right now," said Kimmery. "I need space to figure out what I want. I can't be all overwhelmed and obsessed like the last time."

"I think I've heard enough about that for now."

"Okay."

"But —" I gathered myself, made a plunge into territory far stranger to me than Connecticut or Massachusetts. "I think I understand what you mean about space. About leaving it between things so you don't get too obsessed."

"Uh-huh."

"Or is that the kind of talk you don't want to hear? I guess I'm confused."

"No, it's okay. But we can talk about this later."

"Well, okay."

"Bye, Lionel."

Dial and redial were sitting on a fence. Dial fell off. Who was left?

Ring.

Ring.

Ring.

Click. "You've reached two-one-two, three-oh-four —"

"HellokimmeryIknowIshouldn'tbecalling butIjust —"

Clunk. "Lionel?"

"Yes."

"Stop now."

"Uh —"

"Just stop calling now. It's way too much like some really bad things that have happened to me, can you understand? It's not romantic."

"Yes."

"Okay, bye, Lionel, for real now, okay?"

"Yes."

Redial.

"You've reached —"

"Kimmery? Kimmery? Kimmery? Are you there? Kimmery?"

I was my syndrome's dupe once again. Here I'd imagined I was enjoying a Touretteless morning, yet when the new manifestation appeared, it was hidden in plain sight, the Purloined Tic. Punching that redial I was exhibiting a calling-Kimmery-tic as compulsive as any rude syllable or swipe.

I wanted to hurl the doorman's cell phone out onto the grassy divider. Instead, in a haze of self-loathing, I dialed another number, one etched in memory though I hadn't called it in a while.

"Yes?" The voice was weary, encrusted with years, as I remembered it.

"Essrog?" I said.

"Yes." A pause. "This is the Essrog residence. This is Murray Essrog. Who's calling, please?"

I was a little while coming to my reply. "Eat me Bailey."

"Oh, Christ." The voice moved away from the phone. "Mother. Mother, come here. I want you to listen to this."

"Essrog Bailey," I said, almost whispering, but intent on being heard.

There was a shuffling in the background.

"It's him again, Mother," said Murray Essrog. "It's that goddamned Bailey kid. He's still out there. All these years."

I was still a kid to him, just as to me he'd been an old man since the first time I called him.

"I don't know why you care," came an older woman's voice, every word a sigh.

"Baileybailey," I said softly.

"Speak up, kid, do your thing," said the old man.

I heard the phone change hands, the old woman's breathing come onto the line.

"Essrog, Essrog, Essrog," I chanted, like a cricket trapped in a wall.

★ ★ ★

I'm tightly wound. I'm a loose cannon. Both — I'm a tightly wound loose cannon, a tight loose. My whole life exists in the space between those words, tight, loose, and there isn't any space there — they should be one word, tightloose. I'm an air bag in a dashboard, packed up layer upon layer in readiness for that moment when I get to explode, expand all over you, fill every available space. Unlike an airbag, though, I'm repacked the moment I've exploded, am tensed and ready again to explode — like some safety-film footage cut into a loop, all I do is compress and release, over and over, never saving or satisfying anyone, least myself. Yet the tape plays on pointlessly, obsessive air bag exploding again and again while life itself goes on elsewhere, outside the range of these antic expenditures.

The night before, in Kimmery's alcove, suddenly seemed very long ago, very far away.

How could phone calls — *cell-phone calls*, staticky, unlikely, free of charge — how could they alter what real bodies felt? How could ghosts touch the living?

I tried not to think about it.

* * *

I tossed the cell phone onto the seat beside me, into the wreckage of Zeod's sandwiches, the unfurled paper wrapping, the torn chip bag, the strewn chips and crumpled napkins gone translucent with grease stains in the midmorning sun. I wasn't eating neatly, wasn't getting anything exactly right, and now I knew it didn't matter, not today, not anymore. Having broken the disastrous flow of dialing tics, my mood had gotten hard, my attention narrow. I crossed the bridge at Portsmouth into Maine and focused everything I had left on the drive, on casting off unnecessary behaviors, thrusting exhaustion and bitterness aside and making myself into a vehicular arrow pointed at Musconguspoint Station, at the answers that lay waiting for me there. I heard Minna's voice now in place of my incessant Tourettic tongue, saying, *Floor it, Freakshow. You got something to do, do it already. Tell your story driving.*

Route 1 along the Maine coast was a series of touristy villages, some with boats, some with beaches, all with antiques and lobster. A large percentage of the hotels and restaurants were closed, with signs that read SEE YOU NEXT SUMMER! and HAVE A

GREAT YEAR! I had trouble believing any of it was real — the turnpike had felt like a schematic, a road map, and I in my car a dot or a penpoint tracing a route. Now I felt as if I were driving through the pages of a calendar, or a collection of pictorial stamps. None of it struck me as particular or persuasive in any way. Maybe once I got out of the car.

Musconguspoint Station was one with boats. It wasn't the least of these towns, but it was close to it, a swelling on the coast distinguished more than anything by the big ferry landing, with signs for the Muscongus Island Ferry, which made the circuit twice a day. The "place of peace" wasn't hard to find. Yoshii's — MAINE'S ONLY THAI AND SUSHI OCEANFOOD EMPORIUM, according to the sign — was the largest of a neat triad of buildings on a hill just past the ferry landing and the fishing docks, all painted a queasy combination of toasted-marshmallow brown and seashell pink, smugly humble earth tones that directly violated Maine's barn-red and house-white scheme. This was one shot that wasn't making the calendar. The restaurant extended on stilts over a short cliff on the water, surf thundering below; the other two buildings, presumably the retreat center, were caged in a fussy, evenly spaced row of pine trees, all the same year and model. The sign was topped with a painted image of Yoshii, a smiling bald man with chopsticks and waves of pleasure or serenity emanating from his head like stink-lines in a Don Martin cartoon.

I put the Tracer in the restaurant lot, up on the hill overlooking the water, the fishing dock, and the ferry landing below. It was alone there except for two pickup trucks in staff spots. Yoshii's hours were painted on the door: seating for lunch began at twelve-thirty, which was twenty minutes from now. I didn't see any sign of Tony or the giant or anyone else, but I didn't want to sit in the lot and wait like a fool with a target painted on his back. An edge, that's what I was after.

Edgerog, 33, seeks Edge.

I got out of the car. First surprise: the cold. A wind that hurt my ears instantly. The air smelled like a thunderstorm but there wasn't a cloud in the sky. I went over the barrier of logs at the corner of the parking lot and clambered down the grade toward the water, under the shade of the jutting deck of the restaurant. Once I'd dipped out of sight of the road and buildings, I undid my fly and peed on the rocks, amusing my compulsiveness by staining one whole boulder a deeper gray, albeit only temporarily. It was as I zipped and turned to see the ocean that the vertigo hit me. I'd found an edge, all right. Waves, sky, trees, Essrog — I was off the page now, away from the grammar of skyscrapers and pavement. I experienced it precisely as a loss of language, a great sucking-away of the word-laden walls that I needed around me, that I touched everywhere, leaned on for support, cribbed from when I ticced aloud. Those walls of language had always been in place, I understood now, audible to me until the sky in Maine deafened them with a shout of silence. I staggered, put one hand on the rocks to steady myself. I needed to reply in some new tongue, to find a way to assert a self that had become tenuous, shrunk to a shred of Brooklyn stumbling on the coastal void: Orphan meets ocean. Jerk evaporates in salt mist.

"Freakshow!" I yelled into the swirling foam. It was lost.

"Bailey!" vanished too.

"Eat me! Dickweed!"

Nothing. What did I expect — Frank Minna to come rising from the sea?

"Essrog!" I screamed. I thought of Murray Essrog and his wife. They were Brooklyn Essrogs, like me. Had they ever come to this edge to meet the sky? Or was I the first Essrog to put a footprint on the crust of Maine?

"I claim this big water for Essrog!" I shouted.

I was a *freak of nature.*

Back on the dry land of the parking lot, I straightened my jacket and peered around to see if anyone had overheard my outburst. The nearest activity was at the base of the fishing docks below, where a small boat had come in and tiny figures in Devo-style yellow jumpsuits stood handing blue plastic crates over the prow and onto a pallet on the dock. I locked the car and strolled across to the other end of the empty lot, then scooted down the scrubby hill toward the men and boats, half sliding on my pavement-walker's leather soles, wind biting at my nose and chin. The restaurant and retreat center were eclipsed by the swell of the hill as I reached the dock.

"Hey!"

I got the attention of one of the men on the dock. He turned with his crate and plopped it on the pile, then stood hands on hips waiting for me to reach him. As I got closer, I examined the boat. The blue cartons were sealed, but the boatmen hefted them as though they were heavy with something, and with enough care to make me know the something was valuable. The deck of the boat held racks covered with diving equipment — rubber suits, flippers, and masks, and a pile of tanks for breathing underwater.

"Boy, it's cold," I said, scuffing my hands together like a sports fan. "Tough day to go boating, huh?"

The boatman's eyebrows and two-day beard were bright red, but not brighter than his sun-scrubbed flesh, everywhere it showed: cheeks, nose, ears and the corroded knuckles he rubbed under his chin now as he tried to work out a response.

I heard and felt the boat's body clunking as it bobbed against the pier. My thoughts wandered to the underwater propellers, whirring silently in the water. If I were closer to the water I'd want to reach in and touch the propeller, it was so stimulating to my kinesthetic obsessions. *"Tugboat! Forgettaboat!"* I ticced, and jerked my neck, to hurl the syllables sideways into the wind.

"You're not from around here, are you?" he said carefully. I'd expected his voice to come out like Yosemite Sam's or Popeye's, scabrous and sputtering. Instead he was so stolid and patrimonial with his New England accent — *Ya nawt from around heah, ah you?* — that I was left with no doubt which of us resembled the cartoon character.

"No, actually." I affected a bright look — *Illuminate me, sir, for I am a stranger in these exotic parts!* It seemed as likely he'd shove me off the dock into the water or simply turn away as continue the conversation. I straightened my suit again, fingered my own collar so I wouldn't be tempted to finger his fluorescent hood, to crimp its Velcro edge like the rim of a piecrust.

He examined me carefully. "Urchin season runs October through March. It's cold work. Day like today is a walk in the park."

"Urchin?" I said, feeling as I said it that I'd ticced, that the word was itself a tic by definition, it was so innately twitchy. It would have made a good pronunciation for The Artist Formerly Known As Prince's glyph.

"These are urchin waters out around the island. That's the market, so that's what's fished."

"Right," I said. "Well, that's terrific. Keep it up. You know anything about the place up the hill — Yoshii's?"

"Probably you want to talk to Mr. Foible." He nodded his head at the fishing dock's small shack, from the smokestack of which piped a tiny plume of smoke. "He's the one does dealings with them Japanese. I'm just a bayman."

"*Eatmebayman!* — thanks for your help." I smiled and tipped an imaginary cap to him, and headed for the shack. He shrugged at me and received another carton off the boat.

"How can I help you, sir?"

Foible was red too, but in a different way. His cheeks and nose and even his brow were spiderwebbed with blossoming red veins, painful to look at. His eyes too showed veins through their yellow. As Minna used to say about the St. Mary's parish priest, Foible had *a thirsty face.* Right on the wooden counter where he sat in the shack was evidence of what the face was thirsty for: a cluster of empty long-neck beer bottles and a couple of gin quarts, one still with an inch or so to cover the bottom. A coil heater glowed under the countertop, and when I stepped inside, he nodded at the heater and the door to indicate I should shut the door behind me. Besides Foible and his heater and bottles the shack held a scarred wooden file cabinet and a few boxes of what I guessed might be hardware and fishing tackle beneath their layers of grease. In my two-day suit and stubble I was the freshest thing in the place by far.

I could see this called for the oldest investigatory technique of them all: I opened my wallet and took out a twenty. "I'd buy a guy a drink if he could tell me a few things about the Japanese," I said.

"What about 'em?" His milky eyes made intimate contact with the twenty, worked their way back up to meet mine.

"I'm interested in the restaurant up the hill. Who owns it, specifically."

"Why?"

"What if I said I wanted to buy it?" I winked and gritted through a barking tic, cut it down to a momentary *"— charp!"*

"Son, you'd never get that thing away from them. You better do your shopping elsewhere."

"What if I made them an offer they couldn't refuse?"

Foible squinted at me, suddenly suspicious. I thought of how Detective Seminole had gotten spooked by the Minna Men, our Court Street milieu. I had no idea whether such images would reverberate so far from Gotham City.

"Can I ask you something?" said Foible.

"Shoot."

"You're not one of them *Scientologists*, are you?"

"No," I said, surprised. It wasn't the impression I'd imagined I was making.

He winced deeply, as though recalling the trauma that had driven him to the bottle. "Good," he said. "Dang Scientologists bought the old hotel up the island, turned it into a funhouse for movie stars. Hell, I'll take the Japanese any day. Least they eat fish."

"*Muscongus* Island?" I'd only wanted to feel the word in my mouth at last.

"What other island would I be talking about?" He squinted at me again, then held out his hand for the twenty. "Give me that, son."

I turned it over. He laid it out on the counter and cleared his rheumy throat. "That money there says you're out of your depth here, son. Japanese yank out a roll, the smallest thing they got's a hundred. Hell, before they shut down the urchin market, this dock used to be littered with thousand-dollar bank bands from them Japanese paying off my baymen for a haul."

"Tell me about it."

"Humph."

"Eat me."

"Huh? What's that?"

"I said tell me about it. Explain about the Japanese to a guy who doesn't know."

"You know what *uni* is?"

"Forgive my ignorance."

"That's the national food of Japan, son. That's the whole story around Musconguspoint anymore, unless you count the Scientologists camped out in that damn hotel. Japanese family's got to eat uni least once a week just to maintain their self-respect. Like you'd want a steak, they want a plate of urchin eggs. Golden Week — that's like Christmas in Japan — uni's the only thing they eat. Except Japanese waters got fished out. You follow?"

"Maybe."

"The Japanese law says you can't dive for urchin anymore. All you can do is hand-rake. Means standing out on a rock at low tide with a rake in your hand. Try it sometime. Rake all day, won't get an urchin worth a damn."

If ever there was a guy who needed to *tell his story walking*, it was Foible. I stifled the urge to tell him so.

"Maine coast's got the choicest urchin on the globe, son. Clustered under the island thick as grapes. Mainers never had a taste for the stuff, lobstermen thought urchins was a pain in the ass. That Japanese law made a lot of boatmen rich up here, if they knew how to rig for a diving crew. Whole economy down Rockport way. Japanese set up processing plants, they got women down there shucking urchins day and night, fly it out the next morning. Japanese dealers come in limousines, wait for the boats to come in, bid on loads, pay in cash with wads like I said before — the money would scare you silly."

"What happened?" I gulped back tics. Foible's story was beginning to interest me.

"In Rockport? Nothing happened. Still like that. If you mean up here, we just got a couple of boats. The folks up the hill bought me out and that's that, no more cars with dark windows, no more Yakuza making deals on the dock — I don't miss it for a minute. I'm an exclusive supplier, son, and a happier man you'll never meet."

In the little shack I was surrounded by Foible's happiness, and I wasn't enthralled. I didn't mention it. "The folks up the hill," I said. "You mean Fujisaki." I figured he was deep enough in his story not to balk at my feeding him the name.

"That's correct, sir. They're a classy outfit. Got a bunch of homes on the island, redid themselves a whole restaurant, brought in a sushi cook so they could eat the way they like. Sure wish they'd outbid the Scientologists for that old hotel, though."

"Don't we all. So does Fujisaki — *Superduperist! Clientologist! Fujiopolis!* — does Fujisaki live here in Musconguspoint year-round?"

"What's that?"

"Fly-on-top-of-us!"

"You got a touch of Tourette's syndrome there, son."

"Yes," I gasped.

"You want a drink?"

"No, no. The classy outfit, do they all live up here?"

"Nope. They come and go in a bunch, always together, Tokyo, New York, London. Got a heliport on the island, go back and forth. They just rode in on the ferry this morning."

"Ah." I blinked madly in the wake of the outburst. "You run the ferry, too?"

"Nope, wouldn't want any part of that bathtub. Just a couple of boats, couple of crews. Keep my feet up, concentrate on my hobbies."

"Your other boat's out fishing?"

"Nope. Urchin-diving's an early-morning affair, son. Go out three, four in the morning, day's over by ten o'clock."

"Right, right. So where's the boat?"

"Funny you ask. Let a couple of guys take it out an hour ago, said they had to get to the island, couldn't wait for the ferry. Rented my boat and captain. They were a lot like you, thought I'd be real impressed with twenty-dollar bills."

"One of them big?"

"Biggest I ever saw."

My detour through the middle of Boston had cost me the lead in the race to Musconguspoint. Now it seemed silly that I'd imagined anything else. I found the red Contour and the black Pontiac in a small parking area just past the ferry landing, a tree-hidden cul-de-sac lot for day-trippers to the island, with an automated coin-fed gate and one-way exit with flexible spikes pointed at an angle and signs that warned, DON'T BACK UP! SEVERE TIRE DAMAGE! There was something I found poignant in Tony and the giant each paying to park here, fishing in their pockets for coins before enacting whatever queer struggle had led them to hire the urchin boat. I took a closer look and saw that the Contour was locked up tight, while the Pontiac's keys were in the ignition, the doors unlocked. Tony's gun, the one he'd pointed at me the day before, lay on the floor near the gas pedal. I pushed it under the seat. Maybe Tony would need it. I hoped so. I thought of how the giant had strong-armed Minna wherever he wanted him to go and felt sorry for Tony.

On my way up the hill I felt a buzz, like a bee or hornet trapped inside my pants. It was Minna's beeper. I'd set it to "vibrate" at the Zendo. I drew it out. It showed a New Jersey number. The Clients were home from Brooklyn.

In the parking lot I got into my car and found the cell phone on the seat with the sandwich wrappings, which were beginning to mature in the sun. I rang the number.

I was very tired.

"Yes?"

"It's Lionel, Mr. Matricardi. You beeped me."

"Yes. Lionel. Have you got for us what we want?"

"I'm working on it."

"Working is wonderful, honorable, admirable. Results — now those we truly cherish."

"I'll have something for you soon."

The interior was all inlaid burnished wood to match the exterior's toasted-marshmallow color; the carpet supplied the seashell pink. The girl who met me just inside the door wore an elaborate Japanese robe and a dazed expression. I smoothed both sides of her collar with my hand and she seemed to take it well, perhaps as admiration for the silk. I nodded at the big windows overlooking the water and she led me to a small table there, then bowed and left me alone. I was the only customer for lunch, or the first anyway. I was starving. A sushi chef waved his broad knife at me and grinned from across the big, elegant dining room. The beveled-glass partition he worked behind made me think of the holdup-proof Plexiglas habitats for clerks in Smith Street liquor stores. I waved back, and he nodded, a sudden and ticcish bob, and I reciprocated happily. We had quite a thing going until he broke it off, to begin slicing with theatrical flair the whole skin off a slab of reddish fish.

The doors to the kitchen swung open, and Julia came out. She too wore a robe, and she wore it splendidly. It was her haircut that was a little jarring. She'd shaved her long blond hair down to military fuzz, exposing the black roots. Her face underneath the fuzz looked exposed and raw, her eyes a little wild to be without their veil. She picked up a menu and brought it to my table and halfway across the floor I saw her notice who she was bringing it to. She lost only a little something from her stride.

"Lionel."

"Pisspaw," I completed.

"I'm not going to ask you what you're doing here," she said. "I don't even want to know." She passed me the menu, the cover of which was thatched, a weave of bamboo.

"I followed Tony," I said, putting the menu gingerly aside, wary of splinters. "And the giant, the killer. We're all coming up here for a Frank Minna convention."

"That's not funny." She examined me, her mouth drawn. "You look like shit, Lionel."

"It was a long drive. I guess I should have flown into Boston and — what's your trick, rental car? Or catch a bus? This is a regular vacation spot for you, I know that much."

"Very nice, Lionel, you're very smart. Now get lost."

"Muscongaphone! Minnabunkport!" I gritted back a whole series of Maine-geography tics that wished to follow these two through the gate of my teeth. "We really ought to talk, Julia."

"Why don't you just talk to yourself?"

"Now we're even, since that wasn't funny either."

"Where's Tony?"

"He's — *Tugboat! Tunaphone!* — he's on a boat ride." It sounded so pleasant, I didn't want to say who with. From the vantage of Yoshii's high window I could see Muscongus Island at last, wreathed in mist on the horizon.

"He should have come here," said Julia, without a trace of sentiment. She spoke as someone whose thinking had taken a very practical turn in the past day or so. "He told me to wait here for him, but I can't wait much longer. He should have come."

"Maybe he tried. I think he wants to get to Fujisaki before someone gets to him." I watched her as I dangled the theory, alert for any flinch or fire that might cross her expression.

It was flinch. She lowered her voice. "Don't say that name here, Lionel. Don't be an idiot." She looked around, but there was only the hostess and sushi chef. *Don't say that name* — the widow had inherited the dead man's superstitions.

"Who are you afraid of, Julia? Is it Fujisaki, really? Or Matricardi and Rockaforte?"

She looked at me and I saw her throat tighten and her nostrils flare.

"I'm not the one hiding from the Italians," she said. "I'm not the one who should be afraid."

"Who's hiding?"

It was one question too many. Her fury's crosshairs centered on me now, only because I was there and the person she wanted to kill was so very far away, working her by remote control.

"Screw you, Lionel. You fucking freak."

The ducks were on the pond, the monkeys were in a tree, the birds wired, the fish barreled, the pigs blanketed: However the players in this tragic fever dream ought to be typed zoologically, I had them placed together now. The problem wasn't one of tracing connections. I'd climbed into my Tracer and accomplished that. Now, though, I had to draw a single coherent line through the monkeys, ducks, fish, pigs, through monks and mooks — a line that accurately distinguished two opposed teams. I might be close.

"Will you take my order, Julia?"

"Why don't you go away, Lionel? Please." It was pitying and bitter and desperate at once. She wanted to spare us both. I had to know from what.

"I want to try some uni. Some — *orphan ocean ice cream!* — some urchin eggs. See what all the fuss is about."

"You wouldn't like it."

"Can it be done up as a sandwich of some kind? Like an uni-salad sandwich?"

"It's not a sandwich spread."

"Okay, well, then just bring me out a big bowl and a spoon. I'm really hungry, Julia."

She wasn't paying attention. The door had opened, pale sunlight flaring into the orange and pink cavern of the room. The hostess bowed, then led the Fujisaki Corporation to a long table in the middle of the room.

It all happened at once. There were six of them, a vision to break your heart. I was almost glad Minna was gone so he'd never have to face it, how perfectly the six middle-aged Japanese men of Fujisaki filled the image the Minna Men had always strained toward but had never reached and never would reach, in their impeccably fitted black suits and narrow ties and Wayfarer shades and upright postures, their keen, clicking shoes and shiny rings and bracelets and stoic, lipless smiles. They were all we could never be no matter how Minna pushed us: absolutely a team, a unit, their presence collective like a floating island of charisma and force. Like a floating island they nodded at the sushi chef and at Julia and even at me, then moved to their seats and folded their shades into their breast pockets and removed their beautifully creased felt hats and hooked them on the coatrack and I saw the shine of their bald heads in the orange light and I spotted the one who'd spoken of marshmallows and ghosts and bowel movements and picnics and vengeance and I knew, I knew it all, I understood everything at that moment except perhaps who Bailey was, and so of course I ticced loudly.

"I scream for ur-chin!"

Julia turned, startled. She'd been staring, like me, transfixed by Fujisaki's splendor. If I was right she'd never seen them before, not even in their guises as monks.

"I'll bring your order, sir," she said, recovering gracefully. I didn't bother to point out that I hadn't exactly placed an order. Her panicked eyes said she couldn't handle any banter right then. She collected the bamboo-covered menu, and I saw her hand trembling and had to restrain myself from reaching for it to comfort her and my syndrome both. She turned again and headed for the kitchen, and when she passed Fujisaki's table, she managed a brave little bow of her own.

A few members of the corporation turned and glanced at me again, ever so lightly and indifferently. I smiled and waved to embarrass them out of giving me the once-over. They went back to their conversation in Japanese, the sound of which, trickling over the carpet and polished wood in my direction, was a choral murmur, a purr.

I sat still as I could and watched as Julia reemerged to take their drink order and pass out menus. One of the suits ignored her, leaned back in his seat, and transacted directly with the sushi chef, who grunted to show comprehension. Others unfolded the spiny menu and began to grunt as well, to jabber and laugh and stab their manicured fingers at the laminated photographs of fish inside. I recalled the monks in the Zendo, the pale, saggy flesh, the scanty tufts of underarm hair that now hid behind the million-dollar tailoring. The Zendo seemed a distant and unlikely place from where I sat now. Julia went back through the kitchen doors and came out carrying a large steaming bowl and a small trivet with daubs of bright color on it. With these she threaded past Fujisaki, to my table.

"Uni," she said, nodding at the tiny block of wood. It held a thick smudge of green paste, a cluster of pink-hued shavings from a pickled beet or turnip, and a gobbet of glistening orange beads — the urchin eggs, I supposed. It wasn't three bites of food altogether. The bowl she set down was a touch more promising. The broth was milky white, its surface rippled from underneath by a thick tangle of vegetables and chunks of chicken, and decorated on top by sprigs of some sort of exotic parsley.

"I also brought you something you might actually like," she said quietly as she drew a small ceramic ladle and a pair of inlaid chopsticks out of a pouch in her robe and set them at my place. "It's Thai chicken soup. Eat it and go, Lionel. Please."

Tie-chicken-to-what? went my brain. *Tinker to Evers to Chicken.*

Julia returned to Fujisaki's table with her order pad, to contend with the corporation's contradictory barked commands, their staccato pidgin English. I sampled the uni, scraping it up in the ladle-chopsticks were not my game. The gelatinous orange beads ruptured in my mouth like capers, brackish and sharp but not impossible to like. I tried mixing the three bright colors on the wood, blobbing the tacky green paste and the shreds of pickled radish together with the eggs. The combination was something else entirely: An acrid claw of vapor sped up the back of my throat and filled my nasal cavity. Those elements were apparently not meant to be mixed. My ears popped, my eyes watered, and I made a sound like a cat with a hairball.

I'd garnered Fujisaki's attention once again, and the sushi chef's as well. I waved, face flushed bright red, and they nodded and waved back, bobbed their heads, returned to talking. I ladled up some of the soup, thinking at least to flush the poisons off the sensitive surface of my tongue. Another reverse: The broth was superb, a reply and rebuke to the toxic explosion that had preceded it. It transmitted warmth in the other direction, down into my gullet and through my chest and shoulders as it passed. Levels of flavor unfolded, onion, coconut, chicken, a piquancy I couldn't place. I scooped up another ladleful, with a strip of chicken this time, and let the nourishing fire flow through me again. Until placed in this soup's care I hadn't realized how chilled I was, how starved for comfort. It felt as if the soup were literally embracing my heart.

The trouble came with the third spoonful. I'd dredged low, come up with a tangle of unidentifiable vegetables. I drank down more of the broth, then gnawed on the mouthful of pungent roughage that was left in my mouth — only some of it was rougher than I might have liked. There was some resilient, bladelike leaf that wasn't losing the contest with my teeth, was instead beginning to triumph in an unexpected skirmish with my gums and the roof of my mouth. I chewed, waiting for it to disintegrate. It wouldn't. Julia appeared just as I'd reached in with my pinkie to clear it from my mouth.

"I think part of the menu got into the soup," I said as I ejected the bulrushes onto the table.

"That's lemongrass," said Julia. "You're not supposed to *eat* it."

"What's it doing in the soup, then?"

"Flavor. It flavors the soup."

"I can't argue with that," I said. "What's the name again?"

"Lemongrass," she hissed. She dropped a slip of paper onto the table by my hand. "Here's your check, Lionel."

I reached for her hand where it covered the slip but she pulled it away, like some version of a children's game, and all I got was the paper.

"Lasagna ass," I said under my breath.

"What?"

"Laughing Gassrog." This was more audible, but I hadn't disturbed Fujisaki, not

yet. I looked up at her helplessly.

"Good-bye, Lionel." She hurried away from my table.

The check wasn't really a check. Julia's scrawl covered the underside:

THE FOOD IS ON THE HOUSE.

MEET ME AT FRIENDSHIP HEAD LIGHTHOUSE TWO-THIRTY.

GET OUT OF HERE!!!

I finished the soup, carefully putting the mysterious inedible lemongrass to one side. Then I rose from the table and went past Fujisaki toward the doors, hoping for Julia's sake to be invisible. One of them turned as I passed, though, and grabbed my elbow.

"You like the food?"

"Terrific," I said.

It was the one who as a monk had applied the paddle to my back. They'd been guzzling sake and his face was red, his eyes moist and merry.

"You Jerry-Roshi's unruly student," he said.

"I guess that's right."

"Retreat center a good idea," he said. "You need long sesshin. You got an *utterance* problem, I think."

"I know I do."

He clapped me on the shoulder, and I clapped his shoulder in return, feeling the shoulder pad in his suit, the tight seam at the sleeve. Then I tugged loose of his embrace, meaning to go, but it was too late. I had to make the rounds and touch the others. I started around the table, clapping each perfectly tailored shoulder. The men of Fujisaki seemed to take it as an encouragement to tap and poke me back while they joked with one another in Japanese. "Duck, duck, goose," I said, quietly at first. "Otter, otter, utterance."

"Otter-*duck,*" said one of the men of Fujisaki, raising his eyebrows as though it were a significant correction, and elbowing me sharply.

"Monk, monk, stooge!" I said, circling the table faster, cavorting. "Weapongrass duckweed!"

"You go now," said the scowling paddle-wielder.

"Eat me Fujisaki!" I screamed, and whirled out the door.

The second boat had returned to the dock. I went back through Yoshii's parking lot and down the hill to have a closer look. Smoke still plumed from Foible's shack; otherwise the scene on the fishing pier was completely still. Perhaps the captain of the boat had joined Foible inside the shack for a drink from a new bottle of gin, on my twenty. Or maybe he'd just gone home to bed after a day's labor that had started at three in the morning, Urchin Daylight Savings time. I envied him if he had. I crept past the shack, to the other side of the pier. From what I could see the ferry landing was empty too, the boat itself out at the island, the ticket office closed until the late-afternoon landing. The wind was picking up off the ocean now and the whole coastal scene had a bleak, abandoned look, as though Maine in November really belonged to the ragged gulls who wheeled over the sun-worn pier, and the humans had just gotten the news and taken a powder.

It was farther on, in the tree-shrouded parking lot, that I saw something move, a sign of life. I went silently past the ferry landing to a place out of the harsh angled brightness so I could peer into the shadow and distinguish what the something was. The answer was the giant. He stood between his car and Tony's squinting in the wind and dappled sunlight and reading or at least staring at a bunch of papers in a manila folder, something out of thc L&L files perhaps. In the minute that I watched he grew bored or dissatisfied with the papers and closed the file and ripped it in two, then two again, and walked across the lot to the edge where the pavement was divided from the sea by a wide margin of barnacled and beer-canned boulders. He hurled the torn quadrants of the folder in the direction of the rocks and water and the wind whipped them instantly back to flutter madly past him and disperse across the lot's gravel and into the trees. But he wasn't finished yet. There was something else in his hand, something black and small and shiny, and for a moment I thought he was making a call. Then I saw that it was a wallet. He rifled through it and moved some folding money into his own pants pocket and then he hurled the wallet, too, with more success than he'd had with the papers, so that it arced over the rocks and possibly reached the water — I couldn't tell from my perspective, and neither, I think, could the giant. He didn't appear particularly worried. Worry wasn't in his nature.

Then he turned and saw me: Laugh-or-cry Edgelost.

I ran the other way, across the ferry landing and the fishing dock, toward the hill, on top of which sat the restaurant, and my car.

* * *

The huff of my own exhausted breath, pounding of blood in my ears, squall of a gull and shush of the surf below — all were overtaken by the squeal of the giant's wheels: His Contour scraped into the restaurant lot just as I got my key into the ignition. His car barreled toward mine. The cliff was near enough that he might push me off. I revved into reverse and jerked my car backward out of his path and he skidded sideways to stop, nearly slamming into the nearest of the parked pickup trucks. I floored it and beat him back out of the lot, down onto Route 1, pointed south. The giant fell in right behind me. In my rearview I saw him bearing down, one hand on the wheel, the other gripping a gun.

Minna and Tony — I'd let them both be gently escorted to their quiet murderings. Mine looked to be a little noisier.

I screwed the steering wheel to the left, twitching myself off the highway toward the ferry dock. The giant wasn't fooled. He hung right on my bumper, as if the red compact were as correspondingly huge as his body and could climb over or engulf my Tracer. I veered right and left, contacting the ragged edges of the paved road to the dock in some half-symbolic finger-wagging or shooing maneuver, trying to dislodge the giant from my tail, but he matched my every vehicular gesture, Contour on Tracer now. Pavement gave way to gravel and I ground braking and sliding to the right to avoid riding straight up onto the dock and into the water. Instead I steered for the ferry's parking area, where Tony's Pontiac still sat, where the gun he hadn't gotten to use on the giant still waited under the driver's seat.

Gottagettagun, screamed my brain, and my lips moved trying to keep up with the chant: *Gottagettagun gottagettagun.*

Gun Gun Gun *Shoot!*

I'd never fired a gun.

I broke through the entrance, snapping the flimsy gate back on its post. The giant's car chewed on my bumper, the metal squeaking and sighing. Exactly how I would find breathing room enough to get out of my car and into Tony's to lay hands on the gun remained to be seen. I curled past Tony's car, to the left, opening a moment's gap between me and my pursuer, and rode for the rock barrier. Shreds of the torn file still fluttered here and there in the wind. Maybe the giant would do me the favor of plummeting into the sea. Maybe he hadn't gotten around to noticing it — since it was only the Atlantic it might not have been big enough to make an impression.

He caught me again as I turned the other way to avoid a swim myself, and veered with me around the outer perimeter of the lot. DON'T BACK UP! SEVERE TIRE DAMAGE! shouted the signs at the exit, warning of the one-way spikes meant to prevent free use of the lot. Well, I'd gotten around that one. The giant's car made contact again, rammed me so we both slid off to the left, toward the exit, away from Tony's car.

Suddenly inspired, I darted for the exit.

I hit the brake as hard as I could as I passed over the flexible spikes, came shrieking and skidding to a halt about a car's length past the grate. The giant's car smashed against my rear end so that my car was driven another couple of yards forward and I was slapped back against the seat, hard. I felt something in my neck click and tasted blood in my mouth.

The first blast was the giant's air bag inflating. In my rearview I saw a white satin blob now filling the interior of the Contour.

The second blast was the giant's gun firing as he panicked or his fingers clenched around the trigger in traumatic reflex. The glass of his windshield splintered. I don't know where the shot went, but it found some target other than my body. I shifted into reverse and floored the gas pedal.

And plowed the giant's car backward toward the spikes.

I heard his rear tires pop, then hiss. The giant's rear end slumped, his tires lanced on the spikes.

For a moment I heard only the hiss of escaping air, then a gull screamed, and I made a sound to answer it, a scream of pain in the form of a birdcall.

I shook my head, glanced in the mirror. The giant's air bag was sagging slowly, silently. Perhaps it had been pierced by the bullet. There wasn't any sign of motion underneath.

I shifted into first, swerved forward and left, then reversed into the giant's car again, crumpling the metal along the driver's-side door, deforming the contour of the Contour, wrinkling it like foil, hearing it creak and groan at being reshaped.

I might have stopped then. I believed the giant was unconscious under the air bag. He was at least silent and still, not firing his gun, not struggling to free himself.

But I felt the wild call of symmetry: His car ought to be crumpled on both sides. I needed to maul both of the Contour's shoulders. I rolled forward and into position, then backed and crashed against his car once more, wrecking it on the passenger side as I had on the driver's.

It's a Tourette's thing — you wouldn't understand.

I moved the map and cell phone to Tony's Pontiac. The keys were still in the ignition. I drove it out of the lot through the smashed entrance gate, and steered past the vacant ferry landing, up to Route 1. Apparently no one had heard the collisions or gunshot in the lot by the sea. Foible hadn't even poked out of his shack.

Friendship Head was an outcropping on the coast twelve miles north of Musconguspoint Station. The lighthouse was painted red and white, no atrocity of Buddhist earth tones like the restaurant. I trusted that the Scientologists hadn't gotten to it either. I parked the Pontiac as close to the water as I could and sat staring out for a while, feeling the place where I'd bitten my tongue slowly seal and testing out the damage to my neck. Free movement of my neck was crucial to my Tourettic career. I was like an athlete in that regard. But it felt like whiplash, nothing worse. I was chilled and tired, the replenishing effects of the lemongrass broth long since gone, and I could still feel my head throb in the place the giant had clubbed it twenty-four hours and a million years ago. But I was alive, and the water looked pretty good as the angle of the light grew steeper. I was half an hour early for my date with Julia.

I dialed the local police and told them about the sleeping giant they'd find back at the Muscongus Island ferry.

"He might be in bad shape but I think he's still alive," I told them. "You'll probably need the Jaws of Life to pull him out."

"Can you give us your name, sir?"

"No, I really can't," I said. They'd never know how true it was. "My name doesn't matter. You'll find the wallet of the man he killed in the water near the ferry. The body's more likely to wash up on the island."

Is guilt a species of Tourette's? Maybe. It has a touchy quality, I think, a hint of sweaty fingers. Guilt wants to cover all the bases, be everywhere at once, reach into the past to tweak, neaten, and repair. Guilt like Tourettic utterance flows uselessly, inelegantly from one helpless human to another, contemptuous of perimeters, doomed to be mistaken or refused on delivery.

Guilt, like Tourette's, tries again, learns nothing.

And the guilty soul, like the Tourettic, wears a kind of clown face — the Smokey Robinson kind, with tear tracks underneath.

I called the New Jersey number.

"Tony's dead," I told them.

"This is a terrible thing —" Matricardi started.

"Yeah, yeah, terrible," I said, interrupting. I was in no mood. Really no mood at all. The minute I heard Matricardi's voice, I was something worse or less than human, not simply sorrowful or angry or ticcish or lonely, certainly not moody at all, but raging with purpose. I was an arrow to pierce through years. "Listen carefully to me now," I said. "Frank and Tony are gone."

"Yes," said Matricardi, already seeming to understand.

"I've got something you want and then that's the end of it."

"Yes."

"That's the end of it, we're not bound to you any longer."

"Who is we? Who is speaking?"

"L and L."

"There's a meaning to saying L and L when Frank is departed, and now Tony?

What is it to speak of L and L?"

"That's our business."

"So what is this thing you have we want?"

"Gerard Minna lives on East Eighty-fourth Street, in a Zendo. Under another name. He's responsible for Frank's death."

"Zendo?"

"A Japanese church."

There was a long silence.

"This is not what we expected from you, Lionel."

I didn't speak.

"But you are correct that it is of interest to us."

I didn't speak.

"We will respect your wishes."

Guilt I knew something about. Vengeance was another story entirely.

I'd have to think about vengeance.

Formerly Known

There once was a girl from Nantucket.

No, really, that's where she was from.

Her mother and father were hippies and so she was a little hippie child. Her father wasn't always there on Nantucket with the family. When he was there he didn't stay long, and over time the visits grew both briefer and less frequent.

The girl used to listen to tapes her father would leave behind, the Alan Watts Lecture Series, an introduction to Eastern thought for Americans in the form of a series of rambling, humorous monologues. After the girl's father stopped coming at all, the girl would confuse her memories of her father with the charming man whose voice she heard on the tapes.

When the girl got older she sorted this out, but she'd listened to Alan Watts hundreds of times by then.

When the girl turned eighteen she went to college in Boston, to an art school that was part of a museum. She hated the school and the other students there, hated pretending she was an artist, and after two years she dropped out.

First she went back to Nantucket for a little while, but the girl's mother had moved in with a man the girl didn't like, and Nantucket is, after all, an island. So she went back to Boston. There she found a lousy job as a waitress in a student dive, where she had to fend off an endless series of advances from customers and co-workers. At night she'd take yoga classes and attend Zen meetings in the basement of a local YWCA, where she had to fend off an endless series of advances from instructors and other students. The girl decided she didn't hate only school, she hated Boston.

A year or so later she visited a Zen retreat center on the coast of Maine. It was a place of striking beauty and, apart from the frantic summer months when the town became a resort for wealthy Bostonians and New Yorkers, splendid isolation. It reminded her of Nantucket, the things she missed there. She quickly arranged to study at the center full-time, and to support herself she took a job waitressing at the seafood restaurant next door, which at that time was a traditional Maine lobster pound.

It was there the girl met the two brothers.

The older brother first, during a series of short visits to the retreat with his friend. The friend had some experience with Buddhism, the older brother none, but they were both a disconcerting presence there in placid Maine — vibrant with impatience and a hostile sort of urban humor, yet humble and sincere in their fledgling approach to Zen practice. The older brother was solicitous and flattering to the girl when they were introduced. He was a talker like none she'd ever met, except perhaps on the Alan Watts lecture tapes, which still shaped her yearnings so powerfully — but the older brother was no Watts. His stories were of ethnic Brooklyn, of petty mobsters and comic scams, and some of them had a violent finish. With his talk he made this world seem as near and real to her as it was actually distant. In some way Brooklyn, where she'd never been, became a romantic ideal, something truer and finer than the city life she'd glimpsed in Boston.

The girl and the older brother were lovers after a while.

The older brother's visits grew both briefer and less frequent.

Then one day the older brother returned, in an Impala filled with paper shopping bags stuffed full of his clothes and with his younger brother in tow. After a sizable donation to the Zen center's petty-cash fund the two men moved into rooms in the retreat center, rooms that were out of sight of the coastal highway. The next day the older brother drove the Impala off and returned with a pickup truck, with Maine plates.

Now whenever the girl tried to visit the older brother in his room, he turned her away. This persisted for a few weeks before she began to accept the change. The lovemaking and talk of Brooklyn were over between them. It was only then that the younger brother came into focus for the girl.

The younger brother wasn't a student of Zen. He'd also never been out of New York City until his arrival in Maine, and it was a destination as mysterious and absurd to him as he was mysterious and absurd to her. To the girl the younger brother seemed an embodiment of the stories of Brooklyn the older brother had entranced her with. He was a talker, too, but rootless, chaotic in the stories he told. His talk entirely lacked the posture of distance and bemusement, the gloss of Zen perspective that characterized the older brother's tales. Instead, though they sat together on the Maine beaches, huddling together in the wind, he seemed still to inhabit the streets he described.

The older brother read Krishnamurti and Watts and Trungpa, while the younger read Spillane and Chandler and Ross Mac-

Donald, often aloud to the girl, and it was in the MacDonald especially that the girl heard something that taught her about a part of herself not covered by Nantucket or Zen or the bit she'd learned in college.

The younger brother and the girl became lovers after a while.

And the younger brother did what the older would never have done: He explained to the girl the situation that had driven the two brothers out of Brooklyn, to come and seek refuge in the Zen center. The brothers had been acting as liaisons between two aging Brooklyn mobsters and a group of suburban Westchester and New Jersey bandits who hijacked trucks on small highways into New York City. The aging mobsters were in the business of redistributing the goods seized by the truck pirates, and it was a business that was profitable for everyone associated with it. The brothers had made it more profitable for themselves than they should have, though. They found a place to warehouse a percentage of the goods, and a fence to take the goods off their hands. When the two mobsters discovered the betrayal, they decided to kill the brothers.

Hence, Maine.

The younger brother did another thing his older brother might never have done: He fell in love with the strange angry girl from Nantucket. And one day in the flush of this love he explained to her his great dream: He was going to open a detective agency.

The older brother in the meantime had grown distant from them both, and more deeply and sincerely involved in Zen practice. In the manner of so many spiritual practitioners past and present he seemed to draw away from the world of material concerns, to grow tolerant and wry but also a little chilly in his regard for the people and things he'd left behind.

When the younger brother and the girl were away from the retreat center they'd refer to the older brother as "Rama-lama-ding-dong." Before too long they even began to call him that to his face.

One day the younger brother tried to telephone his mother and found that she'd been taken to the hospital. He conferred with his older brother; the girl overheard some of their bitter, fearful conversations. The older brother was persuaded that their mother's hospitalization had been arranged as a trap to lure them back to Brooklyn for their punishment. The younger disagreed. The next day he bought a car and loaded it with his belongings, and announced he was going back to the city. He invited the girl to join him, though he warned her of the possible danger.

She considered her life at the retreat, which had grown as close and predictable around her as an island, and she considered the younger brother and the prospect of Brooklyn, his Brooklyn, of living there by his side. She agreed to leave Maine.

On the way they were married in Albany, by a justice of the peace at the state capital. The younger brother wanted to surprise and please his mother, and perhaps also wished to offer some excuse for his long disappearance. He took the girl shopping for clothes in Manhattan before they crossed the famous bridge into Brooklyn, and then, as an afterthought, he brought her to a salon on Montague Street, where they bleached her dark hair to platinum blond. It was as though she were the one who should be in disguise here.

The mother's sickness wasn't a trap. She was dead of a stroke by the time the younger brother and his new wife reached the hospital. But it was also true that the mobsters were aware of everything that happened in the neighborhood and were watching the hospital closely. When the younger brother was spotted there, it wasn't long before he was brought in to answer for his and his brother's misdeeds.

He begged for his life. He explained that he'd just gotten married.

He also blamed his brother for the crimes they'd both committed. He claimed to have lost touch with his brother completely.

He ended by promising to spend his life in service as the gangsters' errand boy.

On that condition his apology was accepted by the gangsters. They permitted him to live, though they swore again a vow of death against the older brother, and made the younger promise that he'd turn his brother in if and when he reappeared.

The younger brother moved his new wife into his mother's old apartment and the woman from Nantucket began her adjustment to life in Brooklyn. What she encountered was first intoxicating and frightening, then disenchanting. Her husband was a small-time operator, his "agents," as he called them, a motley gang of high-school-dropout orphans. For a while he installed her as a secretary in a friend's law office, where she worked as a notary public, humiliatingly on view in a shop window out on Court Street. When she protested, he allowed her to recede into privacy in the apartment. The old gangsters paid the couple's rent anyway, and most of the younger brother's detective work was on their behalf. The woman from Nantucket didn't like what passed for detective work in Brooklyn. She wished he genuinely ran a car service. Their married life was chilly and glancing, full of unexplained absences and omissions, no walk on the beach. In time she began to understand that there were other women, too, old high-school girlfriends and distant cousins who'd never left the neighborhood and never really been very far from the younger brother's bed either.

The woman from Nantucket survived, found occasional lovers herself, and spent most of her days in the movie theaters on Court and Henry streets, shopping in Brooklyn Heights, drinking in the hotel lobbies there and then taking slow walks on the Promenade, where she fended off an endless series of advances from college boys and lunch-hour husbands, spent her days any way except musing on the serene rural life she'd left behind in Maine, the faint uncontroversial satisfactions she'd known before she'd met the two brothers and been taken to Brooklyn.

One day the younger brother told his wife a dire secret, which she had to be sure to keep from leaking to anyone in Brooklyn, lest it reach the ears of the gangsters: The older brother had returned to New York City. He'd declared himself a roshi, an elder teacher of Zen, and started a Zendo on the Upper East Side of Manhattan, in Yorkville. This Yorkville Zendo was subsidized by a powerful group of Japanese businessmen he'd met in Maine, where they'd taken over and renovated top to bottom the homely Zen center and the lobster pound next door: the Fujisaki Corporation.

The men of Fujisaki were highly spiritual, but had found themselves in disrepute in their native country, where monkhood is reserved only for those born into certain esteemed bloodlines, and where capitalistic rapaciousness and spiritual devotion are viewed as mutually exclusive. Money and power, it seemed, couldn't buy Fujisaki the precise sort of respect its members craved at home. Here, first in Maine, now in New York City, they would make themselves credible as penitents and teachers, men of wisdom and peace. In the process, as the older brother explained to the younger, the younger then to his wife, the men of Fujisaki and the older brother hoped to do a little "business." New York City: land of opportunity for monks and crooks and mooks alike.

★ ★ ★

We stood at the rail at the sea edge of the lighthouse tower, looking out. The wind was still strong, but I was used to it now. I had my collar up, the way Frank Minna would. The sky out past the island was gray and uninspiring, but there was a nice line of light where it met the water, an edge I could work with my eyes like a seam of stitching between my fingers. The birds harassed the foam below, looking for urchin, perhaps, or discarded hot-dog ends among the rocks.

I had Tony's gun in my jacket, and from this vantage we could see for miles down Route 1 in both directions should anyone approach. I had a strong urge to protect Julia, to hold her or cover her with my presence, so as to feel that I'd helped someone safely through besides myself. But I doubted that the Fujisaki Corporation cared about me or Julia directly. She and I each had been part of Gerard Minna's problem, not Fujisaki's. And Julia showed no interest in my protective urges.

"I know what happened next," I told her. "Eventually the brothers dipped into the till again. Frank got involved in a scam to siphon money away from Fujisaki's management company." That part of what Gerard told me wasn't a lie, I understood now, just an artfully mangled version of the truth. Gerard had been leaving himself out of it, playing the Zen innocent, when in fact he was the wheel's hub. "With a bookkeeper named — *Dullbody, Allmoney, Alimony* — ah, a guy named Ullman."

"Yes," said Julia.

She'd been talking in a kind of trance, not needing me to prompt her more than once in a while. As the narrative got nearer the present day her eyes grew clearer, her gaze less transfixed on the distant island, and her voice grew heavier with resentment. I felt I was losing her to bitterness, and I wanted to draw her back. Protect her from herself if there was no other threat.

"So Frank was hiding the secret of his brother's existence from The Clients," I said. "Meanwhile the two of them are running a number on Gerard's Japanese partners. And then the deal goes — *lemongrass, sourball, fuckitall!*" I was unable to continue until I made a farting, fricative sound into the wind — "blew a raspberry," in the parlance — to satisfy the expulsive tic. Bits of saliva spattered back into my face. "Then Fujisaki figured out someone was taking their money," I said finally, wiping at myself with my sleeve.

She looked at me with disgust. I'd drawn

her back, in a way. "Yes," she said.

"And Gerard fingered — *Mr. Fingerphone! Uncle Sourgrass!* — Gerard fingered Frank and Ullman to save himself."

"That's what Tony thought," she said, distant again.

"Fujisaki must have told Gerard to take care of it, as a show of good faith. So Gerard hired the killer."

Which was where I, innocent stooge, had walked into the story. Frank Minna had installed me and Gilbert there outside the Zendo two days before because he smelled a rat, didn't trust Gerard, and wanted some backup on the street. Warm bodies. If something went wrong he'd bring me and Gilbert up to speed, let us in on the scam, or so he must have thought. And if things went smoothly, it was better to keep us where we'd always been, were born to be — in the dark.

"You know more about it than me," said Julia. She grew agitated now, her storyteller's reverie dissipated, the talk turning to a killer's hiring and all that went with it unsaid. I had to turn away myself now, imitate her pensive searching of the horizon, though my fingers danced idiotically on the lighthouse tower rail, counting one-two-three-four-five, one-two-three-four-five. I'd grown more accustomed to her short new haircut, but those eyes of hers had blazed so long from behind a curtain of hair that without that curtain they blazed too hard. I was drawn and repelled at once, antic with ambivalence. Now I understood that when Frank showed her to us at the end of high school, she was only five or six years older than we were, though it seemed he'd plucked a woman off a fading movie poster. How Nantucket and Buddhism could have made her so old and fierce, I couldn't fathom. I suppose Frank himself had made her old in a hurry, in ways he'd intended, with panty hose and peroxide and sarcasm — and ways he hadn't.

"Let me work out the next part," I said. I felt as if I were trying to get through a joke without ticcing, but there wasn't a punch line in sight. "After Frank and Ullman were gone, Gerard had to make sure he eliminated any link between himself and Frank Minna. That meant you and Tony."

Gerard, I surmised, had been in a panic, afraid of Fujisaki and The Clients both. By having his brother killed he'd damaged a delicate system of controls, one that had kept him safe from Matricardi and Rockaforte for more than a decade. And Fujisaki had announced a visit to New York to inspect their holdings, to enact a little hands-on management (albeit disguised as monks), right as Gerard was frantically trying to mop up the mess. Perhaps they'd also wanted to see Gerard mop up the mess, wanted to feel him squirm a little.

Gerard had reasoned rightly that if Frank confided in anyone it would be his wife and his right-hand man, his groomed successor. Which was to say, Tony. This last part still came a little hard for me. That Tony had paid with his life for being Frank's intimate was a lousy excuse for consolation.

"It was Gerard who called to say that Frank was dead," I suggested. "Not the hospital."

She turned and looked at me with her teeth gritted, tears making glossy tracks on her face. "Very good, Lionel," she whispered. I reached for her cheeks to blot her tears with my sleeve, but she darted back, uninterested in my care.

"But you didn't trust him, so you ran."

"Don't be an idiot, Lionel," she said, her voice vibrant with hate. "Why would I come here if I were hiding from *Gerard?*"

"Idiot Dressfork! Alphabet Tuningfreak!" I cleared the tic with a jerk of my stiff neck. "I don't understand," I told her.

"He arranged for me to use this as a safe

house. He said the people who killed Frank were looking for the rest of us. I trusted him."

I began to see. Lucius Seminole had said that Julia's records showed a series of visits to Boston. "This was your hideaway when you got angry at Frank," I suggested. "Your retreat into the past."

"I wasn't hiding."

"Did Frank know that you and Gerard were in touch?"

"He didn't care."

"Were you and Gerard still lovers?"

"Only when his . . . *spiritual path* allowed it." She spat the words. The tears had dried on her face.

"When did you figure out the truth?"

"I called Tony. We compared notes. Gerard underestimated what Tony knew."

What Tony knew was the least of it, I thought. Tony meant to take over Frank Minna's share of the Fujisaki scam, not knowing that nothing remained to take over. He wanted that and much more. As I ached always to be a virtuous detective, Tony ached to be a corrupt one, or even to be an out-and-out wiseguy. He'd been fitting himself for the darkest shoes in Frank Minna's wardrobe from the moment he learned they existed, perhaps on that day when we unloaded the guitars and amplifiers and were introduced to Matricardi and Rockaforte, perhaps even sooner, on some uglier errand only he and Frank knew about. Certainly he understood by the time Frank's van windows had been smashed. His special glee that day was at having his Mafioso fantasies confirmed, as well as at seeing Frank Minna's vulnerability for the first time. If Frank's fortunes could rise and fall, that episode said, then power was fluid, and so Tony might someday have a share of it himself. The moment Frank was dead Tony envisioned himself playing Frank on both stages, for The Clients in Brooklyn and for Gerard and the Fujisaki Corporation up in Yorkville, only playing the part with greater efficiency and brutality, without Frank Minna's goofy edges, those soft places that caused him to collect freaks like me or that finally led him astray.

Gerard's picture of Tony was another part of that convoluted after-hours story that hadn't been entirely a lie. I suppose Gerard couldn't be the many things he was without knowing how to x-ray a mind like Tony's at a single glance.

"You and Tony compared more than notes, Julia." I regretted it the minute I said it.

She looked at me with pity now.

"So I fucked him." She took out a cigarette and lighter from her purse. "I fucked a lot of guys, Lionel. I fucked Tony and Danny, even Gilbert once. Everyone except you. It's no big deal." She put the cigarette in her lips and cupped her hands against the wind.

"Maybe it was to Tony," I said, and regretted it even worse.

She only shrugged, worked the lighter uselessly again and again. Cars whirred past on the highway below, but nobody stopped at the lighthouse. We were alone in our torment and shame, and useless to each other.

It might not have been a big deal to Julia that she fucked the Minna Men, the Minna Boys, really, and maybe it was no big deal to Tony either — but I doubted it. *You were the original woman,* I wanted to tell her. When Minna brought you home to us we tried to learn what it meant for Frank to marry, we studied you to understand what a Minna Woman might be, and saw only rage — rage I now understood had concealed disappointment and fear, oceans of fear. We had watched women and letters soar past before, but you were the first that was addressed to us, and we tried to understand you. And we loved you.

I needed to rescue Julia now, retrieve her from this lighthouse and the bareness of her story against the Maine sky. I needed her to see that we were the same, disappointed lovers of Frank Minna, abandoned children.

"We're almost the same age, Julia," I said lamely. "I mean, you and me, we were teenagers at pretty much the same time."

She looked at me blankly.

"I met a woman, Julia. Because of this case. She's like you in certain ways. She studies Zen, just like you did when you met Frank."

"No woman will ever want you, Lionel."

"WantmeBailey!"

It was a classic tic, honest and clean. Nothing about Maine or Julia Minna or my profound exhaustion could get in the way of a good, clean, throat-wrenching tic. My maker in his infinite wisdom had provided me with that.

I tried not to listen to what Julia was saying, to focus on the far-off squalling of gulls and splash of surf instead.

"That's not really true," she went on. "They might want you. I've wanted you a little bit myself. But they'll never be fair to you, Lionel. Because you're such a freak."

"This person is different," I said. "She's

different from anyone I've ever met." But now I was losing my point. If I made the distinction between Julia and Kimmery plain to Julia, to myself — *she's not as mean as you, could never be so mean* — I would only be sorry I'd spoken at all.

"Well, I bet you're different for her, too. I'm sure you'll be very happy together." In her mouth the words *happy together* came out twisted and harsh.

Crappy however.

Slappy forget her.

I wanted to call Kimmery now, wanted to so badly my fingers located the cell phone in my jacket pocket and began to fondle it.

"Why was Tony coming to Maine?" I asked, running for cover back to the plot we'd begun spinning together, which suddenly seemed to have little or nothing to do with our miserable fates, our miserable lives exposed out here in the wind. "Why didn't you just get away from here? You knew Gerard might kill you."

"I heard Fujisaki was flying up here today." Again she struck with the lighter against her cigarette, as if it were going to ignite like a flint against a rock. It wasn't just the wind she was fighting now. Her hands trembled, and the cigarette trembled where she held it in her lips. "Tony and I were going to tell them about Gerard. He was going to bring some proof. Then you got in the way."

"It wasn't me that stopped Tony from keeping the date." I was distracted by the phone in my pocket, the prospect of Kimmery's soothing voice, even if it were only the outgoing message on her machine. "Gerard sent his giant after Tony," I went on. "He followed Tony up here, maybe figuring to take out two birds with one flick of his big finger."

"Gerard didn't want me killed," she said quietly. Her hands had fallen to her sides. "He wanted me back." She was trying to make it so by saying it, but the words themselves were nearly lost in the wind. Julia threatened to recede into the distance again, and this time I knew I wouldn't bother trying to bring her back.

"Is that why he had his brother killed? Jealousy?"

"Does it have to be one thing? He probably figured it was him or Frank." The cigarette still dangled in her mouth. "Fujisaki required a sacrifice. They're great believers in that."

"Did you talk to Fujisaki just now?"

"Men like that don't cut deals with waitresses, Lionel."

"It's rotten for Tony the killer found him before he found Fujisaki," I said. "But it won't save Gerard. I made sure of that." I didn't want to elaborate.

"So you say." She paced away from the railing, gripping the lighter so tightly I expected her to crush it.

"What's that supposed to mean?"

"Just that I'm not acquainted with this giant killer you keep talking about. Are you sure you're not imagining things?" She turned and handed me the lighter, plucked the cigarette from her lips and held it out. "Would you light this for me, Lionel?" I heard a weird vibration in her voice, as though she were about to cry again, but without the anger this time, maybe begin to mourn Minna at last. I took them away from her, put the cigarette in my own lips, and turned my back to the wind.

By the time I had it lit she'd taken her gun from her purse.

I put up my hands instinctively, dropping the lighter, to make a pose of surrender but also of self-protection, as though I might deflect a bullet with Frank's watch like Wonder Woman with her magic wristbands. Julia held the gun easily, its muzzle directed at my navel, and now her eyes were as gray and hard to read as the farthest reaches of the Maine horizon.

I felt jets of acid fire in the pit of my stomach. I wondered if I would ever get used to facing gunpoint, and then I wondered if that was really anything to aspire to. I wanted to tic just for the hell of it, but at the moment I couldn't think of anything.

"I just remembered something Frank once said about you, Lionel."

"What's that?" I slowly lowered one hand and offered her the lit cigarette, but she shook her head. I dropped it on the lighthouse deck and ground it under my shoe instead.

"He said the reason you were useful to him was because you were crazy everyone thought you were stupid."

"I'm familiar with the theory."

"I think I made the same mistake," she said. "And so did Tony, and Frank before that. Everywhere you go, somebody who Gerard wants dead is made dead. I don't want to be next."

"You think I killed Frank?"

"You said we're the same age, Lionel. You ever watch *Sesame Street*?" she said.

"Sure."

"You remember the Snuffleupagus?"

"Big Bird's friend."

"Right, only nobody could see him except Big Bird. I think the giant's your Snuffle-upagus, Lionel."

"*Shockadopalus! Fuckalotofus!* The giant is real, Julia. Put the gun away."

"I don't think so. Step back, Lionel."

I stepped back, but I pulled out Tony's gun as I did it. I saw Julia's fingers tighten as I raised it to her, but she didn't fire, and neither did I.

We faced one another on the lighthouse rail, the vast sky dimming everywhere and perfectly useless to us, the ocean's depths useless, too. The two guns drew us close together and rendered the rest irrelevant — we might as well have been in a dingy motel room, with an image of Maine playing on the television set. My moment had come at last. I had a gun in my hands. That it was trained not on Gerard or the giant or Tony or a doorman but on the girl from Nantucket who'd grown into Frank Minna's bruise-eyed widow, who'd chopped off her hair and tried to retreat to her waitress past and instead been cornered by that same past, by Gerard and the giant and Tony — I tried not to let it bother me. I'd been wrong, Julia and I had nothing in common. We were just any two people who happened to be pointing guns at one another now. And Tony's gun had object properties all its own, not a fork nor a toothbrush but something much weightier and more seductive. I slipped off the safety with my thumb.

"I understand your mistake, Julia, but I'm not the killer."

She had both hands on the gun, and it didn't waver. "Why should I trust you?"

"TRUST ME BAILEY!" I had to scream it into the sky. I turned my head, bargaining with my Tourette's that I could let the one phrase fly and then be done. I tasted salt air as I screamed.

"Don't scare me, Lionel. I might shoot you."

"We've both got that same problem, Julia." In fact my syndrome had just discovered the prospect of the gun, and I began to obsess on pulling the trigger. I suspected that if I fired a shot out into the sky in the manner of my verbal exclamation, I might not survive the experience. But I didn't want to shoot Julia. I flicked on the safety, hoped she didn't notice.

"Where do we go from here?" she said.

"We go home, Julia," I said. "I'm sorry about Frank and Tony, but the story's over. You and me, we made it through alive."

It was only a slight exaggeration. The

story would be over at some secret moment in the next few hours or days when something found Gerard Minna, a bullet or blade that had been searching for him for almost twenty years.

Meanwhile, I flicked the safety back and forth, impelled, counting. At five I stopped, temporarily satisfied. That left the safety off, the gun ready to shoot. My fingers were unbearably curious about the trigger's action, its resistance and weight.

"Where's your home, Lionel? Upstairs from L and L?"

"Saint Vengeance Home for Bailey," I ticced.

"Is that what you call it?" said Julia.

Before my finger could pulse on the trigger the way it craved to I flung the gun out toward the ocean with all the force of my overwound-watchspring body. It sailed out past the rocks, but the tiny splash of its disappearance into the sea was lost in the wind and the ambient crash of the surf.

One, I counted.

Before Julia could calculate the meaning of my action I darted as if for an elusive shoulder and grabbed the muzzle of her gun, then twisted it out of her hand and hurled with all the strength in my legs, like a center fielder deep at the wall straining for a distant cutoff man. Julia's gun went farther than Tony's, out to where the waves that would reach the rocks were just taking shape, the sea curling, discovering its form.

That made *two.*

"Don't hurt me, Lionel." She backed away, her shocked eyes framed by the bristly halo of her crew cut, her mouth crooked with fear and fury.

"It's over, Julia. Nobody's going to hurt you." I couldn't concentrate on her fully, needing something more to throw into the sea. I pulled Minna's beeper out of my pocket. It was a tool of The Clients, evidence of their hold on Frank, and it deserved to be interred with the guns. I threw it as far as I could, but it didn't have enough heft to keep from being knocked down by the wind, and so trickled down between two wet, mossy boulders.

Three.

Next I found the cell phone. The instant it came into my hand, Kimmery's number begged for dialing. I pushed the impulse aside, substituted the gratification of flinging it off the lighthouse deck, picturing the doormen in the rental car who I'd taken it from. It flew truer than the beeper, made it out to the water.

Four.

"Give me something to throw," I told Julia.

"What?"

"I need something, one more thing."

"You're crazy."

I considered Frank's watch. I was sentimental about the watch. It had no taint of doormen or Clients.

"Give me something," I said again. "Look in your purse."

"Go to hell, Lionel."

Julia had always been the hardest-boiled of us all, it struck me now. We who were from Brooklyn, we jerks from nowhere — or from somewhere, in the case of Frank and Gerard. We couldn't hold a candle to the girl from Nantucket and I thought I might finally understand why. She was the hardest-boiled because she was the unhappiest. She was maybe the unhappiest person I'd ever met.

I suppose losing Frank Minna, hard as it was, was easier for those of us who'd actually had him, actually felt his love. The thing Julia lost she'd never possessed in the first place.

But her pain was no longer my concern.

You choose your battles, Frank Minna used to say, though the term was hardly original to him.

You also distance yourself from cruelty, if you have any brains. I was developing a few.

I took off my right shoe, felt the polished leather that had served me well, the fine stitching and the fraying lace, kissed it good-bye on the top of the tongue, then threw it high and far and watched it splash silently into the waves.

Five, I thought.

But who's counting?

"Good-bye, Julia," I said.

"Screw you, you maniac." She knelt and picked up her lighter, and this time she got her cigarette lit on the first flick.

"Barnabaileyscrewjuliaminna."

It was my final word on the subject.

So I drove with my gas-pedal-and-brake foot clad only in a dress sock, back to Brooklyn.

Then somewhere, sometime, a circuit closed. It was a secret from me, but I knew the secret existed. A man — two men? — found another man. Lifted an instrument, gun, knife? Say gun. Did a job. Took care of a job. Collected a debt of life. This was the finishing of something between two brothers, a transaction of brotherly love-hate, something playing out, a dark, wobbly melody. The notes of the melody had been other people, boys-turned-Minna Men, mobsters, monks, doormen. And women, one woman especially. We'd all been notes in the melody, but the point of the song was the brothers, and the payoff, the last note struck — a scream? a bloody beat? a bare interrupted moan? — or not even a moan, perhaps. In my guilt I'd like to think so. Let it finish in silence. Let it be, then, that Rama-lama-ding-dong died in his sleep.

We sat together in the L&L storefront at two in the morning, playing poker on the counter, listening to Boyz 2 Men, courtesy of Danny. Now that Frank and Tony were gone, Danny could play the sort of music he liked. It was one of a number of changes.

"One card," said Gilbert. I was the dealer, so I slid his discard toward me and offered him a fresh selection from the top of the deck.

"Jesus, Gil," said the ex-Garbage Cop. He was a driver now, a part of the new L&L. "You're always *one card* or *no cards* — why can't I get dealt anything but crap?"

"That's 'cause you're still in charge of garbage, Loomis," said Gilbert happily. "Even though you quit the force, doesn't matter. Someone's gotta handle it."

"Handle with garbagecrap!" I declared as I dealt myself three new cards.

Gilbert had been released two weeks before, after five nights in the lockup, for want of evidence in Ullman's killing. Detective Seminole had called us to apologize, excessively sheepish, I thought, as though he were still a little afraid. Gilbert's size and manner had carried him through the ordeal pretty well, though he came out short a wristwatch and had involuntarily given up smoking during his stay, having been connived out of every cigarette on his person. He was making up for it now in cigarettes, and in beer and coffee and Sno Balls and White Castles and Zeod's pastrami heroes, but no flow of indulgences could be constant enough to stem his complaints at how we'd abandoned him. Fortunately he was winning hands tonight.

Danny sat apart from the three of us, silent, eyebrows raised slightly between his poker hand and his new fedora. He sat a little farther apart and dressed a little sharper each passing night, or so it seemed to me. Leadership of L&L had fallen to him like an easy rebound, one he didn't even have to jump for, while the other players boxed and elbowed and sweated on the wrong part of the floor. What Danny knew or didn't know about Gerard and Fujisaki was never said. He took my account of the events in Maine and nodded once, and we were done speaking of it. It turned out it was that simple. Want to be the new Frank Minna? Dress the part, and shut up, and wait. Court Street will know you when it sees you. Zeod will put the tab in your name. Gilbert and Loomis and I couldn't have argued. We were Dapper and the Stooges, it was plain to the eye.

L&L was a detective agency, a clean one for the first time. So clean we didn't have any clients. So we were also a car service, a real one now, one that didn't turn away calls unless we truly were out of cars. Danny was even having flyers printed up, and new business cards, boasting of our economy and efficiency to points all over the boroughs. The Cadillac Minna had bled to death inside was clean now too, part of a small fleet of cars making regular runs between the Cobble Hill Nursing Home on Henry Street and the Promenade Diner at the end of Montague, between the Boerum Hill Inn and stylish apartment buildings along Prospect Park West and Joralemon Street.

As a matter of fact, the Boerum Hill Inn had just closed for the night, and Siobhain was at the door, her eyes dark-circled and her posture rather crushed from the effort of tossing out the tenacious flirting crowd. Gilbert put up a finger to say he'd take the job of driving her home, but first wished to lay his poker hand on the table — it appeared to be one he was particularly proud of. Seeing his recent enthusiasm for chaperoning Siobhain I suspected Gilbert had developed a little crush on her, or maybe it was an old crush he had just allowed to let show, now that Frank wasn't around to needle him constantly that she was playing for the other team.

"Come on, you suckers, I'm calling you," said Gilbert.

"Nothing," said Loomis, bugging his eyes

at his hand, trying to embarrass the cards. "Load of crap."

Danny just frowned and shook his head, put his cards on the table. He didn't need poker triumphs just now, he had better things. For all we knew he was folding winning hands just to throw some glory Gilbert's way.

"Forks and spoons," I said, slapping my hand down to show the card faces.

"Jacks and twos?" Gilbert inspected my cards. "That won't do it, Freakshow." He tossed down aces and eights. "Read 'em and scream, like the maniac you are."

Assertions are common to me, and they're also common to detectives. ("About the only part of a California house you can't put your foot through is the front door" — Marlowe, *The Big Sleep*.) And in detective stories things are always *always*, the detective casting his exhausted, caustic gaze over the corrupted permanence of everything and thrilling you with his sweetly savage generalizations. This or that runs deep or true to form, is invariable, exemplary. Oh sure. Seen it before, will see it again. Trust me on this one.

Assertions and generalizations are, of course, a version of Tourette's. A way of touching the world, handling it, covering it with confirming language.

Here's one more. As a great man once said, the more things change, the harder they are to change back.

Within a few days of Gerard's disappearance most of the Yorkville Zendo's students had trickled away. There was a real Zendo on the Upper East Side, twenty blocks south, and its ranks were swelled by defectors from Yorkville seeking truer essences (though, as Kimmery had pointed out, anyone who teaches Zen is a Zen teacher). Those bewildered doormen had all originally been authentic students of Gerard's, it turned out, rudderless seekers, human clay. It was their absolute susceptibility to Gerard's charismatic teachings that made them available to be exploited, first in the Park Avenue building, then as a gang of inept drivers and strong-arms when Gerard needed bodies to fill ranks alongside the Polish giant. Frank Minna had Minna Men while Gerard had only followers, Zen stooges, and that difference might have determined how the case worked out. That might have been my little edge. It pleased me to think so anyway.

The Yorkville Zendo didn't fold, though.

Wallace, that stoic sitter, took over stewardship of what flock remained, though he declined to claim the title of Roshi for himself. Instead he asked to be called *sensei,* a lesser term denoting a sort of apprentice-instructor. So it was that each of the Minna organizations, Frank's and Gerard's, were gently and elegantly steered past the shoals of corruption by their quietest disciples. Of course Fujisaki and The Clients, those vast shadows, crept away unharmed, barely even ruffled. It would take more than the Minna brothers or Lionel Essrog to make a lasting impression.

I learned the fate of the Yorkville Zendo from Kimmery the only time I saw her, two weeks after my return from Maine. I'd been leaving messages on her machine, but she hadn't returned my calls until then. We arranged a rendezvous at a coffee shop on Seventy-second Street, our telephone conversation clipped and awkward. Before I left for the date I took the thoroughest shower I knew how to take, then dressed and redressed a dozen times, playing mirror games with myself, trying to see something that wasn't there, trying not to see the big twitchy Essrog that was. I suppose I still had a faint notion we could be together.

We talked about the Zendo for a while

before she said anything to suggest she even recalled our night together. And when she did, it was "Do you have my keys?"

I met her eyes and saw she was afraid of me. I tried not to loom or jerk, though there was a Papaya Czar franchise across the street. I was pining for their hot dogs, and it was hard to keep from turning my head.

"Oh, sure," I said. I dropped the keys on the table, glad I hadn't chosen to hurl them into the Atlantic. Instead I'd been burnishing them in my pocket, as I had The Clients' fork once upon a time, each talisman of a world I wouldn't get to visit again. I said good-bye to the keys now.

"I have to tell you something, Lionel." She delivered it with that same hectic half smile that I'd been trying to conjure in my mind's eye for most of two weeks.

"Tellmebailey," I whispered.

"I'm moving back in with Stephen," she said. "So that thing that happened with us, it was just, you know — *a thing.*"

So Oreo Man was a cowboy after all, now striding back in from his sunset backdrop.

I opened my mouth and nothing came out.

"You understand, Lionel?"

"Ah." *Understand me, Bailey.*

"Okay?"

"Okay," I said. She didn't need to know it was just a tic, just echolalia that made me say it. I reached across the table and smoothed the two ends of her collar toward her small, bony shoulders. "Okayokayokay-okayokay," I said under my breath.

I had a dream about Minna. We were in a car. He was driving.

"Was I in the Butt Trust?" I asked him.

He smiled at me, liking to be quoted, but didn't reply.

"I guess everybody needs stooges," I said, not meaning to make him feel bad.

"I don't know if I'd put you exactly in the Butt Trust category," he said. "You're a little too strange for that."

"So what am I, then?" I asked.

"I don't know, kid. I guess I'd call you King Tugboat."

I must have laughed or at least smiled.

"That's nothing to be proud of, you radish rosette."

What about vengeance?

I gave it five or ten minutes of my time once. That's a lot, a lifetime, when it comes to vengeance. I had wanted to think vengeance wasn't me, wasn't Tourettic or Essroggian at all. Like the subway, say.

Then I took the V train. I did it with a cell phone and a number in Jersey, I did it standing by a lighthouse in Maine. I did it with a handful of names and other words, strung together into something more effective than a tic. That was me, Lionel, hurtling through those subterranean tunnels, visiting the labyrinth that runs under the world, which everyone pretends is not there.

You can go back to pretending if you like. I know I will, though the Minna brothers are a part of me, deep in my grain, deeper than mere behavior, deeper even than regret, Frank because he gave me my life and Gerard because, though I hardly knew him, I took his away.

I'll pretend I never rode that train, but I did.

The next call that came in that night was a pickup on Hoyt Street for a trip out to Kennedy Airport. It was Loomis who took the call, and he grimaced exaggeratedly when he offered it to the three of us, knowing that according to L&L lore JFK was an exasperating destination. I put up my hand and said I'd take it, just to deny him the point.

For another reason, too. There was a snack I had a hankering for. At the International Terminal at Kennedy, upstairs by the El Al gates, is a single kosher-food stand called Mushy's, run by a family of Israelis, with sauce-spattered metal tins full of stewing kasha and gravy and handmade knishes, a place utterly unlike the chain restaurants elsewhere in the terminal. Anytime I took a passenger out to the airport, night or day, I'd park the car and slip up to Mushy's for a bite. Their chicken shwarma, carved fresh off the roasting pin, stuffed into a pita and slathered in grilled peppers, onions and tahini is one of the great secret sandwiches of New York, redemption for a whole soulless airport. Permit me to recommend it if you're ever out that way.

Kimmery and lemongrass broth hadn't ruined my taste for the finer things.

The ghosts I felt sorriest for weren't the dead ones. I'd imagined Frank and Tony were mine to protect, but I'd been wrong. I knew it now.

It was Julia I couldn't shrug off, though she was hardly more mine than the others, though she'd barely recognized my human existence. Still, my tic of guilt took the form of her shape, standing in the wind on the lighthouse rail, standing still in a mist of bullets and shoes and salt air and my saliva, like the cursed icon from a black-and-white-movie poster she'd resembled when first glimpsed so long ago, or perhaps a figure of Zen contemplation, a mark of ink brush-work on a scroll. But I didn't try to find Julia — simple as it would have been, I knew better than that. Instead I let my obsessive instinct get to work tracing that figure, waiting for it to turn abstract and disappear. Sooner or later it would.

That left who? Only Ullman. I know he haunts this story, but he never came into view, did he? The world (my brain) is too full of dull men, dead men, Ullmen. Some ghosts never even get into your house they are so busy howling at the windows. Or as Minna would say, you pick your battles — and you do, whether you subscribe to that view or not, you really do. I can't feel guilty about every last body. Ullman? Never met the guy. Just like Bailey. They were just guys I never happened to meet. To the both of them and to you I say: Put an egg in your shoe, and beat it. Make like a tree, and leave. Tell your story walking.

The employees of Thorndike Press hope you have enjoyed this Large Print book. All our Large Print titles are designed for easy reading, and all our books are made to last. Other Thorndike Press Large Print books are available at your library, through selected bookstores, or directly from the publishers.

For more information about titles, please call:

(800) 223-1244
or
(800) 223-6121

To share your comments, please write:

Publisher
Thorndike Press
P.O. Box 159
Thorndike, Maine 04986